Praise for t

Dawn of Fire: Avenging Son

by Guy Haley

'The beginning of an essential new epic: heroic,
cataclysmic and vast in scope. Guy has delivered
exactly what 40K readers crave, and lit the fuse on
the Dark Millennium. This far future's
about to detonate...'

Dan Abnett, author of Horus Rising

'With all the thunderous scope of The Horus Heresy,
a magnificent new saga begins.'

Peter McLean, author of Priest of Bones

'A perfect blending of themes – characters that
are raw, real and wonderfully human, set against
a backdrop of battle and mythology'.

Danie Ware, author of Ecko Rising

THE IRON KINGDOM
A DAWN OF FIRE NOVEL

THE IRON KINGDOM

A DAWN OF FIRE NOVEL

NICK KYME

BLACK LIBRARY

A BLACK LIBRARY PUBLICATION

First published in 2023.
This edition published in Great Britain in 2023 by
Black Library, Games Workshop Ltd., Willow Road,
Nottingham, NG7 2WS, UK.

Represented by: Games Workshop Limited – Irish branch,
Unit 3, Lower Liffey Street, Dublin 1,
D01 K199, Ireland.

10 9 8 7 6 5 4 3 2 1

Produced by Games Workshop in Nottingham.
Cover illustration by Johan Grenier.

A CIP record for this book is available from the British Library.

ISBN 13: 978-1-80026-115-0

See Black Library on the internet at

blacklibrary.com

Find out more about Games Workshop
and the worlds of Warhammer at

games-workshop.com

Printed and bound by CPI Group (UK) Ltd, Croydon, CR0 4YY

For Stef.

For more than a hundred centuries the Emperor has sat
immobile on the Golden Throne of Earth. He is the
Master of Mankind. By the might of His inexhaustible
armies a million worlds stand against the dark.

Yet, He is a rotting carcass, the Carrion Lord of the
Imperium held in life by marvels from the Dark Age of
Technology and the thousand souls sacrificed each day so
that His may continue to burn.

To be a man in such times is to be one amongst untold
billions. It is to live in the cruellest and most bloody
regime imaginable. It is to suffer an eternity of carnage
and slaughter. It is to have cries of anguish and sorrow
drowned by the thirsting laughter of dark gods.

This is a dark and terrible era where you will find little
comfort or hope. Forget the power of technology and
science. Forget the promise of progress and advancement.
Forget any notion of common humanity or compassion.

There is no peace amongst the stars, for in the grim
darkness of the far future,
there is only war.

DRAMATIS PERSONAE

Parnius	Knight of Hurne
Klaigen	Knight of Hurne
Henniger	Knight of Hurne
Martinus	Knight of Hurne

Those who are oathed

Morrigan	Brother-castellan, Black Templars, called 'the Unchained'
Dagomir	Sword Brethren, Black Templars
Godfried	Brother-Champion, Black Templars
Anglahad	Battle-brother, Black Templars
Fulk	Brother-Apothecary, Black Templars
Vanier	Shipmaster of the *Mourning Star*
Hekatani	Station mistress

OF ANCIENT KAMIDAR

| Albia | Mendicant priest of Hurne |

RENEGADE ASTARTES

Graeyl Herek	Red Corsair pirate lord and captain of the *Ruin*
Vassago Kurgos	Red Corsair, chirurgeon
Rathek	Red Corsair, called 'the Culler'

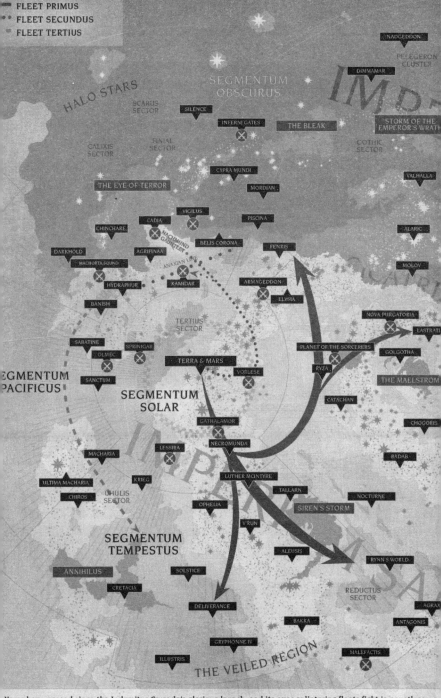

Years have passed since the Indomitus Crusade's glorious launch, and its ever-splintering fleets fight in countless warzones across the galaxy. No cartograph, even this one, should be considered all-encompassing due to the immeasurable scale and fluidity of the crusade as it battles to save the Imperium of Man from total annihilation.

PART ONE

IRONHOLD

Prologue

CORSAIRS

SHIELDBROTHERS

PLUNDER

Sirens rang throughout the deck halls, proclaiming the end of the *Mercurion*. The ship's armsmen ran here and there in a panic, their once fine green-grey uniforms now ragged and spattered with blood. They were trying to close off companionways or seal the bulkhead doors that led deeper into the ship.

Jagra strode through their scurrying masses, the much smaller mortals flinging themselves from the armoured warrior's path. He went unhurried, his naturally long gait propelling him at speed as he made for the oculus chamber at the aft end of the deck. Through the corner of his eye, he saw the debased hordes the enemy had sent ahead to muddy the waters of a clean assault. He had heard of the tactic being used before. It was how they had lost the *Hermes*, rats overwhelming the once proud frigate. Jagra had vowed it would not be his fate, but as the breather-masked and leather-clad cultists swarmed the ship, he could not deny the similarity with what had happened to the other vessel.

In its frenzy, one of the wretches had fought its way into his path, armed with a pistol and a length of chain with a billhook on one end. Solid shots peppered the Space Marine's white armour, casting sparks. Jagra slew the creature, his backhand blow crushing bone.

He moved on, intent on his destination.

'Krilus, Vultu...' his gruff voice rumbled as he activated the vox-unit embedded in his gorget. The signal returns from his battle-brothers chimed before their equally deep replies.

'Brother-sergeant,' uttered Krilus, a faint rasp in his throat a reminder of the flamer he had survived at Tromund.

'Here, brother,' said Vultu in that lilting refrain of his that made him such a potent orator of the nascent Chapter's histories.

'I have need of you at the oculus, brothers. Make all haste.' Jagra cut the vox, not needing to hear their responses. His brothers had been summoned, so they would come. It was the way of the Chapter.

Further into the ship and the fighting grew more ferocious. Las-beams skittered across Jagra's vision, and a troop of men with stern faces, all bearing tall boarding shields, tramped past. He made way for the armsmen, considering it was the least he could do since they were all going to their deaths.

Krilus' voice came through a burst of static. *'They're here,'* he said simply, and wasn't talking about the cultists or the armsmen.

Jagra nodded, reaching for the helmet mag-clamped to his side, donning it as he walked. A slew of data scrolled across his vision. Armour systems, ship schematics, bio-scan, preysight and weapons status spilled out in a flood that Jagra assimilated and analysed in a nanosecond. The oculus was close, the distance ticking down via a counter in his right eye-lens.

Ahead, a gout of flame spewed into the corridor, a squad of burning armsmen thrashing through the pooling smoke. A clutch of cultists followed, their faces hidden behind devilish masks and garbed in bloodstained iron. Their leader carried a flamer, delighting in hosing the scorched corpses of the armsmen as they broke down into blackened nothing, until he saw the Space Marine advancing on him.

Jagra did not blame the cultist for balking at the sight of him, with his white Tacticus armour dirtied by battle and emblazoned with the black double-headed axe and red lightning bolt of the Storm Reapers. Mania flashed in the cultist's eyes, his devotion to the warp making him bold and heedless of his own mortality.

Deluded fools. They thought a reward from the Dark Gods awaited them if they served without question. In truth, it was only damnation that would greet them. Jagra gave it little thought as he unslung the broad crusader's shield from his back, the double-axe-head sigil of the Storm Reapers in the centre.

The wall of fire hit him the second he braced his shield. He charged forward into billowing flames, using the shield to batter them out of the way and crush the cultist, who went down under the onslaught. The other heretics fared no better. Jagra smashed one into a wall, shattering his skeleton. Another he punched, so hard the neck snapped and the decapitated head spun away into darkness. Two more fell beneath the battering-ram force of his momentum, though Jagra hardly noticed, only his helmet's kill-counter acknowledging their destruction. The last cultist tripped as she tried to flee and was crawling on her back like a wounded beast. Jagra slammed the shield down one-handed, its edge sharp enough to sever the cultist's head and end the wild screaming.

The encounter had lasted four seconds and as it concluded, the oculus was in sight at last, a band of wary armsmen holding it with desperate looks written on their soot-blackened faces.

'To your kinsmen,' Jagra said, effectively dismissing them.

The officer in their ranks quickly saluted and they were on their way.

Jagra turned his back to the rune-etched door to the oculus chamber, eyeing the carnage of the ship's last stand with dispassionate eyes. He was about to reach out to his brothers again when two figures appeared at the end of the corridor, marching swiftly towards him. The overspill from the skirmishes taking place in the adjacent corridors impeded them, but not for long. Another twenty cultists lay dead and dismembered by the time Krilus and Vultu were before him.

'You took your time,' Jagra remarked mildly as the blade-veterans fell in, one at either shoulder.

'The ship is overrun,' said Krilus. He hadn't bothered to unhitch his shield and his gauntlets shone dark and wet in the urgent strobe light. Like all Storm Reapers, he wouldn't tarnish his blade with an unworthy opponent's blood.

'The bridge?' asked Jagra.

'Taken,' Vultu replied curtly.

'So, we shall meet the enemy here, and regroup with Ushdu Khan when we are finished.' It was a statement of fact from Jagra, as inevitable as the cold void outside the ship's hull and the slow heat death of the universe.

'Aye,' said Krilus and unslung his shield, a hunger in his grey eyes. He was the last to put on his helmet, crushing a crest of jutting black hair.

Vultu gestured, the belligerent jerk of his chin emphasised by his war-helm. 'Look...'

At the far end of the corridor, having just emerged from the junction, a host of armoured warriors waited. Jagra counted eight – no, ten... more had come to join them. A few wore helms, their trappings the dark mirror of the Storm Reapers, a riot of black and dirty crimson.

The Red Corsairs.

Some went unhelmed, their faces twisted, ravaged by warp exposure; skin stretched like candle wax, melted and reset. The first amongst them smiled, his flesh a mess of iron spikes and hooks, the mark of his gods seared into his forehead. Filed teeth glinted like needles in his mouth as he sent a gaggle of cultists on ahead, carrying flails and rusty saw-toothed blades.

Jagra and his brothers met them, a shield wall to break their bones and their spirits, power-armoured fists and kicks to finish them. It was quick and merciless but just a preamble. Amused, the Red Corsairs leader ordered the attack and now it began in earnest, belt-fed bolters roaring a fierce staccato as muzzle flare chased away the shadows.

Shields forward, Jagra and his brothers drew their swords at last. Thick steel blades slid from scabbards with an eager scrape of enhanced alloys. His heart thundered with the anticipation of true battle. The blades lit, disruption fields flaring for a second, lifting the red dark again with azure brightness before settling into a humming rhythm that crackled every sword-edge as if it were alive.

'Jagun hak sang tal!'

For Jagun I give my blood, a bellowed tribute to their adopted world and a promise to fight until death.

The three fought as one, and in perfect concert, skills well honed over a hard-fought crusade. Jagra made the first kill, splitting his enemy groin to neck. Vultu slew the second, transfixing his foe through the primary heart; there was a loud bang of powered feedback as the disruption field cooked the Red Corsair's organs. Krilus fought two at once, deft swings of his blade and canny shield work leaving the Storm Reaper unscathed as he bested both opponents and cut them down with a criss-cross slash. One fell away, half his skull missing, clawing at the red ruin of his features. The other lost his weapon arm, bolter shells chattering wildly off the ship's walls before the finger released the trigger and it fell silent again. Jagra finished off the faceless renegade, severing head from neck with a simple left-to-right cut. The other fell to Krilus, who bashed in the Corsair's skull with his shield.

Odds evening by the second, the Storm Reapers advanced, shield and sword in peerless union. They had fought together for five years, ever since the crusade began, and were more than brothers by Chapter. Bolt-shells caromed off their shields but did little except to anger them. Three more Red Corsairs died, split apart and sent back to the hells. Vultu hacked down on the head of a fourth, straight through the helm, through the skull and matter within, all the way down to the cavity of the neck. The bifurcated halves slid off one another with horrific slowness but the Storm Reaper was already moving, herding a fifth enemy into the path of Krilus, who cleaved right through the renegade's midriff, separating legs from torso. The Red Corsair mewled as he fell. Jagra ended him with a thrust through the head, his blade still oily and slick as he raised it to the warband's leader.

If the renegade was daunted, he did not show it. He had hung back to watch the battle but smiled now his turn had come, those needle teeth catching the light and turning red. A serrated sword glinted fiercely in the armoured fist, promising an ugly death. Faces had been scored into the blade, screaming, agonised. They distorted the metal unnaturally.

Jagra spat his contempt. He had seen it all before. He wanted this done, the ship cleansed so he could return to a world of sky and air and open plains. A great longing welled up within him at the thought until he crushed it with duty.

Vultu made to step forwards but Jagra warned him off.

'This one is mine,' he growled, and the others retreated, shields down and blades at their sides. 'Do you have honour, dog?' asked Jagra, and levelled his sword.

'No,' came the sibilant reply, then the warband leader rushed headlong, howling like the damned.

The Storm Reaper parried the traitor's first blow, a coruscation of sparks ripping between their blades. Jagra landed a hit to the renegade's forearm, cutting deep enough to draw blood.

It barely slowed him, pain a well-acquainted friend as he hacked back. Jagra took the brunt of the blow on his shield, which he then thrust forward like a battering ram, throwing his opponent off balance. The Red Corsair flailed wildly and lost an arm to a savage stroke of Jagra's blade.

'Submit,' snarled Jagra as his opponent fumbled with one upper limb, 'and I will give you a clean death. More than you deserve.'

'Yours will be ugly.' Blood spewing from the wound, the renegade lashed out savagely, his sword arm still intact.

Jagra swatted aside the attacks, before uppercutting with the edge of his shield. It cracked his opponent on the chin and disarmed him, the tortured sword slipping from the renegade's nerveless grip. The Red Corsair staggered, dazed, and Jagra ran him through before he could realign. It went deep, the Storm Reaper's blade, right to the hilt's cross-guard, so close he stared into the other warrior's eyes. Fathomless hate glared back, though glazing over now with the onset of death.

'You have been found wanting, dog,' Jagra hissed. With a grunt of effort he kicked the renegade off his sword and sent him sprawling several feet down the corridor.

The warband leader landed at the feet of another, and Jagra realised the dying renegade he had just bested had not been the one in charge, after all. This one had a hulking frame, enhanced by baroque armour and a tattered half-cloak of ermine trailing from his shoulder like a wraith. Unlike the others, his face was uncorrupted apart from two small hornlike protrusions pushing at the flesh either side of his forehead.

Jagra took stock at once, shifting to a fighting stance, instantly wary. Then his gaze strayed to the belt of helms strung around the brute's waist.

He recognised one of them.

'Ushdu Khan...'

The words slipped out in a ghostly rasp, so appalled was he

by the sight. Blood still dripped from the severed head encased within. It was then that Jagra saw the axe looped over the butcher's shoulder, a huge single-bladed half-moon of dark metal, rimed with blood.

As the butcher glanced down at his fallen brother, dying as he slumped against the wall, holding the mortal wound in his chest, he almost looked... *sad*. Then he said something in a language Jagra didn't understand but that made his teeth itch and his tongue ache, and he had seen and heard enough.

The actinic tang of powered war plate filled the atmosphere as it geared up to attack. Servos growled, a beast snapping at the leash.

'Jagun hak vun tal!' *By Jagun, I will taste vengeance.*

They all said it; Ushdu's severed head was almost too awful to look upon.

The butcher seemed not to hear. He had sunk into a crouch by the stricken renegade and laid a gauntleted hand to his cheek as he gave him a solemn look. Then he rose and swung the axe around.

'To the killing, then...' he said in Gothic, his voice more refined than Jagra had thought it would be.

'Give me the honour, brother-sergeant,' declared Krilus, his passion overspilling into hatred.

'No,' said Jagra. The desire for retribution was almost overwhelming but something about this warrior before them gave him pause, like the inkling a man gets before a storm. 'As one,' he said.

They attacked, blades screaming.

Krilus died quickly, a sudden shift in posture from the butcher, and the Storm Reaper's head left his shoulders. Jagra was struck dumb, slowed by precious nanoseconds as a fount of arterial blood laced his helm and one side of his vision. He barely parried the next stroke, his shield practically cut in twain as he saw poor Krilus collapse onto his knees and fall forwards a headless corpse. Krilus, who had fought the orks at Ormunga and slaughtered the traitor uprising at Nebeshekar. Five years on crusade, too many victories to count.

His fate – to die without honour, destined to wander the under-worlds headless and blind – was almost too much for Jagra to bear.

He heard a cry of anguish, and thought for a moment it was his until he saw Vultu attacking, his artful blows dodged and parried, the butcher fighting with a swiftness that brutal axe had no right to afford. The blade found its way into Vultu's chest, dug deep, only to be wrenched out in a welter of blood and bone. The Storm Reaper staggered, starving for breath, and ripping off his helm to reveal a blood-spattered face pale as alabaster. He went three more steps, backwards, and fell in a heap.

Undeterred, Jagra threw himself at the butcher, his eyes stinging with tears.

'Jagun hak vun tal! Jagun hak vun tal!'

Every blow swung was fuelled by this mantra. Only half his shield remained, the other shorn off and shucked away like wreckage. It had been his proudest moment when he took up that shield, an honour. And now...

The half-shield skittered away, Jagra unable to process in that second how he had come to lose it. Then he saw the wrist of his left hand spitting blood and realised it had been severed. He fought on. Bereft of the shield, he could move with greater freedom, show this cur how a Storm Reaper *really* fought. Unrestrained, like lightning on the plain, a jagged spear of veng–

He lurched back, having lost his sword arm. Jagra could only stare as blood spurted, too fast for his enhanced body to counter. Unsteadily, he stood before his murderer.

'It gives me no pleasure to see a warrior such as you laid so low,' said the butcher. 'Know no fear, brother, I will end your suffering.'

Jagra's mind went to the plains, to Jagrun. Closing his eyes, his last thought was of rain.

The dead warriors lay about Herek, their offal still steaming. He nudged the one slumped against the wall but he had expired too, his entire midsection caved in and the organs destroyed. He let Harrower fall and the axe embedded in the deck perfectly upright, humming, sated.

The vox in his gorget crackled and a voice hailing him slithered across it.

'Here...' answered Herek, able to tell from the pitch of the comm-feed that his brother was close.

A wretched, lumpen creature shuffled into view. Power armour clung to its body but fleshy growths spilled out to breach it, still crisp with void-frost. Kurgos limped across the deck, glaring at Herek through dark eye-lenses, his head oddly canted on account of the hunch that deformed him. A tooth-bladed bolter hung from his swollen right arm, the hand of the left tucked in his belt.

'Chirurgeon,' said Herek, nodding a greeting.

Kurgos made a grunted reply, looking down with pitying eyes at the dying renegade with a hand across his chest. He knelt, awkwardly and with great effort, eye to eye with the injured warrior. There he muttered a brief exchange to the dying man. Herek had heard the words before. Too often. Then Kurgos took out his knife, pushed it gently through the warrior's ear and proceeded to cut out the vital genetic material.

Herek watched for a few moments before turning his gaze away to stare at his left hand where he slowly clenched and unclenched the fingers. He felt Kurgos' presence by his side when the chirurgeon was done, reeking of that abattoir stench and the waft of tainted unguents.

'Holding up all right?' asked the chirurgeon.

Herek made a fist. 'Well enough...'

'The bridge is ours, engines too,' Kurgos went on, delivering his report. 'Rathek has the last of the security forces cut off and herded into non-essential sections.'

Herek nodded, imagining the carnage the Culler must have wrought. 'Vent the decks with the security forces, have our overseers take the engines and maintain oversight on the original work gangs. Promise clean water, more rations. They'll soon turn coat, swapping one oppressor for another. At least we'll feed them. For as long as it lasts, anyway.'

'I'll see it done. And the bridge crew?'

'Find out who amongst them values survival over devotion to a dead throne, then kill the rest.'

'We're taking her, then.'

'Seems a pity to waste her, she's a good ship. I was considering giving her to Innox...' Herek glanced at the Red Corsair lying dead against the wall, his chest and neck recently and roughly cored out.

'Vyander acquitted themselves well,' Kurgos suggested.

Herek struck up the vox. 'Vyander, consider yourself captain of this vessel. She's yours to defile but keep her hale enough that she can still fight. I want her for the armada.'

The warrior gave a gleeful affirmative and Herek cut the feed. Then he turned his attention to the door.

'Is this it?' asked Kurgos.

Fear bled through the wards, fear and the uncanny.

Herek nodded. 'Oh, yes...' He bent down and hefted Harrower. She felt eager again, the old hunger fully returned like an insatiable cancer. Herek felt it too. Felt it in the wrist of his left arm, burning through the numbness. 'There's little enough time for it but we need what's behind that door.'

Kurgos took a grimy bottle from his belt, holding the neck in a piece of leathery cloth. Then he tossed it and the glass shattered, releasing a shrill keening as something began to materialise in the murky pinkish sludge left behind. It ate the wards, reaching out and draining them with gelatinous tendrils until the sigils flared then grew cold and dead. The daemon ichor turned instantly inert, trembling as it fell onto the deck and discorporated into foul-smelling smoke.

Herek took out the conventional locks with his axe – dirty and undignified work for sure, and she'd make him suffer for it, but it could not be helped. Kurgos shoved the door aside, his bulk equal to the task, and it ground wide enough to reveal two robed and emaciated individuals, one male, one female, cowering behind grav-thrones.

'Please...' uttered one, the male, his voice strange through an elaborate helm. It was massive and ridiculous, a T-shaped encasement of steel with a single gemstone in the centre that resembled a stylised eye. The female went unhooded, a simple band of cloth wrapped around her forehead. She had a shaved skull, the icon of the Navis Nobilite tattooed onto her left temple.

'Now,' said Herek with a smile, his gaze travelling from one to the other, 'which one of you is coming with me?'

Chapter One

MOTHER OF IRON

PROTECTORATE

BURDENS

Orlah looked from the great window of the lunarium upon a firmament of stars, and knew her daughter was out there somewhere amongst them.

The night was bright. Cellenium cast its sickle-edged glow onto the estate below and the cityscape beyond. There was a time, not so distant, that Orlah had stood in this exact same place and beheld devastation. Horror in the streets, entire fiefdoms burning, the pillars of smoke so high they touched the clouds. Those had been dark days when they thought the time of endings had come, when all contact with the Imperium had abruptly and suddenly been cut.

Predators had come, sure as anything, drawn by blood in the water, drunk on the fear of their prey. Except they had been mistaken, these opportunistic bandits. Orlah had raised the household Knights and they had marched out from their ironclad keeps into the palace, through the Gates of Ryn, gates her great grandfather had laid in generations past, out into the city. To fight. To purge.

To cleanse. A night of honour and restoration, the night the Iron-hold had declared her independence.

Kamidar, principal seat of governance and epicentre of martial prowess in the system, had led the charge. And from there, the fighting spirit had spread.

It had been the same across the entire protectorate. At Galius, where the skies had burned red with the light of ten thousand fires. And Vanir, whose ruling family had been slain and its citizens enslaved. Orlah had liberated them, inspired them. To rise, to fight, to endure.

Through it, through the many uncertain nights of horror that followed, of not knowing whether they would live to see dawn, the peoples of the Ironhold had shown their determination to survive. And survive they had. Six years as the hells reigned, Orlah had clenched her mailed fist around her borders and kept them safe.

And now *this*.

Word had reached her, with some of the interpretative unreliability of astropathic messaging, of worlds that had been stripped to the bone and left as hollow shells; of a war machine thoughtless and uncompromising in its hunger to push ever onwards. She knew how voracious a crusade could be. She had fought in enough, but never like this. The stories beyond her borders were sobering to say the least.

She held the esteemed position of queen, and of a Knight world, no less. Kamidar, named for the house that ruled her, a reign that had lasted millennia. That afforded a certain independence, a spirit of self-sufficiency and pride that had only grown during the years of isolation. Ever had the Imperium been careful in its courting of the Knightly houses, for they commanded a martial power few other worlds could equal and possessed a heritage stretching back all the way to the Dark Age of Technology. Such historical provenance was not discarded easily, and though Orlah and her fellow nobles of the many Knight worlds across the galaxy were a part of the Imperium, they considered their relationship with it that of an alliance rather than as a humble vassal.

In her life, both as a warrior and a royal head of state, she had become accustomed to wearing armour. But now, and for the first time, she wondered if it would be thick enough to withstand what was coming.

She had instructed the braziers to be kept low, the dusky light a balm to turbulent thoughts, and the world beyond the window seemed all the brighter for it. The city looked stunning, awash with light and glory. Statues rose above the grand colonnades, their long shadows enfolding Martial Square and Victoris Plaza. Ancestors rendered in marble, fierce, benevolent, their cold eyes turned towards the heavens. There her people went about their business, labourers returning from the fields and factorums of Harnfor, the traders closing up their wares, the watchmen with their long lumen-poles lighting the night darkness. They lived, they toiled, and went about their duties to the protectorate. Together, they had endured. They had *thrived*. By contrast, the palace felt quiet. As a tomb, Orlah thought sombrely.

A patrol returned, not so far from the city walls and beckoned in by pike-armed sentries. Through the gatehouse they went and into the square, the engines of their vehicles idling. A convoy of three transports, a cohort of thirty soldiers alighting from each, dressed in the green and gold of the Kamidarian Sovereigns, begrimed and weary from a long stint out in the wilds.

'Has there been any sign?' Orlah asked of the dark, watching as the Sovereigns unpacked heavy cannon and other armour-shredding weapons from their armoured transports.

'Some...' said Ekria, and came to stand by her queen's side, though she kept a respectful step back. 'It always amazes me how you are aware to my presence,' she confessed.

'Ears of a vulpine,' Orlah answered, giving a half-smile that swiftly faded. 'You would not think Lareoc would be so difficult to find.'

'The wilds are extensive, your majesty. Plenty of places for a resourceful man to hide, even one as conspicuous as the Knight Errant.'

'I rode every inch of those wilds as a girl. I know how far they stretch. And how deep.' She paused a beat. 'And it is *former* Knight Errant,' Orlah corrected, but her interest in this subject was already fading as her gaze returned skyward.

'Former, yes, your majesty. He will be found soon.'

'Which one do you think she is?' asked the queen, abruptly changing subject. 'Sirus, Yemneth, Elynia...' She referred to the stars, winking at the edge of the Kamidar System, already in their death throes.

'I do not know, my queen. She will not be far.'

Orlah stiffened at the name, felt a pang of something in her chest. It reminded her of a knife, twisted and left in the wound.

'Even as a child, she could name them all. Every one. I would tell her stories of how the constellations came to be, of our ancient myths. Dracons and knights. Stories of honour and magick. I never cherished those days enough, before the Rift, before all of this...' She paused, the weight of her silence heavy as a gravestone. 'In a flare of dying starlight, she was gone, Ekria. Silver against the night.'

'You steeled her, trained her – you could have done no more to prepare her, my queen.' Ekria took a step forwards, offering support through proximity, and Orlah was glad of her presence, but her grief was like an ingot of lead in her stomach.

'Am I?' she asked, despair pulling on her.

'I beg your pardon, your majesty?

'A queen,' Orlah answered simply. 'I do not feel like one in this moment, though I wish I could. I wish I could don my armour and have it shield me from the world...'

For a moment, she caught her ghostly reflection in the glass. Tall, a long white-and-gold gown trailing from her silhouette. An ornate guard over her left shoulder, rendered into the image of a gilded dracon with rubies for eyes. A little more silver in her dark hair than there once had been. Dark skin like polished onyx. A handsome woman, she supposed. Powerful, proud. Bereft.

'But I feel like a mother,' she said, 'raw and exposed, waiting for a dawn I wish would never come.'

'At least she returns now.'

'Yes, and I will greet her as her queen, but I will mourn for her as her mother. My dear Jessivayne.'

Her hand strayed to the torc around her neck, and the sharply cut black garnet in its centre. Her mother had worn it, and her mother before her. And so it went. It should have gone to Jessivayne next, but now...

'How long before they arrive?'

'The astropaths estimate six days before they reach high anchor in our atmosphere.'

'Make all necessary preparations.'

'Of course, your majesty.'

'Thank you, Ekria.'

She reached out to clasp her servant's pale hand. It was warm, and supple. The equerry had served House Kamidar for years but had aged little during that time. Orlah felt she had aged a century in a day when she heard of Jessivayne's death.

'This will be the last time,' she said, releasing Ekria's hand and turning her own into a tightly clenched fist.

'My queen?'

'That I show weakness,' she answered sternly, turning her face from the widow of memory and gently embracing the darkness.

Of the many vessels comprising Fleet Praxis, Ariadne's main concern was the *Fell Lord*, its flagship and the war throne of Admiral

Ardemus. It was also where, as one of the quartermasters senioris, she was stationed. Her remit, though, extended far beyond that. To the entire battle group. Fuel, rations, munitions: each had a count, had a cost. Ariadne's job was to levy that against the needs of the crusade. Balancing the mundane arithmetic of war was as crucial as the fighting itself. And not without its frustrations.

'Are you telling me the ship isn't there?'

The ship's bosun nodded, a little breathless as he fought to keep up with the quartermaster.

'Well, Mavik?' Ariadne pressed, turning her stern gaze on the lowly bosun as she marched across the deck towards the bridge.

'That is to say, madam quartermaster,' the bosun gasped, his face flushed with effort, 'the Navigators can find no sign of the *Mercurion*. Both it and the *Hermes* did not emerge from translation with the rest of the armada.'

Ariadne cursed under her breath. 'Both good ships. A goodly portion of our additional fuel and rations were aboard the *Hermes*.'

The *Mercurion* was a warship, effectively the other vessel's minder, but that had counted for little it seemed. She tapped a sequence of icons on her slate's claviboard, prompting a screed of information to appear on the screen.

'This will hurt us.'

Reports fed through on her ocular augmetic, and she blinked from one to the next, assimilating and assessing reams of data in a matter of seconds. It was ugly, her bionic, a boxy, metallic adjunct to her own flesh-and-blood eye that she could never remove. Vanity had never been Ariadne's preoccupation, though she still had her youth, her raven-black hair and jade-green eyes. Men liked her eyes. Ariadne found their attention tedious. She valued efficiency and accuracy – traits useful to a crusade quartermaster – and that was all.

She worked rapidly, a gently flashing runic notification in the corner of her ocular's retinal display reminding her of Ardemus' summons.

'The impatient bastard wants the stars before we've barely had chance to glimpse them,' she muttered.

'Madam?'

'Nothing,' Ariadne snapped. 'We're already stretched. We'll have to make further changes, tighten our belts again.' She began calculating, shifting resources from one place to another, accounting for the loss of fuel and rations represented by the absent vessels. It was possible they would rejoin the armada but her experience of the crusade so far suggested otherwise. Once a ship was lost, it tended to stay that way or else reappear on the other side of Sanctus, minus its entire complement and gutted prow to stern. Even the Mechanicus reclamators left those ships alone, some salvage simply not worth the risk.

'If I may, quartermaster...' ventured the bosun, and again Ariadne gave him the hard emerald of her sharpest glance. Couldn't he see she was trying to ameliorate a crisis?

'Speak then,' she scathed, when he didn't immediately continue.

'What of the Ironhold? They will have rations, fuel. Supplies of all kinds.'

Ariadne's expression softened as she considered the bosun's line of logic before answering, 'We don't know what we can count on from the protectorate. My understanding is the admiral wants to turn it into a forward base, one of the redoubts.'

'I only ask because I heard Usullis is prepping a vanguard to move ahead of the main battle group with Imperial sanction to make landfall on the principal world and begin asset appropriation.'

Ariadne stiffened like a knife in her slate-grey uniform, her rapid march slowing but a fraction at this new information. Usullis was her contemporary, an unsubtle man who had made more than one pass at her over the years. She thought of him as a blunt and brutal instrument.

'Tell me everything. Now.'

'They are scheduled to make landfall two days ahead of the main fleet with a flotilla of resupply frigates and a small Naval escort. There is to be a warship amongst their number, the *Vortun's Ire*. That's a Militarum carrier, madam, it's–'

'I know what it is,' she snapped. 'Throne... he's been given leave to land *soldiers*?'

'That's my understanding, madam.'

'When?'

'Imminently, as soon as the briefing is concluded.'

And he had kept that information from her. Worse, Admiral Ardemus had not seen fit to inform her either; but then again, he had matters on his mind that went beyond how many beans were in the fleet's silo ships. The groupmaster was an ambitious man, capable but ambitious. He would be chafing at this duty, preferring to be out in the void killing heretics and whatever else deigned to stand up to him.

Ariadne consoled herself with the knowledge that nothing could be done in that moment, and besides, the door to the bridge section now loomed, and Ardemus' briefing. The heavy blast doors were open, an angular arch edged with marble statuary beckoning her into a deep, umber gloom. She passed a pair of guards on the way in wearing tan uniforms beneath bronze breastplates. Each had a silver-chased autocarbine held at parade height, eyes forward, glowering from beneath steel helms. Polished soldiers in shining chrome. Other officers had already begun to gather as she took her place amongst them in the oak-panelled opulence of the strategium, exchanging the odd banal pleasantry where it was offered, a nod or a glance to others as she recognised them in their fine Naval and Militarum uniforms.

It was a lavish chamber, low-lit with a hololithic table in the middle. No seats: Ardemus would suffer no one in his presence to slouch or recline when discussing the business of war. The walls were hung with ancient star and seafaring maps, protected behind gently flickering stasis fields. Other navigational artefacts stood upon plinths or inside plasglass cases: a sextant, a brass scope, an ancient compass. Ardemus had assembled this collection over several years, a testament to his vanity and yearning for tradition. Most prominent was a long harpoon, its blade still sharp and held aloft by suspensors above the other antiques.

Ariadne could practically *feel* the admiration and jealousy emanating from the other officers, certainly those who were physically present. One of their gathering showed no interest, however, and Ariadne risked a glance at the Holy Sister in her blood-red plate. Prayer scrolls and miniature skulls hanging on votive chains gave her a baroque, almost otherworldly aura. So armoured, she stood a good head and shoulders above most of the men, and this made Ariadne smile despite herself as they vainly puffed up their chests and straightened their backs in an attempt to match her. None could.

Save for the warrior who followed in slowly on the admiral's heels.

This one made Ariadne's skin crawl, for he was a brutish monster with a slab-like, symmetrical face, eyes like flint and just as sharp. His armour, unlike the Holy Sister's, was a functional, brutalist thing, painted in muddy yellow and black, the sigil of a winged lightning bolt on his hulking left shoulder guard. As he entered the strategium he had to stoop below the arch and had already removed his helm, which he held in the crook of his left arm, his right free to draw the broad blade at his hip should he need to. Violence bled off this man in a near-palpable fume. He was badly scarred, metal plates bolted here and there to his jaw and skull, the remnant surgeries of some injury once suffered. Pitiless, he had the reek of death about him. His name was Renyard, a captain of Space Marines and the admiral's war dog.

Ariadne instinctively retreated a few steps away as Renyard came amongst them, as did many of her fellow officers. Even the Holy Sister fractionally shifted her stance, a predator reacting to another and wary of its intent.

Only the admiral appeared unperturbed by the warrior's presence.

Ardemus was a heavyset man, broad-shouldered even without the golden epaulettes of his light blue Naval uniform. Three gilded chains hung from neck to shoulder and a sword and pistol hung from his belt. He had fair hair, with eyes like storms, and was well groomed. Attractive in a stern sort of a way.

'In four days, the first of our ships will have made landfall on Kamidar, principal world of the Ironhold Protectorate,' he declared proudly. 'Our mission here goes beyond the refit and repair of our vessels. We are to raise a bulwark in the Imperium's name, for the crusade. We shall do so with alacrity and purpose.'

He paused, taking in the room. A few of the assembled worthies flickered, comms distortion rendering their holos indistinct for a second or two before realigning again. A hundred and sixty-three vessels made up Battle Group Praxis, a formidable armada, the majority of which would take up anchorage above Kamidar while the rest would be sent to the other two worlds of the Ironhold. Their captains and officers were many, and all were required to attend Ardemus as he held forth.

'Our hosts here are the Kamidarian royal household,' he went on. 'They are Knights of an esteemed order, a martial culture, led by a warrior queen who commands a small empire. I believe the burden we carry to her is partly the reason for her allowing us to land resupply ships pre-emptively. The Kamidarians have not seen or heard from the Imperium in many years and their customs and beliefs may have diverged from our own during this time. Even at their most loyal, Knights have ever been strong-willed. They are very proud. Be wary, then' – he glanced at the hulking Space Marine at this point, but the warrior gave nothing back save the uncompromising steel of his glare – 'but also understand this is the sovereign territory of our God-Emperor, regardless of its distance from the Throneworld or how long the protectorate has had to endure in the dark, on its own. They are still of the Imperium, proud or not. There is the belief among some quarters that we may find an unwillingness here to comply, but our calling is just, our need beyond any alliance.

'So know this... I will *claim* these worlds and take from them what the crusade needs, what Praxis needs. It is nothing less than our duty. Our *right*. We begin with Kamidar, for that is the seat of governance and the other worlds of Galius and Vanir will follow suit.'

The other officers nodded or murmured agreement at this, like vassals come to pledge their loyalty and swear fealty to Ardemus' throne.

'Are we expecting resistance?' asked Shipmaster Tournis of the *Valiant Spear*. His image flickered, grey-blue, then stabilised. A good-looking man, tight of frame but muscular with a neatly trimmed beard and close-cut hair. A patch covered one eye, an old injury that Tournis wore well. He was a crusade veteran and master of the second most powerful ship in the Praxis armada, second only to Ardemus.

'We should always expect resistance, captain,' answered Ardemus, mildly chiding. His rivalry with Tournis was a poorly kept secret. 'But the protectorate are our kin, at least in kind. We are liberators, bringing sanctity to the Imperium. Our torchbearer fleets have already sown the seeds and now we have come to reap the harvest. It may be distasteful to some, but we have our orders and we are in need of the supplies and materiel they can provide.'

'Is that why you are sending Quartermaster Usullis and a military escort as a vanguard to Kamidar, my lord?' Ariadne spoke, the words on her mind coming out of her mouth before she realised she had uttered them.

A tremor of annoyance flickered over the groupmaster's face. 'We have a long task ahead of us and must work swiftly. Usullis will steal a march for us, requisitioning the materials and resources we need so that we may get underway without unnecessary delay. As such, I have no desire to prolong this meeting further with inconsequentialities, Quartermaster Ariadne.'

'Of course, sir.' Chastened, Ariadne wanted to disappear into the crowd but Ardemus had already moved on. Though she doubted this would be the end of the matter.

'We all know how dark a day it was for the Imperium when Cadia fell,' said Ardemus, casting his eye around the room at the blanched faces, the clenched jaws, the officers with balled fists at their sides. There had been none darker. It had heralded the Rift, after all, and ushered in the blighted era they now fought to overcome. 'A fate no one could have predicted, and one that is the reason we are all here. Our mission is ordained by none other than the Regent of Terra himself.'

From the sudden fervour in his voice, Ariadne could tell on which side of the argument Ardemus fell when it came to whether or not the returned primarch was a god. He believed. Utterly. She had never met the Avenging Son, though she had heard his voice across countless addresses to his troops, to his crusaders. To think he had lived over ten thousand years ago, and had come back to them at mankind's bleakest hour... Man or god, it didn't matter what she thought. He was all that stood between the Imperium and oblivion. Privately, she wondered if it would be enough.

Ardemus nodded to one of his functionaries, who unobtrusively activated the hololith.

And with a flicker of light, Lord Guilliman appeared.

A stilled reverence fell across the chamber, as every officer present knelt. Even Renyard appeared humbled and struggled to meet the primarch's gaze.

'Even now Fleet Secundus fights to hold the galactic north, the first line of defence against our enemy, who pours through the Cadian Gate in droves,' Guilliman said, his tone – even through the holo – so rich and deep it did not seem possible to have been uttered

by a human mouth. But, of course, he wasn't human. Not really. He was so much more.

Massive and dominant in his ornate, gold-edged armour, a laurel about his head like a crown, the iron halo he wore a brilliant gilded sunburst that framed his patrician countenance. Filigree and intaglio adorned his singular war plate, festooned with a swathe of purity seals affixed by the highest ecclesiarchs. Guilliman was something from myth, brought back to fight Ruinous Gods and halt mankind's imminent destruction.

'It is a bitter campaign, grossly attritional, but know that its continued success means nothing less than the safety of Terra. To staunch the threat of attack from this ill-favoured quarter, a robust chain of resupply must be established. Through the strategic positioning of bastion or redoubt worlds, we can ensure Secundus remains well strengthened for the rigours it must face. But should it fail, should our enemy slip through its pickets, then our defences behind it must also be strong. Here then is the wisdom of a hemispherical chain of fortified strongholds, arranged strategically so if one falls another will stand in its place. Each supporting the other. Defence in depth. Our Anaxian Line.'

He stopped to smile, a cold but bracing appraisal of his troops, raising his chin as if to behold them all with his highest regard. Ariadne felt her heart beat faster, her pride and determination swelling. She could appreciate how such a being had once commanded an empire. Some said he still did, and had no inclination to relinquish it.

'You, brave men and women of the Imperium, are tasked with securing our eastern lynchpin, Kamidar and the Ironhold Protectorate,' Guilliman continued. 'There are few greater burdens than this. If Kamidar holds then the Anaxian Line holds and our enemy from the galactic north will be stymied. These redoubts are the crusade's lifeblood. Without them, we cannot hope to prosper so far from Terra. Know that we will have to journey far from the

Throneworld before this is over. Our supply lines are crucial. The acumen of our logisticians and Munitorum adept-generals is crucial. In order to attack with purpose, we must also be sure of keeping what we have already won. This, then, is the singular purpose of the Anaxian Line and its importance to the crusade. I know you shall all undertake this task valorously. Together we shall overcome and light a beacon through mankind's darkest hour. I have sworn it, so it shall be. Ave Imperator. Courage and honour to you all.'

The recording ended, the image stuttering as it stalled in place until the functionary turned it off again.

Slowly, the officers rose to their feet. The Holy Sister ended her genuflection with the utmost poise, making the sign of the aquila. Even the brutal Space Marine grunted his assent. A hush descended, the reverence for the returned primarch slow to fade.

Ardemus was the first to break it.

'And thus is it spoken. From the very lips of our saviour, the Lord Guilliman himself. I hope you feel as humbled as I do in receiving these orders. To live in such times of peril and magnificence...'

His gaze roamed the room, fixing every officer whether present or not. It alighted on Ariadne last of all and lingered, a calculated move and one that said he had not forgiven nor forgotten her outburst.

'Ours is nothing less than a sacred calling, god-given,' said Ardemus. 'What we do is nothing less than the Emperor's will, so be about your tasks without hesitation or doubt. This is the fight for humanity's survival and we shall not be found wanting.' He nodded then, fierce conviction in his eyes as they left Ariadne and roamed again. 'Dismissed.'

A worm of unease coiled in Ariadne's gut as she made her way back to her quarters. She had left some data-spools there and wished to retrieve them before presenting any sort of report to the groupmaster. Ardemus was so full of piss and vinegar that she doubted he would have much time or interest in ration shortfalls or their diminishing fuel, but she had a duty.

She almost missed the armour-clad warrior coming the other way, her head so far into her data-slate and her calculations that they almost collided. An awful sense of disquiet, something only half-fettered but repelling, made her look up. Ariadne pulled up short, and the warrior came to a sharp stop herself as she looked down on the quartermaster like an adult appraising a truculent child. Despite all her years of experience, her esteemed position in the Departmento Munitorum, Ariadne quailed a little before the woman.

She was like some grim, silver goddess from a forgotten era. Not one of the Sororitas like the Sister in the strategium; at least she had radiated grace, even compassion, behind her stern appearance. This one standing before Ariadne was a warrior-queen with dark shadows around the eyes and the aquila marked indelibly into her skin. She wore slight, almost form-fitted, archaic armour. Ariadne knew who she was but dared not speak her name, dared not even think it for fear she would know and disapprove.

Instead, Ariadne uttered, 'My pardon, milady.' She cast her eyes down, humbled and disquieted.

The warrior didn't reply, though gave a slight narrowing of the eyes, and waited for Ariadne to step from her path before striding on. Ariadne let her go, not moving, listening to her boot steps, grateful to hear them receding. The sense of disquiet faded as the sound diminished, and she breathed a sigh of relief.

Chapter Two

PENITENCE THROUGH PAIN

AN ABSENT PLINTH

A BLOODY SIGN

The whip bit the flesh of his back, a hot line left after the sting, bloody droplets spraying with the backswing. Another blow followed, savage, deep, but he did not flinch despite the fact his skin was already a tapestry of scars.

'Again...'

The hooded serfs obeyed, lashing out as ordered. The metal hooks at the end of three-pronged whips caught the light of the braziers that filled the air with the aroma of clove and mugwort.

Sacred. Purifying.

'Again...'

Penitence through pain.

As they whipped him, Morrigan wound the chain. He did it slowly around the left wrist, his sword arm. The metal felt sharp against his bare skin, grating. He bore the pain like all the rest, and wound the links tighter.

'I am an unworthy servant,' he murmured to his watching brethren, their cold eyes appraising. He turned the chain again. The whips lashed him. 'I am found wanting under your regard, oh God-Emperor.' Another turn. Another lash. 'I beseech you, oh Lord of Terra, help me to see your will. Give me the strength to atone.'

Harsh iron bit, drawing blood. It dripped readily onto the black flagstones of the chapel, an offering, penance. Another turn of the chain. Another lash. Morrigan pulled; he pulled so hard the feeling in his fingers fled and his tanned skin grew white where the iron throttled it.

'And let me return to the light of your glory.'

The chain broke, the links splitting against the strain, and Morrigan gasped in relief. In the shadows, he heard both serfs sag, their gasping breaths, their vigour spent. Pain stole across his body as the blood rushed back, great ugly weals left in his flesh by the metal that fell in two split halves either side of his wrist. The chain still entangled him, the broken links a reminder of his broken oath and the deed he must accomplish if he were to reforge it.

A mark of shame.

The eyes of his dead brothers condemned him, their forty-three sightless helms regarding him from their plinths in the chapel's shrine of remembrance. One of those plinths was empty, its absence a sword thrust through Morrigan's hearts.

'Bohemund...' he whispered, an anguish like a burning coal filling his chest with its pain and heat.

We'll take these wretches in short order, Varun... For the Emperor and glory.

'For the Emperor and glory,' Morrigan echoed, a decade too late and Bohemund's headless corpse long turned to bone in the Sturmhal's reliquarius.

He bowed his head, unable to bear the weight of old shame, *their* still eyes burning into him like iron rods from a torturer's forge. He deserved every flagellation. For only through pain could he find the path to redemption.

A prisoner to his own thoughts, Morrigan realised his seclusion had been intruded upon when he smelled oil and lapping powder above the heady incense. The growl of his brother's war plate came later as Morrigan took to his feet with slow deliberation and turned to face the warrior at the chapel's archway.

'Godfried.'

'My castellan.' Godfried bowed, a feat in his armour. He was tall and thick-set, even considering his pauldrons. His stare was penetrating and fierce behind crimson retinal lenses, his voice a soft machine growl through his helm's audio-emitters. 'Sincerest apologies, lord, for interrupting your penance.'

'It is nothing, brother. Speak freely of whatever it is that has brought you here.'

'A fleet has come.'

Morrigan failed to hide his surprise at this news. They had been alone and isolated within the Ironhold for almost six years, ever since Bohemund...

'An Imperial fleet, lord,' Godfried elaborated. 'A great many ships.'

'They have come to yoke the Ironhold.'

Godfried gave a shallow nod. 'I believe so, lieutenant.'

'An emissary must be prepared.'

'The Iron Queen has also sent a summons.'

'I would expect nothing less.' The blood from Morrigan's tortured arm was pooling at his feet but Godfried gave it little heed. The castellan was about to return to conclude his penance when his brother spoke again.

'There is more.'

Morrigan's raised eyebrow bid Godfried continue.

'*He* is here.'

The inflection made it so no further elaboration was needed.

'Where?'

'Our augurs tracked the *Ruin* at system's edge a few hours ago.'

The metal wrapped around his wrist groaned as Morrigan clenched a fistful of the chain links in his hand. Pain flared red but warming through his arm. His hearts thundered in his muscular chest.

'How many...?' he breathed, anger turning to sorrow as he gazed upon the shrine of remembrance and the helms of his dead brothers. 'How many have we lost to keep the Ironhold safe all these years?'

'A number beyond countenance,' answered Godfried simply.

'A number beyond countenance,' said Morrigan, giving his affirmation.

His gaze hardened, drawn to the casket that lay at the heart of the shrine, the ghosts of the slain surrounding it. Blessed chains had been wrapped around the metal, its clear sides wrought of armaglass, the hex-wards shimmering every now and then in the chapel's brazier light. A sword lay within, bound by sanctified iron, festooned with purity seals, and the entire casket filled to the brim with holy oil. A sword with a dark blade and a hilt of gold that resembled roots twisted into the shape of a cross-guard. Blasphemy, they had named it. The hand of its former wielder was still attached to the grip, impossible to remove, impervious to every effort to destroy it. A skeletal hand, long stripped of flesh. The hand of an enemy.

'Are we to be denied this vengeance?' Morrigan asked, of himself as much as the empty helms of the shrine.

'What does the Emperor will?'

He looked over then at Godfried. The Champion stood with his hands clasped together before him, but eager to wield the deadly greatsword sheathed upon his back.

The offering at Morrigan's feet had spilled into a broad pool, his grizzled face reflected in it, all his many wounds and scars turned crimson in this mirror-world of blood. A shape had formed, discernible to Morrigan alone. An eagle with wings outstretched. An aquila. A sign of condoning.

His will.

Morrigan took up his sword with the scrape of metal against stone and signalled to the serfs lurking in the shadows.

'Bring me my armour.'

Chapter Three

MAUSOLEUM

AURIC GODS

A RELIGIOUS EXPERIENCE

A sorrowful air hung heavy in the ship's hold like mist over a forlorn isle. Hardly a fitting place for a memorial, and yet it had become a mausoleum.

She sat alone encased in the Throne Mechanicum and her machine's old cradle, a god of war now reduced to an open casket. A flock of candles, burned almost to their wicks, surrounded her body, a sacristan diligently replacing them whenever they ran to the nub. Fingers of wax trailed down the sanctified mechanisms, settling in congealed pools on the floor. This too would be scraped away and renewed by rote. A pair of old coins, Kamidarian crowns, bearing the heraldic sword of the royal house, covered her eyes. An offering to whatever ferryman would carry her to the Emperor's embrace. Her wounds had been so grievous that a silken veil shrouded her face to spare the grief-stricken the horror of her injured countenance.

Here lies Jessivayne Y'Kamidar, former scion to the throne of the Ironhold, warrior princess of Kamidar.

A chapel or Reclusiam would have made a better resting place, but no chapel could house a shrine of this scale. And the ship had no Reclusiam. After the princess had been moved from the lander, she had been ensconced here in its host vessel, the *Virtuous*, now a funerary barque to convey the deceased and those who accompanied her on the last leg of the journey back to Kamidar.

Magda Kesh had scarcely met Lady Jessivayne's kinsfolk, although she knew they visited the mausoleum in the quiet hours when most of the ship were asleep, so they could weep in peace without anyone to hear it. For a time, one of Jessivayne's house, a stern-faced knight of solemn bearing with sandy hair and darkly weathered skin, had stood vigil until matters of duty beyond those to the dead had called him away. He had worn his grief like a sodden cloak, thick and heavy until it dragged on his noble frame and made him bitter.

Sorrow had a way of leaching into things, Kesh knew. It clung like the whiff of smoke or a bloody stain, hard to remove entirely, its tendrils deep enough to last. Kesh felt it here. This place reeked of it, despite the functional setting. The *Virtuous* was a heavy transport ship. Of the six drop keeps it could carry, only three remained. The House Y'Kamidar had given much to Guilliman's crusade, even its heir, and after six years Jessivayne was finally going home. It would have been sooner but for the demands of the crusade. A bittersweet reunion.

Kesh wondered if she would ever see Mordian again, though she had no family there to speak of and the night world wasn't exactly pleasant. But she knew it, and it knew her. Perhaps a casket was the best she could hope for.

Sacristans busied themselves here and there, stirring Kesh from morbid thoughts, the tech-adepts far enough away and too absorbed in their labours to be considered intrusive. They paid her no mind anyway, her visit sanctioned by the Baron Gerent Y'Kamidar, who had been the one to turn this hold into a memorial to his niece. As such, he granted the rite of observance through prayer but only to those who had fought on Gathalamor, and only on account of the fact that they neared journey's end. Theirs was a proud and martial culture, Kesh had quickly realised, and a warrior's prayer did honour to Jessivayne's memory. Or so Kesh believed, though she would never be so audacious as to suggest she knew the Baron Y'Kamidar's thoughts or will. The honour guard, of which she and several other Mordians, including General Dvorgin, were a part, had largely been confined to the barracks and armoury for the last several days after they had come aboard the *Virtuous*. So as well as paying her respects, it was also a chance to stretch her legs.

The shrine spread out below her and from her vantage on the stairs it looked magnificent but also crushingly morose. The flowers placed there had since perished, their leaves browned to flakes and devoid of life. Kesh had come close to death, back on Gathalamor. The nightmare of being buried alive under the bones of the long-dead had never truly faded. The cardinal world and its war felt almost a foreign country to the pathfinder-scout now, but it lingered in her senses. The blood, the dirt, the fear. It, like sorrow, had a tangibility that was difficult to erase.

She patted the pocket of her unbuttoned uniform jacket, glad to feel the presence of the injector vial. In the darker moments when the nightmares came, the stimm injector had been a lifeline. Every Guardsman had one. It was supposed to be used in combat, to keep you moving, to keep you sharp. For Kesh, it kept her functional. For now.

Faith helped too, she had discovered. And perhaps somewhere in that was a revelation of sorts. Kesh had seen much she could not readily explain or reconcile, her survival probably the least incredible thing amongst them, and that in itself had been miraculous.

Miracles, she thought, *are not such an abstract concept.*

That was just as well, for nightmares had also grown more real in the passing years.

She descended the stairs, her eyes on the princess in state, preserved by the tender ministrations of the priests just as the sacristans tended to her fallen Knight to prevent it falling into greater ruination. The wreckage of the great war engine dwelt here with her, half-destroyed and beyond repair, like a master who is buried with his dead hound or the faraohs of old with their favoured servants. That last reference had come from Dvorgin, who had read it in some old book. Kesh found it sad but oddly appealing.

Even in death, we do not wish to feel alone.

Face to face with Jessivayne, Kesh could not help but feel a pang of sympathy. The veil did little to really hide the injuries. And the rigours of the void, despite the many stasis fields and devices of preservation employed, had not been kind. Her skull had been crushed, this the blow that had killed her back on Gathalamor, and half of her face deformed in the act. It gave a strange dichotomy to her features: one side a broken ruin, a thing of horror; the other still beautiful. *And she had been beautiful.* And though Jessivayne was of noble birth, Kesh found kinship in that damaged visage. Her own scars were underneath, that was all. Half a soldier, a pale version of who she once was.

Kesh ran a hand through her hair and felt the calluses against her scalp. It was closely shorn, cut short so the lack of opportunities to wash it didn't irritate her too much. It kept the lice away too. Her uniform suddenly felt grubby, her fingers grimy with gun oil. To anyone watching, she would present as a soldier in short-sleeved Mordian blue. Short but strong; not stocky exactly, but muscularly framed. Fair-haired, though the Militarum cut made that harder to discern. Grey eyes, with too much pain in them. Younger than she looked. A marksman's cap sat snug under the left shoulder strap.

She missed the weight of her rifle across her shoulder or in her hands, and she yearned to be running fitness drills around the half-deck where they had been quartered. But she was here now   55

THE IRON KINGDOM

and so she would pay her respects and try to learn a little of who this woman had been when she was alive.

Kneeling made Kesh wince, provoking the sharp pain she would carry all her life; a memento from Gathalamor and the price for fighting alongside gods.

'I have no business amongst such beings...' she mused aloud.

'Which beings are those?' answered a gruff voice, causing Kesh to gasp suddenly, and she stood up straight.

'Throne... I thought I was alone.' Flustered, Kesh made to turn and retrace her steps back to the stairs until Vychellan stopped her.

'Do not depart on my account,' he said genially, 'though I can leave you to your solitude if you prefer.'

'Please, no,' said Kesh, still trying to quiet her hammering heart.

His golden armour made a man who was already a giant even more cyclopean. Long hair as white as alabaster and tied back in a neat queue added to the severity of his features, which were framed by a neatly trimmed beard. His azure gaze had the intensity of ice and was just as cold; colder when he wished it to be. The aquila tattooed upon his forehead gave away his vocation, as if any evidence was needed.

Kesh felt herself begin to tremble but rallied. Standing in the presence of one of the Adeptus Custodes was not easy, even one she had fought alongside and witnessed in battle. She knew one of his order would deny it, but to her it was nothing short of a religious experience. And that also applied to the holy warriors of the Adepta Sororitas, who had also counted amongst their number that day. To reflect on it, on what she had seen and done... *blessed* was not really the word.

'I assume you have come to pray?' he asked without obvious judgement.

Kesh nodded. 'Ever since Gathalamor... well, I...' She made a face as if to suggest she had not the words to accurately express the experience, which she did not. 'I am surprised to see you here,' she added, noticing the book in Vychellan's hand for the first time. It was a simple tome, small in his gauntleted hands, no larger than a notebook and bound in simple, supple leather.

'Evidently.' If there was to be elaboration on the point it was not forthcoming.

'I did not know your... *kind* read or needed to read.'

Throne, this was awkward.

'I have no *need* of it. I find it pleasurable.' He gently closed the book, turning it over and back as if to regard it. 'I know every word, every crease and imperfection by heart. I have known it for centuries. Perhaps longer. It is war philosophy. I read it to remember, not words but feelings, and to honour an old friend.'

Kesh thought this must be Achallor, another of the Custodians' singular order, who had perished on Gathalamor. According to Dvorgin, his body had been interred in the cardinal world's soil, an act of resanctification and sainthood for the fallen Custodian who had sacrificed his life for the Imperium's victory.

'It is quiet here,' offered Vychellan, the only explanation she would get or he would give, 'and I am usually left undisturbed.'

Now Kesh wondered if the Custodian was just teasing, though the notion was hard to reconcile with the auric god before her. She did not think the likes of Vychellan possessed something so ordinary as humour.

'A jest,' he said, confirming what she had just dismissed, the smile on his face at odds with its brutal features. 'Please, pray to Him if you must. I will pass no judgement.'

That Kesh definitely did not believe as she settled into a comfortable position.

'It must appear strange to you,' she said, just as she was about to clasp together her hands and make the sign of the aquila. 'For one who has... who knew... *Him*.'

'I cannot say that I or any of my brotherhood ever *knew* the Emperor, though some might claim otherwise.' Vychellan sneered at this, as if the thoughts were a bitter draught on his tongue. 'We were not merely made to be warriors, though. Our true purpose was as companions. Our skills with philosophy and debate were meant to be just as well honed as those with spear and sword.'

'I... I did not know that. Then this must seem foolish to you.'

'I remember Him as a man, a gifted man of vast intelligence and abilities far beyond that of the ordinary mortal range, but a man all the same.' Vychellan had become mildly melancholic, as if spirited to better days and reluctant to return to a bleaker present. He turned his gaze back to Kesh, the softening of sorrow in his eyes swift to turn back to winter ice. 'So, yes, what you are doing is preposterous to me. But I would not deny you if it brings comfort.'

'It does,' Kesh answered truthfully. Since Gathalamor, her faith brought her more solace than it had ever done before.

'Then pray, Magda Kesh,' Vychellan answered as he began to leave, 'and I hope you find whatever peace you seek.'

She heard him depart after he had moved beyond her peripheral vision, footsteps eventually diminishing into echoes.

A religious experience, Kesh reflected, closing her eyes as she murmured the first lines of her prayer.

'Our God-Emperor, He who dwells on Terra...'

Chapter Four

ORDERS
STORM RIDERS
LANDFALL

Another tremble shook the inside of the lander and not for the first time, Ariadne regretted speaking out in the strategium. She had regretted it the moment she had done it. A short missive had been waiting for her upon her return to her quarters. Already unnerved by her encounter with the warrior in silver, this only worsened matters. Orders from Ardemus, conveyed by one of the admiral's lackeys no doubt. A scroll of vellum, sealed with wax: innocuous and ubiquitous enough on an Imperial starship, most might suppose, but Ariadne knew better. She had erred and the bill for that was due. She was to accompany Usullis, join the vanguard flotilla and supervise the requisition effort on Kamidar.

Poor choices, lamented Ariadne to herself, as another jolt ran through her body. They had led her here, clinging to a restraint harness.

The lander juddered again, navigating a minor debris field. Every *plink* of wreckage or rock against the hull thrust her heart into her mouth so hard she thought she'd choke.

Departing dock at the *Fell Lord*'s tertiary embarkation deck had been straightforward enough, almost pleasant. Ariadne had gone to the observation blister in the upper deck of the lander, crowded in with her colleagues and watching the many great vessels of Battle Group Praxis drift past them with stately grace.

A host of ships of varying size and denomination, dominating a great swathe of the void many hundreds of miles across. She had caught but a minuscule fraction of their fleet disposition and so close up it was like passing by an immense face of rock with little to distinguish it. In her mind's eye, cruisers and frigates eased alongside escorts and destroyers whose sleek hulls slid predatorily through the endless black. Alongside the ships of the line were the workhorse vessels, those that ferried supplies and ensured Praxis could function far from the nearest port, keeping its engines fuelled and troops fed; not so different from a military baggage train, she supposed. Ships like the *Hermes*, which Ariadne had been tracking before Ardemus had decided he wanted to show everyone how so very important he was.

The capital ships were by far the most impressive, like immense floating cathedra, bedecked with statues and gothic architecture, festooned with weapons arrays that could decimate worlds. And of the many ships that fit this description, the *Fell Lord* was the largest. It was Ardemus' flagship, an honour he wore vainly, she thought, but wear it he did and it suited him well.

Unlike her own current transportation.

Ariadne had no intrinsic dislike for void transit, she was just more used to the actual transport being considerably larger and more robust. Which was not to say the Colossi-class lander was a small craft. Far from it. The vessel needed to be sufficiently expansive to house not only the hundreds of Munitorum staff and their equipment, as well as the not-inconsiderable military escort, but also for the vast silos that would be packed to the metaphorical gunwales with rations and materiel acquired from the tithed world below. A gargantuan undertaking, and one that would require careful organisation on both a logistical and political level. It was one thing to tithe a world that knew the Imperium was coming, but quite a different prospect indeed to take from one that had been surviving independently for the last several years.

'You cannot move in that restraint,' said the warrior sitting opposite her. She had spoken to him little during the journey, beyond the odd awkward pleasantry she scarcely remembered, but he had seemed intent to engage her. Certainly, he was fairly gregarious for a Space Marine.

'I see...' said Ariadne, eyes firmly shut, her knuckles still whitening as she clenched the vertical locking bars.

'And you might as well open your eyes, *visha.*'

She had learned during their transit together that visha meant 'little one'. She should have been insulted, but right now Ariadne felt very small and insignificant indeed, so the name fit.

'Do you know what that is?' she asked, somewhat tremulously, as another blow struck the hull, sending a resonant clang throughout the hold. Two hundred sat in this section alone, mostly Munitorum, a few Militarum troopers and... *them.* A handful only, to ensure the smooth transition of materiel – or a potent reminder of the Imperium's might. It could be either, probably both.

'I think it is the wind,' he said, gently teasing.

'Don't be foolish,' Ariadne snapped, 'there is no atmosphere in the void.' And realised she had opened her eyes.

The Space Marine returned her gaze, an amused look on his face. He had told her his name was Ogin. A Storm Reaper, one of the Ultima Founding. Primaris.

White-armoured, wearing a sigil of a double-bladed axe and twin lightning bolts, Brother Ogin was an arresting sight. As wide as a ship's door and just as tall, or so it seemed to Ariadne, the ostensibly threatening aura that all Astartes evinced up close was belied by a jovial face, unkempt beard and laughter lines in the corner of his storm-blue eyes.

'Ah, well then,' said Ogin, as if this was some kind of revelation, stroking his long dark moustaches as he pondered it, 'then it must be a *grushälob*.' His eyes went wide, and he leaned back, causing the two Munitorum adepts who sat next to him to shrink away or risk being crushed by his armoured bulk.

'Now you are just mocking me,' Ariadne said.

'Perhaps, but the grushälob is very serious. A beast of Jagun, it can steal upon the unwary wherever they might be.' He made a face as if weighing such a place. 'In your grandest hall, under your bed... even in the cold of the void.' His eyes flashed as the soft lumen light caught them and there was something almost feline in them. Almost savage.

Ogin's booming laughter shattered the silence that followed, and Ariadne thought one of the adepts might have just pissed himself but she chose not to comment.

'But look here,' Ogin said, and gestured to her harness. 'You have no fear, visha.'

Ariadne had let go of the restraint bars without realising, her face flushing with mild embarrassment that she hoped the shadows would hide.

'Very clever, but you still haven't answered my question.'

'Perhaps it is lightning, heh?' he said, somewhat insouciantly and tapping one of the icons on his shoulder guard.

Ariadne gave him a lethal look that was sharper than the *szabla* strapped to the Astartes' belt. A curved-edged sword, the szabla was indigenous to Jagun and forged by its native weaponsmiths. Of the few Storm Reapers she had seen around the fleet, all carried one. She had once seen a curious armsman reach out to touch a sheathed szabla hilt, a student of militaria intrigued by its beauty, only to find it swiftly drawn and pressed to his neck. No words were exchanged, but the meaning was clear enough.

This blade was sacred, and anyone not of Jagun who touched it would meet death. She had steered clear of the Storm Reapers since, but here she was face to face with one wearing the mask of a mirthful fool. Or perhaps it wasn't a mask at all, and the two aspects of the Storm Reapers' character simply contradicted.

As if to prove the point, Ogin held up his hand. 'I apologise, visha. I had only meant to divert your mind. It is a ship graveyard.'

Ariadne blanched almost to the colour of the Astartes' armour as a heavy thud, louder than the ones that came before, had her snapping her hands around the restraints again.

'What?'

'Yes, hundreds of ships, or pieces of ships. Out there.' He sobered at once at the mention of war. 'I have wandered, I have seen all kinds. Ork, aeldari... ships of Ruin.' His face soured at this last one. They had fought little else since embarking on the crusade and Ogin and his kind felt a particular hatred for the worshippers of Chaos. 'Lifeless they are, broken as if on sharp rocks, though here, I think, those rocks are some pretty damn big guns, heh?'

'The Kamidarians have a sizeable fleet, or so Imperial intelligence believes,' offered Ariadne. 'And they have seen to their own defence since the Rift.'

'Let us hope,' said Ogin, turning the intensity of his attention back onto the quartermaster, 'they can tell friend from foe, heh?'

Ariadne felt a mild tremor in her chest to match the one that rang the hull.

'You have a way of simultaneously reassuring and alarming me.'

Ogin smiled again, like the warmth of a young sun. 'It is a gift.'

Ariadne sighed but conceded she did feel better for his presence. 'What are you even doing in this part of the ship anyway?'

Ogin glanced around, as if only really noticing his surroundings for the first time.

'I wanted to sit, I found a seat,' he answered with infuriating simplicity. The restraint had not been made with Space Marines in mind so it remained locked in its cradle above, and in point of fact Ogin took up three berths, not one. Most of the other Astartes on board – and their numbers were little more than tokenistic – either resided on a different floor or stood statuesque, mag-locked to the deck.

'That's it? That's the reason?'

'And I thought you had a friendly face.'

Ariadne frowned at that.

'Underneath, heh,' Ogin clarified, eliciting a long groan from the quartermaster, who realised she was in for a long flight.

They descended on Kamidar in force, an invading army in all but name. Bulky landers, their clawed stanchions impaling the native soil, disgorged a host of Munitorum adepts and Militarum troopers from their bellies, voracious, relentless.

Acquisition stations were raised immediately, a bulwark of tithing engines, there to collate the needed materials for the crusade. Logisticians stood around large maps, considering the local geography with furrowed brows as they tried to determine optimal locations for manufactories or where additional defences could be raised. Hololiths flickered between regions, critical data unspooling alongside images relating to mineral compositions, static defence capability gradings, garrisons.

Servitors and Sentinel-class cargo-walkers did the bulk of the labour and a company of Mordian Iron Guard stood ready, though little danger was expected. Kamidar was a settled Imperial world under a strong ruler. It was a capital or principal world, and one of three in the Ironhold Protectorate. A Knight world, and a powerful one. Beyond the native fauna and the odd bandit gang, there was little to trouble the Imperials.

This, then, was the heart of the acquisitions operation. One of several, from which the arteries of reclamation groups would extend like armies marching into a foreign land.

Or so Ariadne thought as she watched them from the landing apron, her staff busy with setting up her equipment. Kamidar would be the first; it would serve as example to the others of what was expected. Already, the crusade felt heavy-handed. A virtual laager of caskets, cases and plastek-sheathed data-analysis equipment had begun to form around Ariadne, one of many subsidiary adjuncts to the colossal logistical machine need to ensure every bean and bullet was accounted for.

She had lost sight of Ogin in the dust-whirl of engine wake and frantic activity during disembarkation. Her last sight of him after she opened her eyes upon a successful touchdown was of his armoured back as he ventured across the deck to the slowly widening chink of light that was the exit ramp descending. She thought he had said something to her by way of a farewell but it was lost in the roar of turbine fans cycling down.

A blink-click slaved her bionic to the data-slate in her hand, a haptic frame-glove skipping across the glossy surface as she married her archive data of Kamidar to real-time readings. Classed as a viable agri world by the Adeptus Cartographica Astra, the guild of Imperial taxonomers, it had a sixty per cent water mass and a rugged but far-from-inhospitable landscape comprising forests, grasslands and mountains. There were no desert regions, but it did possess a wild scrub that ran along the eastern continental edges, the extreme extent of which bordered on wasteland. A few more years and it would become desert.

She skimmed past the data-inloads for the other two worlds of the protectorate. Neither was as prosperous as the principal but both had their own populations, armies and minor fleets. Kamidar treated them like vassal states, dependants under her protection.

She knelt, taking a fistful of earth. Her haptic augur glove cascaded a rapid analysis to the slate, which Ariadne chose to view via her bionic's retinal display. The soil sample was good, showing healthy concentrations of nitrogen, phosphorus, potassium and sulphur. A fertile land by any reasonable account.

The Munitorum cohort, comprising four Colossi-class landers, had landed at the outskirts of Rund, a border settlement of the Aglevin Province. Kamidar was a median-grade world, around half the size of Terra, broken into four major continental landmasses across six feudal domains, of which Aglevin was one. Victua and Brynof were adjudged the Kamidarian feudal heartlands, though by far the largest of these domains was Harnfor, where resided the Gallanhold Palace and the world's Administratum officium. The others, Wessen and Eageth, lay on the west and east border respectively and had also received landings from the beta and gamma cohorts. As befitted her position as quartermaster senioris, Ariadne had been assigned to alpha along with one of her colleagues.

Ariadne spied him through the milling crowds, having just alighted from a junker. He had an entourage of lesser adepts and servitors tailing behind him, their arms heaped with scrolls and other surveying equipment. For a second or two, she dared to hope he hadn't seen her but then realised he was heading straight for her, an overly genial smile on his face.

'Niova, what a surprise to see you here,' he began, all false bonhomie.

Her jaw clenched at the overfamiliar use of her first name. *You knew I was coming here, and precisely when and where I would arrive.* She expected he had been partly responsible for the assignment too. The unctuous man had ever been a favoured pet of the admiral.

'Usullis, how unpleasantly unexpected it is for us to be breathing the same air.'

He laughed at that, a crow cackling at some barely felt slight, but Ariadne could see the malice thinly veiled.

'Oh, come now, Niova, are we here already? I thought we might at least exchange a few platitudes before the knives came out.'

He drew closer, too close; she could practically feel his breath against her cheek and smell the cured meat he had eaten for his morning repast, as well as the cologne that did little to mask his odour.

Usullis held up his hands, though the lie was drawn all over his narrow face. She had thought him handsome when they had first met. He was taut, like a tightly fletched arrow, with an athletic if slightly rangy build, and greyish hair that he styled in a long ponytail. Like Ariadne, he had an augmetic, his left eye, a chrome-plated piece that spoke to the man's self-aggrandisement, as did his finely tailored uniform. Then he had opened his mouth and Ariadne had taken his measure. Her initial impression had not been favourable and had only soured further with time. Evidently he had taken something of an interest in her, but when her staunch rebuttal had left Usullis with two broken fingers, his interest had turned into harassment.

'It was not my doing. The admiral assigns his assets where he sees fit. I merely came to welcome you to Kamidar.'

'Yes, well, consider me *welcomed*, now leave me alone. I have a lot of work to do.'

His face fell abruptly and Ariadne sensed the danger to come. Her body stiffened as his jaw clenched.

'Oh no, no. I think there must have been some sort of error.' He looked around as if trying to find some functionary to question, but in the end his self-satisfied gaze landed on Ariadne.

'What is it?' she demanded, her fingers pressed into fists all of a sudden.

'Must have been a clerical error. An innocent mistake, to be sure.'

'Usullis!'

'No one likes to be the bearer of unfavourable news,' he said, a smile curling at the edge of his mouth. 'This isn't your station.

You're to accompany one of the requisition groups heading into the cities and industrial regions.'

Ariadne balked at the thought, casting her eye to the long trails of vehicles and trooping adepts, a bodyguard of Mordians in train. There was peril out in the wilds and confrontation with the locals to consider. She had expected her post to be here, at the landing zone, surrounded by Imperial personnel: counting supplies, not obtaining them.

'I was not...' She faltered, heart racing. Why did a voidship hold no terrors for her, yet the thought of venturing into the heart of a foreign land did? 'I was not informed.'

'You're being informed. Now.'

Another wry smile. She wanted to strike him, punch him straight in the face and knock that smirk right off. Her fists were still balled; she could feel her nails digging into her palms where they would leave little half-moon marks.

'You'll need to report to the Munitorum senioris for tactical gear and your protective detail,' Usullis added, handing her a piece of parchment with the order.

'Am I in danger?' She regretted the words the moment she said them – to show weakness to him – but she couldn't deny the sense of trepidation that swept over her.

Usullis made a show of weighing the question, but he already knew the answer and was merely taunting her with this bit of cheap theatre. He was savouring it.

'This is a stable world, part of the Imperial sovereignty, but our outriders and liaisons with local authorities say that bandits roam these lands too, Imperial dissidents. And let us say that the natives haven't exactly been the most welcoming of hosts...'

'We are here to strip their assets and requisition their troops. I imagine that would put a crimp in anyone's geniality.'

'True,' Usullis conceded. 'As per the admiral's orders, our approach has been somewhat stringent.'

Ariadne moaned inwardly. Typical of the man to paint Arde-mus' tactics with a light, forgiving brush. 'Heavy-handed, you mean. This is a delicate matter, Usullis, it has to be handled with the utmost care or we risk losing the cooperation of the populace.'

'Oh, they'll cooperate.' And there it was, a glimpse of the nasty little bastard he really was. He saw these people as defiant lessers, whereas Ariadne saw a proud and independent empire. 'Lieu-tenant Vintar has seen to that.'

Ariadne dreaded to think what that meant but she knew Vintar by reputation. He was one of Renyard's officers, and her blood ran cold at the thought of his ilk unleashed on the Kamidarians.

She glanced upwards, into the sky. Her bionic turned a fraction, magnifying the dusky outline of the warship hanging in low atmos-phere. According to the manifests, the *Vortun's Ire* had brought both the 84th Mordians and 9003rd Solians to Kamidarian soil. She hadn't officially met any Solians yet. From her research, she knew they were originally from the Sol System and had a reputation as finely disciplined soldiers, but the troopers here on Kamidar were primarily made up of natives of Gathalamor, unruly gang-fighters turned regimental reinforcements under an officer called Jordoon. Ariadne found herself wondering again at the admiral's motives, bringing their like and that of Vintar and his men to what was meant to be a non-hostile occupation.

'Magnificent, isn't it?' Usullis had followed her gaze, just two adepts admiring the view – except she was far from appreciative.

'I don't know what it is,' admitted Ariadne somewhat enigma-tically, but she only felt concern at the vessel's ominous presence.

Turning away, she caught sight of one of her staff on the way to some errand or other and grasped the woman's shoulder, using it as an opportunity to disengage herself from the odious Usullis, who looked like he wanted to further outstay his welcome.

'Patrica, find us decent transport,' said Ariadne. 'We're heading into the city with the requisition groups.'

'Madam?' Patrica looked nonplussed.

'Yes, I know. Just get it done.'

The Munitorum aide nodded and went to their duty.

'See you soon, Niova,' Usullis called after her, as she went to receive her gear and find out who would be protecting her and her team out in the wild.

'Screw you, Usullis,' she muttered, flashing a false smile and a two-fingered insult at him from over the shoulder.

His self-assured laughter followed her all the way to the Munitorum armoury.

Chapter Five

TERRORS

FOR BOHEMUND

THE TRAP

Herek ran barefoot through the lower decks of the *Ruin*. He knew the ship like he knew the tracery of scars and tattoos lining his body. Naked from the waist up, he had been in the midst of a meditation cycle when he heard screaming. It echoed loudly, a familiar refrain from a familiar voice. He had not even slowed to take up a weapon, though Harrower yearned to be grasped, her pleas inside Herek's head vying for dominance over the ones outside it.

Only encumbered by a loose pair of fatigues, he moved swiftly through the ship and had entered the lower decks, hearts drumming. And found the first of the dead.

A cultist, a lowly serf who had been in the wrong place at the wrong time. Her neck had been broken. Another, Herek found impaled on an electro-sconce. Several more had been so badly bloodied as to make easily determining cause of death impossible. Herek left them in his wake, crimson footprints leaving a trail as he splashed heedlessly through the dead cultists' leavings.

Deeper he went, into *Ruin*'s very bowels where the mutants and other creatures dwelled. Where less damage could be done.

He is still cognisant then, thought Herek, *that is something.*

The trail ended at the outskirts of the bilge and the corpse of an armoured Red Corsair, his neck twisted and near torn off despite the armoured gorget protecting it. Herek saw finger impressions in the metal around where it had been cracked open like an egg.

Three of his brethren stood farther ahead. Each had a blade drawn and between them they had hemmed in a fourth figure like beast tamers trying to keep a dangerous predator at bay.

And he *was* dangerous.

Rathek, who they called 'the Culler'.

Unarmoured like Herek, his tanned skin glistened in the sodium glare of the bilge lamps. And like Herek, his flesh was a tapestry of ugly scars, brands and marks of the gods. Long hair, lank with sweat, framed a narrow face, the ears slightly pointed, and where Herek was bulky, Rathek was lean, a rapier to his captain's broadsword. He had no weapon, save for himself, though his hands were blood-red claws and his eyes wide with madness. An incoherent scream tore from his lips, and it kept the other three in place. Herek wasn't sure who was actually caging who.

He stepped breathlessly over the threshold, dismissing the others. 'Lower your blades,' he growled, eyes locked with Rathek's.

One of the Red Corsairs, a ragged scrap-armoured warlord called Clortho, half turned as if to check Herek hadn't lost his faculties too.

'Lower your blades, and stand back.'

The dead littered the floor here, cultists and mutants both, the squalid inhabitants of the *Ruin*'s underworld. Prey for Rathek's insanity. Carnage only fit for the bloodiest of battlefields. Clortho obeyed, he and his brothers. They wanted retribution for this. The dead warrior in the corridor behind them was Voga. One of

Clortho's warband. Herek would make it up to him later, find a way to provide recompense.

As soon as the other Red Corsairs backed off, Herek leapt forwards to tackle Rathek. He bore him down, a hand pulling hard on his jaw, the other clamped around Rathek's wrist and twisting his arm around his back. It wasn't gentle. Rathek yelped in sudden agony but Herek held him, ignoring the rabid biting of his augmetic fingers as his quarry bucked and fought.

'Be still, brother,' he hissed into Rathek's ear before glancing back at Clortho. 'Get Kurgos. Be swift!'

Clortho nodded, the mail skirts of his armour rattling as he left his men behind, and was on his way.

He didn't get far. Kurgos was already lumbering through the lower decks and had reached the corridor to the bilge when Herek had called for him. Every pain lay writ upon the face of the chirurgeon, who suffered greatly in the quiet hours whenever the fighting was done. He wore his entire war plate, for he could never remove it, even if he had wished to; a lumpen, terrifying creature. And also the only man aboard the ship who could bring Rathek a measure of peace. The vial was already in his hand, the injector loaded with a hiss of pressure.

'This will hurt,' he rasped through his breather grille, 'I've had to make it stronger than last time.'

Rathek had grown stronger too, and Herek struggled to keep him contained. 'Just bloody do it!'

With a grunt of effort, Kurgos stabbed in the needle and the viscous fluid inside the vial deployed, leaving an oily grime inside the casing.

Rathek shuddered, neck muscles bulging, veins standing out like cords. Herek clung to him so hard he thought he might pass out from the exertion but then slowly, ever so slowly the resistance slackened as Rathek relaxed and grew still.

'The terrors...?' Herek asked him, his voice urgent.

Rathek's eyes held only abject fear and sorrow, but that wasn't an answer.

'The terrors, brother?' Herek insisted.

A tired shake of the head before Rathek slapped at his arm and Herek, reluctantly at first, released him. Both fell back, exhausted.

'Out,' breathed Herek. 'I said, out,' he repeated when the others hesitated.

Clortho nodded, but his anger was plain when his gaze strayed to Rathek and a scowl pulled at the scar across his mouth. 'One of mine is dead,' he growled. 'I am owed.'

'And you shall be compensated in full,' Herek replied. 'Now leave, or Harrower feeds early tonight.'

The three left slowly, not turning their backs until the shadows had claimed them.

Kurgos lingered, but only for a moment. 'May not be wise...' he warned, referring to being alone with Rathek.

'It's all right,' Herek reassured him. 'I'm all right.'

'Such waste,' said Kurgos looking around, but he relented. 'Perhaps I can make use of some of this biological material,' he muttered, grumbling every step of the way back up-ship.

Having slightly recovered, Herek got to his feet and helped up Rathek, who was still a little unsteady. He held the Culler's face, a hand either side, and spoke slow so Rathek could follow the movement of his lips.

'Brother?'

It was an enquiry of identity. Rathek *heard* things, in his mind. Voices from beyond. Sometimes they sunk hooks into his flesh, whispered their madnesses. Terrors, Kurgos had called them. The name had stuck. Seemed fitting.

Exhausted, still coming down from his trauma, Rathek nodded.

'At least you are still whole...'

Sometimes the terrors did more than whisper... Sometimes they *showed* him things.

Herek released Rathek's face, signing to him. *What did you see?*

They know we're here, Rathek signed back.

Is it him?

A nod.

Herek turned aside for a moment, thinking. 'Sooner than I thought.' He looked back to find a perplexed expression on Rathek's face. *It's nothing. Can you fight?*

Rathek gave an ugly smile. *Give me a sword, and I'll kill.*

Herek smirked by way of reply. *All in good time, brother. Put on your armour, there is much to be done.*

They knelt in silence in the still darkness of the hold. Thirty warriors armoured in black, a Black Templars cross emblazoned on white tabards, the chains of their oaths taut around their wrists, joining them to bolter and blade.

Godfried knelt at the front of the congregation, as was his right and duty. He knelt with helm removed and clamped to the deck, as did his brethren. The greatsword he usually wore scabbarded upon his back was held before him like a talisman, the cold metal of the hilt pressed up to his face, his eyes framed by the cross-guard. He was a grim warrior, a scrub of blond hair still clinging to his ravaged scalp, with a face split more times than any could count. It served as a testament to his courage, his resilience, his utter determination never to fail.

An effigy stood before them, rendered in gold: the Holy Emperor seated upon His Throne. One hand was raised in benediction surrounded by a halo of light; the other held a sword aloft, its blade alight with leaping flames. They prayed to it, their stentorian voices filling the hold with the solemn fervour and conviction of the Black Templars of the Morrigan Crusade.

The crusade's namesake sat at the rear of the gathering, his own bindings broken and hanging loosely. The Unchained, they called him, a mark of his shame that he should not be so bound as his brethren, untethered from his faith, a self-imposed punishment meted out in the aftermath of what had happened to Bohemund. The castellan stiffened at the memory, his features cold as stone. A broadsword sat firmly in his armoured grip, the blade held up to his face like a penitent's cross.

'O God-Emperor, most holy lord and Master of Mankind...'

As Godfried began the Prayer of Oaths, serfs dressed in charcoal-grey robes and scapulae began to shuffle reverently around the hold.

'Grant us the will and strength to smite our foes, to enrich your glory and find honour at your side in eternal grace...'

They moved in pairs, one carrying a plain metal bowl, the other a thick marble-handled brush.

'We pray we are not found wanting in your sight, oh God-Emperor, and that when called upon to serve we follow the example of Saint Sigismund and prove steadfast in our faith...'

One by one, the serfs visited each of the Black Templars, who lowered their upraised swords at their approach in order to receive the benediction of the oath: a simple black cross daubed across the eyes, nose and cheekbones.

'May the Throne endure, everlasting, and our pledge to you, God-Emperor, be unswerving in the face of heretic, xenos or daemon. We are the willing sword, the stalwart shield. This is our oath.'

As the serfs retreated, their duty performed, the congregation chorused, *'This is our oath. Ave Imperator,'* and a field of swords rose up to touch the light.

The frigate listed badly in the void. A lone supply vessel. Several miles out, but sensorium magnification told Morrigan all he needed to know about the stricken vessel and the signal they had followed to reach it.

'A trap.'

Anglahad nodded, scratching his greying beard. Prematurely

greyed, for all of the Black Templars of the Morrigan Crusade were Primaris Marines and as such had not the decades to be considered old. He liked how it made him look distinguished and played up to the fact.

'Not the vessel we were expecting. He must have laid a false signal.'

'Difficult to discern,' conceded Dagomir, his arms folded across his broad chest.

'I see little other recourse here,' Anglahad concluded. 'We have to be sure. And yet...'

Morrigan cocked his head a little. 'Trap.'

'Yes, most likely.'

'He wants to find us as much we him,' offered Dagomir, stepping closer to the armaglass as if through proximity he could garner some of the ship's secrets. Smooth and as hard as marble, the Sword Brother's scalp shone in the dull ship lights. 'There may be more to this, something we can manipulate to our advantage.'

Morrigan turned to Godfried. 'You are as taciturn as ever, brother, what say you?'

Of the four Black Templars standing in the gunship's observation bay, only the company Champion had not yet spoken since they had found the *Hermes* drifting in the void. He had a pensive air about him, his mood ever guarded.

'If it is him, it is worth the risk,' he said finally.

Anglahad murmured in agreement. 'A token landing party would be wise. Perhaps you should–'

'I am going,' Morrigan said firmly, pre-empting the argument and ending it before it had been given voice. 'But I agree, we should proceed with caution.'

'Six swords then,' answered Anglahad, 'tactical insertion. With your leave, captain, I will make the roster.'

His eyes still on the frigate, Morrigan gave a curt gesture of concession and Anglahad departed, allowing them all to move a little more freely. The Overlord was a tough vessel of not inconsiderable size, one of the finest Cawl had engineered, but it was a troop transport and the observation bay a nominal concession at best.

'Dagomir, what are you thinking?'

The broad-chested Black Templar shrugged, his mountainous shoulders shifting like tectonic plates. 'I am wondering what he wants. He took Bohemund, and you took his hand. A beggar's price,' he said, one eyebrow raised.

Ever blunt was Dagomir. Morrigan didn't deny it.

'*This*,' said Dagomir, gesturing to the frigate through the magnified armaglass, 'feels elaborate. He has always been cunning, but this is theatre. He may not even be aboard.'

'And yet he knows I will not be able to resist...'

A regicide board laid out with all the pieces in the middle of a game stretched before Morrigan in his mind's eye. He had been playing for years, move matched by counter-move, and so it went. His opponent had just made his latest gambit. Now it was Morrigan's turn.

'So it stands to reason he wants *something* from us,' he finished.

Dagomir scratched at his crag of a chin. 'A fair amount of ship to cover with only six.'

Godfried gave a gruff retort. 'Then we had best be about it, had we not?'

Silence reigned in the observation bay for a few moments, until Morrigan nodded. Thinking about a gambit of his own.

'Our move...' he said.

Kurgos cycled the ocular lenses strapped to his skull via a metal frame. A rare thing to see the chirurgeon without his helm. It was not a pretty sight, Herek reflected as he took in the myriad deformities and tumours. Exposure to the warp *twisted* a man, even one as enhanced as an Astartes. It had a way of worming into his flesh and remaking it, sometimes subtly, sometimes dramatically unsubtly. Kurgos' ravaged appearance owed as much to the wars he had fought as the pervasive influence of the empyrean. Even so, he was a hardened and simultaneously hideous creature.

'They will be expecting a trap,' the chirurgeon muttered, tending the finger joints of Herek's bionic where Rathek had actually managed to do some damage. 'Gods, he really took a bite out of you, didn't he?'

'I know.'

'Which one?'

'Both.'

Kurgos grunted, but whether it was in disapproval or agreement was impossible to say. 'He's getting stronger too, by the way,' he said.

'I know.'

'Then you must have considered–'

'No. I won't put him back down there.'

'He killed Voga,' said Kurgos, his tone pointed as he dealt with aligning the delicate servos and haptic interfaces of the bionic. 'Snapped his neck.'

Herek watched him work but betrayed no emotion, save what was revealed by his words. 'I know what he did.'

Kurgos adjusted one of the ocular lenses. 'And if he snaps my neck, if the serum fails?'

'You are entirely too leathery and ancient for that,' said Herek with a hint of a smile he didn't truly feel. 'I'm sure he would find you as unyielding as star iron.'

'And yet, I am not reassured...' muttered Kurgos under his breath. He leaned back painfully, his work finished. 'That's as best as I can do. Alas, I am no warsmith.'

'No, brother,' said Herek, flexing the fingers of his bionic and finding it to his liking, 'you are Vassago Kurgos, worth ten warsmiths by any measure.'

'Only ten...' Kurgos glanced up from gathering his tools, and Herek followed his gaze to the Red Corsair standing at the doorway to the infirmary.

'They are herded, captain.'

Herek nodded, standing. 'Fed and well watered?'

'As per your orders.'

'And lots were drawn?'

'They were, captain. The choosing was fair, according to the fate of the gods.'

'Then all is well and true.' Herek half turned to Kurgos. 'See this, Kurgos? Obedience. I hope you are taking notes.'

'Copiously,' the chirurgeon grumbled before shuffling away into the gloom of the infirmary with its vials and alembics, its bell jars of matter, its briny foetor thick enough to pare with a knife. Kurgos' domain, as vile and disturbing as its master.

Herek let him be, turning his attention back to the Red Corsair standing at the doorway.

'The mutant, does it still live?'

'Barely, captain. It appears the rigours of following its kin through the empyrean has taxed it almost unto death.'

Herek was moving, his mind already drifting to the coming encounter.

'Bring it. I have a further use for it.'

Grainy swathes of sensorium light washed across the aft lower deck of the *Hermes*, overlapping and repeating as a flock of servo-skulls busied themselves. They drifted ahead of the Black Templars in their preconfigured murmurations, chirruping and bleeping in idiot machine cadence. They were crude creatures, their biological matter once having belonged to priests and other Ecclesiarchal worthies. But they served in death as they had in life, dutifully and without complaint. It was the only sound, barring the chugging of the minimal life support systems.

After tactical insertion, during which the Black Templars had breached the lower hull aft of the frigate where the armour was thinnest and sealed off the immediate section, they had discovered the *Hermes* was functioning on nominal power. Motes hung in the air, globules of unidentified particulate, metal shavings and the dust from finely shed human skin.

Atmosphere sensors in Morrigan's helm read amber and showed unhealthily high concentrations of carbon dioxide, suggesting the air filtration systems had malfunctioned. It gave him little hope for the ship's crew, some twenty thousand hands or so.

He had expected the *Ruin*, not this workhorse vessel. The *Hermes* was more supply tender than warship and it showed in its boxy, functional design. A repositorium with an engine. Few guns, save a battery or two of anti-torpedo turrets and its prow-mounted laser batteries. Whatever had taken her had done so swiftly and with little resistance. What it was even doing here, at the very edge of protectorate territory, was a mystery.

It was a ghost ark, haunted by echoes.

A rune appeared on Morrigan's retinal lens, flashing intermittently amongst all the other data of the captain's auto-senses. It was a request to break vox silence. Though they had found signs of disturbance, tools and weapons discarded, bullet and shell impacts, blade gouges in metal, they had neither met nor seen another soul in the last two hours of traversing the ship and the servo-skulls' bio-scans read as negative. He granted the request.

'*Ship narrows ahead, brother-captain,*' Anglahad's voice crackled across the vox, rich despite the fragmentary feed. '*And we are approximately a mile from our initial ingress. It would be prudent to make another breach.*'

'For rapid egress,' Morrigan assumed.

'*Precisely, brother-captain.*'

'I have no intention of leaving early, Anglahad.'

'*Nor I...*'

The rest of his sentence remained unspoken. *But if it is a trap...*

Morrigan had Quillane and Halbard set breaching charges. They were dense, heavy blocks of fused incendiary. Enough to core even ship armour if the situation called for it. The process of setting them took time, as did the subsequent burn, during which the Black Templars took defensive positions. Anglahad remained ahead as scout, monitoring the servo-skulls that hovered in dormant/tracking mode, whilst Godfried took up a rear sentry position, his unsheathed sword swung downwards before him, point to the floor.

That left only Dagomir and Morrigan.

'What will you do,' asked the burly warrior, who leaned his broadsword against his left shoulder, 'if he is here?'

'Kill him,' Morrigan answered flatly.

'And if you cannot?'

Morrigan turned on him sharply. 'Do I lack purpose, brother? Am I not the warrior who has fought and bested every one of our company?'

'Every one except Bohemund.' The barb was not meant as such but stung nonetheless.

'He was surprised. Caught with an unready sword. Emperor... I put it in his damn hands.'

'Then let us not be caught unawares and use every advantage we possess.'

'Are we not? Am I not?'

'You want to challenge him.'

'I *will* challenge him.'

'Then you will die as Bohemund died, an arrogant fool.'

Morrigan gripped the hilt of his sword, the joints in his armoured gauntlet creaking he held it so fiercely. 'Are you determined to insult me, Dagomir? Insult Bohemund? Do you seek to provoke me,' he spat, inwardly raging, 'or are you intent on having me strike you, brother?'

Dagomir turned slowly. 'He will say far worse and not wear an ally's face. If I may be frank?'

'Have you not been so already?'

Dagomir went on, 'Your humours are misaligned. Find the temperament to look inward and you will see this, by the Emperor's grace.'

Morrigan's hearts thundered. Sweat pricked his skin, the anger pulsing through his chest. He knew Dagomir was right and slowly relaxed his grip.

'I am not entirely myself, Dag,' he confessed. 'Perhaps Anglahad was right, and I should have remained on the Overlord.'

'You grieve, Morrigan, as do we all. Your grief is worst because you were there. You saw that bastard cut him down and take his head. An unclean death, and no way for a warrior to die.' He paused. 'And I know you believe you led him to that fate. But you are where you need to be. Godfried and I would not have agreed to it if either of us thought otherwise.'

Morrigan glanced at the company Champion, but if he heard any of their exchange he gave no sign.

'I am blessed with the finest Sword Brothers,' said Morrigan, clapping a gauntleted hand on Dagomir's shoulder. 'And *when* we find him,' he went on, 'we take our vengeance as one. Kill him together.'

'Yes, brother-castellan,' answered Dagomir, 'that is precisely what we will do. For Bohemund.'

'For Bohemund.'

Anglahad was approaching, an auspex in his hand slaved to the servo-skull flock.

'I have something, or rather... *had* something.' He passed the handheld scanner to Morrigan. Contact flares, small feathery pulses of white light, appeared and disappeared on the green screen.

'What am I seeing, brother? Have we found something or not?'

'A signal, yes. Not clean, but a signal. It's being impeded.'

'A jammer?'

'Perhaps, though it doesn't appear to be affecting internal vox. Seems to strengthen with proximity. I think they're bio-signs.'

'Then they're coming from deeper in the ship?' Dagomir had one eye on the two Black Templars still setting up the charges that would burn through the hull.

'A few hours ago we thought we had tracked down the *Ruin*, but that signal return proved false and led us here. I assume nothing at this point. They are, however, all concentrated in the same area,' said Anglahad.

Morrigan handed back the auspex, bringing up the ship schematic. 'That's a large chamber,' he said, aligning what he had seen with the wireframe overlaying his retinal feed.

'Refectory, if I had to guess,' said Anglahad.

'How many?' asked Dagomir.

'Hundreds.'

'Alive?' asked Morrigan.

'Bio-scan is faint but that could be the interference, brother-castellan.'

'Alive then,' Morrigan confirmed, and Anglahad nodded.

Quillane and Halbard had finished with the charges and were returning to the others. Godfried, evidently sensing they would soon be moving on, had left his position as sentinel.

'Could be cultists,' Dagomir ventured, as an aside rather than a comment on the potential numbers he and his brothers faced.

'Do you really think he would send cultists?' said Morrigan.

'No,' Dagomir conceded, 'he would not.'

The bodies lay heaped alongside each other, swaddled in darkness.

Hundreds of them.

Every lumen in the refectory had been meticulously smashed, shattered plasglass crunching noisily underfoot as the Black

Templars cautiously entered the large chamber. The flock of servo-skulls preceded them, panning grainy red light across twitching human forms. Many lay unmoving or slumped in alcoves. The ship's crew, or a portion of it. Faint heat signatures via retinal lens suggested they did not have long. Those still alive gibbered in the throes of madness or else softly murmured, their voices ghostly. Sweat and the rank odour of stale urine and other foulness threaded air already made wretched by the malfunctioning atmosphere cyclers.

Morrigan headed for the middle of the chamber, keenly aware of the widening gulf of darkness either side of him as he crossed the threshold. It felt unnatural, the dark, almost too thick, and hindered the reach of his auto-senses. The other Black Templars followed their captain's lead but fanned out, two on either flank with Godfried as rearguard.

'Are your auto-senses impeded?' queried Anglahad across the feed.

'Aye,' confirmed Dagomir, the others chorusing their agreement after him.

'Slowly now,' Morrigan hissed across the vox, tracking the languid trajectories of the servo-skulls as they scoured every inch of the room. The sword in his hand felt heavy, as if it might slip his grasp at any moment. Untethered and unbound, it was a reminder of his shame. He shook the feeling off, recognising his weakness, and tried to focus on the voices of the stricken crew but discerned only ravings.

Approaching the centre of the chamber, Morrigan held up his clenched fist. The Black Templars halted at once.

'Castellan...' ventured Dagomir.

'A moment, brother. I hear something.'

Nearby, towards the middle of the room... a plaintive weeping and the first cogent utterance Morrigan had heard from the crew since they had entered.

'Hold position,' he voxed and edged forwards, careful not to step on anyone and crush them as he followed the voice.

'Alight, aflame, it is He in agonies unbound, encircled by shadow...' It repeated in this way, over and again, sibilant, afraid.

A heat signature – stronger, but still weak – presented itself and Morrigan followed it, his auto-senses stunted but alert to threats and the servo-skulls still drifting through the shadows ahead. His breathing was even, calm, but a minor adrenaline spike revealed by his biometrics hinted at the heightened danger of the moment.

'Be on your guard,' he warned the others. The path to the cogent speaker in the middle of the room was clear, as if an invisible bomb blast had gone off and this one knelt at its epicentre. Except there was no crater, no evidence of explosion; something else had sentenced these poor wretches to death.

A figure: cloaked in midnight-blue velvet, female, her arms bound behind her back. She was collapsed onto her knees. Her head lolled forwards, her bald scalp gashed and bloody.

'Alight, aflame, it is He in agonies unbound, encircled by shadow...'

Wiry and misshapen, her limbs overlong and bent at unnatural angles, she had the look of the void-born. She gasped when she felt Morrigan's presence, a shuddering breath dragged through half-poisoned lungs, and the mantra halted abruptly.

'I tried not to... I tried...' she rasped through sobs and hikes of rancid air.

A grey beam of light illuminated her face as Morrigan snapped on his bolt pistol's lumen, her head still low as she whimpered like a scalded canid. She was a mutant, one of the Navis Nobilite, the tattoo on the side of her head confirming it. Even cowed as she was, Morrigan saw how wide her eyes had grown, the foaming around her mouth, the blood drool eking to the floor in a long, gelatinous tendril.

'Please...' she begged, and slowly began to raise her head.

The bodies nearest her were cold; that's how Morrigan had

contorted as if they had fought against their fate.

'Please... I could...'

Another lay curled in on herself, her fingers blood-soaked where she had tried to core out her own eyes.

'I couldn't help...'

A snapped wire tether hung around her neck where it had been used to pull her head back, leaving a sore crimson weal in the flesh like a hangman's kiss, raising her head, a slit opening above her eyes...

'I couldn't hel... hell... hell...hellhellhellhellhellhe–'

The boom of Morrigan's sidearm crashed like a pealing bell, shredding the shadows with jagged muzzle flare as he ended the Navigator's pain, her head disintegrating with the shell's explosive impact.

Everything happened quickly after that.

Quillane shouted a sudden warning and swung around his bolter, but he fell before he had a chance to fire, the two halves of his cleaved body landing two feet apart as he hit the ground.

'Morrigan!' roared Dagomir, as a host of chain-fed and powered blades activated in the darkness.

But Morrigan was alive to the threat, lurching back as a blade missed his throat by mere inches. He had parried a second blow before he even saw his attacker.

He emerged from a black, unnatural fog. A sword in either hand: one long with a serrated edge; the other short like a maingauche. Horn-helmed, armoured in red and black with the Tyrant Claw emblazoned across his chest.

Red Corsair. Renegade.

Dagomir barrelled into the renegade like a battering ram before they could swing again, and the two Black Templars stood shoulder to shoulder.

'Where is he?' snapped Morrigan, the old anger rising, his eyes on the renegade, who had regained his footing and held them both at guard.

'Here...'

The severed head of Halbard rolled noisily towards Morrigan's boots and the memory of Bohemund returned with unwelcome clarity.

The smoke and chaos of the incursion, confusion and fire as his restraint cradle refused to open. Trapped in the burning assault ram as Bohemund raced on, eager for a traitor's scalp. Then the clash of steel and Morrigan getting free at last. Running alone through the Ruin, *killing cultists by the score until he reached the last hall at the end of the deck. A bright oval of armaglass looking out onto the poisoned void beyond, and the light of fell stars shining on the duel within.*

Bohemund and him.

Blade to blade, and the Black Templar losing. Humbled, then struck down, a head suddenly absent its body as Bohemund slumped first to his knees and then over onto his chest.

Then Dagomir dragging Morrigan back and Godfried taking up the Champion's fallen sword. The head, taken. The body, fought for bitterly and reclaimed.

Shouting from deeper in the ship, the call to arms of many guttural, barely human voices.

Too many.

A retreat inevitable, and the screams of grief and anguish as Morrigan was denied his vengeance.

His decision to attack the *Ruin, his* failure.

A rush of memory condensed into a second of remembered pain before the false darkness dissipated as if on command, revealing the one the Black Templars had come to kill.

Bareheaded except for two small horned protrusions, handsome for a fiend, his armour bedecked in spikes, slabs of ceramite laid on hulking shoulders. The double-bladed axe hefted in both hands proclaimed him as an executioner, the heads strung to his belt further evidence of the fact.

Graeyl Herek.

Morrigan cried out, his fury a hot iron embedded in his chest. 'Godfried... Anglahad!'

Reunited, the Black Templars stood as one. Four against two, but the odds felt far from certain.

'For Bohemund,' Morrigan uttered simply, and then it began.

Under pressure at once, Anglahad gave ground before the dual-wielding renegade and Godfried stepped in to prevent him being cut down. Morrigan lost sight of them both after that, as they peeled off into the shadows, blades flashing sparks. Oaths stung the air from Godfried's mouth and he knew the Champion was already hard-pressed despite the supposed advantage of two versus one.

He and Dagomir had the same odds and again found their foe the equal to it. A heavy blow from Herek separated them, nearly hacking off Dagomir's arm but for the veteran's hasty parry. The axe embedded in the deck and Morrigan seized on what he thought was a mistake, believing that the blade would be stuck fast. But it slid free like hot steel through wax, the backswing cutting off an ornamental wing from Morrigan's faceplate and pushing him to retreat.

No guns; Morrigan had already holstered his pistol and his brothers did not draw either. This would be blade to blade. Even the Red Corsairs would respect that.

Two fighters against one was not always the boon it seemed. One fighter had a single mind, a single purpose; he could plan knowing he need only account for his opponent. An ally muddied the tactical waters, and success relied on shared instinct and mutual understanding only born from years of fighting side by side.

Morrigan and Dagomir had drawn swords together for over

a decade. They were one blade. As Morrigan feinted, Dagomir thrust, catching Herek between spaulder and rerebrace, the slightest gap brutally exposed. The renegade gave no utterance of pain but did recoil, edging away with wide swings of his dread axe, which moved with some of its own animus.

A possessed weapon, Morrigan could feel it, the oily passage of its blade slick on the air.

The two Black Templars advanced, a downward swing from Morrigan's sword, Pious, catching the axe haft and raking across its length with a screech that was more than just metallic. Dagomir hacked into his opponent's flank, but Herek had already adjusted his footing and the blade glanced across his side before he trapped it between his upper arm and body. A jerk of the waist and the sword ripped from Dagomir's grasp, but only as far as the chain manacled to his wrist. Even still, it unbalanced him and the axe moved like summer lightning. A sudden thrust hit Morrigan in the chest, splitting his plastron. Blood welled in the cavity, hot and urgent, and the castellan staggered.

The upswing took Dagomir's arm, chain and all.

The veteran's sword clattered, untethered. The arm fell nearby and Dagomir roared as blood spurted from his stump.

Morrigan pressed his attack, unleashing a flurry of blows but none of them telling. Herek rode the assault, but was driven back. Distance yawned between Morrigan and Dagomir. He was alone now, as he had always desired to be, with his enemy. With Bohemund's killer. His brother's head taunted him from the renegade's belt. He had no awareness of whether Anglahad or Godfried fought on. He heard sword clashes, but either could be dead. His focus had narrowed to a single point: the end of his blade and the heart of Graeyl Herek.

The axe came in fast, leaving heat in its wake, searing air. God-Emperor, he could practically taste the evil on that blade. Another blow, meant to decapitate, but Morrigan lurched back out of harm's way. Barely. He landed a kick, a brutish short snap from knee to foot that could shatter bone. Against power armour it merely dented, but Herek felt it, and his right side briefly crumpled. Long enough for Morrigan to punch Pious into his opponent's chest. He had aimed for the heart, but even reeling, Herek managed to turn and the blade sank into his pectoral muscle instead. Painful but not fatal.

Herek smashed the haft of his axe into Morrigan's faceplate, a quick, heavy blow that left the Black Templar dazed and with one lens crazed. The upswing from Pious was wild but bought a few seconds, enough for Morrigan to correct his stance, but the axe hove in again and he was forced to parry, on the back foot once more.

A vox signal crackled in his ear and Morrigan blink-clicked an affirmative.

Relentless, Herek attacked again and snapped Morrigan's sword from his grip. The broken chains clattered uselessly against the Black Templar's vambrace as Herek kicked the weapon away. Lashing out with a hand, Morrigan grabbed the underside of Bohemund's helm and tried to wrench it free of the Red Corsair's belt. Somewhere behind him, bleeding and missing an arm, Dagomir grunted, but Morrigan knew he was on his own as he was pushed away.

Staring the Black Templar down, Herek swung his axe into a two-handed grip. He glanced at his belt, at the damaged cord, then at the prize Morrigan regarded like a holy icon.

'You would sacrifice a sword for a rotting skull,' said Herek, judgement in his eyes. 'Never learn... do you, brother?'

'I learn,' said Morrigan as the port side of the refectory suddenly burned red, turned molten and sloughed inwards. Atmosphere vented instantly, a host of bodies sent tumbling towards the breach where a gunship hove into view, Black Templars clambering across its extending gang ramp.

Herek took one glance at the reinforcements and ordered the retreat. The honour duel was over and both sides pulled guns, snap-firing across the refectory floor in tight explosions of muzzle flare. He gave a nod to Morrigan, backing off as the shadows renewed themselves in his wake.

Morrigan gave chase, firing his bolt pistol into the unnatural darkness.

'Take him!'

The Red Corsairs fell back into a narrow corridor aft of the refectory. Morrigan was first to the threshold and caught a last glimpse of Herek twenty feet away when a chain of devastating explosions rocked the *Hermes*. Breaching charges, Morrigan realised, thrown back from the blast, enveloped by smoke and a hail of small shrapnel. Alerts cascaded across his retinal display, notifying him of a dozen minor injuries. He ignored them, clambering to his feet, but a crack shuddered through the ship. Eyes widening with disbelief, he saw the *Hermes* break into two, its sparking ends like a severed limb. Bodies sluiced through the ragged tear in the hull like a mudslide.

Dagomir pulled Morrigan aside before he was taken with them. Mag-locking their boots to the deck, the Black Templars could only watch. And on the other side of the rift stood their enemies, as still and calm as statues.

'He wanted this,' said Dagomir, his breathing laboured across the vox. He had Pious slid through his belt and a bolt pistol in his remaining hand.

'We had him, Dag,' said Morrigan. 'We had him, and the bastard still got away.'

Herek clamped on his helm as the icy touch of the void pricked his hardened skin. He glanced at Rathek but his brother looked little the worse for wear.

He was good, signed the Culler, sheathing his blades. *Worthy of his title.*

'You fought a Black Templars Champion,' said Herek, knowing his audio feed would be turned into text on Rathek's retinal lens. 'There are few better.'

And you, captain, what did you learn?

'That Morrigan doesn't carry the sword, which means he's keeping it elsewhere. Somewhere he thinks is safe.'

They will certainly have a larger vessel than that gunship we saw.

'Agreed, but I don't think it's on a ship. They're out here somewhere.'

A stronghold.

Herek nodded. 'All we need do is find it.'

A vox signal chirruped in his ear. Kurgos, reliable as ever. He was bringing the ship.

'Let's move out,' said Herek, watching the other half of the *Hermes* as she tumbled slowly and gracelessly through the silent dark, her old crew spilling out with all the other wreckage. 'They'll be coming for us now.'

He opened a vox-feed to Kurgos so they could talk.

'The Black Templars are on us.'

'Isn't that the idea?' came the chirurgeon's reply.

'No sword yet.'

'Ah, I see. Then we'll need to dissuade them.'

'Vyander has a ship of his own now.'

'And your orders to him?'

'Tell him to hurt them but not kill. Not yet.'

Chapter Six

REUNITED

THE GIRL WITH VIOLET FLOWERS

BRIGANDS

Another hump jolted the back of the junker and Ariadne cursed as she hit her head against the hold interior for the third time.

'I believe I may have preferred the void journey,' she confessed crankily, rubbing the back of her bruised skull.

It was warm in the transport's hold, the atmosphere a bad soup of body odour and gun oil only partially alleviated by the open hatch at the back.

'Ah, but breathe in that air... It is reinvigorating, heh?'

It was Ogin. Of course her protective detail would be him. Irony had thrown them together, or so it seemed to Ariadne, and now the Storm Reaper would dog her steps throughout the entire reclamation campaign. It was fated. No point in trying to fight it.

She did anyway.

'It reeks of fyceline and dirt,' she grumbled, determined to be awkward.

They were on their way further into Aglevin Province, as part of the sixth reclamation group, on one of the arteries that threaded out from the landing zone at its border. She should be back there still, helping to coordinate efforts, but instead she was here on this dirt road, thudding and jolting across the rugged terrain. All because she had broken some arsehole's fingers and ruffled a few eagle feathers on an admiral's uniform. Sullen was not the word for how she felt at that moment; enraged might have been more accurate but would have served just as futile a purpose, and so she chose to engage with the task instead. Her 'protector' seemed determined to make that more difficult.

'I smell earth and wind, fresh water...' said Ogin, and took a deep breath.

'You are smelling something I can't,' she said.

He tapped his nose knowingly, saying, 'Heightened senses,' as if that explained anything – or why he was even here.

'Isn't it rather profligate to assign one of your kind as a body-guard?' she said, giving voice to the thought. 'Wouldn't you be happier running battle drills or something?'

He frowned at her, mockingly, though a few of the soldiers in his immediate vicinity balked at how she spoke to one of the Astartes and he to her, but whilst Ariadne felt the so-called trans-human dread that all mortals experienced when faced with one of the Emperor's divine creations, she did not fear him. Not really. Yes, he was scary – the violent potential was obvious and she imagined her feelings might change if she ever had the misfor-tune to see him in combat – but she felt no danger. He treated her like an amusing oddity – or perhaps it was fondness? The mores of the Astartes were difficult to fathom, she had decided. Human, and yet inhuman in so many ways.

'Anyone would think you do not enjoy my company, visha,' he said, a faux-hurt expression on his face that swiftly turned into a broad, perfect-toothed grin. 'It is my honour and duty to pro-tect you. You are an important woman, heh.'

'It feels like overkill, is all I'm saying.'

Ogin leaned against the junker's interior wall. That insouciant look was back again as he answered, 'I say, do not overthink it, heh. There is air, there is grass and trees. I for one am glad to be off a ship, my feet touching earth, not metal.'

Ariadne shrugged, unwilling to concede the point openly out of principle. Privately, she supposed Kamidar, or at least this region of it, had some rural charm. Many Imperial worlds were cities, literal hives of industry where sun, clear air and clean running water were afterlife fictions promised to the weary. This was nothing like that. It had the trappings – the manufactories, the silos, the cyclopean statues to the world's dead saints and rulers – but it was also wild. There were forests, mountains, scrubland, even marshes. It was sparsely colonised, according to the Imperial census data Ariadne had accessed. There was a vitality to Kamidar, a place that had allowed nature to grow over its scars and retake what it had lost. They had passed several ruins on their way to Illect, a large township. Aglevin was one of the major provinces responsible for grain production, amongst other things, and therefore prioritised by the crusade. It had weathered war, this place, and insurrection. It had endured the Days of Blindness and the anarchy that followed, and it had survived. In the native Kamidarians they had seen en route, Ariadne did not see a people defeated nor one ready to surrender to the will of their Imperial sovereign; she saw a proud people willing to fight and keep the independence they had. One way or another that was a situation that would definitely change.

And Ogin's presence here was proof of that belief, if nothing else.

A shout from the driver's cab up ahead announced they were close and that all passengers should prepare to disembark. Ariadne had around twelve staff with her, all Departmento Munitorum, all in drab, functional fatigues and tabards, each charged with collating and tabulating the required yields from the Illect store yards and silos. Metals, fuels, grain, even weapons were all priorities.

The Kamidarian yields were impressive, their warehouses well stocked. They had believed they were fighting a siege, albeit one seemingly without end and imposed upon the entire planet, and as such they had made substantial provision. Ardemus had practically salivated at the prospect during the initial briefings. His quartermasters and their adepts would have their work cut out for them, but quotas would have to be met and it all started here at the outskirt provinces.

The rest of the transport harboured a squad of Mordian Iron Guard, part of a regiment that had been posted at Gathalamor several years ago but who had acquitted themselves with honour. Ariadne liked the dour, slightly over-starched Mordians, who were ever polishing their brass buttons and brushing the road dirt from their navy-blue uniforms. The last seat went to Ogin, the Storm Reaper a hunched, white-armoured giant whose head almost touched the hold's ceiling despite his best efforts to appear relaxed. As ever, he looked unperturbed but Ariadne could sense the unease in the Mordians, who did their utmost to remain professional yet couldn't help but be awed and cowed by the hulking Primaris Marine in their midst.

Gratefully then did they receive the news that they were soon to reach their destination, and the moment the engine stopped, they began to alight with the urgency of men and women who had spent the last hour or so in a cage with a genial carnodon.

Ariadne leapt down from the back of the transport, taking the hand of a friendly Mordian soldier to steady her before her boots touched soil and they went off to their duties after a crisp salute.

At once, she surveyed her surroundings. They had arrived later than the rest of the reclamation group, and the acquisition effort was already well underway. Illect was overrun with adepts and servitors loading crates and drums onto grav-skiffs that would be drawn by Mechanicus cyber-mules and led off in train once they had reached capacity.

There were also more soldiers – Mordians again, from the same platoon as the squad aboard Ariadne's transport, and small knots of Solians, ragged-looking ex-gang fighters wearing drab tan uniforms and flak armour. One whistled at Ariadne as she walked past, a narrow-faced youth with piercings and old gang tattoos, but her icy glare backed up by her augmetic soon silenced him.

As she passed through the Imperials, a young girl with straw-coloured hair and dark eyes, dressed in rugged work overalls and a hardy smock, caught her eye. She stood in front of a field of flowers, her and the rest of her family, the mother and father of which were arguing with one of the quartermasters minoris about some tithe they felt they should not have to pay. It was hard to hear the exact nature of the complaint, the air was so filled with the noise of bickering and activity. But the girl seemed apart from all that, watching Ariadne as she watched her, her bare feet muddy from her morning's labours, earthy handprints smeared down the front of her clothes from where she had wiped them after planting. The blooms were staggeringly beautiful, with vibrant violet petals shaped like teardrops that tapered at the edges into a languid tendril.

Ariadne smiled despite herself, a concession to the beauty of the girl's harvest, but the girl turned away without smiling back and left a hollow feeling in her wake.

They see us as invaders, Ariadne realised, and with the army that had descended upon this rural haven, why wouldn't they? Soldiers stood around in groups, watching warily, the ones from her transport and the dozen or so others that had made the trip. Mordians and Solians both. They weren't alone either. One of Vintar's men stalked the edge of the acquisition zone, cold retinal lenses appraising and assessing. He was a grim effigy, his bolt rifle held loose but ready in his armoured hands, a slow menace in his careful movements. Yellow and black: warning colours in every system, whether that be natural or artificial. Ariadne thought that apt and noted how even the Mordians gave the forbidding Astartes a wide berth, and that wherever discord sprang up amongst the native populace it quickly died like a fire suddenly denied oxygen when Vintar's man drew near.

'You need not worry about him, visha,' said Ogin, so close that Ariadne clutched her chest in sudden panic.

'Throne of Terra, you are infuriatingly quiet when you want to be,' she gasped, and tried to catch her breath. 'And isn't he one of yours, a *Space Marine*? Aren't you a closely bonded brotherhood even across the different Chapters?'

'He is of the Marines Malevolent. They are bastards of the lowest order.'

Ariadne stared for a moment but the Storm Reaper did not elaborate, he merely looked to the horizon and soaked in the wildness of it. She could not imagine that was a good sign, though any animosity the Storm Reaper might feel for the Marine Malevolent was kept firmly under the surface and well fettered.

Illect's warehouses were being emptied, grav-skiffs loaded and acquisitions tallied. The booted feet of adepts, menials, soldiers and servitors, along with the tracks of tyres, left churned earth in their wake and oil spills and other detritus. The wreckage raised shouts from many, a large consortium of farmers, minor guilders and labourers. Like the land, they were a rugged people. A few had brought old lascarbines and the odd stub pistol, presumably used to scare off predators, but were wise enough not to reach for them.

From what she had read, and judging by the layout of the province, Kamidar based its industry on a feudal system run by merchanteers and guilders, who paid the workers and ensured the tithes to the crown were met. These slightly better-heeled individuals, with their fine cloaks and gold-and-silver shoulder guards, kept their distance from the masses, watching carefully. Guards stood around them protectively, wearing flak-carapace hauberks, visored carapace helms and long-handled fusils they had slung across their shoulders. They kept up a stern enough facade, but Ariadne had no doubt they would be vastly outmatched by the hardened crusade soldiers of the Astra Militarum. She did not even want to think about what the likes of Ogin and the Marine Malevolent could do to them if provoked. Regardless, it left an uncomfortable mood in the air, one of tension and distrust, and for the next few hours, as the Imperium essentially plundered and denuded the Aglevin store yards, Ariadne kept her mind on her work.

By the time it was done, and the trucks and transports were moving on to their next destination, and the trail of grav-skiffs wound off into the distance like a metal serpent with no tail, the earth lay ruined underfoot. Though she had tried to curb the zeal of her own adepts, the other Munitorum staff had been less kind, the soldiers even worse. It was as if a storm had raged through Illect, tossing drums and breaking crates. Weary, and not just from fatigue, Ariadne clambered back aboard the junker. The shouts and jeers of some of the bolder natives chased her and the others as they left without ceremony, her last sight that of a field of trampled violet blooms and a native girl staring back at her coldly.

'God-Emperor,' she breathed, 'can we truly claim to be their allies...?'

Illect faded as the reclamation group headed off to less-violated pastures and they had travelled a mile or so down the dirt road when the first transport exploded.

It took a moment for it to sink in even as her own transport shuddered to a halt and the shouts of soldiers took over. Smoke was on the air, and cries of the wounded too. She met the gaze of Unna, one of her adepts, across the hold space. Saw fear in his eyes, but Ariadne was trying to make sense of what had hit them.

Something heavy-calibre, she thought distantly, still detached.

Ogin was rising, reaching over to her. She flinched back, suddenly fearful that he would crush her, until the blast hit and fire and noise roared through the junker like a tornado. Only then did she realise he had been trying to shield her.

There was blood on her face. Ariadne didn't know if it was hers – deep down she suspected it was Unna's – when she felt herself lifted up. Then came a brief sense of weightlessness before the fiery wreckage of the transport dissipated and she was in the open air again.

'Are you injured, visha?' Ogin asked her calmly, but it was clear he was juggling a dozen or more different scenarios in that second of concern.

Dazed, ears still ringing, Ariadne shook her head and caught a glance beyond the Storm Reaper's formidable silhouette to the burning junker. A junker was made for transport, not war. It had stood up poorly to attack. Bodies still hung in the wreckage, twisted like the metal chassis. Some were on fire. Too late, Ariadne turned away. Her eyes must have been wide with fear because Ogin laid a gauntleted hand on her shoulder as gently as if he were touching a paper flower.

'You get safe,' he told her. Dully, Ariadne followed his eyes to where a small group of Mordians had begun to herd some of the Munitorum staff behind an improvised barricade of vehicles. The other soldiers, including a half-company of Solians, had started to take up defensive positions along the edge of the road, finding gullies and ditches to hunker down in or else sliding onto their bellies and stabbing at the distant fog with beams from their lasguns.

The Marine Malevolent was already there, two of his battle-brothers having joined him from elsewhere in the mist. Rain was falling, a strange counterpoint to the hard bangs from the bolt rifles that shook the air, a cascade of starburst flames flaring with every burst. Fog lay heavy on a bank of distant fenland, where the shots were coming from. A faraway tear of light and suddenly jags of red tracer fire came whipping forth. Several soldiers took hits, those more exposed than their comrades, and spun and jerked as little red patches appeared on their uniforms.

Ariadne stared. She had been in battle before, but that was aboard ship and dealt with swiftly by capable armsmen and so it had remained an abstract concept. This was different. It was loud and it was near. Death felt just a hand's breadth away. Closer even.

Ogin's stern voice snapped her out of it. 'On your way, visha.'

She ran then, stumbling, one of her staffers, Yenn, helping her to her feet.

'We can make it, quartermaster,' she said, managing a half-smile. It brightened her face, Ariadne thought, reaching for anything to detach her from the moment, to hide her from her own terror.

As she fled, Ariadne tried to see what the troops were firing at, but there was just fog and mist. The light rain persisted, the sort that's good for soil, for growing, and Ogin ventured off into it, calling to his own kin, who had taken positions farther down the line. The Mordian sergeant who she had met earlier, the friendly one who had helped her from the junker, was urging them to join the cluster of Munitorum adepts behind the vehicle barricade. She reckoned there were thirty or so people hiding there, the act of calculation the only thing that was keeping her mind from shutting down. Eight soldiers, seven lasguns, one pistol. A dozen explosive munitions, six buttons for each jacket, four adepts wearing rainslickers, three with data-slates, and so it went on.

She and Yenn, a capable tertius-grade adept, were twenty feet away when burst fire raked across the side of the vehicle. It practically sliced the junker in half, stitching and scything at the same time. The friendly sergeant disappeared, a puff of crimson left in his wake. The others too, torn up and ripped apart, limbs severed, torsos ruptured. Blood misted the air, smeared and diluted by the rain. Smoke and fyceline clung in dense motes, drifting like errant cloud. The engine block took a hit, and Ariadne was already grinding to a halt, effecting an abrupt reverse in direction as the fuel tank went up. A bright flash in her peripheral vision, the feeling of heat against the side of her face, her back, Yenn's hand clutched in hers and her screaming.

'Move!'

The blast threw Ariadne forwards and she felt a hail of small shrapnel follow. A piece stung her cheek and it began to bleed instantly. She crawled, and sensed Yenn with her. They left the vehicles, too much of a target for the deadly guns out in the mist, and found a gulley into which Ariadne clambered. Yenn appeared to be having some trouble, so Ariadne reached for her and dragged the adept in with her. Only then did Ariadne see the chunk of hull plate embedded in Yenn's back. It was a miracle she had made it this far, but her fatigues had turned crimson and her face was like ice. For a second, just a second, Ariadne buried her head. She wanted to scream, to give in, to cower and die in this hole just to make it end, but instead she turned her gaze from poor Yenn and scrambled to the edge of the gulley.

Her bionic still functioned and, in addition to data-assimilation, it had ranging capabilities. As she peered over the lip of the gulley, through clouds of aerosolised soil and blood, she saw the with-ering defensive line of the Imperial troops. Several lay dead, more injured, but numbers were hard to track in the carnage. The Astartes had moved up, taken advanced positions. One – a Storm Reaper, but not Ogin, she thought – was slumped against a low boundary wall with a hand against his chest where the armoured white had changed to red. Alive, but incapacitated. The Marines Malevolent tried to concentrate fire, the heavy rattle of their guns chugging in concert.

A blink-clicked magnification of the visual feed, and she saw Ogin. He was alongside his other kinsman, the two of them snap-firing into the mist, always moving, making it hard for the distant guns to track them, but whatever was out there seemed uncon-cerned about their presence and kept laying down swathes of high-calibre munitions across the length of the reclamation group. Several junkers were on fire now. A servitor blundered around dumbly, far beyond the Imperial defensive line, until a shell clipped it and it fell.

Ariadne increased the magnification again, tried to filter some of the visual noise of the mist and spoiled air. There *was* something out there, several somethings. Her distance gauge read close to four miles and even with her vastly enhanced sight, she could only make out a rough bipedal outline, two long cannons at either arm, and a hunchbacked carapace. The walker canted forwards, revealing reverse-jointed legs that propelled the war engine gamely across the mist-shrouded fenland. Three more went with it, emitting dull flashes of light as they unleashed those cannons and riddled the Imperial line. It hit like rain, like deadly weather. By now the troops had got better at knowing when to hunker down, but the bullet hail still felled a dozen or more.

God-Emperor, thought Ariadne, *who are they, and do they mean to kill us all?*

Her only hope was the Astartes, those who were more than human and bred for war. She had heard a single Astartes warrior could take a world, or so the saying went. Surely they would deliver them?

That was when the Marines Malevolent started to fall back, and then Ogin and his kinsman too. They retreated in good order but moved quickly, rejoining the main Imperial line in less than a minute. Ogin and the other Storm Reaper slowed to gather up their fallen comrade but joined the Marines Malevolent a few seconds later.

Ariadne trained her bionic on the distant mist, concerned at the sudden shift, and saw then what had prompted the fallback.

It loomed, behemoth-like, out of greying fog, mist tendrils clinging to its towering form, reactors crackling with little flashes of corposant as something in its arsenal took on power. Much larger than the bipedal walkers and slightly more anthropo-morphic, it had armour plate and sweeping pauldrons, a masked helm for a head. The simulacra of a warrior-giant. But there could be no mistaking it for anything other than a weapon of supreme potency. The decision to retreat by the Astartes was the only sane response when facing a Knight.

Steadily, it began to walk.

Ariadne quailed, unable to move, barely able to breathe as the massive war engine strode towards the scattered reclamation group. It ate the distance greedily, all the while that crackling lightning coursing over one of its weapon mounts, revealed as it closed to be some kind of thermal cannon. That was a Knight-killing weapon, Ariadne didn't need to be a princeps to know that. Against infantry and basic transports it meant annihilation.

Some of the Imperial troops were fleeing, running past her position, not looking back. Munitorum adepts too. A handful of junkers hared off; Ariadne heard their engines and the protests of those left behind that the transports were only half-full. An understandable act of self-preservation. Utterly pointless.

She still couldn't move, her feet like stone, anchoring her down as the Knight forged on. Ariadne saw its pennants now, the besmirched heraldry of its armour, the gold sword of Kamidar replaced by a stag's skull on a forest-green field. Its other weapon arm was a great chain-toothed blade, raised up like a lance before the charge.

Ogin found her in the gulley, the Storm Reaper sliding down the rocky side to join her. Blood spattered his armour, shock-ingly stark and crimson against the grimy white. He didn't look injured but his expression was grave.

'Visha...' he began. He made it sound like an apology.

'We will die here,' said Ariadne, her voice hollow. 'Won't we?'

'Close your eyes, visha,' Ogin replied. 'You do not have to see this.'

But Ariadne could not look away as the Knight slowed to a

halt. It roared, war-horns blaring, and even a mile away it was loud enough that she had to clamp her ears. It stood there unmoving, an inviolable fortress lashed by the rain, reactor humming, puffs of steam rising from the barrel of the thermal cannon. A dread engine, it had no true soul – and yet, as Ariadne cowered in its presence, she felt it *glower*, the eye slits of its helm gateways to anger.

Slowly, inexplicably, it turned and walked away, the great sweeps of its legs stomping heavily back through the mist until it was gone.

Ariadne was incredulous, her heart a tangible lump in her throat. 'What... what happened? Why did it leave?' The tears on her face mingled with the rain.

Ogin didn't answer. He was still watching the mist for the Knight.

That's when the war-horn blew behind them, several miles distant but still loud, and Ariadne turned. Ogin's hand went to his bolt rifle, but Ariadne wondered what he could do with it against a god-engine.

Two of them stood silently behind the shattered reclamation group. Those Imperials who had been fleeing stopped in the no-man's-land between the old defensive line and the forbidding war machines that had just appeared in their path. Metal golems: faraway iron giants to the men and women on the ground, but to Ariadne, through her bionic, they were Knights, resplendent in the white-and-gold heraldry of Kamidar, the sword emblazoned on their plastrons and pennants. Larger than the other war engine, bristling with weapon systems.

They lingered for a few seconds more, before turning and disappearing into the mist.

That's why the other Knight had retreated, Ariadne realised. It was being hunted.

Chapter Seven

VANDALS

A SUNDERED NAME, FOR A SUNDERED HOUSE

THE BEGGAR-KNIGHT

Orlah's face stayed neutral as she read the report on Ekria's data-slate.

'Tell me again,' said the queen, her tone calm as she handed back the device. Inwardly, she was a tempest.

They rode in a repulsor-barque, large enough for the queen, her equerry and an escort of Kamidarian Royal Citizen Sovereigns. In addition, four other vehicles, tracked and heavier armoured, drove alongside. Two in front, two in the rear, flanking.

Despite the barque's powerful and inbuilt refractor field, it was open to the elements and Ekria swept a few errant strands from her face as the wind tousled her red hair. She had a pale countenance, lacking sun, and the perpetually pinched look of a scholar. A scar running down the middle of her face was like a crack in porcelain but did little to detract from her simple beauty.

'An attack on one of the Imperial convoys,' she said. 'Witnesses claim the attackers were Armigers and also a larger engine.'

The equerry wore rugged clothing, well suited to this excursion, a flak-armoured vest over a russet tunic and breeches, a bronze-chased laspistol belted at her hip. The silver band around her forehead bearing the sigil of the Kamidarian *oighen* was failing to keep her hair in order, and Orlah could tell from Ekria's annoyed expression that she wished she had chosen something more practical.

'How many dead?' asked the queen. She was the epitome of poise but also ruggedly dressed, wearing a simple gold breastplate that perfectly accented her dark skin. It had the same sword device on it as her equerry's band but with a matching shoulder guard that cinched a half-cloak of green velvet. It snapped fetchingly behind her like a dracon's tongue lapping at the air.

'None of the Illectian citizens perished, your majesty. Though the Imperials were less delicate with the province itself. The damage is apparently egregious. The crown has already received several claims for recompense and petition for redress by a council of guildmen.'

A tremor of annoyance crossed Orlah's face and she gripped the hilt of the ceremonial sword at her hip a little tighter. An ancestral blade, the oighen had once belonged to Grandsire Laughlen, whom she partly blamed for the pain currently dragging at her, a pain she fought to keep locked away in the vault of her grief. Its name was Justicus, which felt apt.

'And the Imperials?' she said casually, as if asking about the weather, pulling her shoulders back, the wind bracing against her skin. Unlike Ekria, her long, black hair was well pinned and appeared sculpted to her head, which was encircled by a simple gold mitre.

'Dozens killed, your majesty. We have no accurate tally as of yet, but blood was shed, and weapons fire exchanged.'

'Lord Baerhart?'

'Was present for the aftermath.'

The repulsor-barque canted suddenly to avoid a rise in the terrain and Ekria scrambled a little to keep her feet. Even the Sovereigns, who were like tin soldiers in their shining armour, had to adjust their footing.

Orlah remained statuesque, imperious. 'Raise the Kingsward now.'

'At once, your majesty.'

The hololithic feed flickered to life through a projector node located just behind the driver. Green monochrome light established the grainy render of a veteran Knight pilot with a neatly trimmed beard and wearing padded fatigues. He had light armoured plates on his shoulders, chest and knees, a visored helm hooked to his belt, and all the straps and connectors that joined him to his engine were loose and free.

Baerhart DeVikor, of the *Martial Exultant*, Kingsward, and sworn protector of the royal house of Kamidar.

'My queen...' Baerhart began, his voice gravelly across the feed, and bowed deeply from the waist.

'Well met, Lord Baerhart,' said Orlah, a lightness to her tone that hadn't been there before.

'It was him, my queen,' he said and, after the royal formalities had been observed, his mood darkened at once. *'I am certain of it. Lareoc was abroad.'*

'A sundered name, for a sundered house,' bit the queen, 'I would not hear it spoken again.'

'Of course, my queen. But he was there nonetheless. The dog caused quite the ruckus. He killed forty-three of the Imperials. I took the tally myself.'

'I assume the fact you have not told me that the cur is either dead or in your custody means he evaded us.'

'Regrettably, we saw him only from a distance and the moment he detected us via augur, he quit the field. He knows the wilds of Kamidar better than anyone.'

'Ever the coward.'

'Yes, my queen,' Baerhart agreed, the gravel in his voice with a little extra grit in it.

'I want him found, Baerhart. But I want him alive. I want to look him in the eyes before I kill him.'

'As you wish, my queen. There is little to be gained with further pursuit now but I will send the Sovereigns out afresh come the morning and see if we can stir up his spoor.'

'I have faith in you, Baerhart. Emperor guide your sword.'

'I am ever your devoted servant,' Baerhart replied, a smile on his lips that stayed overlong before he bowed again and, at the queen's subtle urging, Ekria cut the feed.

They were closing on their destination, the smoke trails already visible and the signs of an army having passed along the churned roads. Orlah regarded the ruination, her pain at her people's suffering obvious.

'Are they all like this?' she asked.

'It would appear so, your majesty.'

'And how many have we allowed onto our sovereign soil?'

'Six, your majesty.'

Orlah bit back an old curse. The wind-whipped silence held a question.

'Out with it,' she demanded.

Ekria gave a shallow, respectful nod. 'I have no wish to be impertinent, your majesty...'

'And yet whenever one of my advisors prefaces whatever they are about to say with such a statement, they are invariably so.' She turned to look the equerry in the eye, her face hard but not entirely unkind. 'You are amongst my most trusted advisors. No secrets, we promised. Are you about to renege on that oath?'

Ekria conceded the point with a look of mild contrition before she glanced at the nearest Sovereign.

'Do not worry about them,' Orlah reassured her. 'These men and women are my lifewards and as such my will is their will. You can speak freely. Please, Ekria...'

'Why allow them to make landfall at all? These armies of soldiers and logisticians announce themselves in the deep void, claim Kamidar as a vassal world and proceed to despoil it. And all of that before their fleet proper is even at anchor in our atmosphere.'

Orlah held the equerry's gaze as she considered her answer. 'In these benighted times, many worlds would welcome the return of the Imperium. For protection. That Terra endures should be a cause of joy.'

'I rejoice at the Throneworld's survival, but this fleet is not Terra, and it has not come here as a protector or even a friend. They are... *vandals*, your majesty. Trampling wherever they may and taking what is not theirs to take.'

'A tithe charter signed and witnessed by my elders would suggest otherwise. We swore oaths, the blood of my house binds us to them.'

'But to tread so rampantly, with such disregard?' argued Ekria. 'Is this how the Imperium treats its vassal worlds? Have we not prospered on our own? Did we not survive the darkest of days? When they sent their torchbearers, they did not even deign to send a missive.' She paused. 'Are we not Kamidar first, Imperium second?'

Orlah found herself unable to disagree with any of it. The mysterious torchbearer fleet had left the fate of the Imperium as open to conjecture as its purpose for coming to the Kamidar System. It had not lingered, and vox had proven impossible. It was only later when she had spoken with Castellan Morrigan that she had learned the small flotilla of ships had visited Cellenium and then abruptly departed. Even then, it had felt like a snub and left more questions than answers.

'Have you not given enough?'

Orlah held the equerry's gaze, a sudden pang of emotion stilling her, curdling, churning; becoming something akin to anger, only worse. It passed but did not entirely depart.

'It shall be put right,' said the queen, her eyes cold, her face like ebony.

Ekria bowed low out of respect for her queen, their frank exchange at an end.

Orlah turned back to the wind, but the roar of it surging past failed to stifle her thoughts. Ahead, the provincial border of Victua came fully into view and the township of Crathe. Its people lined the roads, their complaints writ clearly on their angry faces.

And Orlah muttered bitterly, 'Let us see what carnage our protectors have wrought...'

They left Victua late in the morning and went on to visit major townships of two other provinces that had suffered during the first Imperial landings. In each settlement, the domains of Orlah's vassal lords-minoris and guildmen, the story was much the same. Fields trampled, stores ransacked, her people close to uproar.

'More will come, your majesty,' said Ekria quietly, her face ashen as they drove through the carnage.

The citizens of Kamidar had begun to try to set matters right, mending what they could, repurposing what they could not, but the loss was staggering and difficult to justify, charter or not.

'They mean to strip our world of everything of worth,' Ekria went on, getting louder, more animated. 'Where will it end, how much must they take before–'

'Enough,' the queen uttered simply and Ekria checked herself immediately.

'I apologise, your majesty, I forget myself.'

'They have come, they are here, and nothing else matters now. They will do a lot more than sequester our mills and manu-factories. Plunder is the least of it, I fear.'

'Then what can we do, your majesty?'

The edge of the last province dwindled to a dark speck behind them as they made for the edge of the wilds. Few roamed out in these parts; it was unsafe. Brigands were not so uncommon but it was one in particular that interested Orlah, or at least his old familial estate. Anything to take her mind off what was coming next.

'For now, we accommodate them. I will make a petition to the admiral of the Imperial fleet, express my concerns.'

It was thin gruel and hardly a fitting demonstration of a sovereign's power, but caution was wise until she got a measure of whom she would be dealing with.

Ekria's silence said everything it needed to. Orlah felt the same, but a queen did not have the luxury of being impolitic.

'And to that end,' said Orlah, 'I need you to go back to Gallanhold and begin preparations. Gather the nobles.' Her mood darkened, grew sombre. 'I would have my daughter well received upon her return. Everything must be ready.'

'Of course, your majesty.'

'Captain Gademene will escort you back to the ship.'

The captain of the Sovereigns gave a stiff salute upon hearing his name and his queen's order. Orlah nodded and the barque slowed then stopped so Ekria could alight and climb aboard one of the armoured transports. Only two would remain with the queen.

'This is unsafe territory, your majesty,' ventured Ekria as she was leaving. 'Is it wise to thin your protection detail. I am sure I could manage with a handful of–'

'These have been my lands since I was a girl, and my kingdom since my husband, the High King Uthra, joined the Emperor's side,' Orlah replied, waving away the equerry's well-meant concerns. 'I shall never fear it, whoever or whatever might roam its wilds.'

With that, she bid Ekria farewell and two of the escort vehicles peeled away to the north and Gallanhold. Orlah watched them go, her reduced guard waiting on her order to move out. She gave it silently and the repulsor-barque stirred, ferrying her and her retinue deeper into the wilds.

* * *

It had been beautiful once, Orlah remembered as she stood before the ruins of the old manse. Formerly a magnificent building but merely a preface to the larger palatial manor that rose up beyond. Dilapidation and neglect had reduced them, their marble opulence stained by windblown grime and overrun with creepers and voracious growths of lichen. The wilds had reclaimed this place and were slowly, surely pulling it back into the earth. Its fields had run fallow, the bone-white carcasses of cattle-beasts left to degrade to dust, its stone promenades choked by weeds.

As Orlah passed the manse and approached the manor on foot, she was aghast at how ramshackle it had become. She had not been here in some time, content to let it rot, determined to never revive the estate and condemn it to perpetual ruin. Her wrath felt cold, even to herself, on past reflection. She felt it stirring again now but for different reasons.

A fallen coat of arms lay just inside the gaping threshold of the manor. The building's main gate had long since rotted, now fit only to be gnawed upon by predators. A few skittered from the light as Orlah pushed the portal wide, giving it a first touch of fading sun in a long time so she could properly regard the heraldic shield lying on the ground in front of her. A crack ran through it, the stone likely shattered upon impact. A gauntlet laid upon a blaring sun rendered in granite, it was the heraldry of the House of Solus, once a proud barony of Kamidar. The stonemason had fashioned a scroll along the bottom and carved into it was the name *Lareoc*.

'A sundered name, for a sundered house...' uttered the queen, disturbing a few raptors who had taken roost in the rafters. The birds took flight, spiralling up through a cleft in the roof, their shrill cawing like screams. Orlah watched them depart dispassionately. Empty and hollow, the old estate of Lareoc had become a lair for craven beasts and nothing more. She hadn't expected to find anything, but the attack on the Imperial convoy had been bold and, she suspected, designed to cause her discomfort in her negotiations.

Orlah gave the place one last look and left the manor behind. As she walked out into the last of the day's light and the slowly encroaching foliage, she stared into the wildness. To the forests and the highlands, the sweeping hills and caves. Kamidar had its share of hidden places.

'I hope you were watching, you bastard,' she said to herself, lingering only a little longer at the entranceway of the manor before heading back to the barque. Two of her guards fell into lockstep behind her as she went, though Orlah paid them little mind. They were a formality, she could take care of herself.

'Baerhart...' she said into the vox built into her gorget.

'My queen.'

'Seems he did not take the bait.' She cut the feed, but when she returned to the clearing where she had left the barque and the rest of her protective detail, she found a message waiting for her. Vox was unreliable at range and through the Veil, but rudimentary missives could get through and were easier to conceal. Orlah felt herself tense upon reading it, a gauntlet seizing her heart.

It was from Gerent, her brother. The Imperial fleet had reached the Iron Veil a day earlier than expected.

And then five simple words.

We are bringing her home.

Lareoc watched her through a mag-scope, like a sea captain trying to chart uncertain waters. The device was stretched to its limits and as such he could not see every detail, but the queen appeared upset. He smiled, shutting up the scope and putting it back into the pouch on his belt.

Twelve of his followers surrounded him in the darkness of the woods, their armour and fatigues dulled with dirt and arboreal foliage so as to blend in. They turned as he turned, following

Lareoc back out through the narrow poacher's trail and away up the crags and along the hills towards the footings of the east mountains. They ranged on foot, draped in dense black cloaks, their war engines far too conspicuous to use so brazenly. Besides, Lareoc suspected he wasn't the only one watching. The bastard Kingsward would be out here somewhere, waiting to spring his trap. No, Lareoc was cannier than that. Hit and run, disrupt, menace. These were not the tools of a Knight, he conceded, but he had not truly been worthy of that appellation for many years. He was what he needed to be, to survive.

Besides, he had a different plan in mind for Baerhart: a trap, well baited.

By the time they reached the mountains, night had fallen and darkness swaddled the hills like velvet. Lareoc found the cleft in the crags, one of two ways in and out of his outlaw's fastness, and navigated the narrow channel downwards in abject darkness, water from an underground stream splashing quietly underfoot. His warriors took his lead, as they always did, voices hushed and hands near their holstered weapons. After a short while, a faint light wavered ahead like a thin candle flame that blossomed into a fire-bright maw.

Through this natural fissure the channel opened out into a massive, vaulted cave.

Sacristans and a few of the house servants still bonded to him looked up at the baron's return. Even unkempt and thick-bearded as he was, Lareoc still had their respect. *I am a beggar-knight,* he thought, descending the rough-hewn steps that led down into the cauldron. He gave nods of greeting to the men he passed, clasped forearms with others. They hated the queen almost as much as he, and loved him for it. Outlaws had the luxury of being uncompromising, he supposed.

Parnius was waiting for him, his old squire turned friend and co-conspirator, with a grave look on his youthful face. The

men-at-arms and footmen dispersed as the two of them came
together, fearful of whatever volatile alchemy might be unleashed.

'A bold deed,' said Parnius – without greeting, Lareoc noted.

'Spying on the queen?' Lareoc replied, being deliberately obtuse. 'It was child's play.'

Parnius scowled, and scratched at the tufts of rust-coloured hair that sprouted from his head like plucky flames. 'You know what I'm referring to. Attacking the Imperials. It was bold.'

'You've mentioned that,' answered Lareoc casually, striding past the squire to stand in the shadow of his war engine.

'Overly so,' Parnius clarified. 'You risk much.'

'I do,' Lareoc agreed, basking in the reflected power of the machine. *Heart of Glory*, an engine of the Knight Errant class, a soaring edifice of martial magnificence and undeniable power. Its great reaper blade lay dormant, its thermal cannon reduced to less than a whisper. But it was far from dormant. Even without the connection of the Throne Mechanicum harboured within its indomitable chassis, Lareoc could feel the stirring of his ancestors. It had once borne the colours of Kamidar as well as the Solus house crest. All that was history now, and the forest green of the Knight's armoured plates served as testament to the fact.

It was a king amongst lesser machines, eight Armiger Knights that still stood more than three times the height of a man and could cripple armies with their power and ferocity. The hunched engines appeared to bow before the larger Knight, vassals paying homage to their lord. Nine engines in all, a formidable force by any reckoning but not nearly enough to challenge the queen. There had once been more.

'Perhaps you risk too much...' said Parnius and tapped one of Lareoc's shoulder guards with the dirk he had been using to clean his boots.

Names had been scored into the metal, one for every warrior they had lost to the cause. Every man and woman that Baerhart had tracked down and killed since they had begun their little rebellion.

'The greatest risk is to not risk enough,' Lareoc replied, his jaw stiffening as he glanced at the names, 'or their sacrifices will be for nothing.'

'The Imperium are here, Lareoc. That changes things.'

'It does. She's distracted. We can use that to our advantage.'

'And attacking them, how does that advantage us?'

Lareoc turned and grabbed Parnius by the shoulders in gentle urging. 'You worry too much, my friend. Trust me. The Imperium is no friend to the queen. She is too proud for any of that.'

'I have heard talk that their quartermasters have left townships ravaged. Revolt is in the air.'

'Then all is well,' said Lareoc, clapping him on the arms as he started to walk away.

'They have an army, several armies.'

Lareoc gestured expansively to the warriors and bondsmen in the subterranean hall, their Armigers and *Heart of Glory*. 'We have an army.'

'It is a crusade, Lareoc. They say the largest in history. How can we fight against that? I fear we'll end up trading one tyrant for another.'

Lareoc became serious, the old anger rising, warring with the shame of past misdeeds. He came back to Parnius, a hand firmly behind the back of his former squire's neck as he looked him in the eyes.

'No more tyrants. Only strength and the means to chart our own path, here or elsewhere. That is what I promised these men and women who followed me, and I won't fail them.' He leaned in, eyes conveying the utmost sincerity. 'I won't fail you.'

Lareoc released Parnius, his mood lightening with each second like a cloud departing the sun.

'Now, come, my friend.' A host of warriors had gathered behind them, the men-at-arms and mercenaries in the robber baron's employ, the pilots of the Armigers. 'Albia will be expecting us.'

It was a hidden place amongst hidden places, a deeper well that led to an ancient part of the mountain. Even the air felt old, primordial, and there in a rough-hewn chamber Albia waited for them.

Crouched like some sculpted gargoyle, the old priest went hooded as ever, stray wisps of greying hair protruding from the folds of his cowl, his brown robes plain as a friar's habit.

'Well met, Lareoc and the Knights of Hurne,' he said in the croaking cadence of a venerable bird as the baron and his warriors trooped into the chamber. Albia had lit torches, which lifted the gloom somewhat and cast trembling shadows across a low stone table and nine seats that were little more than round rocks smoothed by the erosion of ages. A sigil had been carved into the table of a leaping stag impaled on a hunter's spear. It was part of Kamidar's elder lore, Albia had told them, and predated the Imperium, even the Emperor.

'These are the old ways,' he had said when Lareoc had first taken him in, a mendicant priest hunted for his aberrant beliefs and the baron a fugitive from his queen's wrath. Lareoc had listened to the priest's preachings, his embittered mind an eager repository. For Albia had promised him the one thing he needed to set matters right: strength.

In the priest, Lareoc found an ally with motives not so dissimilar to his own. Albia wanted a return to the old ways, for Kamidarians to be free to worship as they would, to worship Hurne, he of the wild places.

'Hurne is of the earth and we are his children,' said the priest warmly, watching his flock as they took their seats.

Lareoc watched him back, fascinated by the old preacher's eyes, one green, one brown. The light threw the muddy daubings on his weathered face into a hazy sort of relief, the sign of the stag and spear. He was thin, Albia, with arms like wizened branches and wrapped in leather bindings reminiscent of soft bark. A bowl sat on the stone table before him, the same substance churned within as was painted on the mendicant's forehead. It made the room smell of loam and wet roots, the earthy flavours of the deep wood.

The warriors exchanged a few nervous glances: this part was still fairly new. They had listened, they had learned of the old god's name, now they would be baptised by his blessed spoor, the heart soil of Kamidar.

'Come forth, then – destiny awaits for those who have the will to seize it,' invited the priest, casting back his hood at last to reveal the vigour in his eyes, and the sigil upon his skin. It had crusted as it dried and flaked as he moved, little motes of it drifting down onto the table as he leaned forwards with the bowl. Lareoc went first, he always went first, transfixed as Albia reached into the drab-green unguent and with two fingers reached up to make the benediction.

'We are his children...' Lareoc returned, and swore he felt a thrill of power trickle through him just as he closed his eyes and the unguent touched his skin.

Chapter Eight

DAUGHTERS

THE HISTORITOR

MIRACLES

Kesh took aim down the targeter. She felt the contours of the lasrifle, appreciated its heft, the length of the barrel. Her breathing was even, her focus narrowed to the head of a pin as she lined up the target. The latent hum of the charged power pack was soothing, and it stilled her thoughts.

Squeeze trigger, simultaneous exhale. The jolt of power discharge, compensated for by her marksman's aim. The magnesium flash, the smell of ionisation as the bolt of light sped through the air, trembling it, searing it.

Six shots, six targets. A burn hole the size of a fist from the heavy charge in each one.

The burst spent the power pack, which Kesh ejected smoothly before hoisting the rifle against her shoulder in one fluid motion so she could inspect her handiwork. She did it automatically, the routine instinctual after years of campaigning.

The sixth target was off. Not just off. Wide. Frowning, Kesh set down the rifle and had to clamp one hand against the other to stop it from shivering. The tremor was mild, and it came and went, but to a marksman it made a world of difference.

Throne, Gathalamor was years ago, but ghosts seldom faded with time.

'Expecting trouble, sergeant?'

Dvorgin had just walked into the armoury, passing a row of empty battle cages with their deactivated servitors before joining Kesh at the shooting range.

'Always, sir,' said Kesh, hiding her earlier concern behind a mask of duty. 'Just as you taught me.'

'That I did,' Dvorgin conceded.

Grizzled and scarred to the point of worn leather, the general had a stout frame and walked with a limp. He smiled, the warmth there genuine. He had led the Mordians on Gathalamor, seen horrors that Kesh knew kept him awake at night. More than once, she had seen or heard him pacing the decks of the ship as the old memories came a-haunting. He had not seen what she had seen, but every soldier's burdens were personal, a battle fought but never won, only hidden behind the eyes. Pain recognised pain, though, and Dvorgin's was clear enough to Kesh. A child he could have had but never did, the wife he had denied that he would never see again, and Kesh as a substitute daughter, she supposed. She didn't speak of it or use it to her advantage, but the affection was there, a small comfort but a welcome one.

Dvorgin picked up a lasgun Kesh had been cleaning and left in the adjacent booth. He glanced over, as if to seek permission.

'Be my guest, sir,' said Kesh.

Barring the dead-eyed servitors slumped in their battle cage cradles, they were alone. It was late and only the harrowed walked the halls of the *Virtuous*.

Dvorgin took the lasgun in a well-seasoned grip, snugging the stock into his shoulder and aiming down the iron sights. His

targets were much closer but he didn't have a scope like Kesh.
He fired four shots, a two-second gap between each.

'Rustier than I thought,' he remarked, reviewing his efforts. Then he glanced over at Kesh's targets. 'Not like you to miss one...'

'Something on the lens,' she lied.

'Not like you to have a dirty lens.'

'Having an off day. I'll endeavour to do better, sir.'

Dvorgin laughed, trying to placate. 'I'm only joking, Magda. Off day or not, you're the best damn shot in the regiment and I'm including myself in that assessment.'

Kesh blinked once, unsure how to act. She could name at least six other better marksmen than Dvorgin.

The general laughed again. 'Another joke, sergeant. You seem a little uptight.'

'End of a long journey.'

Dvorgin nodded at that, empathetically. 'And the start of another.'

'I am just glad she will finally be at rest.'

'To lose a daughter...' Dvorgin began, his expression drifting to some faraway pain only he could touch. He returned after a few moments, smiling at her. That affection again.

'How long until planetfall?' asked Kesh, eager to change the subject.

Dvorgin checked his chron. An antique piece, it had been given to him by his wife. One evening, a long time ago when he had been somewhat in his cups, Dvorgin had shown Kesh the inscription.

Luthor,

Make us always proud, my fierce protector,

Marie.

Kesh had never seen a picture of her, nor had he offered to show her one. She assumed he didn't have one. Dvorgin clung to this instead. *Strange, the mementos that anchor us.*

Dvorgin glanced at the face before snapping the chron shut and returning it to his pocket.

'Another twelve hours. We're to accompany the casket as part of the honour guard.'

'I am surprised the baron has allowed it, sir. The Kamidarians seem fiercely protective of her.'

'I've come to understand he's a reasonable man. He actually insisted, and that's not all he allowed either.'

Kesh's frown held a question.

'You didn't think I was here practising my aim, did you, sergeant?'

'Sir?'

Dvorgin stepped aside to usher in another figure, a willowy man with a long and sombre face and wearing a plain black military uniform.

'Historica Verita,' said the man, extending a hand that Kesh took warily. His fingers felt like bird bones in her sturdy Mordian grip, liable to break under the slightest pressure. The metallic brace that supported his frame creaked audibly above the groans of the ship. Void-born, she assumed, with a body unused to the rigours of gravity.

'I have heard of you...'

'Theodore Viablo.'

Kesh let go of his hand and looked to the general but Dvorgin was already on his way.

'This man wishes to know something of you, Kesh. I spoke to one of his colleagues a few years ago but I think they want to talk to the one who was actually there...'

'*There*, sir?'

'In the catacombs,' Viablo supplied, 'alongside the Custodians.'

Kesh groaned inwardly. She began stripping back her rifle, and would move on to the second one just as soon as she was done. 'You have until I've finished with these two.'

'Of course. I have no wish to keep you overlong. I am in pursuit of truth. That is our role in the Logos Historica Verita, the task the primarch has given us.'

'What truth?'

'Of how you survived. No one I have spoken to can account for it.'

Kesh stopped, poised with the partially disassembled pieces of the rifle in her hands. They were shaking again. She stilled them with anger.

'Why does it matter how I lived? I don't know. I thought I was dead for sure, but one of the Custodians rescued me. Talk to them, if you want to know the truth.'

'I have. Or rather,' Viablo corrected, 'I *tried*. They wouldn't speak to me.'

'What makes you think I will?'

'You already are, aren't you? Besides, I have the mandate of Roboute Guilliman and you are not a Custodian.'

Kesh set down the rifle pieces and slowly turned. 'You're pulling rank on me?'

'No, I'm not even sure if it works that way. I just want to talk.'

His solemn face seemed open enough. Kesh had seen little of the historitors, even since joining the crusade and Fleet Primus, but she had heard of their mission, an undertaking to preserve knowledge and present an accurate account of the war. As a lowly sergeant, she had hoped she would fall beneath their notice but this Viablo appeared very interested in her story.

'Tell me about the catacombs,' he went on. 'What did you see?'

'Miracles, horrors... Throne, I cannot begin to fathom it. I saw a warrior's faith undo evil incarnate, is that what you want to hear?'

'I only want the truth.'

Kesh snapped, 'I can't rightly say what that is!' She composed herself, steadying her breath, calming her nerves. 'Sorry, I don't like to return to it. The memory.'

'I appreciate this must be difficult for you. It is why I sought you out here.'

'On the target range?'

'In familiar surroundings.'

Kesh glanced at the rifle. It was how she felt, disassembled and only partly put back together. A piece missing or in the wrong order.

'I saw the dead,' she told him.

'As in corpses reanimated?'

'No, their... *spirits*, I suppose. Old, not really there. They could hurt us, though our weapons passed through them at first.'

'I have heard similar accounts. My colleague, Historitor Guelphrain, took statements after Gathalamor.'

Kesh kept her eyes on the rifle pieces. It was easier that way. 'Then why talk to me at all?'

'I wish to corroborate, and there's the matter of your survival.'

'We found a way to fight them.' She laughed, but it was hollow, bitter. 'Would you believe me if I said it was faith?'

'I would. I do.'

'It was the Holy Sisters at first. They struck what the rest of us could not. And then we followed their example. We *believed*, we invoked His name and it was like fighting something flesh and blood. They could be... *undone*. I won't say killed because they were already dead. I can't explain it, just like I can't explain how I am alive, standing here and talking to you.' Kesh faced him but found no scorn in him, only patient interest.

'And do you believe in divinity, Sergeant Kesh?'

'Are you asking if I believe in the God-Emperor?'

'Not exactly. We all believe in the Emperor. I am talking about the literal power of faith. In living saints and He on Terra moving through His subjects.'

'Are you a priest as well as a historitor?'

'I am merely a student of truth. By your own admission you saw miracles in those catacombs, acts that defy explanation. Your own survival cannot be explained. Is also miraculous.'

'I'm not sure what you're trying to imply.'

'Nothing. I'm just trying to find out what you remember and make an accurate account.'

'I don't *want* to remember. I was fighting beside those auric gods, the Custodians. Fighting and climbing. An actual mountain of bones. Death was in the air. I was terrified. I fought, I fell, and the bones swallowed me and one of the Custodes. I honestly thought I was dead. The next thing I remember, I was walking back to camp and the war was over.'

'And there's nothing more?' said Viablo. 'Nothing between when you fell and when you awoke?'

Kesh shook her head. She had decided to pack up the rifles. Finish them later. She wanted out of this conversation. 'That's it,' she said, readying to be on her way. 'There's nothing else.'

Except that was a lie.

Chapter Nine

THE FEUDAL COUNCIL

THE IRON VEIL

A CLANDESTINE ORDER

Orlah waited quietly as the feudal council bickered.

Their voices carried in the vaulted chamber, which was tiered like an auditorium with the queen's place at the apex of the tiers looking down on her subjects. Immense statues lined the edge of the hall, their ornate plinths the size of battle tanks. They were the rulers of Kamidar, its nobles of days gone, pristine in white marble, untouchable by time. An emblem, the unsheathed sword of Kamidar, was prevalent in the room's heraldry and spoke to her house's pre-eminence, reminding the queen's vassal lords of their place.

Orlah had exchanged her rugged travelling attire for something more regal and stately. A gown of green satin fell from her supple shoulders, a silver lion-faced pauldron over the left. Voluminous sleeves hid the queen's hands, which she folded in front of her. Patient, serene. Cuffs of silver matched the shoulder guard, and the black garnet she wore on the torc around her neck glittered in the soft lumens of the hall. Wire had been worked into the fabric of her gown, fanning it out artificially at the edges, and the long train that trailed behind it had the iridescent shimmer of dracon scale. Orlah's hair had been coiffed into an ornate headpiece, shaped like a crescent moon and fashioned into a long, thick braid that ran the length of her back.

Ekria stood by her side, as composed and watchful as her liege. She had likewise changed her attire for something better befitting the Hall of Sovereigns, and though elegant she was a pale and sombre thing matched against the queen's magnificence. She had gathered the conclave following news of the imminence of the Imperium's arrival. Alas, the nobles had taken it as their opportunity to vent grievances.

Let them, Orlah thought.

'It is tantamount to invasion,' one of her lords, Banfort, was saying. A noble of House Vexilus, he wore the red-and-gold livery of his ancestors, the rearing falcon of his household heraldry accented with the sword of Kamidar to show his fealty to the ruling faction. Banfort had the look of a hawk, with his sharp beaklike nose and his hair swept back and styled into almost spike-like feathers. The man was ever agitated, shifting from one foot to the next and glancing between the attendees.

'That is too far, entirely too far,' replied one of his contemporaries, Lady Antius, baroness of House Orinthar. She had a strong but compassionate air that was immediately calming, her manner less animated than the baron's as the cyber-canids padding around her feet nuzzled her ankles. The long dress she wore, together with a breastplate of enamelled bronze, flowed elegantly like a silver cataract.

None who were summoned here would ever sit. The Hall of Sovereigns was a place for debate and the resolution of issues that affected the protectorate. Such things were accomplished on one's feet. If nothing else, it improved the briskness of discussion.

'Then what would you call it, *milady*? I see troops on our native soil, and armies marching through our townships. It is occupation in all but name.' Banfort turned to the crowd, imploring his other nobles, some of whom met his declaration with supportive nods or murmurs of agreement.

'There have been reports of extensive damage, and heavy-handed tactics,' uttered a third: Ganavain, the baron of Harrowmere. Ganavain represented the last noble house of Kamidar now that Solus had been excommunicated, and he wore a black, lacquered breastplate with dark blue tunic. His heraldic sigil, a prancing horse, was emblazoned on a silver talisman hung from a chain around his neck. Hands behind his back, he had the look of a military man and raised an eyebrow as he looked askance at the queen, an invitation to participate in the debate. 'I have heard talk of riots. As of yet only threatened, it is true, but the mood sours by the hour.'

More agreement here, almost unanimous, even from the Lady Antius, who had counselled caution from the very outset.

'Are they not our allies, though?' Antius ventured again. 'Let us call for restraint, seek diplomatic address.'

Banfort scoffed. 'Evidently, her ladyship has not seen the flotilla of warships lingering at the edge of our domain in the void,' he said. 'They are not here to establish diplomatic ties. They mean to dominate us, make us vassals of the Imperium anew.'

'And are we not?' uttered the queen, and all eyes turned at once. 'That is how they see us, as subjects of the Throne. That is what we are. But we are also survivors. We have endured. For the last six years, we have endured. The Iron Veil is testament to that. Our continued existence is testament to that.'

Her gaze roved the chamber, taking in each and every face, imprinting her invisible will and confidence upon them. In truth, many of these nobles had passed their prime. Most of the warrior-lords had departed years ago, called to the crusade and glory, honouring the age-old oaths to which Kamidar and her sons and daughters were bound. They had strength still but it was faded, and soon it would be the scions who ruled in their stead, though she would fester. Her lack of a successor had guaranteed that, and she had no inclination to give the throne to her younger brother. Gerent was a gifted tactician but had no head for statecraft.

Feeling her mind wandering, she pulled herself back into the moment.

'Lord Gerent returns, and brings Sir Sheane with him,' the queen declared. 'Our other Knights have been sequestered to the lord primarch's armies. They honour us. Perhaps it is time for Kamidar to return to the Imperial fold also and be embraced as one of its subjects, but we will show them strength, not this quavering and bickering,' she said, face souring. 'That is unbefitting of the Kamidarian nobility.

'Every courtesy shall be extended to our guests and allies. I will speak to their lord admiral and gain assurance that greater restraint and care will be taken in the acquisition of the crusade's needs.'

'And can we trust this lord admiral, your majesty?' asked Ganavain, the question an honest one.

'I have to trust him, Lord Ganavain, and take him at his word.'

'And what if he refuses?' said Banfort.

'I must believe that our desires are aligned and that he will not refuse,' countered the queen. 'What other choice is there? The *Virtuous* is amongst the Imperial fleet. My daughter resides aboard.'

At this, the other nobles fell into a respectful silence, the mood abruptly sombre. They had all learned of the princess' fate. It had been years but their grief had been held fast, like a sword blow poised but yet to fall.

'I will have her returned to me. Nothing will prevent that.'

After a moment's respite, Antius spoke up, changing the subject.

'Has the brigand been apprehended? His continued *sorties* will do little to assuage the Imperial faith in our intent.'

'Baerhart will have him soon,' the queen assured them, 'and

of a lone discontent. For now the matter is closed.'

And so none raised it further, but there was one more issue for
the conclave to discuss.

'And what of the Black Templars, your majesty?' said Ganavain. 'What stake do they have in all of this?'

Orlah's lip quirked in annoyance, but she quickly masked it.
A void stood out amongst the throng of nobles and Kamidarian
worthies. Even the representatives of Galius and Vanir were in
attendance, though as little more than silent observers, looking
nervous at all the talk of invasion. The vassal worlds of the protectorate owed their continued existence to Kamidar and its queen.
They had little agency of their own. Unlike the Astartes. Though
not for lack of trying, the Black Templars had been unreachable
for several days, since before the fleet had been detected at the
Mandeville point at system's edge.

'Castellan Morrigan is oathed to Kamidar, sword-sworn to this
house. His stake is our stake,' she said.

'I would feel much reassured if the Black Templars were here,'
said Banfort.

Orlah turned her gaze on him, a lance tip marking its target.

'We are here, Lord Banfort. And that shall suffice. This is not occupation or subjugation, it is reunion. Let us be mindful to act thusly.'

'I have received petitions, my queen, from those who have lost
their lands, had their livelihoods trampled, their crops denuded,'
said Antius.

'The crown shall reimburse every loss. I have been to the provinces, reassured their citizens. I will trust all of you to do the
same in your own fiefdoms. We must be united in this.' She let
the silence linger, allowing the other nobles to nod their assent,
and then made a surreptitious gesture to Ekria, who ended the
conclave with a curt statement and the queen's consent to depart.

Several of the lords flickered out of existence, those who had attended via holo from the more distant provinces of Wessen and Eageth, and the seneschals from Galius and Vanir. Others, with their retinues in tow, departed gracefully with polite bows to their liege. A few lingered, finishing cups of wine, but soon Orlah was alone with Ekria. Even her own house had quit the hall.

'Tell me how that went, Ekria,' said Orlah, glad the counsel was over but eager to be rid of her uncomfortable trappings. She hated the politics, even though she was good at it.

'I believe you showed a fair and even hand, your majesty.'

Orlah quirked an eyebrow at her. 'Meaning I did not go far enough?'

'Not at all, your majesty. Only that a true ruler shows strength through restraint and caution. To react aggressively will only provoke aggression in turn, and matters are already volatile.'

Orlah held her eye. She did not flinch.

'I have a Kingsward, admittedly abroad hunting that brigand, a host of household troops that would put most Militarum regiments to shame, and six lances of Knights at my beck and call. I do not need the protection of my equerry. Speak your mind.'

Ekria gently smoothed down her gown. 'Very well. Between the attack on the Imperial convoy and foreign troops in the townships, I think the people feel abandoned.'

Anger swelled up in Orlah like a burning sea, but she held it back. Just. She had asked for candidness, she could hardly remonstrate her equerry for doing as her queen had bid.

'They are unprotected.' She looked away, taking in the spectacle of the old lords, silently beseeching their wisdom.

'I heard murmurings to that effect, your majesty, yes.'

'Fail to protect my subjects, and I will appear weak. Demonstrate strength, and I risk escalation of an already hostile situation.' Orlah scowled, not liking where this line of reasoning was taking her. Grief was muddying her thinking, however much she tried to deny it. She turned back to Ekria. 'What is your counsel?'

'The House Armigers would send a potent message, your majesty.'

'Too potent, I fear, and I don't want war engines in the townships. Those days are supposed to be behind us. A cohort of Sovereigns will suffice.'

'In every township, your majesty?'

'Without exception. I want the citizens of Kamidar to feel my presence, my will, to know they are looked after.'

'And if matters escalate?'

Orlah's face darkened. 'Then we ford that river if and when we need to. Now,' she added, straightening up and raising her chin, 'how do I look?'

'Regal and powerful, your majesty,' Ekria replied without hesitation.

'Good,' said the queen. 'I am about to speak with a lord admiral.'

The wreckage of ships spread across the void like a sea of dead iron.

Ardemus saw freighters, warships, heavy transports, every class and scale of vessel under Sol. Hundreds of them. Many were xenos in origin, others bore the marks of the Archenemy. Void erosion made it difficult to tell how long each ship had drifted like this, their gutted carcasses crusted with hoar frost and savaged with scars. Several had been broken in two, their listless halves floating in sombre orbits around the pieces of lesser vessels. Fragments glittered in the silent sea like false stars, flotsam left behind after warp core detonation. Corpses floated, disgorged from ruptured holds, little pieces of brittle driftwood gently colliding and slowly breaking apart. Other ships had been seared black through the violent chemical reaction of short-lived fires.

Whatever the cause, it was a fearsome tally and Ardemus could appreciate why they had been left like this, unclaimed, unsalvaged. It was a warning.

The sea of wreckage was also riddled with defences, mines, auto-turrets and more besides. He added paranoia to the ruler of Kamidar's character traits.

It would make approach difficult but not impossible. For the smaller and more nimble landers he had sent on ahead, it had proved no impediment. It had him hoping the compliance of the natives would be straightforward. Their sovereign had accepted the Decree Imperialis, which effectively repatriated the system of worlds and re-established the tithe charter. As the given representative of Terra, Ardemus could prosecute his duties in any way he saw fit. He ached to be back with the main fleet and had begun to hope that return to the forefront of the crusade and glory would be swift. Then he had seen what awaited him beyond the so-called 'Iron Veil'.

An armada of warships stood at silent anchor, a host of cruisers and frigates, monitors and gun-festooned orbitals. The Kamidarian fleet.

'Quite the array...' he muttered, his appreciation honest if begrudging.

Ardemus believed in the superiority of the Imperial Navy, in its power and importance. Of course, man for man, the Astartes were the pre-eminent troops in Guilliman's arsenal, but the ships of the Navy, her iron-willed captains... *That* was where the true strength of arms lay. A Space Marine could conquer a world, given time. A company of Space Marines could arguably conquer a system. But a warship of the Emperor's Imperial Navy, that could vanquish a world in one fell stroke. They were gods in all but name, ageless leviathans of the void.

The thought of it stirred Ardemus' blood and made him pine for the simple honesty of battle and not this theatre of diplomacy in which he had become embroiled. From his position seated in the command throne of the flagship, *Fell Lord*, he absently regarded the threat assessment presented by the other fleet – the other *Imperial* fleet, he forcibly reminded himself. It was grave.

Praxis had emerged from the warp bleeding from dozens of

wounds, its ships low on fuel, its crews with groaning bellies. Every hull plate had been patched, every breach sutured and stitched. The crusade had stretched them all and the farther from Terra they ranged, the harder the challenges would become. It needed Kamidar and the resources of the protectorate; it needed her ships and her warriors too. Ardemus meant to take it all.

He rose from his ornate throne, a leather-cushioned and gilded affair, as ostentatious as a man like Ardemus warranted, a tangible symbol of his importance, and approached the wide oculus that faced towards the prow of the *Fell Lord*. It offered an unparalleled, near-panoramic view of the void beyond the ship. As he walked the slender companionway between the cogitators and stations of his diligent bridge crew in the pits below, his second-in-command and first lieutenant, Haster, followed in train.

Litus Haster had been in Ardemus' service long enough to recognise when the admiral wanted company and when he did not. He was a slight man, of average height, his dark hair shaved to military precision and his green eyes ever alert. Hands behind his back, shoulders straight, he could have come straight from the parade ground.

'What do you make of this, lieutenant?' Ardemus asked as he reached a few feet shy of the oculus, its surface an armaglass curve like a super-hardened bubble.

Haster cleared his throat, making sure he spoke clearly. Ardemus liked his crew to be clear and declarative at all times.

'They have been on their own for some time, admiral. I would say they are being cautious.'

Ardemus nodded, though more to some inner determination of his own rather than what Haster had just said. 'Do you sense resistance?'

'We have had warmer welcomes, sir.'

Ardemus laughed at that, his humour rueful.

'But they have accepted the Decree Imperialis,' Haster went

on, 'and our landers are already on Kamidar's native soil, so that at least bodes well.'

'And the other matter?' Ardemus asked, a half-turn to bring the lieutenant, who was a step behind, into his eyeline.

'Two more ships lost, though that might be a signal issue. We are spread across a wide cordon and half of Praxis isn't even in system.'

Ardemus made a face that suggested he had just swallowed something he didn't much like the taste of.

'Do you think it is a signal issue, Lieutenant Haster?'

'No, sir. I do not. I could task some destroyers...'

'And have them chase shadows on fumes and dwindling munitions...?' Ardemus gave a curt shake of the head. 'No. They're snapping at the edges, taking out the strays and the weak from our herd. Have the cordon brought in. Even the ships at Galius and Vanir. Tighten our ranks. Strength in numbers will give the dogs greater pause than our exhausted destroyers. Once we're hale and hearty again, we'll run the perpetrators down if there are any and gut their vessels to the bone.'

'As you wish, admiral.'

'Very good, and then there's this of course...' He gestured to the graveyard of ships floating several miles beyond the prow of the *Fell Lord*. 'That's a narrow passage between those wrecks.'

'Helm estimates we can fly two abreast, with minimal clearance. Three is... well, it's untenable, sir.'

'Almost as if they wanted us to thread the needle's eye.'

'I think that's exactly their intent, sir.'

'What about the Mechanicus breakers? Could they widen the gap?'

'A lengthy process, especially given that manpower is somewhat light. Also, we have no accurate assessment of what might still be on those ships. Nor visibility of any hidden defences.'

Ardemus nodded again, this having already occurred to him but wanting it confirmed anyway. 'And we've ruled out a volley, turn the larger pieces into smaller ones and push through the debris?'

'The paucity of our munitions notwithstanding, sir, we could risk triggering a volatile chain reaction. This many unknown ships with unknown technologies, the possibility of void-mines and this close...'

'Any response to our hails?'

'Beyond signal acceptance of the Decree Imperialis, our vox has been quiet, sir. Until recently, of course.'

Haster referred to the overtures from the royal household of Kamidar. Ardemus knew why. One of the ships in the flotilla, the *Virtuous*, bore precious cargo. The honoured dead. At least it would allow him to open a dialogue and gauge the ruler of the protectorate for himself.

'Then we thread the needle,' Ardemus decided, though this recourse had never truly been in question, 'and assume good intentions.'

Haster didn't answer. It wasn't a question, and didn't require one.

A presence had just joined them on the bridge. She strode the companionway, her tread raising almost no sound despite her being armoured.

'Sister Syreniel,' Ardemus welcomed her.

The warrior in silver warplate stood a full head taller than the admiral and radiated a disquieting aura. Shaved to the skin at her temples, she had a black crest over the middle of her scalp and crown. A scar ran from her left ear to the edge of her lip, a gift from a Traitor Astartes, or so the story went. She wore kohl around the eyes, her stern features made more severe by its application, and a tattooed aquila graced her forehead, inked in blood red.

She inclined her head to the admiral, her gaze wintry as she stood before the oculus, both hands by her sides, her armoured legs slightly apart. Syreniel was Ardemus' truth seeker, for she had an eye for mendacity and would root it out however well veiled. She was also one of the most potent and palpable symbols of the Imperial Faith, and therefore the Emperor's will, on the entire ship. Let the Kamidarians see from whom his authority stemmed.

Haster on one side, the Silent Sister on the other, Ardemus received the notification via the slate on his vambrace that the queen was ready for them.

'Well then,' he said, raising his chin and inhaling a long, imperious breath, 'let us not keep her majesty waiting.'

A large pane of the oculus flickered as an image shimmered into being, a visual signal from the surface of the world below. And there she was, as indomitable as the line of warships ringing her domain, the queen of Kamidar herself.

'Greetings from Fleet Praxis, your majesty,' Ardemus began genially with a modest decline of his head to the queen.

Queen Orlah replied in kind.

'You are welcome here, Lord Admiral Ardemus, it has been long since the Imperium came to our borders.'

'And yet the reunion has not been easy, has it, your majesty.'

The queen stiffened at this, doubtless unused to being addressed in this manner. Ardemus wanted to demonstrate his power, that her sovereignty meant little when matched against the greater authority of the Imperium. He had cowed kings and queens before. He knew the routine.

'I do hope the actions of an outlaw do not colour our relationship, lord admiral.'

Ardemus was about to reply when the queen undercut him. A deliberate manoeuvre on her part.

'Though I agree that there have been mistakes.'

'Mistakes?'

'Yes, indeed. Can we both agree that a certain measure of delicacy

on the behalf of your men would be conducive to the satisfaction of
both parties and the expediency of your task?'

Ardemus bristled. He didn't like being talked down to but he salved his pride with the one major card he had to play in this exchange.

'Urgency has forced my hand, your majesty. The needs of the crusade are paramount, I am sure you can understand.'

She nodded her assent, though to what exactly was left unclear.

'Nothing less than the sanctity of the Imperium is at stake,' he added, and continued, deciding at last to play his hand, 'I am confident we can resolve any and all disputes, just as I am confident that Praxis can return your daughter, who lies in state aboard a ship in my fleet.'

The queen's countenance became stone.

Through taut lips, she replied, *'Every accommodation shall be made.'*

Ardemus nodded, a slight smile curling the edges of his mouth. *I have you now.*

'I thought so, your majesty. I thought so.'

The conference ended, casting Orlah into darkness again as the hololith faded to black. Crackling electro-sconces barely lifted the silence and threw fingers of shadow against the walls of her private chambers, hinting at velvet and silk. She was alone and this was good, because no one saw her clenched fists or heard the roar of anguish and fury spill from her lips. No one saw her draw her oighen and use it to destroy the vintage writing desk that had been in her family for generations. It was over quickly, the queen a master of her outward emotions again, and when she called on Ekria she was calm and stately as ice.

Their exchange was brief, the equerry having only just returned from relating her majesty's orders to the Sovereigns. What she heard upon greeting the queen paled the equerry despite her best efforts to appear unmoved.

'It will be difficult to retreat from this, your majesty,' said Ekria after she had received her instructions, with just the slightest glance at the hacked-apart writing desk within the queen's chambers.

Orlah's expression showed she had no intention of retreating and she nodded that she had both heard and understood the equerry's words of caution.

'And I need to reach my brother in the fleet. As soon as possible.'

'I assume the vox transmission should be veiled, your majesty?'

'Use every precaution. It will not be easy to conceal.'

'I shall see it done, your majesty,' said Ekria, bowing as she made to depart before the queen stopped her with the raising of a hand.

'And, Ekria,' Orlah said, her scowl back as her mind returned to other things, 'find out what has become of Morrigan. I may have need of the Black Templars. What good are oaths if they are unfulfilled?'

Chapter Ten

OATHS FOR THE DEAD

HUNTING

RUIN

He had sworn it to Bohemund, to the headless corpse they had dragged from the bowels of that damned ship.

Vengeance. Retribution.

Morrigan swore it again now in the shadows of the Reclusiam aboard the *Mourning Star*, a silent promise to the sightless helm he had so nearly retrieved. Bohemund's helm. Morrigan's armoured fingers shook as they formed a fist. The honoured dead would know peace. It would come with Graeyl Herek's death.

'I swear it,' he rasped to the dark, spittle flicking from clenched teeth.

He looked up from his impassioned reverie, and saw Godfried waiting at the threshold as he always did. The Champion nodded once. Morrigan unclamped the helm from his belt and donned it purposefully.

They had caught up to the *Ruin*.

* * *

Morrigan strode through the halls of the grand cruiser with purpose, the shattered chains of his broken oath swaying from his wrists like old rags. Godfried kept pace, a step behind his lord, arms by his side. Dagomir would not join them. He had been taken to the apothecarion to tend his wounds and see what could be done about his severed arm.

Anglahad joined them at the companionway to the bridge, also helmed for war. None spoke, for no words were needed, and they emerged onto the bridge of the *Mourning Star* without ceremony.

'He burns hard, my lord, but ours is the stronger ship,' declared Shipmaster Vanier, a veteran of several centuries, and almost more augmetic than man.

The black-clad crew that served him went about their duties with quiet resolve, not one looking up from their station at the Black Templars. That took training and obedience. Vanier had instilled both.

Morrigan approached the wiry old ship captain. The veteran's uniform hung off his wizened frame like a funerary suit but there could be no mistaking the steel in his eyes and the strength of his mind.

'How long?' asked Morrigan, staring through the forward oculus, eyes narrowing behind his retinal lenses at the distant speck ahead of them that was the *Ruin*.

'They will be in close range of our lances imminently, my lord.'

'Cripple them, Vanier. I want them dead in the void.'

Vanier gave a curt salute and turned his attention back to the task at hand.

After a few seconds, an alert sounded. The *Mourning Star* had the enemy in range. Commands issued back and forth across the bridge, a sequence of call and reply as the crew responded with ready status affirmatives to their orders. In the servitor pits below the main crew stations, the cyborganic creatures relayed power to weapons, monitoring the ship's outputs and the status of every system. Void shields crackled into being and the forward oculus clouded marginally as the *Mourning Star*'s defences were raised.

Far below and to the aft of the ship, in the enginarium, labour gangs would be toiling to maintain the vessel's speed. On the weapon decks, munitions would be breeched and spare shells cycled up ready for reload. None knew how the *Ruin* would react. She might stand and fight, but though she was a nimble vessel, she could not withstand a duel with the *Mourning Star*. The *Star*'s sheer strength of arms and brutal engine power would overwhelm the traitor ship.

But Morrigan did not want to destroy her. He wanted her hamstrings cut, her motive agency hobbled. He wanted to face Herek again, and kill him in combat.

The alert klaxons ratcheted up to a fever pitch, as the *Mourning Star* reached optimal weapons range.

'Fire,' uttered Shipmaster Vanier without hesitation.

A lance blast spat from the prow, bright as sunfire. It seared across the void in a burning beam, so fast it was quickly lost to sight. The *Mourning Star*'s augurs tracked it, the beam's trajectory illuminated on tactical screens throughout the bridge. Morrigan watched it pensively, his fist tight around the hilt of his sheathed sword, as a penumbral silence fell over the bridge like a held breath.

A cheer rang out amongst the crew as the lance volley hit the *Ruin*'s void shields and they collapsed in a flare of distant light.

'Another volley,' Shipmaster Vanier demanded, hands clenched around the arms of his command throne as he leaned forwards, eager for the scalp. 'Then give them a spread of torpedoes. I want that ship limping and bleeding.'

The second volley spat forth, all eyes on its impact as they waited to see if their enemy would manage to re-engage its shields. Another impact, another luminous flash like a star detonating in a faraway system. No cheers this time. They watched the torpedoes, surging across the void on bright contrails, a deadly and unerring flight seconds in the wake of the second lance volley.

'Ha!' roared Vanier, lurching out of his throne to pump his fist. 'That's it, you bastards!'

A bellicose cheer rose up as an explosive detonation registered on every screen.

'They're wounded, my lord,' said Vanier, sagging back into the throne after his impromptu surge of vigour had sapped him.

Morrigan didn't speak. He turned on his heel, Godfried and Anglahad parting to allow him to leave the bridge then following in lockstep. Only as they were stalking out, bound for the assault rams, an urgent cry came from the main augur station.

'Second vessel detected, captain,' snapped the officer.

Vanier took it on his screen. Morrigan paused, already turning towards the shipmaster. His stance held a mute enquiry.

'Imperial designation,' said Vanier, frowning. All the while, the enemy ship floundered in the void, her crews doubtlessly toiling hard to reignite her engines.

'Hail it,' Morrigan commanded after a moment's hesitation.

Vanier gave the order to his voxmistress who immediately attempted to open a channel.

'What is the name of that ship?' said Morrigan, edging back into the heart of the bridge.

'Something amiss?' asked Anglahad over a private channel.

'A feeling,' Morrigan replied, his response similarly masked from the crew at large.

'The *Mercurion*, my lord,' said one of the crew. 'A warship, Mars-class.'

'Allies, my lord?' ventured the shipmaster to Morrigan but the Black Templar did not answer.

'They have raised void shields and are powering up forward laser batteries,' added the crewman.

'Any response to our hails?' asked Shipmaster Vanier.

'Negative, captain.'

'What about proximity and heading?'

'Within weapons range, and coming abeam to intercept the *Ruin*, captain.' The crewman sounded relieved: two ships against one and Herek was theirs.

Morrigan exchanged a glance with Godfried but the Champion was like an armoured statue. Anglahad looked restive, his stare enquiring even through his retinal lenses. The pinch of indecision held Morrigan, the sudden shift from what was known to what was unknown infecting him with paralysis.

Anglahad pressed, 'Shall we embark, brother-captain?'

'Wait...'

'The *Mercurion* is closing on the *Ruin*, my lord,' offered Shipmaster Vanier. 'Still no response to our hails...' He was about to give another order when his augur master spoke up.

'Captain, the *Mercurion* is firing its broadsides!'

'Throne of Terra...' hissed Vanier. 'Brace for impact.'

Two ships against one, except the *Mourning Star* was the one.

'It's a looted ship,' snarled Morrigan, giving voice to what they already knew.

The *Mourning Star* fired its thrusters hard, but they had been hitting full burn at the *Ruin* and momentum was hard to arrest. A slow inertial turn pulled their power towards the broadside volley, their stoutest armour and thickest shields. Impact flares rattled across the forward oculus a few minutes later like stone splashes in water as the heavy munitions detonated harmlessly but fouled the immediate view.

Shipmaster Vanier went to his instruments. The augurs had the *Mercurion* skirting aft of the *Ruin* as its engines took it in a looping arc that kept its broadsides very much facing the *Mourning Star*.

'They are priming for another volley...'

'Shield strength at fifty-three per cent, captain,' called the helm.

'Lances at readiness,' said another.

'Fire on the *Mercurion*,' ordered Vanier.

They were still burning for the *Ruin*, albeit at an oblique angle and at half power, but now the Mars-class ship was matching their aspect and coming on at speed.

The lance volley went wide, fired in haste, a warning shot across the bow.

Vanier swore. 'Helm, pull us about,' he commanded, 'and get those broadsides ready. I want all cannons run out and in unison!'

The *Mercurion* showed no intent to change its facing, content to run alongside the *Mourning Star* whilst gamely exchanging fire. A second broadside lit up the other vessel's flank, magnified on the bridge's tactical screens.

'Brace!' snarled Vanier and a few seconds later the *Mourning Star* trembled as it took the full volley. Distances narrowing by the moment as the trajectory of both vessels brought them on an intersecting course, alert klaxons sounded as shield integrity plummeted to less than twenty per cent.

The shipmaster raged. 'Restore void shields, and fire back, damn it!'

Morrigan could only watch. This was Vanier's domain now.

A return volley thundered from the starboard weapon decks, shot out into the silent void. The *Mercurion* took the hit but she was already turning and almost half the guns slid wide of their target.

As the *Mourning Star* saw to its shields and its broadsides recycled for another turn, the augur master called out, 'Third ship detected, captain. Coreward, and coming into our battlesphere.'

Vanier glared at the officer, demanding more.

'It's a traitor ship, captain. The *Vindictive*. Inferno-class.'

And then from another section of the bridge, 'The *Ruin* is reigniting its engines. They're underway again.'

'The *Vindictive* is firing lances, captain!' cried the augur master.

They were already pulling away from a third broadside volley from the *Mercurion* when the distant beams from the third ship arrowed into the night-black.

'Where are those damn shields?' Vanier demanded as the *Mourning Star* loosed a reply from its weapon decks, but three-to-one they were outmatched.

The lance burst glanced abeam of the *Mourning Star*, taking out long-range augur, but the damage was minimal. Explosions rippled through the lower starboard decks, felt as a deep seismic tremor on the bridge as the ailing shields capitulated under sustained barrage from the *Mercurion*'s laser batteries.

'Starboard shields down, captain,' came the swift report.

Vanier's face crumpled in frustrated anger as he turned to Morrigan. 'They are pulling us apart, my lord.'

His gauntlet creaking at the stress of gripping his sword hilt so hard, Morrigan tore Pious from the scabbard and slammed it into the deck, where it split the floor.

'Withdraw,' he uttered, taking long breaths between sentences. 'Get us out of here.' Morrigan wrenched the blade free with a twist, about to turn when he looked back at the damage and said, 'And my apologies for that, shipmaster.'

He stalked off the bridge under blood-red light and to the clarion of alert klaxons.

As the *Mourning Star* retreated from the fight, none aboard noticed a fourth ship trailing at the edge of their wake, at the very extremity of viable augur range. It was a sleek ship, not as favoured as the *Ruin* – for she had seen Herek through uncounted battles and had more victories to her name than any vessel he had ever known – but the destroyer was fast and could move unnoticed. It was a dagger, this ship, one he would thrust into the heart of the Black Templars and take back what was his.

Chapter Eleven

DISCORD

A BRIEF MOMENT OF SERENITY

GRUSHÄLOB

A large mob of protesters had gathered at Runstaf: farmhands, drovers and labourers. Their guild overseers and landlords looked on with their armed militias, a step removed from the rowdy peasantry. Runstaf was the last and one of the biggest Aglevin townships and as such the toll required of it was steep.

Ariadne reviewed the projected Munitorum tithes on her dataslate and frowned at the numbers. Then she looked from the back of the junker as it rumbled along the road to the acquisition site to the unhappy hordes that were gathering and felt a tremor of unease.

She had hoped Ardemus would have pulled back the logisticians after the incident at Rund; certainly it had made the Marines Malevolent jumpy, the Astartes practically prowling up and down the Imperial positions ready to dispense lethal violence at the merest perceived infraction. But the admiral had declined all extraction requests. An understanding had been reached, the perpetrator of the carnage a brigand being dealt with by the queen's warriors. No further harm would come to them.

Ariadne knew the truth: Ardemus had deemed it worth the risk. Praxis needed these supplies more than it needed its Departmento adepts, and it would get them regardless of the potential price. Her heart leapt every time she heard a bellicose word. It had been thundering around her chest for the last half-day or more.

Even Ogin, relaxed at the start of the expedition, appeared withdrawn and on his guard. He watched her still, when he wasn't staring into the wilderness, and smiled kindly when she met his gaze, but there was something like concern behind those eyes that hadn't been there before – or else he had just hidden it better.

'You can feel it, can't you?' she said. 'Something in the air.'

'Heh, you sound like you are from Jagun.' His offhand mood was a little forced. She noticed his hand was never far from his szabla. 'What can you feel, visha?'

'Discord. Trouble.' A few of the other Departmento adepts were listening and shared dark glances. 'They can feel it too.'

'And yet here we are,' answered Ogin, his easy words at odds with his expression.

Ariadne leaned forwards. She could practically taste the heat coming off his armour. 'Tell me, Ogin. When you look out there, what do you see?'

He looked. 'Do you remember the grushälob, visha?'

Ariadne sighed. She had been hoping for a useful insight, not more deflection from the Space Marine. 'The child's story you made up? I remember.'

'Heh. Grushälob is very real. It lives in the hearts of men, a beast that can take on any form, and thrives on weakness. It is envy, cruelty and fear, a poison to anyone who heeds its whispers. That is what I see. I see the grushälob and it is everywhere.' He turned back to her, and his vehement expression chilled her.

Ariadne remained silent the rest of the way, and thought about the grushälob and what havoc it might wreak.

She alighted the transport as soon as it came to a stop and went to work. Other adepts had arrived ahead of her cohort and were busy making tallies and investigating silos. For their part, the natives of Kamidar kept out of the way. Mostly.

One elderly farmer wearing worn but hardy breeches and a long duster coat with a wooden-stocked shotcannon over his shoulder was arguing with Usullis, and the veteran quartermaster looked close to losing his temper. He was a leathery old soul, the farmer, his stubbled face like grey gravel and the wisps of hair clinging to his wrinkled pate like tendrils of white smoke. He was also loud. Several other Kamidarians in the crowd had heard the brewing altercation and were taking notice. So had a trio of Solians, who were heading in the direction of Usullis and the farmer.

Ariadne hustled over to them first, showing her palm hand up to the soldiers in a gesture that said, *I'll handle this*. Her gaze strayed to the disgruntled natives who eyed her and Usullis with disdain, their ire for the Imperial invaders obvious.

'This silo and its contents are property of the Imperium and the Regent of Terra himself,' Usullis was saying, 'I have *every* authority.'

'That doesn't give you the right to take what's mine,' the farmer replied, the grip on his vintage shotcannon an obvious threat but one that the quartermaster thankfully missed. 'I owe fealty to the Iron Queen and Kamidar, not to you... *interloper*!'

Usullis glanced around, probably hoping to find a trooper to help get his point across but found Ariadne instead. 'Everything is in hand here, Ariadne. I don't need any further Munitorum help.'

'Looks that way,' answered Ariadne, in a tone that suggested she thought opposite.

Usullis shot her daggers, his previous geniality when they had first arrived on Kamidar exposed for the thin façade it was. He felt thwarted and wanted to impose his will on this man, to cow him.

Ariadne decided on a different approach but not before she hissed in Usullis' ear, 'Calm down, Beren.'

He started, perturbed, but his burgeoning anger bled to nothing when he caught the look in Ariadne's eye.

'Carry on like this and we'll have another incident.' She jerked her head surreptitiously in the direction of the crowds. Hundreds of Kamidarians. 'See those people there? They are already angry. Keep this up or go further down the road I think you're on and it'll spill over. No one wants dead natives, especially not Ardemus.'

At the mention of the admiral's name, Usullis seemed to remember where and who he was. He nodded, near imperceptibly, and moistened his lips.

'Very well,' he said, smoothing down his hair, and mustering a little composure to save face, 'have at it then.' He backed off, saying to the farmer, 'I'll allow my colleague to explain the details of the tithe that your ruler has acceded to.'

Ariadne shot him a glance that could have cut ceramite before turning her attention to the farmer.

'I promise you we will not take more than is needed,' she said to the farmer, aware that if it came to it she couldn't actually back up that claim. 'The crusade has come to protect Kamidar but is in sore need of resupply.'

The farmer laughed, a croaking rasp. 'Ha! Kamidar needs no protection. The Iron Queen has seen to that.'

'It will not last, I assure you,' Ariadne replied, and meant it earnestly. 'I have seen what lies beyond your borders and no world, however strong, can survive against it alone. Even Cadia fell, and I know you know what that is.' The farmer lowered his gaze a little at the mention of the fallen world. 'You have survived, and by the Emperor be thankful for that, but worse is coming. I don't say it to scare you or goad you, it is simply a fact.

The Imperium has been shattered. It has to unite. All of it. But to endure there has to be sacrifice. Grain can be resown, minerals mined anew, livestock rebred, but worlds cannot be remade after they are lost.

'What is your name? I am Niova. It was my mother's name before mine.'

'Malik...' uttered the farmer, tears in his eyes as Ariadne gently clasped his hand in both of hers.

'I *promise* you, Malik,' she said, 'no more than is needed.' She hoped that was true.

Slowly, reluctantly, the farmer gave a shallow nod. He sagged, appearing suddenly older than he had before, and as she released her own breath Ariadne caught Ogin looking at her. The Astartes had the slightest smile on his lips, with what looked like approval in his eyes.

It was in that brief moment of serenity that the Kamidarian Sovereigns arrived, in their tanks with their guns and pikes, and everything became immeasurably worse.

Tension rippled through the crowds, some cheering belligerently for their apparent saviours. The queen had sent her warriors from the palace. They would keep their property safe. They would send the invaders on their way. Let them take from other worlds. Let them leave Kamidar alone. It was as if a pendulum had swung, and the old farmer snatched his hands away with its sudden movement.

'Liar,' he snapped, backing off, an eye on the armour-clad Sovereigns deploying from their vehicles. 'You're all liars!'

'Please... just wait.'

It was too late. The three Solians who had been sweeping in to take matters into their own hands returned with interest. About twenty of them now, with more coming and a few squads of Mordians too, preparing to face off against the Sovereigns, who had begun to move through the crowd. One with a laud hailer attached to his gorget declaimed for calm, that all natives of Kamidar should be at ease. It only stirred their jingoism further.

Ariadne felt herself hustled aside as the Solians went past her and she reached to try and grab one of them, to tell them to stop, to wait, but her fingers slipped and she could only watch as the Imperial soldiers collided with the natives to force them back.

The old farmer fell as he tried to back away, caught up in his own feet, his own fear. The shotcannon, an old and temperamental weapon that he probably used to scare raptors from his fields, went off. It boomed, deafening even in the growing clamour. Someone cried out, bleeding from the shin, and in the confusion others in the crowd who had brought out-of-service rifles and vintage revolvers thought the Imperials were attacking, and fired on them.

The bullets lacked the strength to really trouble the Solians' armour or else missed entirely, but Ariadne had been around enough munitions to know a powder keg when she saw one.

The Imperial soldiers fired back out of instinct, lasguns snapping. Men and women died, for these troopers had been trained to kill and fighting in the crusade for the last five years. Even had they tried, they could have done nothing else.

'God-Emperor, no...'

Ariadne found herself lurching towards the troopers who had ranked up in a firing line and were going at the natives like they were culling greenskins. Bravely, madly, the natives charged with picks and hoes: tools, not weapons. The odd bolt-action gun fired, a sharp crack here and there ultimately drowned out by the fusillade of las-fire from the platoon of trained soldiers.

Ariadne tried to intercede, place herself between them. A suicidal notion, but none present were thinking straight.

Save one. She felt a strong hand on her shoulder, then a thick arm around her body that lifted her up and out of harm's way as the natives broke and fled and the Kamidarian Sovereigns took over.

Then there was true madness and she saw the grushälob, and
knew that it was real.

Chapter Twelve

A QUEEN'S BURDEN

SECRETS OF ANCIENT KAMIDAR

OLD TECHNOLOGY

Orlah moved silently through the cloisters of the inner palace, the train of her dress a wraith chasing in her wake. No electro-sconces here, and only the pearlescent gleam of Cellenium to guide her with shafts of moonlight spearing through the lancets of the undercroft. She went unhurried but with purpose, following the old paths laid down by her ancestors into the deeps of the Gallanhold where few had trod since the eldest ages of Kamidar. It was a gift, the knowledge of this place and how to reach it, from the rulers who preceded her. When her reign ended, she did not know to whom it would pass. Perhaps it would be lost and forgotten. The thought chilled her, and Orlah upped her pace.

A warren of passageways and nooks unfolded, her path wending inexorably outwards and down, and she took them unerringly until she reached a narrow stairwell that descended even farther into darkness, a great well of it coalescing at the bottom. Here, she slowed, for the steps were steep and she would not be the first of her house to have slipped and broken a neck. The scent of oil, of old mechanisms flavoured the air, the domain of sacristans and tech-priests.

Soft light bloomed in this deepening space, emanating from an arched portal at the end of a long corridor. Here then was the nadir of the palace, right above the heart of the world. A spiritual place where the voices of her ancestors rose loudly in Orlah's mind, as clear as when she mounted her Throne Mechanicum.

As a mother, Orlah had experienced the pain of loss, as a warrior she realised that strength was nothing without will, but as a head of state she knew that compromise was the only way to ensure safety and sovereignty for her people. Long years had Orlah's ancestors ruled this world. None alive could recall the day when it had been named in honour of their house, and no records existed that could teach of it.

What the ancient annals did recount was the pioneering spirit of the original Kamidarians and how they explored every nook and cranny of the world they had colonised and would make their holdfast. They were also industrialists and mined the rock for its mineral wealth, putting it to use in their settlements and armoury. The delves had led to more than just ore and gems: in the deepest parts of the world, at its very heart where its planetary capital would be raised, they had produced something from an era so ancient it did not have a name.

As Orlah approached the honey-rich glow of the light and stepped through the portal she thought of those elder days and realised they had come again.

A sacristan met her at the threshold, an immense and vaulted room, a place of reverence and genuine foreboding. In recent times, Orlah had found herself visiting this chamber often.

'My queen,' uttered the sacristan, bowing low in his blood-red robes.

She could taste the actinic tang in the air emanating from the heart of the room, as she acknowledged the serf and moved inwards. Flocks of servo-skulls haunted the high rafters of the chamber, a dome-shaped vault, where crimson sensor arrays shone like bloody stars. At ground level a cohort of sacristans took readings, swung incense from thuribles or otherwise sung hymns into the shadows. A dingy room, the only illumination came from the two devices in the middle. They were rad-shielded and ancient, sunk into a shallow pit. More tech-adepts busied themselves here, protected by hazard suits, wielding scanners.

The queen stopped at the force field, which marked as far as she could approach without the need for shielding. And there she stayed and stared.

'During the darkest years, both in the distant and recent history of our world,' she began, addressing Thonius, the chief sacristan who had met her at the chamber entrance, 'the rulers of Kamidar were forced to utilise every advantage in order to survive. It was their duty, you understand. We face a similar crisis, one that could end everything and cast us back into that darkness. Like my forebears, I will do everything I must to preserve our way of life.'

'Your will is our will, my queen. Name it, and it shall be done.'

It was technology, that was what her ancestors had realised during those formative days. Technology from before the fall of Old Night and the repatriation efforts of the Great Crusade. Forbidden, proscribed by every Imperial diktat and edict, and it had lain in the bedrock of Kamidar for aeons.

The lambent glow of it, sitting there now in the pit, filled Orlah's eyes like a glamour from which she had no hope of escape. She touched the black garnet around her neck almost subconsciously. Her grounding rod, her north star.

As a ruler, I must compromise to ensure safety and sovereignty for my people.

'Listen very carefully, Thonius. This is what I want you to do...'

Chapter Thirteen

DELEGATION
A SHOW OF STRENGTH
A ROYAL WELCOME

Kesh held her breath in the crimson-tinted darkness of the hold. Landfall happened with a thud of the drop-ship's metal stanchions and the jerk of deck plate underfoot. No one spoke as the engines cycled down, a dull cataract roar that fell to a feline purr as the turbofans slowed. This wasn't a deployment, a hostile insertion, though her heart drummed all the same and she felt a tightness in her chest that was like a belt strap. Fifty Mordians stood to attention in that hold space in neat ranks, one of five identical cohorts made up of the men and women who had fought at Gathalamor, one of several nominal companies to represent the regiment entire, waiting for the walls to stop shuddering and for silence to resume.

She caught Dvorgin's eye, the general standing a few places to her left in the middle of the formation. Finely attired in his dress uniform, an ornate sword scabbarded to his hip, an antique pistol in his holster, full brocade and medals. Some men might have seemed like prancing peacocks in such a situation; he looked born to it. Solemn but proud. He gave her a quick nod by way of recognition. It was a big moment for the general. He hadn't met a queen before either.

To her right, at the outer edge of the finely trimmed and attired Mordian square, was the historitor. Viablo had his own entourage, a retinue of scholarly types but wearing something akin to loose military garb rather than a clerk's robes. They looked lean, and eager to record history. She supposed this was a big moment for them too.

Unreadable as ever, Vychellan stood slightly apart from the others, an indomitable golden slab of auramite, wearing his plumed war helm, with a red half-cloak draped over one shoulder and his guardian spear strapped to his back like a gonfalon. Even the sober lighting couldn't dull his aura. The Custodian was magnificent.

Only one other figure could draw focus from him, and she was as different to the Custodian as ice is to fire, despite the fact they shared the same designation as 'Talons of the Emperor'. Kesh had learned her name was Syreniel, an Oblivion Knight of the Palatine Vigilators. One of the soulless, so the rumours around the ranks persisted, whatever that actually meant. She had never met one of the Silent Sisterhood before. On reflection, it was quite the day of firsts. Tall as a battle standard, much slimmer in frame than Vychellan but no less hardy, she wore silver war plate with a bronze gorget that rose up around her mouth and nose to shield it entirely. A huge greatsword hung from her back like a threat, barely sheathed in black synthleather, and votive scrolls trailed from her cuirass and greaves, the parchment stained with age. Those black-ringed eyes of hers held fathomless, pitiless nothing. She was more instrument than human being.

Apparently, Ardemus called her his 'truth seeker'. Kesh found her gaze repelled from the Sister of Silence, almost sliding off her like oil on water, and noted the ring of empty space surrounding the warrior despite the otherwise cramped confines. Even to look at her made Kesh's guts churn.

Vychellan betrayed no discomfort, if he even felt any, but the tension between the two was palpable. He had a sour look on his face whenever his eye strayed to Syreniel, which it did more often than was usual for the Custodian. Kesh assumed he did not agree with the presence of the Oblivion Knight. She had not been a part of the campaign on Gathalamor and her inclusion in the delegation felt like an act of cynicism by Ardemus, a means of gauging the intent of the Kamidarians, whom the admiral had further snubbed by declining their invitation and sending First Lieutenant Haster in his stead. This Kesh had learned from Dvorgin prior to embarkation, a quiet drink in the mess hall before they went to their duty. She wondered what Ardemus hoped to gain by deploying the Sister of Silence, and prayed it wasn't the ire of the queen.

For his part, Haster had donned his finest fleet uniform, an ornamental shoulder guard over his jacket and red piping down his breeches. He looked almost as gilded as the general, though he lacked the number of medals. A Naval cutlass with a gem-encrusted hilt hung from his hip and a long-nosed laspistol sat snugly in a holster down his left leg. A peaked cap emblazoned with a gold aquila finished the ensemble but failed to hide the nervousness in the man's eyes.

Then, as the ship's engines stilled and the embarkation ramp began to open, Kesh exhaled. This was it.

Praxis had managed to send a dozen vessels beyond the Iron Veil by way of an honour guard. They stood at anchor like still sentinels, across from the line of Kamidarian ships a hundred miles opposite. Close, in void terms. It made Ardemus nervous as he watched the native fleet roll out their guns for the honour salute. A second line was manoeuvring to join the first, all warships, all aimed at the fathomless nothing of the void.

As he watched them move into formation, a sombre funereal

procession that would discharge their guns once the Lady Jessivayne had been interred, he wished he had more ships on this half of the Veil. The others lingered nearby, relatively speaking, broken up into smaller formations. Some of Praxis had already driven on deeper into the sector to Galius and Vanir, those with fuel and munitions to do so, but like the rest they would need resupply soon and Kamidar would be the depot to provide it. A redoubt, a lynchpin in the Anaxian Line. Thinking of it only reminded Ardemus of how far behind schedule he was and the urgent need to launch the hundreds of landers readied for deployment behind the Veil.

As soon as the funeral was over, he would send everything. Then they'd move on to the other protectorate worlds. It risked the further annoyance of the queen, who had been somewhat... frosty during their last exchange, but she would have to understand. At least the delegation demonstrated her desire for consolidation. Ardemus had been mildly surprised at that, allowing a cohort of Imperial troops and officers into the Kamidarian planetary capital and royal palace no less, but it would give Syreniel opportunity to gauge the intent of the queen and whether she would make the necessary transition difficult.

Sending Haster had been unavoidable and Ardemus felt like he was missing his right arm with the first lieutenant gone. It was either that or venture to the surface of Kamidar himself, but his place was with the fleet and not at the beck and call of a grieving queen.

Through the oculus, the admiral could just make out the distant trail of the first landers coming up under the flotilla of Kamidarian ships as they returned from the world below. It would be several hours yet before they docked and days or even weeks before Praxis was at full capacity again. Months before a vital piece of the Anaxian Line was properly established.

A lengthy, drawn-out process.

When Ardemus turned his gaze back onto the Kamidarian ships

arranging in slow, stately manoeuvres he felt every second of it and his face soured.

'Let's just get this damn thing over with.'

A vast plaza unfolded before her as Kesh took position in the Mordians' formation and began to march. Stone had been quarried from the mountains and reshaped for the colossal slabs. The Imperials had left behind the massive landing platform almost immediately upon leaving the ship, and the cool Kamidarian air was like a balm to Kesh after so long stuck in a stuffy transit hold with fifty other soldiers. These were joined by five hundred others, including a contingent of Pyroxian tanks, in a funerary honour guard of the troops who had fought on Gathalamor alongside the late Princess Jessivayne and her Knights. All who had fought barring the Adepta Sororitas, who had remained behind, and the other Custodians, who were represented here by the dour figure of Vychellan. He walked slowly alongside the other troops, in all respects a being apart.

In Kesh's peripheral vision, the sun faded in the east, a warm orange orb taking with it the heat of the day, a chill creeping in its wake. It bathed the walls of the Gallanhold in a rich, caramel hue. Braziers had been lit against the slowly advancing dark, wrought in the shape of huge bronze gauntlets and jutting from marble pillars that lined the processional way at precise intervals. White-and-gold hued stone glinted underfoot, the sword of Kamidar worked into the design and twice as long as two men lying head to toe. This image repeated several times, the blade tips like a series of arrows pointing to their destination, though they were hardly needed. The triumphal arch was immense.

Two statues, Kesh assumed they were former kings, held up an impressive span ornately carved with shields and crests. It soared above her, dwarfing the Mordian scout, but it was only as she passed through its shadow and into the outer precincts of the palace proper that she saw the true glory of Kamidar arrayed.

As with every son and daughter of Mordian, composure had been bred into Kesh at birth, but even she struggled to contain her awe. The great square beyond the triumphal arch was immense, drowning the Imperial delegation who saluted the thousands of onlooking Kamidarians proudly. A colonnade of soaring statues flanked the Imperials either side and from tiered auditoria the worthies of Kamidar paid their solemn respects to the fallen princess.

Jessivayne went at the head of the procession, transferred to an anti-gravitic funerary barque and attended by the daunting presence of two Imperial Knights, Baron Gerent and Sir Sheane. Kesh could scarcely catch sight of the barque through the throng, but the massive war engines stood out easily enough.

As the last of the delegation passed beneath the arch and into the square, a veritable army of choristers struck up a lament. They sang in ancient Kamidarian, a language unknown to Kesh, but their sorrow was clear without the need for translation. Huge banners almost as tall as the Knights hung from the high walls of the auditoria depicting the noble houses of Kamidar and the heraldic creatures of its long history. As the procession passed by, the mourners cast violet petals that were caught and tossed gently on the breeze, settling throughout the square in forlorn drifts.

The Mordians had a banner too, but theirs paled into insignificance against those arrayed around the square, as did their four-hundred-strong battle company compared to the mustered Kamidarian war host. Battalions of soldiers in white livery and polished gold armour stood either side of the processional to receive the princess, their fluted helms topped with pale feathers; tank brigades by the score, their turrets turned in solemn salute; a host of Royal Armigers, the so-called 'Swordsworn', their heads dipped in respect; and a lance of Kamidarian Knights towering above the rest, their pennants cloaked in black. All for her. Their beloved Jessivayne.

As her company formed up alongside the rest and with Kesh in the front rank, she recognised this for what it was: an outpouring of grief but also a demonstration of martial prowess. For as the long ranks of troops and war machines reached a conclusion, there stood at the heart of it all this world's general.

The queen of Kamidar waited upon a dark metal dais at the end of the processional where the square met a great door, tall enough to admit one of the Knights and wrought from engraved bronze. Like everything else, the door was ornate, the queen no less so. She wore a gold cuirass, the sword of Kamidar engraved in the middle in silver intaglio. A high gorget forced her chin into an imperious angle – it suited her – and a skirt of mail hung down from her waist, where a scabbarded blade was buckled, to the knees of her armoured legs. Neither the head of state nor a grieving mother but instead a warmaster who possessed the power to conquer worlds.

She could only have been more impressive had she ridden in the Knight war engine she doubtless commanded, but she greeted the Imperial delegation as a woman of flesh and blood, rather than a goddess-machine. At first, Kesh wondered why. It was only as the funeral barque came to a solemn halt and the queen descended the dais that Kesh understood. The queen had come to be reunited with her daughter.

Orlah felt her hand begin to tremble as she alighted from the dais but knew this was just in her mind. As she walked down the few steps, she kept her eyes on the funerary barque and nothing else. Despite what she had said to Ekria in the lunarium, it took supreme effort to remain dispassionate, as cold as the marble of the square. She could show no weakness, and only barely acknowledge the dip of *Lance of God*'s war helm, the Knight of her younger brother. Gerent had offered to meet her in the flesh but Orlah had forbade it. Far easier to pay homage to a machine god of war than to a brother she would want to embrace, to cling to in her grief. It could not be so. Only iron would serve now, and in the face of the Imperials she would offer nothing more yielding than that.

Let them see strength.

But she felt far from strong and wished the eyes of the world were not upon her in that moment. Her face did not betray the lie, however. Chiselled from alabaster, she looked down on her daughter as she lay in state, surrounded by the violet blooms of the nightvein that had settled upon her casket, and merely *glanced* before turning to the Imperial delegation.

'You have my gratitude, and the gratitude of Kamidar,' she told them, a vox-amplifier in her gorget boosting the volume of her words, 'for returning the Lady Jessivayne Y'Kamidar to us. I know the journey was difficult and long, and that our reunion has been challenging, but the fact you are here is testament to your courage and does honour to my noble house. You are welcome here, Imperium, and I request you stay with us to observe my daughter's final rites and honour her sacrifice as we honour the martial bond you have shared with our house.'

The queen turned after her speech, and though Haster had moved forwards to reply, she showed no inclination to acknowledge any individual, and the first lieutenant went to his place red-faced and insulted.

Kesh conjectured some of this; she couldn't know Haster's mind, but Naval officers were proud and the queen's actions could not have been construed as anything but a slight. The gates parted then, admitting the queen as she slowly walked away flanked by her Royal Citizen Guard and a pair of Royal Armigers. The rest of the army remained in place like a forest of mismatched statues before the captain of the guard stepped up to provide instruction about what would happen next.

Chapter Fourteen

THE NEED FOR STRENGTH

THE DRAUGHT

KEEP A SHARP EYE

The draught had a tinny aroma but appeared innocuous enough. Lareoc stared at the cup, a simple wooden vessel, the dark liquid within gently steaming the air. He could still feel where the unguent had been applied to his face in the mild tingling of his skin. He gazed across the surface of the draught to the one who had made and offered it.

Albia looked back at him, the old priest inscrutable but open.

'What's in it?' Lareoc asked.

'What you need. Strength.'

Lareoc stole a glance at Parnius, his squire and friend as apprehensive as the rest in the cave.

They had travelled several miles from the subterranean holdfast in the mountain to a different location, but one still very much in Kamidar's untamed wilds. Lareoc and his siblings had played in these caves as children, a cause of much vexation for his mother, who thought them dangerous. They were. That's why Lareoc had done it. The old beasts who had once laired here were dead now, or else driven out by the barons and their warriors. Now it was just a cave, and the ideal meeting place. All nine of the Knights of Hurne were there, Lareoc and his squires.

'It smells like blood,' said one of the men, Klaigen. His long nose wrinkled in distaste, his shaggy beard failing to hide the sour curl to his lips.

'In ancient days, primordial tribes ate raw flesh and drank the blood of their kills,' the old priest said mildly, 'it made them strong.' He smiled, leathern flesh creasing into spiderwebs and crow's feet. 'But, it isn't blood. Well, not *only* blood. There are herbs, roots, the old things of the earth, forgotten by many but not by Hurne or his followers. Sup of it, be refreshed. Find keen-ness of thought, sharpness of touch.' He looked directly at Lareoc. 'You will need it for what is to come. If you are to prevail.'

Lareoc hesitated a moment longer, then drank. It was bitter with a coppery tang, but he tasted some of the promised herbs too.

The others drank too, even Klaigen, wiping their mouths after draining their cups. Only one remained, the dark broth still steaming, and Lareoc saw Parnius' back as he disappeared up the carved steps that led out of the cave.

He found Parnius a short while later, sitting on a rocky outcrop overlooking an old mere. The water within the withered lake was brackish and stagnant. A rot had set in, fat flies buzzing in noisy cohorts around dead animals fallen into the pool from the cliffs above.

'I remember this place,' said Parnius as Lareoc went to sit beside him.

'Lochramere.'

Parnius nodded, smiling at the name. 'My father brought me on fishing trips. He'd bring rods and nets, and I would while away the hours with him. We never caught much, and I was too young then to properly appreciate it for what it was – a chance to bond, and build roots with my father.'

'I know this story, Parnius,' Lareoc uttered gently. 'And I knew your father too. He was a brave man. The war took too many, and too heavy a toll.'

'And what did he die for then?' asked Parnius, and turned to face Lareoc. Tears stung the corners of his eyes but they did not spill.

'Freedom, I hope. Survival, I fear.'

'You really believe Orlah is such a tyrant.'

Lareoc's expression hardened, his eyes moving from his friend to the tainted mere. 'I do. Like the water below, she festers in Kamidar's soil. She says protection and sovereignty, I see only more subjugation and her endless rule.'

'Then what is the alternative, this pact with the old priest? What do we really know of him and his ways? My mother told stories of old Kamidar, the cults of the first settlers. They were pagan men, Lareoc.'

'They were hunters, tribes of the earth. And if there is strength in that, the means for us to rise above our oppressors...' Lareoc shook his head, as if the answer were obvious. 'Why should we not reach for it and take it? She burned my home, Parnius. She abandoned us to death. We did the only thing we could, survive, and she burned us. She excommunicated my house and saw it cast to dust.' He looked Parnius in the eye again. 'If that is what she does to her allies, what fate do you think she envisages for her enemies?'

'But is this the way, through old rites and old gods? It feels blasphemous. What of the Emperor?'

'The Emperor has come, old friend. He has come aboard His warships and through His armies. He has landed upon our soil as an invader beaches a foreign shore. And make no mistake, He means to take it.'

'Take what?'

'Everything we have.'

'And so why fight for them?'

'I'm not. I'm fighting *against* her. Let them kill each other, but let them leave us alone. If she dies then I shall consider my house and honour avenged. I have no desire for power beyond that to defend myself. That is what Albia offers us. The strength to make our own choices. To fight back.'

'And that's why you took the cup.'

'I am more interested to understand why you didn't.'

Parnius turned his attention to the water. 'When my father and I fished the mere, he always told me to keep a sharp eye. Things other than fish swam the depths, back when it was hale and full. I wanted to take a rod and ply the waters myself, but he always said to me that one must watch and keep the sharp eye because you can't do that and fish at the same time. I am keeping a sharp eye for you, Lareoc, in case there are things under the water, things you can't see.'

And as they watched together in silence, something slithered beneath the murky surface of the mere. It wrapped a tendril of itself around a putrid carcass and sleekly pulled it under.

Orlah found her waiting in one of the lower halls. She had been brought here by a cohort of loyal retainers, the Royal Citizen Guard, and now she lay in the quiet dark. Unmoving. Dressed in half-shadow and a thin shift of white cotton, she looked peaceful in repose. The side of her facing the queen was her 'better' side, the one not ruined by horrific wounding, and so the illusion persevered as Orlah crossed the floor towards where the body was lying on a stone slab.

The queen had shed her stately garb, now wearing plain robes with a simple circlet upon her brow. Nearby, having gone ahead of his ruler, Gademene stood to attention at the back of the small chamber. Swathed in darkness himself, the guard captain had refused to leave his queen unprotected, even in her own palace. The arrival of the Imperials had put everyone on edge.

'She is ready for you, your majesty,' he said, a slight quaver in his voice. Jessivayne had been beloved by all.

Orlah nodded, shackling her emotions to her duty, and approached the corpse of her daughter.

Sacristans had stripped her of her armour, and the palace chirurgeons had done their best to conceal and mend Jessivayne's grotesque injuries. Orlah felt her breath suddenly hike at the sight of them close up and took a few moments to regain her composure. Gademene made to assist her but she held him off with a raised hand. Unwavering.

A silver basin of fragranced water and a cloth and sponge had been left out for her. She would cleanse her daughter's body before it would be re-dressed and made ready for what came next. It was a mother's duty. Dipping her hands into the warm soapy water, cloth at the ready, Orlah hesitated as she went to touch Jessivayne's pallid skin.

Her daughter had... *withered* in the void, despite the stasis fields and preservatives and unguents. It was slight, but noticeable, a tightening and greying of the flesh, the shrinking of decay. It had aged her in a way, stolen her beauty. And her wounds... *Blood of Kamidar.*

The tears came unabated, unashamed.

Orlah had promised Ekria she would never show weakness again, but she broke that promise now. It would not be the last she would be forced to break.

'They let her rot...' she uttered, voice faltering. A tentative hand, trembling, went to stroke Jessivayne's cheek but came up just short. Too afraid to touch. 'My child...'

The hand became a fist, clenched tight. Strong again, as her grief burned up in the face of hot, righteous anger.

'This cannot stand.'

'No, my queen,' Gademene agreed.

Silence then for a few moments. Cold and dead as a heart hardened, turning to thoughts of retribution.

'My will has changed, captain,' said Orlah.

'Speak it and I will see it done, your majesty.'

And Orlah did, her every order to him starkly given, and to his credit not once did Gademene balk at what she was asking him to do. She spoke as a queen but felt as a mother. Pain, fury. It was primal. Irreversible. She had no hesitation. And when it was done, she said simply in a quiet voice, 'Leave us, captain. I wish to be alone with my daughter.'

Gademene bowed, and left.

Chapter Fifteen

A MOURNING FEAST

HISTORITOR

THE SILENT SISTER

The queen had spared no expense with the feast. It was a grand affair inside a great, dark hall lined with tables of victuals. Fine meats, luscious fruits, and vegetables sourced from Kamidar's bountiful farmsteads were arrayed in abundance. Another proud boast from an even prouder world.

Kesh felt her mouth salivate at the prospect of food, her campaign diet of protein sticks and cured trail meat like dirt and boot leather compared to this offering of plenty. Even Dvorgin couldn't help but moisten his lips at the prospect, the general the epitome of decorum in every other respect. His honour guard, of which Kesh was a part, shifted in their starched uniforms. They were hungry. Kesh could relate.

She reckoned on about fifty left in the Imperial company, just those who had fought on Gathalamor, and even then only officers and their entourages had been permitted to this mourning celebration. The rest of the troops had been directed to barrack houses elsewhere in the city, where it was assured they would receive similar treatment. Kesh couldn't fault the Kamidari-ans' hospitality, which was surprising considering how things had started. Reports had bled through to the troops of discontent and even hostility towards the crusade's arrival in some of the fringe settlements. Here, in the heart of the queen's empire, all was well. Even Haster and his Naval retinue looked at ease, exchanging friendly words and nodding eagerly at the burgeoning platters and carafes.

'A long journey...'

Kesh looked up at Dvorgin's voice.

'From Gathalamor to here.'

She gave a quick salute.

'No need for such formality. We're not in the field any more.' Dvorgin came alongside her with a smile. Some of the tension had bled out of him, leaving his grizzled features a little softer, though he still absently stroked the chron his wife had given him. Her last gift, and a reminder of the one he had not been able to give her.

'Of course, sir. Apologies.'

'Perhaps a nip of this will help.' He offered Kesh a small silver flask wrapped in red leather. 'It's *rupka*, the good stuff,' he added with a genuine smile.

Kesh hesitated. She hadn't seen this side of Dvorgin before. It was a little unsettling.

'Go on, sergeant,' he said. 'It's not a test.'

Kesh took the flask with a nod of thanks and then took a surreptitious pull. It *was* good. Hot, spiced wine, almost syrupy in texture. She felt it coat the inside of her mouth.

'Better?'

'Yes, sir,' she replied, and went to hand back the flask.

Dvorgin held up his hand to her. 'Keep it. Consider it a gift.'

'Thank you, sir. Very kind.'

He gave a wry smile. 'Still struggling with that formality, eh?'

'It's a hard habit to break.'

'As it should be, I suppose,' he replied, then changed tack. 'How did it go?'

Kesh raised a querying eyebrow. 'Sir?'

He gestured to the lithe figure of the historitor, clad in black, a serious, almost solemn air about him. 'The scribe. He wasn't too intrusive?'

'He asked some annoying questions,' Kesh admitted, 'but no, he was fine. It was odd to be the subject of his interest.'

'How so?'

'I am just a lowly footslogger, what say do I have in the great affairs of the war? I am no lord general... or queen for that matter.'

'Every perspective is a valid one, the experience of the soldier on the ground perhaps more so.'

Kesh nodded at that, conceding the point. She didn't mention that Viablo had asked her about faith and miracles. The remembrance of it made her uncomfortable and she was glad when a master of ceremonies, one of the queen's major-domos, mounted a podium at one end of the hall, preparing to speak.

Banners hung from every wall, depicting the many victories of Kamidar – both ancient and those campaigns they had fought whilst estranged from the Imperium. The later ones were visceral, fierce. War had tempered these people, honed them to a hard, resilient edge. Every banner had been bordered in black out of respect, though the hall was dark and sombre in its general decor. Servitors and robed serfs bustled here and there, making use of the shadows. They held platters and moved through the crowds offering aperitifs.

Dvorgin reached out and took one, the crystal glass catching the glow from candelabras and iron sconces. The light hit the major-domo's breastplate as he cleared his throat, and made the metal glint like warm gold.

All eyes were upon him as he raised his chin, taking the role of imperious orator. The man had a martial aspect, as did all

Kamidarians Kesh had seen so far. She supposed it was required of them, for their nations to be ever prepared for war. The major-domo reiterated the queen's welcome. He was urbane, well spoken. He went on to explain that her majesty would join them presently but for now they should eat, rest and take solace in the camaraderie of shared allegiance as citizens of the great Imperium. A cheer met this part, at odds with the solemnity of the occasion.

Once his address had ended, the major-domo climbed down from the podium and disappeared in the throngs of natives, who easily outnumbered the crusaders. Kesh felt suddenly surrounded and wished she still had her rifle. Her only weapons were a hol-stered pistol and a short sword, but both were more ceremonial than functional.

'No need to look so wary, sergeant,' said Dvorgin.

'More old habits, sir.'

Dvorgin finished his drink. 'Be at ease, sergeant. Enjoy it, if you're able.' He cupped her shoulder, his manner fatherly, and not for the first time Kesh wondered if the man still nurtured the same regrets. 'Go on,' he said, indicating the feast, 'it'll be a long while before we eat as well as this again. If we *ever* eat as well as this again.'

Kesh saluted and felt immediately ridiculous given the infor-mality of the moment. 'Sir,' she said, her voice clipped, and turned on her heel to hide her embarrassment. The rest of the troops were already tucking in; none amongst the delegation could hide their eagerness. Kesh joined in.

A mouthful of cooked fish practically melted on her tongue and she luxuriated in the sensation. She had never tasted food like it and, after a few more tentative bites, ate with gusto.

'It is something, isn't it. All of this, I mean.'

She turned, trying and failing to deftly wipe the meat juice trick-ling down her chin, and saw Viablo standing next to her.

'It's delicious,' she replied, her voice muffled with a half-mouthful of venison and gravy.

'Not just the feast,' the historitor replied, and gestured expansively. '*This*, the hall, the army of Kamidar, the ceremony and the camaraderie. In truth, I expected us to come here and meet a hostile force, a clenched fist not the open hand of friendship... And yet.'

'And yet,' Kesh agreed, though as she looked around the immense room and raised her head above the fog of hunger, she noticed other things.

A pair of ceremonial Swordsworn stood in sentry alcoves by the grand doors at the south end of the hall, opposite the entrance through which the Imperial guests had been ushered. The Armigers were decked with pennants, again edged in black, and stood sombrely. Armoured guards in breastplates and helms, holding tall electro pikes, stood in every niche, unmoving but watchful. The Custodian, Vychellan, watched them back and she realised he had not deigned to eat. She didn't even know if his kind *needed* to eat, but regardless his gaze swept the room for threats, like a beacon scouring the sea for rocks. He looked on edge, almost poised. Perhaps it was his habit. She wondered if she should exercise more caution, but then Viablo interrupted her thoughts.

'It is fascinating,' he said, still observing the general hubbub, the odd pitch and yaw that these kinds of celebrations usually possessed, with some of the guests mingling easily and others sticking to their own. Kesh counted herself amongst the latter, more at ease with a scope in her hand than a silver fork. 'I had thought to join Praxis to see the inner workings of the crusade,' Viablo went on, 'to record its endeavours, the banners raised, the worlds liberated, the victories... but, this is something I had not expected. A foreign dignitary, an independent sovereignty more or less, welcoming the crusade so warmly. Fascinating.'

'They are still Imperial,' said Kesh, only half engaged in the conversation as she continued to enjoy the victuals on offer.

'By Terran law and charter, yes. But look around... Tell me

we are still in the Imperium and not a different empire entirely. Allied, yes, but not kin. Not really.'

Kesh had visited only a handful of worlds and exclusively when they were at war against some hostile alien or warlord of the Arch-enemy. She had seen little of peace and diplomacy, and although every place of foreign soil she had set foot upon had possessed its own cultures and creeds, they had still been unmistakably Impe-rial. Kamidar felt different, not markedly so but just enough as to be discernible.

Deciding these were matters for those with higher concerns than a lowly Militarum sergeant, she said, 'I'm surprised you're not recording this,' returning her attention to the feast, for what need was there for an additional sentry when a Custodian of the Emperor was keeping vigil? She ate, tried to relax as much as her soldier's conditioning would allow. 'Don't you historitors have stylus and slate attached at the hip?'

Viablo tapped an ocular lens he was wearing over his eye. A subtle device, shaped similarly to a monocle, only thinner; Kesh had missed it at first.

'Who says I'm not?'

Kesh shrugged, as if to say *I should have known,* and took another mouthful. 'Have you tasted any of this? It's incredible.'

'I will, though I am ashamed to say we are fed well in the Logos Historica Verita. Nothing as extravagant as this, mind you. It's remarkable how well preserved Kamidar is. Though, Knight worlds are known for their independence and martial strength. Still,' said Viablo, unpicking his own line of thought as Kesh kept on eating, 'to have survived the Rift so intact. That's a feat few other worlds have managed.'

'They have a sizeable army,' Kesh conceded, trying to add something of value to the conversation, especially if the historitor was on a different track to miracles and her survival at Gath-alamor. She wanted to forget politics and the war but Viablo was determined to draw her in. Besides, she conceded to herself, she liked him. He had a quiet way but he was intelligent, empathetic.

'As I understand it, they also have a bonded alliance with a company of Adeptus Astartes,' he said.

'Then you have your answer, historitor,' she replied, wondering how such an alliance had come to pass but keeping her thoughts to herself.

Viablo smiled. 'Please,' he said, offering his hand for Kesh to shake, 'Theodore.'

'Very well,' Kesh replied, shaking the man's hand. Yes, she found him very likeable. 'Magda.'

'Magda.'

'I do hope this isn't a clumsy preamble aimed at getting me to talk more about my experiences on Gathalamor.'

Viablo held up his hands plaintively. 'You have made it clear that subject is closed and I will respect that. I merely seek pleasant company.'

She smirked, still chewing the latest morsel. 'Are you sure you've latched onto the right person, Theodore?'

Viablo laughed loudly, genuinely. She had not thought such a sound could emanate from the willowy, void-born historitor, but then people could surprise you. She found herself warming to him further, especially now that his investigative eye was turned elsewhere.

'I have a feeling, Magda,' he said, 'that you and I will become good friends.'

'Let's not get ahead of ourselves.'

He laughed again, and Kesh found herself smiling in return until Viablo shuddered like a trickle of ice water had rolled down his back.

'What's the matter?'

He didn't need to answer as Kesh saw Syreniel stalking through the hall. She must have been here the entire time though the sergeant hadn't noticed her at first, which was incredible given how imposing she was, a silver goddess wrought for death. She loitered in Haster's vicinity, having evidently just conducted a sweep of the immediate perimeter, and now returned to her body-guard duties. At least that's what Kesh assumed she was here for.

'What do you know of them?' she asked in an unintended whisper, careful not to meet Syreniel's gaze.

Viablo did not turn, though he knew to whom Kesh referred.

'Other than the oath of silence and the propensity to be deeply unnerving, not much,' he said, and Kesh's attention was drawn to the void around the Sister of Silence where no guest, Imperial or otherwise, would willingly trespass. 'A few of the historitors have tried, but their... *language* is coded and extremely difficult to decipher. Then there is the... *aura*. I knew of one amongst my order who attempted to interview one of the Sisterhood but could not physically enter her presence without voiding his stomach. It got so bad, he had to be taken to the medicae. That story got around the fleet and no one has attempted it since. With good reason. Naturally, I am curious, but she is forbidding and I'd like to keep the contents of my stomach on the inside if at all possible.'

Kesh nodded at that, finding comfort in the solidarity of their shared unease towards the warrior woman.

'Why do you think she's here?'

'A representative of Lord Guilliman, perhaps?' ventured the historitor. 'The Talons of the Emperor are singular in their ability and reputation. Or more likely she is a protector for the admiral's proxy.'

'I thought the same,' Kesh confessed. 'I think she unsettles me more than Lord Vychellan.'

Her eye strayed then to the Custodian, who, she realised with a start, was looking right at her, as if he had heard his name despite the noise and the distance between them. Hastily, she averted her gaze.

'Are you sure about that?' Viablo said, gently chiding.

Kesh made a sour face at him.

'Tell me this, Magda,' said the historitor, changing the subject, 'what do you make of these Kamidarians?'

Kesh thought on the question, weighing up their hosts between mouthfuls of tender beef. 'Honourable, I think. They are soldiers all, whether they wear a uniform or not. Proud too. I see much of Mordian in them, though this world is a paradise compared to my own.'

'To have survived thusly, it speaks well of them, do you not think?'

'Undoubtedly, though there is a... *tightness*, a sort of practised camaraderie.'

Viablo frowned, genuinely intrigued. 'How do you mean?'

'I don't know, I have no gift for words. I let my rifle speak for me. It's as if they're trying too hard, or even warning us.'

'A warning about what?'

'To take them seriously, to see them as equals. I don't really know, it's just a feeling.'

'An instinct.'

'Something like that.'

'Reunions are difficult, I suppose, and this is no different. How long has it been since the Imperium has set foot on Kamidar?'

'Dvorgin would say we had never left.'

'True, but the Imperial representative on this world is the queen, and she speaks as an independent sovereign.'

'Meaning?'

'Only that rulership breeds power, and power, once obtained, is not so easy to relinquish.'

'Is that what we're doing here, taking power?'

'Nothing as crude as that, though to the Kamidarians, to their queen... That sabre rattle upon our arrival, do you know what it said to me?'

Kesh shook her head, and felt her appetite waning.

'We are strong,' said Viablo, 'and this world is mine.'

A chorus of trumpets blared then, clearing for Queen Orlah as she entered the hall at last.

Chapter Sixteen

BURY THE DEAD

INTERFERENCE

TAKING A STAND

The slain still lay strewn across the battlefield. Imperial and Kamidarian, soldiers and civilians both. It took almost three minutes for an officer to call for calm and order to be restored. One of the Mordians, a major judging by his rank pins, climbed atop one of the transports and bellowed for a ceasefire. The shots whipping back and forth diminished then ebbed away to nothing, leaving the living to count the dead.

At least fifty on both sides, by Ariadne's reckoning, making the rapid calculation via her augmetic. It could be more. A proper accounting would have to wait. Mercifully, the Astartes had stayed out of it. Had they not, it would probably have ended sooner, but she dreaded to imagine the carnage. Her heart stilled just thinking about it. Let alone the political ramifications. The fleet's time on Kamidar so far had been, to put it lightly, fraught.

Her excursion to the Knight world had not been anything like how she had envisaged. She knew Ardemus had sent her here as a punishment, but the admiral could scarcely have predicted any of this. Or perhaps he had and didn't care. The implications worried her, and more than ever she wanted nothing more than to board a lander and get the hells back to the fleet.

With thoughts of Praxis on her mind, Ariadne turned her attention to one of the officers nearby. He stood ramrod straight, waiting to be connected to the ships in orbit, but the voxman in his service kept shaking his head and retrying his instruments.

'Is something wrong?' Ariadne asked. She had some knowledge of engineering, picked up from many years of being around the inner workings of a starship as a fleet logistician, and thought she might be able to help.

The Mordian captain gave her a side-eye until he realised who she was and her position within the fleet.

'Ma'am,' he offered, sketching a deferent bow to Ariadne, who returned a curt nod. 'I need to make the admiral aware of the skirmish with the natives. He'll want to be apprised of everything happening on the ground.' He looked down then to glare at his sergeant who was having so much trouble.

'Nothing, sir,' complained the voxman, frowning. 'It's dead as Sebastian Thor's mummified corpse.' He gave the boxy device an experimental tap then a much harder smack, but the dead air kept on coming, wheezing like the last breath of a corpse.

'Is it the same across the other landing parties?' Ariadne asked.

The sergeant nodded, not having thought to check, and proceeded to flick through the different channels. His frowned deepened.

'What is it, Maddox?' the captain demanded, getting flustered and frustrated with the lack of apparent progress.

'It's across every channel, sir.' He scratched at his head, slipping his cap back to claw at his thinning hair. The sergeant looked up at Ariadne and the captain both. 'Almost as if there's some interference.'

'Keep trying, Maddox,' said the captain, who nodded to Ariadne by way of farewell and turned his back.

With little else for it, she moved on.

The injured were being rescued and tended to by now, the two sides keeping to their own but operating under an unspoken truce. At least at the moment. With no beans to count, Ariadne rallied her staff and set to helping the medicae officers. She led by example, mucking in though she had little knowledge of field medicine beyond what she'd seen the armsmen employ after a skirmish in the void. In truth, those encounters were so brutal, they seldom left much to patch up.

A Mordian medicae who saw her hovering quickly snapped her up and before she knew it she was kneeling by the side of a Solian on a stretcher, pressing a wad of gauze to a red wound in his stomach. He'd gazed at her glassy eyed as she'd held him, and reached out a hand. At first Ariadne hadn't known what to do, but then she realised he was afraid and she clutched his outstretched hand and didn't let go.

She prayed then, prayed for the ex-ganger's life, seeing past the tribal tattoos, the roughness of his upbringing until just another human being lay before her wanting to live.

'Oh Emperor, protect this loyal soul and keep him safe, heal his wounds and make him whole so that he might live on in your light and glory...'

He had wept, the injured Solian, out of fear, perhaps out of gratitude, his mouth murmuring his own prayer, and Ariadne had held his hand as if she held his life at the same time. Instructions came like bullets then, barked from the mouth of the chirurgeon trying to save the man and triage whoever else followed.

The next hour drifted over her in a daze, like half-remembered memories, but she nodded numbly as every order was given. Such waste, such pointless, idiotic waste. It was one of many reasons why Ariadne had always preferred things to people. Things were dependable, they had clearly defined limits and functions. If a thing malfunctioned, the reason could be discerned, the problem fixed. People were unpredictable and cruel, they didn't need reason and in high-pressure situations seldom operated with enough – or any. Case in point, the carnage in which she was red-elbow deep.

If this was how the requisition of Kamidarian assets had begun, she dreaded to imagine how it would end. And as she knelt alongside the next patient, seemingly more of their blood on the outside than the inside, she allowed her attention to wander.

Away from the site of the skirmish, she caught a glimpse of Ogin. A dim memory of him pulling her from the firefight as it erupted swam hazily through her mind. He appeared to be having a heated debate with a Storm Reapers officer, a warrior she hadn't seen before but who had evidently been part of the cohort that accompanied Usullis. She assumed the Space Marines were experiencing similar communication issues.

Of the insipid quartermaster she had seen little sign, barring him skulking back and forth at the edges of the crisis, doubtless preparing to resume his bean counting as soon as the blood had been sluiced from everyone else's hands. That had all ceased for now, the requisition teams' activity, on orders of the Storm Reapers. This edict came from the same officer engaged in the altercation with Ogin. Both appeared to be unhappy but shackling their emotions as they spoke in their native Jagun. Or so Ariadne assumed. She could only speak Gothic and had no gift for languages.

Beyond that particular exchange, the Kamidarians had begun to gather. The Sovereigns remained on nervous tenterhooks, eyeing the Imperial soldiers, and wary of the Astartes – especially the Marines Malevolent, who numbered twenty. Mustard-coloured armour prowled the edges of the Imperial camp, ostensibly to maintain the peace. Ariadne thought they just wanted an excuse to draw down on the natives. Whatever the reason, it was working for now. Fear held the Sovereigns in check. Many of the civilians had retreated to some of the more distant fields, conducting solemn ceremonies by torchlight as they buried the dead. Night crept in, hiding the worst evidence of what had happened here, but the gentle moans of the injured and the weeping of the grieving persisted.

Ariadne watched them as they faded into black, swallowed by the night. As she did, wading through the fog of her thoughts, she felt the hackles on her neck rise and then smelled the cloying aroma of sweetmeats on his breath.

'I have need of you, Ariadne.'

Still using her surname. She would have appreciated it but for the fact that the bastard used it like a weapon instead of a respectful means of address.

'I am busy here, Usullis.' She glared back at him, over her shoulder, hands and forearms lathered in another wounded soldier's blood. 'Or can't you see the blood behind all that ignorance?'

As she turned back, his face began to screw up into a wrathful scowl.

'Medicae,' he said, and the Mordian glanced up from his stitching, 'I need you to release the quartermaster. Immediately.'

The medicae looked annoyed but resigned, too weary to put up any sort of fight, and dismissed Ariadne with a couple of flicks of his hand. He did nod as she stood, acknowledging the help she had provided.

'Am I to work a data-slate with blood on my fingers, quartermaster senioris?' She stood her ground, eager to square off. Taking a stand against Usullis was something she had promised herself for a long time.

Usullis, feeding off his own power, raised his chin and straightened his back so he stood a little taller. He knew others were watching and chose to use it as an opportunity to exert his superiority. 'I'm glad you can recall my rank.'

'It is the same as mine.'

'And yet, the admiral had given me operational authority. That means I rank above you.'

Ariadne balled her fists, and it took every ounce of her composure to keep her arms by her sides. Treating her silence as compliance, Usullis went on.

'We have a task to perform and need to be back to it. *You* need to be back to it.'

Exhaling a long breath between her teeth, she replied, 'The dead are literally lying at our feet, Beren. Some of them are not yet cold. Have some compassion.'

'I haven't time for compassion and nor have you. And do not refer to me by my first name again. I let it slide the first time but when we are in the field before sanctioned Departmento work, you will call me Usullis, or senioris.'

'Or what exactly?'

Usullis reddened, his shame quickly turning to anger in which to hide his own inadequacy. 'You have been pulled up on your insubordination once, *Niova*,' he sneered, getting in so close that his breath was the only thing she could smell, 'and don't think because of our history that I won't drag you up before the admiral and petition to have you flogged, because I—'

The blow to his jaw that felled Usullis onto his rump arrested the tirade, Ariadne standing over him rubbing her bruised knuckles.

'How's that for seniority,' she said.

Usullis had turned a deep shade of crimson, and was purpling by the moment.

'The admiral will hear of this,' he snarled, wiping away a line of red from a cut lip. 'You're finished in the Departmento, Niova. I'll see to it.'

'You'll have to postpone the celebration, Beren. Vox is down. There's no one going to be contacting the admiral, least of all a jumped-up shit like you.'

She walked away, back towards the medicaes where she could

feel useful. Usullis was all talk, though as she left him raging impotently in her wake, she considered that it wasn't his threat that put her suddenly on edge, it was the reminder that the vox was out.

Of all the devices in the Militarum armoury, it was the humble vox that was the most reliable, at least in terms of its function. It could not always guarantee a clear signal, but it could be relied upon to work faithfully. To have it fail so dramatically and across every channel, it made Ariadne wonder what exactly had caused the outage and whether it was a rare malfunction or something more deliberate.

Tiberion Ardemus paced. He paced until he felt the polished floor of his observatory wear down beneath the relentless passage of his boots. Of his many virtues and talents, patience was not one. He had needed to learn it, but the lesson had never come easy. Back when he had been a humble captain of a single warship and not the master of an entire fleet, it had been easier. He hadn't needed to exercise as much patience. He certainly hadn't been concerned with the whims of prideful queens or staunchly headstrong colonies.

He missed those days, of tearing across the void, engaging any foe that should stray into his path. The thrill of a broadside barrage, the satisfaction of witnessing the silent death of an enemy vessel. He felt powerful, vigorous – as if he were the ship, its will, its anima, and its weapons his fists or a sword wielded by his hand. Even with void warfare being conducted as it invariably was, at distance, there was an intimacy to the dance. No doubt, he had become a most powerful man indeed, and Ardemus craved power above more or less anything else. But invigorating as commanding a fleet was, and despite the frisson of self-satisfaction that came when his orders were carried out, it did not quite match up to the thrill of those old days when he had been a younger man with a younger man's foolish ideals.

Honour. Victory.

Politics came with the territory now, the trappings of power threaded through with their own inescapable caveats. Ardemus wanted glory and he had thought advancement the best route to it, but of late he had begun to question that assumption. Stranded here on the outskirts of some petty potentate's domain, forced to engage in rude diplomacy... The Kamidarians should give up what they had for the crusade and uphold their Imperial oaths so Ardemus could get on with upholding his. The Anaxian Line would not miraculously manifest, it had to be wrought, hammered, tempered. And for Ardemus that was the least of it. Until Kamidar and the protectorate had been established as one of its lynchpins, he could forget meaningful void warfare. There were enemies out in the dark to engage and destroy, a great surfeit of them since the galaxy had split in twain and all the devils of all the hells had spilled out roaring conquest. He had already put many to the sword. Not him personally, though, and this was at the root of the unspoken gripe that had dogged him for the last decade or more, but it barely scratched the corrupted surface.

Mankind had been edged right up to the brink and it had teetered, almost fallen, but here they were at the spear's tip, fighting for every bloody yard. It was invigorating. At least, it had been before the crusade ground them between its teeth and supped of their supplies. Though he would admit it to no one, Praxis was a ragged battle group in its present state and in urgent need of resupply. Campaigners driven to the limits of endurance, they needed what the Iron Protectorate had. And Ardemus meant to get it by any means.

He paused in his pacing for a moment to cast a glance through the large oculus window dominating one wall and the entire ceiling of the domed room. It provided a stunning, near-unparalleled view of the void beyond the *Fell Lord*. Ardemus liked the observatorium, and would often come here when he needed to think. He found the expansiveness of the void, its many stars and nebulae, both beautiful and soothing. It had been hard for Praxis, reaching the Ironhold. Loath as he was to admit it, even in this private oasis, the farther the fleets ventured from Terra, the more difficult the task of maintaining momentum and cohesion became. Outposts, these so-called redoubt worlds like Kamidar, would be increasingly crucial to the lord primarch's aims.

'Magnify...'

His voice echoed off the glass as the machine spirit that governed the mechanisms of the room brought up a closer view of the scene ahead of the fleet.

'There you are...'

Ardemus allowed himself a grim smile. Several miles distant, the fleet of Kamidar loitered at high anchor, poised to unleash a lance salute in honour of the fallen princess. *Still poised.* They held in good order, he conceded, the shipmasters evidently well drilled, the crews serviceable. The vessels were old but well kept. In better circumstances, he would have liked to tour one or two and witness first-hand these naval relics. But matters were less than cordial at the present and Ardemus had a schedule to keep.

Not for the first time, he considered whether he and not Haster should have descended to the world below. He quickly dismissed the notion. His first lieutenant was ably suited to the task. Placate the queen, assert Imperial authority then get on with the damn task at hand. She would surely come to realise, this Orlah Y'Kamidar, that she really had no choice other than compliance. Haster would see it done, Ardemus had every confidence. He just had to navigate the mire of local customs and traditions. State funerals could be *delicate*.

'Sir...'

A voice behind him drew Ardemus' attention to the glass where his second lieutenant, Renzo, stood reflected.

'You may be at ease, shipman.' He caught his own reflection

too, proud and imposing in his full Navy regalia but with a tired sag to his features that hadn't been there before.

We really need to move on...

He noticed the second lieutenant clutched a data-slate in both hands. Not usually a good sign. Ardemus scowled.

'Out with it.'

'Another three ships are unaccounted for, sir.'

Ardemus turned on his heel to face the petty officer. 'Elaborate, lieutenant.'

'The master of augur cannot locate them in the battlesphere, sir.'

'A starship doesn't simply disappear, lieutenant. Have the master of augur check again and think before you bother me with such inconsequentialities.' He was about to turn back to his view when the lieutenant replied.

'With respect, sir, he already has. Three times.'

The admiral's scowl deepened, his brow knotting in discontent. *Perhaps Haster had been right about deploying those destroyers... No, then there'd be two more missing ships.*

Ardemus felt his jaw tighten. Most of the fleet was spread out across the sector, a handful of his finest vessels segregated from the rest by the damned Iron Veil. They were at a disadvantage but could do little until matters on the surface had been resolved and the ready flow of supplies resumed.

'Have the fleet close ranks, destroyers to the outer void markers. It could still be a comms error, but every ship is on yellow alert until stood down. Understand?'

Renzo gave a crisp salute, nodding sharply afterwards.

'And have the master of vox open a channel to First Lieutenant Haster. I want to know what's going on down there.'

At this, the second lieutenant frowned. Ardemus sighed, a headache already forming.

'What is it?'

'Vox to the surface is currently down, sir. All efforts are being made to restore communication.'

'Cause?'

'Unknown at present, sir. The master of vox thinks it's some kind of interference.'

An inward groan preceded Ardemus rubbing his temples with the fingers of his left hand. 'Is the Kamidarian fleet sending vox to the surface?'

'I'm not sure, sir.'

'Find out. And can we listen in to their communications?'

'Without their signal cipher, no, sir. Just as they can't listen to ours.'

'But we can tell if a vox carrier signal is going from one of their ships to somewhere on the ground?'

'Yes, sir.'

'Good. Have the master of vox monitor frequency of vox-traffic sent and received by the fleet.'

'Anything else, sir?'

'That will be all, second lieutenant.'

Ardemus turned back to the void and the magnified image of the Kamidarian fleet, silent, still. Poised.

Chapter Seventeen

STEEL AND LEADERSHIP

A DEBT IS OWED

HASTER'S FOLLY

She had not come alone. The barque upon which her dead daughter lay in gentle repose followed her. She wore her armour; they both did. Orlah's a more ornate version of the suit she had donned to greet the Imperial delegation and only a little less belligerent in its cast and form; Jessivayne was in the patched-up breastplate and greaves she had worn inside her destroyed Knight, a veil of golden chain to hide the hideous wounding of her face and head that the chirurgeons had been unable to mask. A sword had been clasped in her gauntleted hands, the fingers worked with wire to prevent them from slipping.

Orlah walked slowly, her manner stately and stern, an emerald cloak sweeping behind her like dracon scale. She too carried a sword, her oighen, strapped to her waist on the left side as if ready to be drawn. Her crown shimmered in the firelight of the hall and all eyes watched her as an expectant hush stole over the crowd. Only the dulcet hum of the funeral barque's anti-gravitic motors intruded, that and the crackle of a hearth or a spit of flame. It felt ritualistic.

Guards came in train after Jessivayne's body, Royal Citizen Sovereigns. They wore fluted helms, their faces covered, horse-hair manes spitting from their crowns in gold-and-white crests. Silver armour, so bright as to be almost white, shone like star fire, and they clasped ornate pikes in leather gauntlets. Then came the knights, not the larger cousins of the dread war machines holding station at the end of the hall but the warriors who piloted and dominated these engines, who rode them, with all the knowledge and will of their forebears at their command thanks to the miracle of the Throne Mechanicum. Led by Gerent Y'Kamidar, who looked resplendent in gold and blue, they walked with solemn purpose, heads high, eyes hooded. Armour-clad, like their queen, the knights of House Kamidar and the lords of the houses inferior had come in grim observance of this direst of days.

Two burly and gene-bulked servitors brought forth the throne of Kamidar itself, a chair of hard, dark metal and uncompromising edges. It did not look a comfortable seat, but it spoke the word 'power' in every contour. Creatures had been wrought into the metal, hard to discern until the light touched them just so: gryfons, basilysks and, of course, dracons. These mythical heraldic beasts adorned much of the Kamidarian architecture, reminders of an elder time when warriors rode horses not machines and lances were shafts of wood tipped with steel, not deadly energy cannons that could render entire armies to dust.

Such change and transformation, yet tradition endured, and this was Kamidar.

Orlah took the throne as it was laid down, a nod of respect to the hooded servitors who knew nothing of it but who instead sloped away into the shadows. She mounted slowly, taking a moment to settle herself, her poise effortless because it had to be.

Let them see me, she thought as she touched the black garnet almost subconsciously, her lips pursed as she swept her gaze

across the silent crowd. *Let them see the warrior-queen. Let them*
see steel and leadership.

Jessivayne reached the end of her funeral procession, the humming of the mechanisms inside the barque finding quiescence at last and slowly drifting down until her deathbed touched the polished floor. Only then, once the torches had been lit around her daughter, only then as the guards had fallen into position and the knights had arranged themselves as honour dictated, a row of kneeling champions bowed before their queen, did Orlah begin.

She addressed the Imperials first. 'A debt is owed,' she said. 'For the return of my daughter, the Lady Jessivayne, aslumber forever more, her light drawn to the side of the Emperor.'

Orlah did not glance at the barque; her eyes remained fixed on a point in the hall, a crest, a pair of crossed swords upon a kite shield, two eagles clutching at the edges. She knew every banner, every piece of heraldry and emblem associated with her world and its long history, but for the life of her she could not bring the name of that old house to her mind.

'We have waited and are glad to be reunited, though our grief outweighs the peace a reunion should bring.

'I want to honour those who fought beside her, and so' – she gestured to the feast – 'I offer the bounty of Kamidar, for which you must each take your fill. A worthy gift for a worthy host.'

At this remark, an officer in uniform stepped forwards, thinking himself an ambassador. Orlah recognised this peacock for the one the admiral had sent in his stead, his proxy and puppet. He sketched a courtly bow, which she generously acknowledged though her eyes remained as steel.

'Your honour us, your majesty,' he said. 'I am First Lieutenant Litus Haster, of the *Fell Lord*, Imperial Ambassador at the behest of Lord Admiral Ardemus, and master of ordnance for Battle Group Praxis.'

She smiled indulgently at the man's use of his hollow titles. *He thinks himself an equal.*

Haster then cleared his throat. Apparently, there was more.

'Lord Ardemus has asked me to convey his deepest sympathies for your loss and hopes the return of your daughter will provide some solace in the days ahead now that she is at rest, her duty ended.' He bowed again, the slight flicker of the tongue as it touched sweat-dappled lips. 'But,' he said with no little trepidation, 'matters must turn now to the crusade, for which the Lady Jessivayne gave her life in honour, and the needs of the fleet. I say this with the utmost respect.'

Orlah's skin was as ice, her heart just as cold. She turned it on Haster and saw the man shiver.

Then she thought of her daughter, six years dead, only preserved through the arcane science of the sacristans and suddenly what she had to do next came easy.

Ardemus watched the Kamidarian fleet. He had not moved for over an hour, his hands clasped behind his back, his gaze fixed like a targeter.

An aide stood nearby, the same one from earlier, and informed him that the Kamidarians were receiving vox instruction from the world below.

'Any news from First Lieutenant Haster?' he asked without much hope.

'Still nothing, sir.'

Then he saw the weapons of the other fleet beginning to power up, their lance capacitors filling. The honour salute must be imminent.

'Thank the Emperor...' Ardemus murmured, but his sense of relief was short-lived when he noticed something slightly awry about the elevation of the Kamidarian guns. Difficult to detect, even via magnification, but the admiral had been a voidfarer for most of his adult life and had gained a sixth sense about such things.

In that moment, right before he turned to bellow at the aide, he remembered his very first combat drop. All Navy cadets had to do it, had to experience the stomach-lurching terror of dead weight and the inexorable pull of gravity before the engines kicked in and a fall turned into a descent. He was trapped in the fall, in that stomach-lurching terror he had never forgotten. A sense of the world slipping away beneath, leaving only the plunge into uncertain, existential dread.

Ardemus was moving now. He moved quickly for a big man, his heavy body still mostly muscle.

'Get me the helm and the master of vox right now. All channels. Every ship in the fleet. Right now!'

Chapter Eighteen

OPPRESSORS
LET NONE LIVE
AN OLD LITANY

On later reflection, Kesh could remember exactly when the tone of the queen's words had changed. Standing in that ornate hall, solemnity lying all about her like a heavy cloak and the bookish historitor beside her drinking in every word and gesture, she experienced a change in the air. A cold wind blew as if a window had slipped its shutter, allowing in an infiltrating gust.

'Such respect is well received, Lieutenant Haster. For we are a proud house of a proud people,' stated the queen, her words thick with implication. 'And we are honoured to be a part of the Imperium. Even in the days of our isolation, we never forgot our oaths of allegiance.'

Kesh felt something then, an instinct kicking in or perhaps something else, something warning her. Abruptly, she was aware of just how many Kamidarian guards were in the hall.

'And in the name of such honour, we make humble request, your majesty, here representing the will of the pri–'

Orlah did not let Haster finish, her raised hand wrapped in chainmail enough to silence the Navy veteran.

'Our world has suffered in your absence,' she said.

Kesh glanced around for Vychellan, and found the Custodian edging towards the middle of the room, his mood impossible to gauge but his actions telling. He was unsettled. He could be reaching for his sword, but in the crowd, Kesh couldn't tell for sure. She couldn't find Syreniel either, but then the Silent Sister had an uncanny knack of disappearing, despite her ostentatious appearance. Dvorgin caught the sergeant's eye, evidently noticing her discomfort, too far away to speak to her directly but his expression querying.

'Magda...' Viablo murmured under his breath, keen not to intrude on the solemnity of the moment. 'Is something wrong?'

'I don't know.'

A ceremonial pistol and short sword... God-Emperor, how she wished she had her rifle.

'Your hand is on your weapon,' said Viablo, looking down.

'Is it?' Kesh replied, following his gaze, and found that was true.

The queen had continued, citing the invasion of the Lord of Curs, the greenskin rampages that had left swathes of Vanir uninhabitable, the Days of Fire when the entire protectorate had burned. The rampant civil disorder, fostered by the Nine Cults of Destiny, whom she had personally seen purged at great cost to her lands and peoples. On she went, listing the many trials and tribulations Kamidar had endured during the Days of Blindness, though she called it 'the abandonment'. Any attempt by Haster to intercede was doomed to failure for the man had not the presence nor the will to interrupt a queen of Orlah's calibre.

'And through this horror,' she went on, 'we endured. Kamidar endured. Our swords grew slick with our enemies' blood. Their ships hang in desolation around our world as a reminder of all we had to sacrifice to survive.' She spoke to the room, her cold eye appraising all. 'And now, we are assailed again. Despite our honourable fealty.

She turned her attention back on Haster, who looked pale.

'Milady, I must protest. There is no–'

'*I am no lady!*' the queen roared, standing up out of her throne. 'I am queen of Kamidar. Ruler of this world and matriarch of this house. I gave *my daughter* to your crusade, *sir*. She fought with honour and died with glory. I have given my armies, my Knights. And yet you come here in false ceremony acting as if you bring us a gift, a favour to gild the deal. Like an open-handed ally and not the thieves and vandals that made landfall upon our sovereign soil so that they could *pillage*.'

She spat the last word, and Kesh felt the venom in it even from where she was standing at the opposite end of the hall. She noticed several of the Mordians and other soldiers had started to shift uneasily, reaching for weapons they didn't have. Vychellan was still moving, edging towards the queen, and for a moment Kesh dared not imagine what he intended. She saw a glint of metal that could only have been a blade.

'I can assure you, your majesty, that no ill intent was meant,' said Haster, mustering every ounce of deference he possessed but chafing at the queen's sudden turn.

'Ill intent, meant or not,' uttered the queen, quieter now as she took her seat again, 'has been felt.' Kesh didn't know which was worse: the storm or the calm. Orlah raised her chin imperiously. 'And we do not take kindly to vandals or thieves. The Ironhold is not a fortress to be ransacked, by any foe...'

Kesh felt a pall of fear clench her chest during the pause.

'Even by the Imperium.'

'You are the Imperium,' said Haster, finding some backbone at last.

The queen fixed him with a stare that had all the vehemence of a spear thrust.

'We will not bow down to *oppressors*.'

* * *

And in the depths of the void, the command rang out, clarion-sharp across every Kamidarian vox-channel. *Oppressors.*

The word was given and so the deed was done. A trigger phrase every shipman had been told to watch out for.

Aboard the heavy cruiser *Honour of the Sword*, Shipmaster Ithion looked up from the vox to his master of ordnance.

He only needed to nod.

In the feast hall, Queen Orlah raised her hand, such a subtle thing, a surreptitious thing, and unleashed violence on them all.

Vychellan roared an oath, and managed to draw his misericordia before the first blow struck his beauteous armour. The pike skidded and then shattered as it met master-crafted auramite. Ten guards had moved to intercept him, a field of pikes angled inwards like they were trying to herd a beast.

The Custodian swept his blade in a wide arc, beheading half the weapons and batting away the others. He leapt forwards, gutted one of the guards and stepped aside to hack the arm from another. More guards joined in, electro-staves crackling. Vychellan took apart another two, slipping from one fighting kata to the next, as slick as molten gold. It was the work of seconds, so swift and unexpected that the rest of the delegation could only watch, unsure of what they were seeing. Kesh felt her mind slow, like how a crash can stretch time like elastic. Horror pinned her in place.

Blood painted the pale stone, floor and columns as Vychellan made for the queen. A cohort of guards interceded and the Custodian looked ready to take on the entire room if necessary. But then they parted in what had to be a prearranged manoeuvre. And that was when the blast rang out. A beam of thermal lethality that scorched the skin as it passed. Those too close to its path recoiled.

Vychellan took it in the shoulder.

He staggered, the room shocked into silence and disbelief.

Kesh gasped. Vychellan was bleeding, his golden war plate

seared through. She didn't know they could bleed. A second beam hit him. It tore off his right arm. A third followed swiftly, coring his chest and he fell, slain.

The rest happened quickly, the Swordsworn stalking forward like hunting dogs, thermal cannons venting even as their other weapon mounts started up. Shouts echoed from the Kamidarian guards, a call to arms, to death and execution.

'Let none live! Let none live!'

Then came the painfully slow scramble as Imperial soldiers who had been disarmed, at ease, realised they had not left the war so far behind after all.

Ceremonial or not, a pistol was still a weapon, and Kesh drew it even as she dragged Viablo behind an upturned table as the gunfire erupted in earnest. She felt him shudder in her grasp, but she didn't have time to figure out why as she was heaving him out of harm's way.

Over the edge of the table as las-fire whipped back and forth, and comrades she had fought beside for years were ignominiously shot and killed, she caught sight of Syreniel. The Sister of Silence leapt from the throng like a shadow. Where the Custodian had edged forward, she had moved unseen and sprang at the queen, her short sword raised. Even divested of her greatblade, she was still immensely dangerous. And she had something else clutched in her grasp, small, fist-sized. Another weapon, hidden. Even a queen, even one as formidable as Orlah Y'Kamidar could not withstand a Talon of the Emperor. As Syreniel soared through the air, intent on murder, Kesh discerned the Silent Sister's role at last. Ardemus had placed an assassin in their ranks, maybe even two, and for a fleeting moment all of the Iron Queen's hatred for the Imperium didn't seem so unjustified.

The killing blow never fell. There was the hard flash of a refractor field and Syreniel was thrown, blade hilt a smoking ruin in her hand, whatever she was carrying skittering away into the masses. Orlah was left unscathed but thronged by her knights. Kesh caught sight of Baron Gerent, a man whom she had spoken to little on the *Virtuous* but one she felt was just and honourable. He protected his queen, his sister, but his face had paled like winter snow.

In moments, he and the others were gone, their charge surrounded by shields and ushered from the hall.

Syreniel had rolled out of her fall, gunfire whipping at her as Kesh watched from behind the upturned table. She grabbed Haster. A secondary mission to get the first lieutenant out. The Navy man had been shot and stabbed more than once. A clutch of pike-armed guards tried to get in her way. She fought them hand-to-hand. At least eight lay dead or critically injured in the Silent Sister's wake, her own armour dented and scored in places.

Kesh could scarcely take her eyes off Syreniel before a terrible whining struck up and one of the other tables being used by a squad of Mordians as a makeshift barricade disintegrated, a hail of bullets from one of the Armigers turning it to kindling. Servitors were caught in the crossfire, twitching and spinning, still clinging to their platters with idiot obedience as they were slowly deconstructed by conflicting streams of las and solid shot.

Kesh had to find Dvorgin. She reckoned twenty or more must be dead and what was left of the Imperial delegation was trying to hunker down and make a break for the exit. The Kamidarians had begun to encircle them, and now Vychellan was dead – and God-Emperor that was a sobering thought – the Armigers had no equal. Kesh doubted even Syreniel could take down one of those war machines. It appeared she had no intention to, fighting a single-handed breakout action with Haster's punctured body slung over her shoulder. Whatever weapon she had once possessed, she either had it no longer or it was no use here.

Then Kesh heard Dvorgin. Rallying the men, trying to impose order. She saw him a second later, his uniform ripped, bloody, missing his hat. He looked old but defiant. They were fighting back. The Kamidarians had fought many foes, but she doubted these palace guards had ever locked swords with a Mordian. A flush of pride came then, partly dousing her fear.

'Historitor, come on,' urged Kesh. If they could just make it across the room and reach Dvorgin and the others... 'Viablo,' she said again, gauging the distance between where they were and where she needed them to be. She snapped her head around to him when he didn't move a third time, despite her tugging on his sleeve. 'Theodore!'

Theodore Viablo was dead. Eyes like dirty glass regarded Kesh, a sad, scared look etched forever on the man's face, his now nerveless fingers clenched around the bullet wound to the heart that had killed him. Such a small amount of blood. It seemed so innocuous really.

A stray las-beam that seared her cheek brought Kesh around. She let him go, his limp arm falling like a tree's dead limb, and scurried from her hiding place. Shots chased her like angry hornets, undirected and just a consequence of the fearsome firefight.

She scrambled across the gap. It seemed to yawn before her, and she caught her ankle in some debris. Slamming hard into her face, Kesh lurched up onto her hands and knees, head turned towards the Armiger that would surely kill her.

The war machine's thermal cannon built to critical mass. No way could she dodge that beam.

Then a misfire, pluming smoke and vented heat and the weapon stalled. She scrambled, knowing providence when she saw it, but the Swordsworn, not to be denied, swung around its other weapon. Solid shot peppered the ground around Kesh, who expected a bullet any second but felt no impact.

She made it to the other side, frantically patting her body down to check for injuries. Emperor's mercy she wasn't hit. *A miracle*. Poor, dead Viablo's old words came back to her and she quashed them.

Less than fifteen Imperial soldiers remained, a mix of Mordians and Pyroxians. They had almost reached one of the doors out of the hall. Kesh had no idea where it led, deeper into the palace she assumed, but she trusted Dvorgin and he was leading the escape.

Syreniel had disappeared again. Perhaps she had found a different way out or maybe she had succumbed too. Kesh thought she would feel it if she had, the absence of that awful presence that they so relied upon now.

Dvorgin bellowed orders, mad shouts against an unforgiving storm as the Kamidarians closed. The only saving grace was the Swordsworn had withdrawn along with their queen, guarding her exit and laying down suppressing fire that the Imperials had no desire or capacity to test. The Sovereigns showed no sign of restraint.

Let none live! The words rebounded in Kesh's subconscious. God-Emperor, what had they done to earn such vitriol?

It took six troopers to breach the door, carved wood hacked apart with blunted blades and pistol shot. It was ruined by the time it fell, and several died just to get them this far. A handful remained, the Kamidarians' fire intensifying now as they realised the massacre neared its end. Kesh, Troopers Willem and Garrod, a captain's adjutant she didn't know, three Pyroxians and Dvorgin himself.

She caught a glimpse of Viablo again as they were retreating, the historitor's outstretched hand just visible though the rest of him was obscured. His fingertips were dabbed red.

'Move, move!' roared Dvorgin, taking potshots with his ceremonial pistol. He looked more alive than he had done in weeks, a man bent on survival – or rather the survival of his men. He killed another Sovereign, a hell of a shot through the gap in the woman's gorget, and exulted with a shout of triumph despite the horror of it all.

'I warrant,' he cried, 'that they haven't had to fight Mordians before, eh, Sergeant Kesh?' He grinned wildly.

Willem was shot in the back and killed as he tried to make for the broken door. 'Let none live!' The cries redoubled from the Kamidarians.

'Give me a single Mordian against ten of theirs,' Dvorgin said, and was shot in the chest before he could fire another burst.

Dvorgin went down, Garrod at his side, shielding the general with his body. He fell next, his back shot to pieces. Kesh scrambled over to them. The captain's adjutant was trying to get Dvorgin to his feet as the three Pyroxians fired back to keep the vengeful Sovereigns at bay.

He looked pale, the old general suddenly seeming every one of his many years and more. But he was alive. The wound in his chest looked bad, though.

'Get him up, up!' snapped Kesh, and between them they heaved. God-Emperor, he felt heavy, his booted feet slipping on blood and unable to support his own weight.

Together, Kesh and the adjutant bundled Dvorgin to the ragged portal, the door frame now hanging in splinters. A grenade went off behind her; Kesh could feel the overpressure of the explosion as it pushed her forwards then down onto the tiled floor. She held on, reduced to dragging Dvorgin, her senses still askew and ears ringing. The adjutant was dead, killed in the blast. The Pyroxians could still be fighting, but she couldn't tell. Sight blurring, she got Dvorgin out just as a section of the lintel above the shattered door collapsed down onto it, effectively cutting her off from the hall, and any Imperials left alive from her.

She paused, unsure whether she should go back, and felt a hand grip her wrist. Kesh looked down at Dvorgin, his face as grey as thin cloud.

'You need to keep moving, sergeant.'

She blinked, still not processing what had happened, what was *happening*.

'I'm getting you out, sir,' she said, barely recognising her own voice. 'We're getting out.'

Up ahead, the shouts of guards, speaking in their native tongue. Kesh didn't need to be a linguist to know they meant her violence.

'Why have they done this?' she said.

'It doesn't matter...' Dvorgin was fading, his grip less assured as he slumped against her, bleeding out. Dying. 'Magda...' he breathed.

Kesh had one eye on the corridor ahead, and the pile of rubble to one side where the open door had been.

'Listen to me... You have to get out. *You*,' he rasped. 'Tell the fleet what happened. The vox... They won't know.'

He gripped her hand, pulled her close until their eyes met. Kesh felt a welling of tears but suppressed them. Dvorgin had trained her to be strong in the face of adversity. She wasn't about to betray that now.

'Magda...' Dvorgin said again. He pressed the old chron into her hand. 'From me to you...' A smile, sad despite its warmth. 'If I had made a different choice all those years ago... I would very much like to have had a daughter like...'

His last breath escaped in a long, trembling sigh and his grip fell slack, his body a dead weight.

Kesh bowed her head, the tears she had fought to stifle running freely now. Her pain quickly gave way to anger as the four guards appeared from around the corner at the end of the corridor. Gently laying him down, she held out her pistol.

'For Luthor Dvorgin,' she whispered. At least she would go down fighting. Then she saw the charge gauge on her pistol read empty. She almost laughed at the irony of it.

Sensing her vulnerability, the guards slowed and drew swords. They wanted to hurt her, and make her end a bloody one.

'You'll regret that,' she told them, about to reach for the sabre but finding the belt empty, the scabbard ripped away and lost in the panic. She hadn't even realised. Releasing a long breath, she balled her fists instead.

'I am a daughter of Mordian, born in darkness, I fear no shadow, not even death.'

It was an old litany, but then again she liked those ones the best. It felt fitting in the circumstances.

Chapter Nineteen

CHAINS

ESCAPING THE VEIL

A ROYAL DECLARATION

The chain was a sacred instrument, each link a symbolically inviolable promise. To never retreat, to never turn a blind eye to injustice, to never break an oath. Its purpose was to bind, in both a literal and metaphorical sense.

Oaths too were sacred. To an order like the Astartes, and even more so to the Black Templars of Sigismund, the words spoken in the making of an oath were as intractable as if inscribed on parchment or chiselled into stone. By uttering them, they attained permanence. In ancient times, millennia ago, those of the old Legion would swear their oaths before battle, witnessed by their brethren or those whom they would fight alongside. They would take the knee, blade rested upon their forehead or laid upon their lap, or sword point to the ground with head bowed, depending on the warrior's individual custom, and an oath of moment would be spoken. And in speaking it, it would be binding until the oath was fulfilled, or the warrior was killed and thus the oath broken.

The chain was a reminder, fastened to their weapons, wrapped around gauntlet and vambrace. Never yield, never lay down your arms. Never break your oath.

Morrigan had failed in that charge. He had let Bohemund die, both oath and chains broken in one colossal moment of being found wanting. He had become the 'Unchained', those trailing links a tangible reminder of his failure. He swore that day in the reliquarius that he would not fail again; that any oath he made would be fulfilled or he would die in the attempt.

And so it was that the Unchained had bound himself for good or for ill, for an oath has no conscience, nor once spoken can it be unspoken. It merely *is*. The only certainty was the weight it carried, like the weight of the chain. Only some burdens were heavier than others.

Shadows filled the strategium of Sturmhal, a spare, stone-clad room filled with serfs at metal consoles, their faces lit by the penumbral green light from many vid-screens. Morrigan stood amongst them, a giant in black war plate, his helm clutched under one arm, his other hand on the pommel of his blade, Pious. Recyc fans did their best to filter the air and cool the generator heat, and stirred the purity seals of his armour.

'Run it again.'

In his absence, whilst hunting for the traitor Graeyl Herek, the lunar fastness of the Black Templars had received a second transmission. They had also been alerted by deep-space augur to the presence of the large fleet currently at anchor outside Kamidar's orbit. As Godfried had warned several hours before, the Imperium had arrived.

The hololith projector whirred as it came back to life, spilling out a cone of hardened light in which the queen's aide was rendered in grainy grey monochrome. She was armoured, in breastplate and shoulder guard, her attire and manner that of a warrior. Morrigan knew she did this to appeal to the Black Templars' martial sensibilities and could hardly fault the sagacity in that.

'*Noble warriors of the Black Templars order, I come to you humbled and in need of counsel. I speak on behalf of Queen Orlah, who has convened the royal court of Kamidar and beseeches your presence. Great matters are afoot, nothing less than the sovereignty of the protectorate at stake. The Imperium has come. It has come.*'

There the recording ended, stalled in awkward freeze-frame, the image juddering as if broken.

Morrigan gave a shallow nod and the hololith shut down, the darkness sweeping back in its wake.

'And the fleet,' he asked, 'how large is it exactly?'

The station mistress, Hekatani, answered. 'It is sizeable, my lord, the exact composition difficult to determine at this time but the ship signatures are all Imperial. It carries the designation "Praxis", which leads us to believe–'

'It's part of the crusade,' Morrigan said for her, but he already knew that.

Hekatani had served the Black Templars for many years, first aboard ship, and now here in the lunar fortress they occupied in the Ironhold. She was a gifted logister and ran a tight crew. Her tenure on the *Mourning Star* had ended when she had lost her left leg in an accident in one of the cargo holds. They had not been in battle and the accident wasn't combat related. It was simply unlucky. Hekatani had accepted and learned to live with it. She had refused a bionic, even when the sacristans of House Kamidar had offered one, stating the injury would not define her but serve as a reminder to be more careful in the future.

As such she did not rise when she addressed Morrigan, and had sequestered herself to Sturmhal when the rigours aboard ship became untenable. Instead, she mastered the strategium and became the conduit through which all information pertaining to the lunar fortress and its immediate environs was relayed.

'Yes, my lord,' she replied, turning in her chair so as to better face the Black Templar. 'It has been six years, but they are here.'

Morrigan said nothing at first, scrutinising the large vid-display in the middle of the cramped room. The screen looked like polished onyx and depicted the fleet relative to the various celestial bodies of the protectorate. Strange to see these great ships, several capable of single-handedly destroying entire worlds, rendered to nondescript markers accompanied by their Navy designation codes.

'We have determined the flagship as the *Fell Lord*, an Emperor-class vessel. Archives point to a storied history,' Hekatani went on.

Morrigan didn't recognise the name, but a vessel that size meant a significant deployment.

'Efforts have been made to contact the fleet but have so far failed. There is...' Hekatani reached for the right words. '*Interference,*' she concluded.

Morrigan looked at her quizzically.

'The master of vox believes there is some kind of jamming, my lord.'

'To what end?'

'That is an extremely good question.'

'Something feels off here,' said Dagomir, stepping into the cast-off light from the vid-screens so he was at his captain's shoulder.

Part of the reason the strategium felt so cramped was that Morrigan had not come alone. Three fully armoured Black Templars, Godfried still wearing his helm despite the stifling confines of the room, stood at ease behind him. They had cracks in their war plate and were gently bleeding onto Hekatani's otherwise pristine floor. She scowled, her gaze meeting Morrigan's, who gave a tilt of the head by way of apology.

'I agree,' he said, feeling that sense of powerlessness rise anew, uncomfortable, unfamiliar. He wanted to take a ship, several ships, and intercede in whatever was brewing here, but they had no time. The *Mourning Star* would need repair. For now, they were grounded. Perhaps he should have sent that emissary after all?

The deep-space augurs that orbited the lunar fortress were

coming into closer proximity again, completing their patrol arcs. They were only seconds from a visual.

Hekatani relayed it to a mosaic of screens dominating the east wall of the chamber. The iconographic representation of the Imperial fleet blinked away, replaced by a static-impaired image of the deep void and a host of distant starships at anchor.

'One moment, lord,' she said, adjusting her instruments deftly before the image resolved more cleanly.

Even partially obscured by the debris of the Iron Veil, the Imperial fleet looked potent. Rarely had Morrigan seen this many ships and not a one at battle stations, their turrets lowered, their broadsides shuttered. By contrast, a line of Kamidarian vessels anchored at the edge of the planet's high atmosphere had rolled out their guns. Black pennants adorned every one, stiff in the airless void.

A funereal honour guard.

He exchanged a look with Dagomir. Missing a limb, he should have been in the apothecarion but Morrigan knew not to argue with the stubborn veteran.

'The return of the honoured dead,' said Dagomir. 'One of the royal household.'

A dozen vessels stood apart from the armada's main complement, separated by the dense barrier of the Iron Veil. A narrow channel led through these defences. The Black Templars, as allies of the protectorate, knew of others, routes through the minefields and weapon arrays, but for the outsiders this was the only obvious way through. They faced off against the Kamidarian ships, several miles between them.

'Is the vox silence meant as a sign of respect?' asked Anglahad at Morrigan's other shoulder. Godfried remained sentinel behind his brothers. His lens-sheathed gaze did not leave the vid-screen either.

'It's possible...' muttered Dagomir.

Morrigan stared without answer. The magnification did not

allow for much in the way of detail but he could imagine the Kamidarian ships powering to fire, the subtle shift in their aspects an indication of such.

'Something is happening,' said Anglahad.

'The Kamidarian fleet is preparing to fire, my lord,' said Hekatani, her face close to her instruments as the power signatures she was monitoring began to spike.

'A salute to the fallen,' said Dagomir.

Then, abruptly – but also in stately slowness that only a great vessel of the line could effect – the Imperial fleet rolled out its own guns. It was done without coordination, as if an urgent order had come down the line. Turrets spurred into motion, prow lances glowed.

The image abruptly cut out at the worst possible moment, turning to static.

Morrigan quirked an eyebrow, perturbed. 'What happened? More interference?'

Hekatani interrogated her instruments, a hand held to the vox-bead in her ear as she listened to the reports of her crew.

'Not sure, my lord. We have lost the feed. It could be the same jamming that is hindering the vox just catching up.'

Morrigan had seen the vid-feed up to the point it failed. He had seen two small flotillas take aim with their guns. He had seen the flare of imminent weapon ignition. He exchanged a look with Dagomir, whose face was grave.

'I don't like the look of this,' he confessed.

Morrigan gave a faint shake of the head. 'Nor I.'

Ardemus shut down the klaxons, siphoning away residual panic, anger, any emotion that would cloud the next few critical moments.

Bridge crew hustled to enact his orders, pulling the *Fell Lord* from the firestorm that had erupted around her and the other ships in the Imperial vanguard. According to the short-range

augur, one vessel, the *Venetor*, had taken critical damage. A static-
hazed visual showed her listing in the void, venting fuel and lower
decks crew. Ardemus had sent transports in response to her distress hails, but the ship itself was lost. Alert icons flashed on the
data-slate built into his throne's armrest, minor damage reports,
shield integrity updates and other chatter. He swept them away
with his fingers, focusing instead on what was operational.

They had taken a few hits before the shields went up. Ardemus had given the order to raise them whilst running from the
strategium. He had coded it with an emergency cipher and had
it widecast across the entire armada with his emergency command ident. The order to open fire had followed. He had seen
the enemy's intent through the oculus.

A subtle thing, easily missed, the gentle shifting of aspects, a
minor adjustment in turret elevation. The Kamidarians had turned
their guns. They had deafened Praxis first, cutting off vox-comms,
and then they had angled to fire upon them.

Ardemus cursed himself for not seeing it sooner. Orlah had
betrayed the Imperium. She had put her sovereignty above the
empire.

And now he had a real problem.

His pre-emptive salvo had been only marginally effective. Only
the *Fell Lord* herself and the *Valiant Spear* had acted quickly enough
before the Kamidarians had launched their planned attack. This
side of the Iron Veil, they outnumbered the Imperials more than
four to one. Simply put, it was an engagement they could not
hope to win. And the bottleneck of wreckage behind made retreat
complicated.

Nonetheless, five vessels had engaged, prow lances spearing
into the void in angry jabs of light. Shield impacts registered several minutes later. In void-faring terms, the two lines of opposing
ships were close.

Return fire came with interest, the Kamidarian ships moving

abeam to unleash their more powerful broadsides. The *Bellicose Hunter* took the worst of it, a shield failure leaving the cruiser exposed. Her prow armour weathered the salvo well, but her flank exploded across several decks.

Torpedoes launched, a thick spread, as two more Imperial vessels joined the five who had engaged. The first true hit on a Kamidarian ship was met with cheers from the bridge crew of the *Fell Lord*, which was moving into a fresh aspect of attack as the nova cannon in her prow built to critical mass.

Pledges of assistance flooded the admiral's vox as the rest of Praxis behind the vanguard began to jockey for position to navigate the bottleneck through the Iron Veil. He curtly denied them all. To attack through such a narrow aperture would only prevent the ships in the vanguard from withdrawing. The signal from the master of ordnance declared the nova cannon at readiness. Ardemus gave the order to fire.

The immense shell blazed through the darkness like a fired comet. It took a Kamidarian cruiser amidships, overwhelming its shields before punching a gaping hole through its hull. After a few minutes the ship began to list badly, its engines guttering and then failing. Lights went out across the entire starboard side and the turrets dipped. A critical hit. She was dead in the void.

Another cheer from the crew. Despite himself, Ardemus clenched a fist but knew the battle was already lost. Reinforcements were joining the honour guard, ships that had been kept at a remove but not so far away that their presence would not immediately be felt in the battlesphere.

Two Imperial ships, the *Venetor* and the *Ardent Saviour*, drifted in the void. A third had been destroyed, sundered in two. Together with the *Bellicose Hunter*, whose desperate crewmen were still fleeing the stricken ship in transports and saviour pods, that left eight operational vessels in the Imperial vanguard. Now the odds were five to one.

Ardemus leaned forwards in his throne, declaring into the master vox, 'All ships, all ships, withdraw behind the Veil.' He bellowed at his helmsman, 'Mister Blake, pull us out at half power. In good order, Mister Blake, a panic now would be just as calamitous as facing those Kamidarian guns without shields.'

Via data-slate, he relayed concise instructions for withdrawal to all shipmasters. The *Brutus* had already moved up ahead of the *Fell Lord* to shield the flagship. The *Brutus* was a hefty vessel, well armoured, a warhorse of the void. She would withstand whatever the Kamidarians threw at her, but rather than press their advantage, if anything the native fleet appeared to back off, their fire lessening.

'They want to chase us off...' muttered Ardemus, the thought pricking at his pride more than it should. But what then? Several landers and their troop complements, not to mention the delegation led by Haster, still remained on the world, as well as the *Vortun's Ire* at high anchor. He had heard from none of them and so was left to imagine their fates.

Syreniel, his assassin, evidently had failed in her mission. *Any sign of aggression, terminate without hesitation.*

A bold strategy but boldness won wars or, in this case, negotiations. She was not his only ploy. One must always have a reserve.

He had done his research on Kamidar; he knew the Knight world could be a glittering jewel in the Anaxian Line, as good a redoubt as any, but for the queen. Bringing back the corpse of her daughter and heiress had not been the peace offering he had hoped. In retrospect, the decision to send Haster had been a shrewd one or it would be Ardemus in shackles, or even worse, perhaps, and the armada at the mercy of the natives.

Another salvo exploded against the shields, sending ripples of impact through the *Fell Lord*'s frame that had it groaning from prow to stern. The *Brutus* had performed her task well, though she burned from a hundred fires or more, guttering like a defiant candle against a storm wind. A bulwark, she advanced inexorably on the Kamidarian line, momentum more than true engine power giving her speed. Sheer mass gave her threat, until the Kamidarians destroyed her. Ardemus' last sight of the *Brutus* was of her breaking apart under heavy bombardment, a fireship that would never reach her quarry. Five vessels lost in a single disastrous engagement.

He said a prayer for the captain and the crew.

Then the Iron Veil was sliding by either side, visible through the port and starboard viewers but glacial in its slowness. In such peace and quietude did starships walk the void. It belied the violence. Ardemus had always marvelled at that. It was why he sought out a Navy commission in the first place. His thoughts drifted, unmoored from the moment, and he was swift to drag them back.

The *Fell Lord* was the first to enter the ring of wreckage and the first to leave, back into the embrace of the rest of Praxis, whose ships all chafed at the bit to take on the Kamidarian fleet themselves. Ardemus still had no desire for any of his captains to fight in a bottleneck, so reined them back.

She had chosen her battleground well and seized the initiative, and as he left the field, away from immediate danger, he thought about those stricken husks in that graveyard of vessels Orlah had surrounded her world with and privately confessed he was glad not to be amongst them.

Ariadne should have seen it coming. In the moment, in the aftermath of the skirmish, it seemed incomprehensible but later, when she was able to reflect on the events of that day, she would realise how inevitable it all was.

'I need water here.' She was still running the lines of injured Mordians and the odd Solian caught in the earlier skirmish. Absently, she noted a vox-trooper still working to restore communications, the woman's face crumpled with a frown at every thwarted attempt.

At least four different vox-stations laboured at the problem, their officers ringed around them in expectant silence.

An orderly in a medicae's cadre handed Ariadne a flask and she took it gratefully. There was still much to be done, though she spared a glance for Usullis, who had recovered from his shaming. Her knuckles still ached from when she had punched him, but it was a good pain. She smiled inwardly at the thought of it as the other quartermaster senioris skulked off to lick his wounds and, doubtless, plan his revenge. Such a petty, small man. She had met many during her service. All of them craved power, recognition, but had neither the will nor the wit to deserve either.

As she bent down to offer a sip of water to one of the wounded, her eye drifted to the night and the ranks of the Sovereigns. Mercifully, they had withdrawn, their gold armour softened in the moonlight. Such quiet tension now, so different from the horrors of before. But as she looked, she noticed something else and the flask she was carrying slid down to her side. The Sovereigns were gathering, almost mustering, their strange accents faint on the air as they called back and forth. A few glanced to an even more distant and, to Ariadne's eyes, more forbidding horizon.

The Marines Malevolent were moving – no, *stalking*. She saw them edging into her peripheral vision, their cold retinal lenses on the Sovereigns. Battle-sign flashed back and forth. Suddenly, Ariadne wanted to find Ogin.

Something was moving up ahead, into the Runstaf hinterlands, far away but getting closer.

The air felt febrile, thick with anticipation. Conversations stopped abruptly. Even the rowdier Solians fell silent. Troopers gazed northward into the night, experiencing the same sense of encroachment as Ariadne had felt.

A hand on her shoulder made her start, and she suppressed a yelp. A face with all the severity of a storm-tossed sea looked down on her.

'You should get behind me now, visha...' uttered Ogin, somewhat ominously, and it stole away the rebuke half-formed on her lips. He had appeared as if from shadow, moving like the wind, like lightning without thunder. A drawn szabla sat in his hand. In the other, his bolter. His eyes seemed to focus on something Ariadne could not see as he shifted them to the horizon.

'What is it?' she asked, chafing at the querulousness in her voice.

The Storm Reaper gently ushered her into his wake, and then she saw others of his Chapter following him as he advanced northward into the darkness. A pregnant stillness fell like winter frost or an ocean becalmed. It deafened her, numbed her, and the fear of it seized her in unseen talons.

Static roared, an unwelcome intruder, and then came voices. Vox-troopers at their stations, all talking in a cascade.

The Marines Malevolent sped up, a purposeful advance turning into a light run.

Realisation sunk in then; it swept around the troops like a plague, infecting all with its terror.

No one would ever know how the word had got out from the palace. Maybe it was an officer leading a daring escape or maybe it was dumb luck or an act of self-preservation that had turned into something else. It didn't matter. The message relayed was the same.

The Marines Malevolent charged at some unseen signal, ripping through the Sovereigns who had bravely chosen to engage them. The Astartes gave no quarter, they barely slowed. Men in the white and gold of Kamidar broke apart against this onslaught, shredded and dismembered. The brutality of it stunned Ariadne, who had never seen Space Marines at war. Such cold and terrifying efficiency, the utter destruction of their enemies. It wasn't just death, it was *dissolution*.

And then Ogin was amongst it all and so were his kin, and

she dared to hope they had come to stop it, to stop the inhuman butchery but they ran on, beyond the melee and out the other side to something else, to something in the darkness. The encroaching fear.

Ariadne grabbed a Mordian trooper who was being called to arms. 'What in the hells is happening?'

He was a young man, dumbstruck at first, struggling to comprehend.

One of the Storm Reapers, Ogin's captain, bellowed a phrase in his native Jagun. It carried despite the distance.

'Ung tar vuk!'

Only later would Ariadne learn its meaning. 'It is war.'

Bright lights flared in the night, brighter than summer flame, and they stabbed through the dark like lances, illuminating a towering form. A Knight. Steam plumed from its engine stacks, heat glow clung to its weapon mounts in a throbbing aura. The grilled mask of its helm, so pitiless, so familiar and yet simultaneously inhuman. A god-machine strode the night, an avatar of war incarnate. It had not come alone. Two of its equally terrifying kin stood alongside it.

A trio of war-horns answered the Storm Reaper's challenge, so loud Ariadne pressed her hands over her ears.

The trooper found his voice at last. 'She's declared war on us,' he said, fighting back a stammer of fear. 'The queen of Kamidar has declared war on the Imperium.'

PART TWO

IT IS WAR

Chapter Twenty

BITTER DRAUGHTS

A RECKONING

AN UNLIKELY REPRIEVE

As Lareoc sat in the darkness of his Throne Mechanicum, he reflected on the events that had led him here. With the haptic and mental connection to the machine, he perceived the susurrant voices of the ancestors of House Solus in his mind, the warriors who had piloted *Heart of Glory* before him. This communion was unique to Knight pilots and a means of connecting to the noble lineage of the past. It was a repository of sorts, of knowledge and tactics, history. A means of connecting man, or woman, to the machine. Some of the voices raged at the callousness of the queen and ruling House Kamidar, others counselled caution; most were silent and left the baron to his own thoughts.

These thoughts came thick and heady, like too much smoke from a burning house. In seconds they resolved from the abstract into the rampant flames of a battlefield...

Heriot was dead, the blaze licking through the eye slits of Sword of Valour *the only sign Lareoc needed that they were outnumbered and possibly outmatched. Two blasts of his war-horn heralded the retreat.*

'We're going back, my lord?' asked Idrius of Shield Maiden, *one of only three Knights of House Solus, including* Heart of Glory, *left on the field. It stood like a giant iron sentinel, several hundred feet between it and Lareoc's own war machine. Both cut a lonely figure, their legs wreathed by low-hanging smoke, their bodies limned with firelight. Everything as far as the eye or the augur could see was burnt amber and shadow. They had been ordered to hold the line and await reinforcements. The world was ending and they had been ordered to stand their ground.*

'Stay and we die, Lady Idrius,' Lareoc replied simply, his voice coming to her through the internal vox-network. 'If we can reach the hills, we can use the natural terrain to slow them down.'

By 'them', Lareoc referred to the horde. Barely visible advancing through the flames, which was all that remained of the farms and homesteads the invaders had put to the torch, were monsters. Infernal engines, wrought by madmen, had come to Kamidar. It was a great host, and not the first since the Astronomican's light had gone dark. Some said these were the end times. Swathes of smoke obliterating his lands from sight, the sound of murder and suffering on the blood-hot breeze, Lareoc could believe it. He stilled a tremulous thought, the words of his ancestors through the Throne Mechanicum steeling him. The shadows out in the blazing fields grew closer. He almost missed the fact Idrius was speaking.

'...we could make a stand at the manse,' she was saying, her voice clarion clear across the vox. He liked Idrius, always the optimist. 'The outer precincts are well defended and–'

'I won't draw the enemy there, too many of our citizens have taken refuge in its arbours and would fall beneath the sword. The fight must stay between us.'

'And what of the queen?' asked Golen, the third of the Solus Knights. His tread shook the earth as he walked up alongside the

others. Even through his own machine's oculus, Lareoc could see Golen had seen serious combat but wore every scar like a medal. He rode War Herald, *a Castellan and one of their most powerful remaining engines. 'Is she coming?'*

Lareoc didn't answer at first. The vox connection to the royal army had been silent for the last few hours. His last communication had come from Martial Exultant, *that bastard Kingsward as curt and ignorant as ever. He had hoped to speak with the queen herself, to implore her aid, but Baerhart was having none of it.*

'We're on our own for now,' he said, unable to mask his bitterness.

'If we leave now,' said Golen, 'there will be nothing to halt the destruction of our lands. The horde will run amok.'

Lareoc gazed blankly at the last of the Armigers and the few armoured cohorts of household troops as they gathered nearby for an ordered retreat. 'They are already running amok, Golen.' He sighed with resignation. 'We're headed for the hills. There, we may stand a chance.'

'You'll never reach it,' said Golen flatly. 'They're close and picking up momentum. Soon as they've picked over Sword of Valour's *corpse, they'll be on us. I'll stymie them,* War Herald *and I.'*

'That's a death sentence, Golen.'

'It's all a death sentence now, my lord.'

The crackling of flames and distant screaming filled the brief silence. Lareoc knew the Castellan was right.

'It has been an honour and a privilege.'

'Likewise, my lord.'

Lareoc and Idrius raised the reaper blades mounted on their war frames in grim salute before Golen turned, issuing a horn blast, and walked back into the night.

A shudder ran through him, then a soothing word from the elders brought Lareoc back around. The present loomed again, stretched out before him with all its potential and threat. Lately, he reflected, he had been spending too much time in the past.

Memory was a bitter draught, he'd found, worse even than the priest's elixir running through his veins. The concoction had put him on edge, like a naked blade resting against his skin. Even his breath came out hot – but then again the confines of his Knight were stifling. He tried to imagine the cool rain tinkling against the chassis of his war machine hitting his skin instead, dappling it in bright starlit globules. It didn't work. The morning was early and the valley was cool with predawn dew as green as any on Kamidar. But within, the heat reigned.

Like that battlefield from years ago. Such pointless, stupid valour. All of it.

Orlah had seen the crisis as a chance to consolidate her power. Those who craved ambition were often best at seizing opportunity. Her brother, Gerent, a man for whom Lareoc had great respect, had once tempered his sister's tyrannical leanings, but he had been sent away to distant wars, and the upholding of old oaths. How they had become slaves to their ancestral past. It would be laughable were it not all so tragic.

Orlah had taken over. She had claimed it was for the sovereignty and security of Kamidar, but Lareoc saw through all of that. Rulers wanted to rule, it was that simple. And Orlah was nothing if not a ruler. Now he had to end it. He had no desire to overthrow an empire. Even had he wanted to, he did not have the martial might or the influence. He merely wanted a return to days gone, when the monarch was a servant of the people and not a tyrant. Orlah stood in the way of that. Her will, her stubborn refusal to relinquish power and dilute it amongst the nobles. Kamidar could become a republic again and not the sole dominion of Orlah Y'Kamidar.

All he had to do was kill a queen.

Getting to her would not be easy, though, especially with her bloodhound ever hungry and in search of him and his kin. She called Lareoc brigand, outlaw, a rabble-rouser turned enemy of the state. He was all of this and none of it.

I am a liberator, he thought, sad that freedom could only be bought through blood. To remove the queen was one thing, a distant glint in the firmament of his plan; first he must lure and kill the hound.

He had not been entirely truthful to Parnius about the attack on the Imperial convoy. Yes, he had wanted to stir up trouble, but it was more calculated than that. He knew Baerhart would not be able to resist returning to the site of the ambush and find there what his attendants could not. For as long as he had known him, the Kingsward had been a consummate warrior, but he was also supremely arrogant.

The valley was an obvious place for a trap and the ever-so-subtle trail Lareoc had left leading to it could only have been found by a hunter as dogged and observant as his prey. The prize it promised is what would draw him, an elusive quarry harried into a mistake. Too late the hunter would realise the mistake was his.

Baerhart had come, as Lareoc knew he would. The Kingsward feared no brigands, even one with a god-machine. He had brought his own, his *Martial Exultant.* An immense war engine, one of the largest in the entire Kamidarian host, a Warden that had seen many battles. It strode up to the valley mouth, the early morning mist peeling away from its bulky chassis like a deep-sea leviathan rising through a pall of ocean fog. Its reactors bled steam into the air and its thermal cannon hummed dully in the gloom.

He had come alone, not wanting to share glory, and that would be enough even for what Lareoc had in mind. His own engine had an injury to its left leg, oil and smoke venting. An added enticement to his prey; also a fiction, and a well-wrought one by the few sacristans still loyal to House Solus. It didn't matter if Baerhart believed it or not. He would not be able to resist the bait.

'He will kill you, Lareoc,' Parnius said through the internal vox.

Lareoc had chosen not to comment on his friend's refusal of the ritual. It was his right, after all, for Lareoc could not claim to espouse freedom if he didn't allow it to his comrades, but it had put Parnius slightly apart from the rest of the Knights of Hurne.

'Then at least I will die gloriously and be a burden to you no longer, my friend.'

'Can you not take even this seriously, Lareoc? He will kill you. You are a fine warrior, one of the best I have known, and lucky with it, but this is Baerhart DeVikor, the Lord of Harrowkeep, and the Kingsward. There is no better fighter in all of Kamidar.'

It was true. In plain terms, Baerhart was a master swordsman, only his sword in this case was a Knight which he wielded with deadly precision and aggression. He also wielded an actual sword, a rare piece delved in ancient days and repurposed by the royal sacristans. He named it Seeker, for some men can only truly possess a thing if they first name it. An apt title, for in Baerhart's hands it was unerring.

'You trust too much in that old priest's tinctures,' Parnius added, and Lareoc thought he detected a note of regret... No, not regret. Sadness.

'Live or die, Parnius,' Lareoc answered and raised his reaver blade in challenge. 'We are about to find out.'

The two Knights stood over half a mile apart, their sheer size making them easily visible. Baerhart had the larger engine, a brute of a thing bristling with weapon mounts and that devastating power sword, which he raised in a gesture, as if willing the Knight Errant's destruction. His faceplate had been shaped by an ironsmith to represent a portcullis and one of the pennants that snapped beneath the engine's legs depicted a spiked crown in silver against a red background, Baerhart's personal sigil. Next to it hung a second pennant with the gold sword of Kamidar upraised on a white field. His carapace was red, like dark wine, and emblazoned with honour markings, campaign badges and icons of fealty.

A squeal of static preceded the activation of vox-emitters, and floor like a tidal wave.

'*A sundered knight from a sundered house, bereft of honour.*'

Despite his earlier insouciance, Lareoc felt his teeth gritting at the repeated insult.

'*You have been found wanting, Ser Lareoc,*' Baerhart continued. '*I am sent here to bring you to heel to stand before the queen, shamed, but I think I will just kill you instead and save the trouble of carrying your sorry carcass back to Gallanhold.*'

After that, Baerhart was all business and didn't wait for a response. He had made his declaration as honour dictated. He let off a blast of his war-horn and began to advance.

To fight the Kingsward was to fight death itself. Any man knew that, but in the strange solemnity of the Throne Mechanicum, Lareoc smiled. The draught had started to bite. He felt enhanced strength in his limbs, his focus honing to a sharp and deadly point. Whatever the priest had put in his concoction, he had harnessed the natural vigour of the earth.

'Come on, you bastard...' Lareoc urged, and answered with his own horn blast.

A sense of utter confidence filled him, growing with every second. A few voices of the past protested but Lareoc scowled at them, master of his own will.

'I don't care if it isn't honourable,' he muttered, 'I only care that he is dead at the end of it.'

Martial Exultant fired a salvo from its gatling cannon. Muzzle flame flared as the high-calibre rounds splashed against *Heart of Glory*'s ion shield in shimmers of iridescent light.

'You'll need to do better than that, old man...' Lareoc replied, engaging the heavy stubber. Bullets ripped up the valley floor, stitching a line all the way to *Martial Exultant*'s flank. It was meant as a desultory sting. Baerhart didn't raise his ion shield but let the rounds rattle his Knight's armour. Sparks cascaded, scorch marks marred his perfect livery but otherwise left him unscathed. It was a show of power, a strut before the reckoning. Baerhart wanted to gut *Heart of Glory* up close and fed power to the engines of his god-machine.

Lareoc stood his ground, *Heart of Glory* champing to be unleashed. Belligerent voices from the past willed him to charge. He quelled them, charging up his thermal cannon instead.

'Parnius...' he ventured. *Martial Exultant* was still coming.

Out on the valley floor, they had laid a line of staves, nearly invisible to the eye unless you were looking for them. *Martial Exultant* had just reached them.

'He's across, he's across!'

'Then do it now,' Lareoc answered urgently, spurring his own engines to anger. The feigned injury to his leg faded away to nothing, its duplicity revealed.

'If you do this, you'll be trapped in here with him.'

'That is the entire point. Do it, Parnius!'

Heart of Glory had begun to advance, slow at first but building momentum. Lareoc aimed straight at *Martial Exultant*. The reaver blade began to churn; he felt it like a sympathetic nerve tremor in his arm.

Numerous threat warnings flashed onto his heads-up screen as *Martial Exultant* closed. Lareoc unleashed a burst from his thermal cannon, the air searing in its wake, but the other Knight took it on its swiftly raised ion shield, barely breaking stride.

'Damn it, Parnius!'

The end of the valley exploded a second later, the entire mouth collapsing in a heave of rubble and flame. A magazine of incendiaries ensured it was sealed and at the other end of the valley a cliff of ink-dark granite effectively boxed them in, a natural arena from which there was no escape. Only now did *Martial Exultant* falter, but only fractionally, as Baerhart resumed his headlong charge.

But there was more...

Hidden within a pair of natural caves in the rock, hard to see from the valley mouth and veiled with dust-drenched tarpaulins, came two smaller engines. *Pledge of Fealty* and *Noble Son* were Armigers, ridden by Henniger and Martinus. Both were kinsmen and fellow discontents. Both were newly christened Knights of Hurne.

Too late for *Martial Exultant* to retreat, Baerhart came at *Heart of Glory* with even greater vigour, heedless of the Armigers attempting to encircle him. Lareoc had committed also, both Knights tilting at each other like their forebears of old. They were seconds away from striking a blow when a ray of sunlight breached cloud, catching the edge of *Martial Exultant*'s armour. It looked glorious, its panoply gleaming, and for a fleeting moment Lareoc felt doubt.

Seeker struck, a fork of lightning against the day. Lareoc felt it gouge carapace, tear strips from his armour. A pained grimace turned his features sour and he bit back a cry. His own reaver blade cut but poorly, the teeth skidding against *Martial Exultant*'s shoulder and making an ugly mark but little else. The impact was huge, sending tremors throughout his body, the world shaken to its bones. A desperate flash of light and pain, and it was over, momentum carrying the two Knights well beyond the exchange of blows.

As they were pulled apart, *Heart of Glory* dug in its heels and turned. Together with his brothers, he would close the trap on Baerhart. Three engines against one, even one as superior as *Martial Exultant*, and with the priest's draught giving them the edge... the Kingsward had no chance.

But rather than stand its ground or opt for defence, *Martial Exultant* had kept moving. It bent straight at one of the Armigers, haring off its straight course and taking a wash of hard rounds against its flank.

Baerhart replied with a terrifyingly accurate burst of gatling fire into the Armiger. *Pledge of Fealty* had been gaining on him but hadn't gauged for how far momentum would carry *Martial Exultant*. Henniger had inadvertently outflanked himself. The raking salvo from the gatling cannon tore up the Armiger's side, severing an arm mount entirely and leaving it with just its chain-cleaver burring impotently.

Instinctively, *Pledge of Fealty* backed off, a wounded animal reacting to its pain, before a servo blew and it ground to a halt, effectively nullifying its threat.

Noble Son strode in from the opposite side, heavy stubber chattering wildly but far enough away that it scored few hits, the small explosions rippling down *Martial Exultant*'s armour little more than insect stings.

Wise enough not to get too close, Martinus kept up the pressure and switched to *Noble Son*'s thermal spear, but Baerhart swung the ion shield around to preserve his war engine and a dense flare of light lit up the near-invisible barrier. Rather than slow his momentum even then, he redoubled his speed to chase down the second Armiger. Martinus evaded at first, his lighter engine nimble compared to the hulking Warden, but the valley was tight and rock-strewn. Its thermal spear throwing out ragged beams of heat, *Noble Son* ran into Baerhart's sights, the Kingsward catching it full on with a burst of gatling fire.

The lighter engine staggered and jerked as it was struck, first losing an arm then a leg before it collapsed in a fiery heap. Loosing a blast from his war-horn, Baerhart would have made sure of the engine kill were it not for the vengeful *Heart of Glory* now bearing down on him.

The thermal cannon's beam went wild, a fog affecting Lareoc's aim. Anger clouded his thoughts, the tang of guilt bitter in his mouth as he witnessed the two Armigers practically unmade in a matter of seconds. The voices counselled caution and he raged at them too. Blood pulsed in his head, a heavy throb like the tattoo of a drum.

Martial Exultant turned to face him, a deft manoeuvre few pilots could pull off with such precision. Gatling cannon roaring, Baerhart strafed at the other Knight's midriff, trying to sever it at the narrow junction between legs and torso. Hastily, Lareoc still had enough about him to lift his ion shield to intercede, but the Knights were close and the heavy impacts rocked him on his giant servos. Thunderclaps resounded within the Throne Mechanicum.

Baerhart met him with *Martial Exultant*, sword swinging. Lareoc parried, or as much as a god-machine can parry, turning Seeker aside in a heady churn of sparks and squealing metal. A slow but brutal ballet of sorts ensued, one Knight striking at the other, the larger Warden using its bulk to crowd the lesser Errant and force it back.

Warning klaxons drowned out all sound, his heads-up screen a mass of damage reports and proximity warnings. Many a Knight had died in such savage chaos. Lareoc stepped back a pace, the heat was stifling, letting his opponent come at him and used the half-breath of space to get his reaper blade under *Martial Exultant*'s guard.

The cut was deep, telling. He'd wounded it. A clenched fist celebrated the small victory but it was far from over. The return thrust near tore *Heart of Glory*'s thermal cannon from its mount and Lareoc blinked, scarcely able to accept what had happened. He had barely seen the blow. Arm half-cleaved, *Heart of Glory* staggered, a chorus of voices in Lareoc's ear telling him to retreat. It near overwhelmed him.

Martial Exultant backed off too, a tiny isthmus growing between the Knights. Baerhart filled it with the gatling cannon's fury, spearing *Heart of Glory* through the torso, cleverly skirting his salvo around the raised ion shield.

Numerous systems failing, hydraulics, targeting, a haze of nerve-shredding static fouling his screen, Lareoc had the deep sensation of impending defeat. He railed at it, at the injustice, incredulous at how Baerhart had escaped the trap and bested them all.

Unable to resist a final gloat, Baerhart's vox-emitters crackled to life.

'You live like an outlaw cur, you will die like an outlaw cur.'

He levelled Seeker, proclaiming death. No longer feigned, *Heart of Glory*'s leg faltered as Lareoc tried to flee.

'A whipped dog knows when it is beaten. Lareoc the coward, the shamed.'

Martial Exultant advanced slowly, drawing out the moment.

Through his cracked vision slit, Lareoc's eye was drawn to the battery of missiles atop the other Knight's carapace. The only one of his weapons Baerhart had not yet employed. He wondered then if he and *Heart of Glory* would die in a storm of fire. An ignoble end, to burn like that and only ash remaining. The futility of it all lengthened, stretching back to every moment of defiance, every pyrrhic victory. Perhaps he should have stayed and fought on that battlefield all those years ago, at least he would have died with honour.

'Tell me, cur, is this how you imagined you would die?'

It was enough of a barb to halt *Heart of Glory*. Lareoc raised his reaper blade in a last, defiant salute.

'You serve a tyrant, Baerhart. The Iron Queen is a blight on all of Kamidar.'

'She is our sav–' The words stopped mid-flow as *Martial Exultant* teetered at the brink of the killing thrust.

In the near distance, *Noble Son* was moving again. It shambled uncertainly towards the two larger Knights, its roaring chaincleaver declaring its intent. Baerhart scarcely heeded it. The missile battery activated, and for a moment Lareoc thought his end would be in fire after all, until the slightest elevation in Baerhart's aim suggested otherwise. In a plume of white smoke and screeching rockets, the missile soared from its mount, arrowing into the valley mouth, where it exploded with shocking force. The earth trembled and as the smoke and flung dirt settled it revealed a ragged hole, large enough for a Knight.

Martial Exultant began to walk. It didn't turn to its defeated foe or stop to slaughter it, and Lareoc was left wondering at his reprieve, at what could have stalled Baerhart's blade at the last moment.

In seconds, the Knight had passed him entirely, unafraid to show its back and intent on some unknown purpose.

Lareoc engaged the vox, one of the few systems still functioning on the *Heart of Glory*.

'Parnius, what has happened?'

Noble Son staggered into view as Parnius replied at length. *'Are you all right, Lareoc? God-Emperor... I thought you were dead. The sacristans are coming. We're a little way off, so we'll need time. They'll get you out of that rig, get Henniger too, and–'*

'Parnius, listen to me. The Kingsward doesn't just abandon a fight, especially not one he has won.' The last part tasted thick and sour in Lareoc's mouth. 'Tap into the feeds, find out what's going on.'

There were a few seconds of dead air as Parnius did as he was asked. When at last he came back, his voice sounded haunted.

'You won't believe it.'

Chapter Twenty-One

IN HIDING

IRON GODS

CAPTURED

The end did not come. Kesh had been ready to meet it and join Dvorgin in whatever awaited her beyond the night's shroud in the afterlife. Instead, a silver storm blew through the hall.

The air was still thick with dust from the recent explosion, the dead still lay at Kesh's feet. One of the Sovereigns cried out and another threw up onto the floor, seized by sudden retching. That was the first sign. The second was Syreniel, a short blade in hand, whipping through the armóured guards like a scythe threshes wheat. She de-limbed them, her cuts precise and eco- nomic, those eyes like ice chips above the unforgiving snarl of her gorget. Crimson slashed against white walls, the perfection of Kamidar violently marred. They died swiftly but in pain, their blood merging with Dvorgin's on the cold palace floor.

She turned when it was over, a gruesome work of seconds, her gaze piercing flesh and into Kesh's very core. The Silent Sister had not emerged from the battle in the feast hall unscathed. Her once pristine armour had dents in several places and a heavy blade had cleaved the metal, revealing cloth then skin beneath. Bloodied, ragged, she looked even more ferocious. Then, sheathing her sword with a bell-ring of steel against scabbard, she crafted a series of curt, precise hand gestures.

Not many of your kind can speak thoughtmark. You understand Signum Gothic?

Kesh replied in the affirmative. She had a brother, Liter, who was deaf, and she had learned the language for him. Her hands were naturally dextrous so it had come easy to her. It had proven useful too, not just in the life she had left behind on Mordian but as part of the Astra Militarum.

Good. We leave. Now.

At least five hundred men were still unaccounted for in barrack houses and halls around the wider palace precincts.

'What about our troops? Some could still be alive.'

We cannot help them nor worry about their fate. The fleet must know what has happened here.

'But, inside,' Kesh protested, turning to the collapsed doorway and imagining her comrades within trying to get out. 'They might be alive, they might...' She trailed off, her gaze finding Dvorgin's body slumped against the wall, his life's light long since extinguished. Only a greying shell remained, the simulacrum of a man. She wanted to take him with her, to see him buried, returned to Mordian with honour.

A hard hand gripping her shoulder put paid to all of that, the gauntlet's edges biting flesh, and Kesh winced in pain as she looked up at the Silent Sister. Even with her limiter cuff engaged, Kesh could still feel the *otherness* of the Oblivion Knight, that awful sense of repulsion that had unmanned the Sovereigns before she'd killed them. It kept her sharp at least; the adrenaline of the moment was fading and she felt the first stirring of shock in the trembling of her arms.

No helping them now. No helping him. The living, not the dead, must act. You and I.

Syreniel looked up suddenly, head turning like a bird of prey to the direction of the empty corridor.

More coming. We move.

'Where? I have no knowledge of this place, no map.'

Inward for now. They will be searching for us. For me. Though I am not easy to perceive if I do not wish to be.

Kesh didn't know what that meant but she recalled how Syreniel had slipped through the hall unseen, unnoticed, and she considered how little she knew of the Sisterhood. By comparison, it made her feel ordinary, insignificant.

'Why risk coming back at all? Why save my life? I am no one in the grand scheme, just a sharpshooter without her rifle.'

Syreniel had been half on her way when she glanced back. *I saw you,* she signed, *back in there. You should be dead. You are not.*

Kesh remembered, and thought the same, but didn't like the implication.

'It was a weapon jam. Happens all the time. Just luck, that's all.'

Perhaps... Live now, worry later.

And then she was moving, sylphlike through the marble corridor, her long strides eating up the distance to the next junction. Kesh followed, pausing only to stoop and grab a rifle from one of the Sovereigns. It felt strange in her hand, ornate and unfamiliar, not like her long-las, but it was well made and had a full charge. It would serve.

As she ran away into the corridor in Syreniel's wake, she considered the Silent Sister's words. The living, not the dead, must act. Kesh should be dead several times over, as far back as Gathalamor. Yet she lived. Again. Another miracle.

They hid, another alcove, another moment of half-held breaths in the shadows. This time the patrol came much closer. Kesh felt Syreniel slide the short blade she carried from its scabbard. Almost no sound, just a silent whisper.

Six guards in all, armoured in gold, electro-pikes fizzing. Two with ornate lascarbines held loosely at waist height. They were jogging through the hall, searching quickly. Hushed chatter went back and forth between them, stablights searching shadows for the survivors.

They were almost touching, the two fugitives, and the proximity of the Silent Sister even with her uncanny abilities dampened caused the sniper's gorge to rise. It took an effort of will to maintain her composure, not to retch and give away their hiding place. To Kesh, it almost felt like drowning.

A vox-flare provided a needed reprieve, a loud crackle of sound signalling a potential sighting. And something else, too. The Sovereigns turned before reaching the alcove, moved away. Syreniel sheathed her blade. Kesh sighed in relief and staggered away from her ally.

'Too close...'

Syreniel nodded, already surveying the room.

Another banner hall, deep alcoves lining the walls, soft light from flickering electro-sconces that filled the air with a low hum. Statues stood on plinths, wrought from marble and encrusted with precious stones by some master lapidarist. A sword crest hung at one end of the hall, partially shrouded by a dusty cloth. The entire room lay thick with dust.

Kesh collapsed. It took her by surprise, her legs giving way seemingly of their own volition. She flung her hand out, only partly arresting her fall. The immensity of it all, the betrayal, the slaughter, Dvorgin's death... Viablo's blood-soaked fingers... It overwhelmed her. She shook, huddling her knees to her chest, fighting against the tremors.

Syreniel turned sharply to regard the stricken soldier, her eyes pitiless, annoyed.

'I n-need... a m-moment,' stammered Kesh, reaching into her uniform where she kept the small injector of stimms. She'd forgotten she still had it. Ramming the needle into her arm, she felt better almost instantly though her heart thundered, pushing her beyond shock and into forced battle focus. She'd pay for it later, come down even harder, but right now she needed the edge.

'Let's just...' she said, breathing deep, letting the stimms do their job, 'let's just take a minute. They've just searched this room, they won't be coming back immediately.'

About to protest, Syreniel apparently thought better of it and gave her assent. Despite her preternatural abilities, she was weary. Wounded. Blood leaked from her upper arm, pooling at the edge of her vambrace before languidly dripping onto the floor. A light spatter but it shone brightly in the flickering glow of electro-sconces.

'You need that binding.' Kesh was shucking off her jacket as she said it, and started to tear at her shirt for a makeshift bandage.

Syreniel regarded the wound disdainfully. *It's nothing.*

'Not if it gives away our position.' Kesh gestured at the blood. They had been lucky the guards had missed it. *Or was it more than that?* Putting the thought out of her mind, she pointed to a plinth, the edge wide enough to sit on. 'It won't take long.'

Reluctantly, Syreniel sat and unclasped her armour. First the vambrace, unhooking the leather straps and then the bronze buckle and seals. She winced as it slid off, gummed blood sticking to the underside and pulling threads of gory matter with it. Then the mail beneath and the thin padded layer under that, drenched crimson with the Silent Sister's blood. The wound was deeper than either woman had realised. Syreniel scowled.

Kesh went to work. She was no medicae but had field training and knew how to stitch. Without needle or thread, a tight bandage would have to do. She cleaned the wound first, as best she could. The rupka served as counterseptic but the sight of Dvorgin's flask brought a pang of unwanted memory.

'He gave me this...' said Kesh, staring at the whorls and sigils wrought into the metal. It was a beautiful piece, wasted on a soldier. 'Merciful Throne...' She gasped as it all came back in a horrifying rush. 'They killed him first. Vychellan, I mean. Dvorgin and the others had no idea what was happening, but you did. And so did he.' Kesh looked up at Syreniel, having only half wrapped the binding, and saw some of the frost thaw. 'This was planned as soon as we arrived. What were your orders?'

Syreniel hesitated, a natural inclination towards secrecy. It passed quickly.

To kill her, if she moved against us.

'I saw a device, something in your hand. Was that a weapon?'

Syreniel pulled a small gold disc from where she had attached it to her armour. A red gem blinked dully in the centre.

You are observant.

'What is it?' asked Kesh, fascinated.

A last resort.

Kesh's interest waned as she thought of the dead. 'It didn't work,' she said bitterly.

I didn't get a chance to use it. I wasn't expecting her to have a personal shield.

'And the soldiers caught in the crossfire, did you expect that? Was any thought given to them or the ones in the barrack houses?'

None.

It felt even more callous delivered via sign language. Kesh finished the bandage, tying it off and making it tight.

'I know my place,' she said, still a little unsteady as she got back to her feet. 'I am one of billions, where as you...'

We die as you die. Under this armour is flesh and blood. Fewer and fewer of my Sisters survive, yet the need for us has never been greater. I wonder if any of us will still be alive when all of this is over.

'I'm sorry,' said Kesh.

Don't be. I know my place, too.

Kesh smiled sadly at that. Perhaps they weren't so far removed after all. The latent disquiet of the Silent Sister's presence, even with her limiter cuff engaged, gnawed at her, warring with the adrenaline rush of the stimms and reminding her of the gulf between them, even as part of one species. She had to grit her teeth against its effects.

'That cuff.' Kesh gestured to the bronze ring around Syreniel's left wrist. 'Does it hurt when you turn it on?'

A frown wrinkled the Silent Sister's brow as she considered the question.

It does not feel... pleasant, like being surrounded by ice, numbing every nerve. But it is worse for others if I do not use it.

Kesh could scarcely imagine. These warriors, these Talons, they were beyond mortal. Again, she considered the meaning-lessness of her own existence. How small she was compared to these... demigods. It was foolish to think otherwise.

Another shout from somewhere close echoed down the stone corridors. Their momentary respite neared its end.

'What now?' Kesh held out the purloined rifle and used it to gesture to Syreniel's empty sheath. 'I have this, you have your fists. And whatever that thing is attached to your armour. We can't fight them.'

Stay hidden, infiltrate deeper and find a way to signal the fleet.

'You're going to try to kill her again, aren't you.'

Syreniel nodded. *If an opportunity arises.*

'How will you even find her?'

Follow the most important-looking servant. She will have an aide or someone of that nature.

'And then what?'

A ruler is always vulnerable in their own chambers. Once I know where they are... She drew her left thumb across her neck in a slitting-throat gesture.

Kesh sighed inwardly. 'She will be well protected, regardless.'

Yes.

And the unspoken reply from Kesh, *And you will likely die in the attempt*, but what she actually said was, 'On the vox, did you catch that last remark?'

Syreniel nodded. *They won't be looking for us long. They'll be readying their armies for war. No time to worry about two survivors.*

Kesh let that sink in and they moved on.

The Marines Malevolent were dying. She saw one cut in half by a focused beam of heat from a thermal lance. His armour parted, simply *melted* apart, with only strings of liquefied metal holding it together until the bifurcated sections fell in two separate heaps. Another fired gamely with his bolt rifle, feet braced and unyielding as the colossal war machine loomed. The heavy-calibre rounds spanked the Knight armour, flattening but scarcely denting, the ricochets kicking up fat sparks. He may as well have been hurling stones.

Ariadne watched as the war engine swung its leg and the Marine Malevolent stood his ground, still firing as he was crushed by a stamping foot. Others came on undeterred, muzzle flares sparking. They roared and jeered, spat invectives, adapted, fought. Over and over. They managed to affix an incendiary charge to a Knight's leg. The explosive blew, the Space Marine responsible for the act of reckless bravura throwing himself clear. He died seconds later, ripped apart by the thrust of a massive chainblade.

They charged again, spewing hate, like raiders rushing an enemy rampart. A weapon mount swung out, an arm sweeping away pests, and three of the Astartes spun feet over apex, flailing through the air, bolt rifles still discharging even as their bones were shattered on impact.

In another section of the field, a squad fell back in good order, loosing controlled bursts only to see their fusillades caught and blunted on an overlapping shield of stark, iridescent light. Each hit was like a bruise, rapidly healed and ineffectual. A booming cannonade answered, dense shells pinwheeling from the ammunition exchange, arcing groundwards to land with heavy thuds. Each spent casing was the size of a Space Marine's helm. One of the shells roared like a comet straight through a Marine Malevolent aiming a shoulder-mounted tube launcher. It obliterated the torso entire, leaving legs still crouched, limbs and head blasted to a ragged mess, scattered at the kill-site like offal. The others in the squad drew together, filling the gap in their ranks as old instincts to make a phalanx kicked in. Knights had no such survival memory. They fought as apex predators, giants against ants, stalking and roaming the field between belligerent blasts of their war-horns.

A missile salvo launched from a carapace mount exploded amongst the surviving warriors and tore them asunder. Fire engulfed them. Nothing much remained in its aftermath, save scraps of bent and broken ceramite and smoke oozing from where the hellish rain of incendiaries still smouldered.

Elsewhere, a band of intrepid Marines Malevolent scaled the legs and back of one of the Knights using combat knives as picks. They rode the war engine like a drover rides a wild horse or an errant steer, hanging on with grim resolve, searching for a weak point to exploit. A grenade went off, shooting a dirty plume of grit and oil skyward, and the Knight's leg faltered. Servos damaged, it staggered and a brief flare of hope kindled in Ariadne that they might prevail. It gave out a bleat of alarm from its vox-emitters, drawing the eye of a fellow iron behemoth, which sprayed the injured Knight's back with heavy stubber fire, unpicking the scrabbling, scrapping warriors. They fell, the Marines Malevolent, some cored through, others trailing broken limbs or bleeding. An intense burst from a thermal lance finished them as they foundered, too slow to regroup. Bodies shrank and disappeared in the hot flare of light.

Ariadne turned away. To see the indomitable Astartes so undone, even the brutish warriors in yellow ceramite, appalled her. It terrified her.

But there was no escape.

She ran, scurrying really, as a search-lamp roamed across her position behind an upturned junker. She was out of breath, unused to such frenetic activity, preferring a data-slate and a ship's hold to a battlefield.

'They're trying to kill us...' Usullis trembled, his voice quavering as he trailed after Ariadne. Hand on her side, sucking in air like it was in short supply, she tried to remember at what point he had glommed onto her. Most of the Munitorum adepts had clustered, a natural instinct. They were all scared, Ariadne included, but his quivering fear was pissing her off. She didn't need a reminder of how imminent their death was. Besides, he was wrong.

'They're hunting *them*.' She pointed to the Astartes, after scrambling into a ditch with a dozen other Imperials. A few Solians were there, and an injured Mordian captain half carried by his adjutant. Most of the former bone-gangers had bolted already, taking to the hills until their commissar started shooting. A stray missile blast took him out, but by then the Solians had stopped running. A few even fought back. The Knights weren't the only threat. The Kamidarian Sovereigns, emboldened by the presence of their liege lords, had renewed their assault. For what it was worth, the Militarum engaged them.

Usullis made to run again. Ariadne grabbed his collar.

'Stay down.'

Fear fuelled his limbs and he struggled against her grip, almost broke free. She slapped him, hard across the cheek.

'They're not after us,' she said, the firmness of her words breaking through, 'but we need to stay down. Keep clear of them until the Astartes can...'

She trailed off, sick at herself for doing it, but what could the Space Marines do against those... *gods*? Up close, seeing them in action, it was difficult to think of them as anything *but* gods, albeit forged of steel and iron with an atomic reactor instead of a heart. To imagine a single pilot at the helm of such a machine, exerting his or her will, each limb an extension of their own. A starship had a crew of thousands, even the bridge was a careful choreography of overlapping systems and co-dependent masters. The Knight had but one, and yet its capacity to inflict damage was colossal.

Throne, she was tired, and her body screamed at her as she pushed it beyond its limits. She wished she'd kept up her daily training regimen, but the fact was adepts of a certain classification could be less stringent about their physical fitness. Her back ached, and her shoulders, stress playing a part in that. Wait until the adrenaline wore off, then she'd *really* feel it. Inwardly, she groaned. Then she groaned outwardly as Usullis kept up his bleating.

'We need...' he said, still seemingly punched drunk by that slap and blathering, 'we need to... to use the vox. Signal reinforcements.'

A few of the other adepts nodded, mainly his own staff.

Nearby, a Mordian comms-officer with a vox-cup over one ear tried to reach the other forces on the surface. If they couldn't get through to the fleet, maybe they could coordinate a fight back on the ground. Despite the distant clamour of the battle, Ariadne could hear every word. It amounted to little, save that every one of the requisition groups had been attacked. Some had broken free, were falling back to the landing sites. Others were simply non-responsive and that could not be good. Across the length and breadth of Kamidar, the Imperial interlopers fought for their lives. This had been coordinated and far from reactionary. Any expert in logistics could see that.

'They mean to exterminate us,' she said, the grim reality of their situation sinking in, 'or at least purge us from their lands.' Even as she uttered the words, she wondered what the difference was. Perhaps the latter would allow some small measure of survival. She hoped she would be amongst those survivors.

Ariadne dared a glance over the lip of the ditch. Three heavily armoured war engines stalked the darkness, moving through smoke and churned-up earth. The air was thick with it, and not for the first time Ariadne wished she had a rebreather. Her bionic locked onto the heat signatures of the machines, the Knights like blazing lanterns in her enhanced vision. They worked in concert, well drilled, warriors with the vast experience of fighting many battles together.

She was looking for the Storm Reapers, for Ogin. A flash of pale white in the gloom drew her gaze...

Unlike the Marines Malevolent who hammered at the Knights relentlessly, trying to find a chink, the Storm Reapers roamed the flanks hoping to outmanoeuvre. They attacked, withdrew, attacked again, constantly recycling. Hit and run.

One of the Knights bled smoke, its armour ruptured in a dozen places but still functional despite its wounding. A pack of Storm Reapers sped away from it, crouching low and running fast. A detonation went off a moment later. Its ankle torn up, the Knight hobbled. It strafed them, sweeping its cannon around in a wide arc. It caught the trailing Storm Reaper before he could go to ground, chewed him up and left the remains for dead.

The other two Knights stomped over in support of the stricken machine, washing the field with flame, engine stacks spewing smoke.

The Storm Reapers withdrew, and now Ariadne found Ogin. He was by the officer's side, the two men urging the others to disperse. Snap fire flickered from bolt rifles, hot dagger flashes cutting the night. Insect stings to Knight armour.

Heat beams threaded the darkness, peeling back the shadows. The thudding reports of rapid-fire battle cannons resounded like seismic thunder. The Storm Reapers wove through it, moving deftly. A Storm Reaper left behind and overlooked in the initial retreat flung himself at one of the Knights, lodging a spiked charge in an arm joint before he was shaken loose. A second war engine gutted him in mid-flight as he sailed through the air, like a huntsman shooting clays. Pieces of the Storm Reaper fell in place of an intact body as the charge went off. It near severed the weapon mount: a victory, but a pyrrhic one.

Two more Storm Reapers died to a salvo from an immense rotating cannon, their Tacticus armour punctured numerous times by the heavy rounds. The warriors staggered and fell, before being lost to sight.

Most of the Astartes were dead. Only a handful of the Marines Malevolent remained from the original complement and those that lived, clad in both yellow and white, were falling back. There was nothing the Astra Militarum troopers could do, both Mordians and Solians shoulder to shoulder in the ditches and behind the wreckage of junkers trying to keep the Sovereigns at bay. In this they failed, the Kamidarians quickly encircling their positions even as the Knights herded the remaining Astartes into a killing field.

They fought to the last, the Emperor's Angels, roaring their defiance. A storm of fire engulfed them and Ariadne had to close her eyes against it.

Ogin... Despite her fear of him, she felt the anguish of his loss and then the terror that followed, knowing their protectors were gone. She was about to cry out, to urge the ones around her to run, when she saw the Sovereigns had them surrounded. Any thought of fighting their way free evaporated when the shadow of the Knight fell across them.

It stank of machine oil and heat, white pennants fluttering in the night breeze even as it lowered its armoured head as if to regard the Imperials like a peasant uprising it had only just quelled.

'It is over,' a voice declared from within, loud and resonant through vox-emitters. '*Citizens of the Imperium, you are now prisoners of Kamidar. Do not resist and no further harm shall come to you. Obey my commands and no further harm shall come to you. I am Lord Ganavain of Harrowmere, and it is my solemn vow to you that you will be treated fairly and humanely.*'

It had a name, man not a machine after all, so why did Ariadne still feel that atavistic fear crawling through her gut?

After that, the Knights withdrew. Vehicles appeared on the horizon, the guttural roar of their engines announcing them. Several stopped in the vicinity of the war engines and Ariadne saw a cohort of tech-adepts, those known as sacristans, emerge from their holds. They had brought equipment for repairs. She lost sight of them as the Sovereigns closed in, slowly rounding up the prisoners, urging them with the sharp end of pikes or the butts of rifles. A few of the Militarum soldiers protested, but they had been divested of their weapons by then and had little choice but to obey.

Further transports, armoured with metal grating over the windows, pulled up nearby and Ariadne shuffled towards one, caught up in the press of bodies. Her last glance just before she was herded into a shadowy hold was of a burning circle of scorched earth where the Astartes had made their final stand.

Chapter Twenty-Two

AN OLD SHIP
A MOST VIOLENT CARGO
DIRE MEASURES

It had not always been called *Vortun's Ire*. In the earliest days of its creation in the shipyards of Jupiter, its name had been *Invincible Wrath*. A bellicose name for a bellicose ship that matched its captains aptly. No man or woman who became master of the *Wrath* was anything but a warmonger and a belligerent commander. The ship, it was said, would tolerate no other. Most notorious on its honour roll was Katphur Vortun, a bloodthirsty and entirely unreasonable man who never spared an enemy, never gave any quarter and, most crucially, never retreated from a fight. As such, his war record was exemplary, the *Wrath*'s list of confirmed kills both impressive and daunting. So successful was Vortun that both of his ship's appellations appeared entirely appropriate for the man.

Until the Rift.

Everything changed when Cadia fell and the galaxy tore open. Where some shipmasters who were caught in the tides of hell unleashed by the Cicatrix Maledictum turned engines in reverse as they sought to survive calamity, Vortun embraced it. He spat at the denizens of hell, standing braced upon his ship's bridge like a sea captain of old might grip the wheel as he faced down a storm. For this was a storm, the greatest and most terrible in the Imperium's history, and Vortun would not blanch from it.

The *Wrath* added seven traitor vessels to its tally in the days following the appearance of the Rift. All capital ships, all scalps that would have made any captain's career.

In the end Vortun did not die from a lance salvo or a hostile boarding force. No, as he was spewing his fury and hatred at the enemies of the Imperium, avowing their painful deaths at his hand, his heart gave out and he died in that moment, upon the deck. A man with water for blood was second-in-command, and he pulled the *Wrath* from what the accounts would say was certain destruction. Nonetheless, he was stripped of his captaincy and forgotten by history. To honour the fallen shipmaster, the *Wrath* was rechristened *Vortun's Ire*.

All of this Renyard knew, for he was, if nothing else, a student of history. Just as the Marines Malevolent also knew that Vortun had raged at the original design of the ship and had seen to the stripping out of what he called 'redundant sections', repurposing them as war decks. Here then was where Renyard and his warriors had waited whilst the rest of the reclamation forces deployed for the ground. This part of the ship was registered on no schematics and known to only a handful of officers in the Praxis battle group. Fewer still knew of its contents. Only one, in fact: Lord Ardemus, the groupmaster himself. Renyard's orders had come from the admiral direct with vermilion-level encryption. Such was their level of sophistication they could bypass any jamming system.

The orders were simple enough, a single word, the true meaning of which would condemn an entire world.

Engage.

As the code-key inputted into Renyard's vambrace unlocked the cipher, he activated his armour. A low growl rippled in the silence as the generator kicked in. The suit looked old like its bearer, owing to wear, and was patched in places. The helm had a plough-blade faceplate, the metal already scored and scratched. Not unlike Renyard himself. He had crossed the Rubicon Primaris, emerging on the other side *changed*... greater. He knew what he was, a sociopathic warmonger. He was no mindless slayer, but he had killed innocents that were in his path and slaughtered men who had tried his patience.

Once, a Guardsman had dared to touch the pommel of his sword. It was a brutal thing, a thick-bladed gladius, but the hilt had a large flawed emerald in the pommel and this had caught the trooper's eye. He wasn't attempting to steal it; the man could scarcely have drawn let alone lifted it. He was reaching towards something beautiful. Renyard had killed him. Then and there, a cross-cut blow with the selfsame sword that had severed the upper and lower portions of the Guardsman in a diagonal. He had gone on to murder the trooper's comrades, his entire squad, as a salutary lesson for others. No one had challenged him afterwards, not even the regimental officers. He had merely gone on his way, untroubled, his actions as automatic as repairing his armour or sharpening his blade. It had not been the first man he had killed for a slight, nor would it be the last.

A warrior of the White Consuls Chapter had challenged him to an honour duel after Renyard had made some insulting comment about his provenance. A sword thrust through the Space Marine's gut rammed upwards and into his hearts had ended the contest whilst the challenger was still mid-utterance. He hadn't lingered to face the consequences; his deployment was imminent. Again, he gave it little thought. Just another fool who thought battles were glorious and war could be honourable.

A veteran of a hundred wars, Renyard's roll of dishonour was long. Flint-grey hair, hard blue eyes, the Belisarian technologies had done little to soften his looks. If anything, the myriad scars were more pronounced. Not for the first time did Renyard wonder at just how bad things were if warriors like the Marines Malevolent were being offered advancement and reinforcement.

Dire measures, he thought and clicked a switch on the side of his brutish war-helm.

Retinal lenses flared crimson, two hostile candle flames in the darkened sea of the war deck. Others followed, like a wild fire taking hold and spreading. Thirty warriors in Tacticus plate, muddy yellow and black, a contrast to the wine-red of their twenty power-armoured comrades. A most violent cargo.

Renyard regarded their leader as he closed the vambrace display. The gaze that returned his smouldered with fervour. *Hatred.* Scars told the story of her wars too, the worst a jagged wound of old pinkish tissue that cut through her right eye. She donned her helm and the lenses lit green. As one, the Sisters clasped their weapons in salute.

'We are called and so we answer,' uttered Renyard, his voice carrying.

How prescient of the lord admiral to hive away this interdiction force. Cautious was Ardemus, and predatory.

Behind the ranks of Astartes and Sororitas, three gunships idled on the cusp of readiness. Tech-adepts and servitors attended them as engines warmed up, building to a roar. Hold lights blinked on, running from one end of the deck to the other in relay. Sirens started up, and the light hue went from red to green. The maintenance crews departed and a launch ramp began to open, pressure venting as it admitted the cold void.

Renyard stared at it, boots mag-locked to the deck as his warriors stomped to their transports.

'Hate,' he said, uttering his Chapter's mantra, 'is the surest weapon.'

Smiling to himself, though with the darkest humour, he thought
Katphur Vortun would have approved.

They made landfall under an hour later, approaching with sensor baffles engaged and zeroing in on a remote location where they would not be detected.

Renyard was first out, the gunship barely touched down as he leapt off the gaping ramp to the firm earth below. A rugged land stretched in every direction, hills and rocks and low-lying mist. He stalked off into it, grey-white wisps coiling around his feet and shins. The others aboard followed as the other two gunships sought out their landing zones. This was primus, led by Renyard himself, and they fanned out into combat squads. One remained behind to protect the transport, should their landing site be discovered.

That happened quicker than anticipated.

A farmhand, by the look of his thick, hardy attire and stout physique, stood gawping. He looked terrified but determined to protect his lands, a wooden-stocked carbine in his hand. Six others joined him, all natives, all people of the land. One wore a pot helmet and carried a shotcannon in a nervous grip. Then came six more, the edges of agrarian buildings emerging through a slowly evaporating fog. Renyard saw a waterwheel, stables, fields for crops. There were more men here too, converging on the five strangers. With greater numbers, they grew bolder. No vox-tower. The lines didn't reach this far out. Regardless, word could not slip of his arrival.

Staring coldly at the first man, who had dared to take aim at the warrior in mustard-yellow ceramite, Renyard uttered, 'Burn it.'

They left the farms and fields a scorched ruin, smoke still spiralling skyward in a thick column in their wake. They would need to move quickly now, and force march across the hardy terrain. Smoke would draw investigation eventually and that would lead to attention. He could have spared them, he supposed, but Renyard preferred the lesson of pain.

He had written a message in their blackened bones and broken bodies. It read, *Fear us, we are coming.*

All combat squads were accounted for, dispersed across a few miles. Their first target was close. He had begun tracking it the moment they made landfall. It had been given to them before embarkation, Ardemus again proving his prescience. He smiled, sickle-sharp, at the thought of what would come next. It had been years since Renyard had fought like a guerrilla. A ruthless and deadly art. He had missed it.

'Come then,' he said to his comrades, the vox turning his gravel-voice into a low rasp, 'let's kill some god-machines.'

Chapter Twenty-Three

THREE COUNCILS

A CHANCE FOR PEACE

CIRCLE OF BLADES

Orlah slowly removed her trappings. First the ornate breastplate, a cumbersome thing that looked the part but would not stop an assassin's knife. Her crown, which she laid gently on a cushion of white velvet, was more effective in this regard. It had a refractor field generator built into its circlet, so powerful it could stop even an Emperor's Talon. The emerald cloak she took off last, releasing the draconhead clasps one by one, and let the thick garment fall heavily to the floor like the shedding of scales.

So divested of her ceremonial weight, she looked at herself in a long crystalline mirror. The black garnet hung around her neck on a chain and she touched it with weary fingers. Orlah had worn these clothes for the last sixteen hours as the brief war had raged. Her military strategists had brought her reports of the engagements. Across Wessen and Eageth, fields and holdings burned. In Pragan an army of Imperial troopers had dug in against three cohorts of Sovereigns and a lance of Armigers from House Vexilus. Only when Lord Banfort had sent in his Knights was the impasse broken. Another force had destroyed a major bridge into the township of Krate and withdrawn to regroup in the hinterlands of Brynof. Several others had been routed. A few destroyed entirely. Lord Ganavain himself had taken captives at Runstaf. In every engagement, the Space Marines had proven particularly tenacious.

She knew something of the Astartes. She had fought alongside them, and they were dogged fighters. But this breed that had been unleashed on Kamidar were particularly brutal. Thus far, none had surrendered, though Orlah had read reports of some falling back to more tactically advantageous positions. They left carnage in their wake, setting fires or leaving rudimentary booby traps. House Orinthar had lost a pair of Armigers to these tactics. The Imperials had been chased back but their ravages were costly. Her people bled, and not only those in armoured war machines. But what choice had this lord admiral given her?

She felt a burn on the side of her neck where the refractor field had touched her skin. Her fingers traced the line of the newly made scar as she stared into the glass. There were comforts in her private chambers, balms that could ease her suffering. Orlah wanted none of them.

'Am I ever to be plagued by men who wish me dead?'

Ekria, who had recently returned to the queen's side and now waited quietly in the low-lit shadows, answered, 'It is the unfortunate lot of the sovereign to bear such burdens, your majesty.'

Orlah quirked an eyebrow as she turned to look at the aide over her shoulder.

Without her stately attire, the queen was a woman in a silken shift, corset, leggings. No different in appearance to any woman, and yet she was much more than that. Her strength of will radiated. Her poise undeniable even given her close scrape with death, for the feast hall was not so long in the memory.

'My own words as counsel, is that it?' asked Orlah, but not unkindly.

Orlah smiled and saw it reflected in Ekria's face.

The aide went on, 'It is bold, your majesty. Bolder than I believed you would be.'

'Is it? Is it truly?' She returned her gaze to the mirror. 'There is a hostile army in my lands. It is murdering my people, laying waste to their holdings, stealing what is theirs and what is mine.' Her face had darkened but there was also sadness behind her hard eyes. 'They sent assassins to murder me. In the circumstances, I have acted with restraint.'

'I believe your brother, the baron, may see it otherwise.'

'Let me handle him. He has been away playing at crusader and leaving the protectorate to me. He will abide by his queen's will. If nothing else, he is loyal.'

As she cast her eye over her reflection, Orlah remarked on other, older scars. They had been well stitched and sutured over the years, the finest chirurgeons employed to patch her hurts with the minimum of evidence of their healing, but she saw them and remembered every blade or bullet that had made them.

Ekria demurred, head bowing. 'As you say, your majesty. Will you gather the council anew?'

Orlah busied herself finding something else to wear, something practical. Leather, real armour. A weapons belt for pistol and blade. The time for ceremony was over.

'As soon as I have spoken to my brother. I assume he is on his way.'

'Imminently, your majesty.'

'Have my armourers meet me in the Hall of Swords as soon as we are done.'

'Of course, your majesty, as you will it.' Ekria bowed again but did not leave immediately.

'There is more?' asked Orlah, sensing the pregnant pause.

'I merely wished to say, I was surprised.'

Orlah paused in what she was doing, hands on a padded leather undercoat. 'Surprised? How so?'

'You... *lured* them, your majesty. And then you killed them.'

Orlah returned a gaze of steel but found no hint of reproach in her aide's eyes. 'You think me reckless, driven by emotion.'

'I think you *righteous*, my queen, driven by necessity. I simply did not appreciate the lengths to which you would go. I applaud it. It shows strength.'

'For Kamidar, for the protectorate...' *For my daughter*, she omitted saying. 'I would go to *any* length. They have mistaken us for meek vassals. We are not. I have shown them the error of that way of thinking.'

'And now you have brought us war,' a strong, deep voice cut in.

Gerent Y'Kamidar had entered the royal chambers without invitation or announcement and stood with arms folded, a sour look curdling his noble features.

'Don't scowl, brother, it ruins your patrician jawline,' said Orlah, a quick glance at Ekria effectively dismissing her.

He had dark hair and a cloak that draped his right shoulder and went to a silver clasp on his left. A stout man, he had a burly frame and honest, brown eyes. Yet to shed his crusade gear, he wore silver half-armour with the sigil of Kamidar proudly emblazoned on the cuirass. His oighen sat in a black leather sheath, the rubies in its pommel glinting in the soft light.

He said nothing for a time, exercising decency and waiting until the aide was gone before continuing.

'You said you intended to hold them captive, not slaughter them.'

Orlah turned her eyes from him and went back to the leather coat, trying to feign indifference. 'I knew you would not approve.'

Gerent came closer so she couldn't ignore him. 'You lied to me.'

'The facts changed. *I* changed. I acted as I needed to.'

Now she faced him, gripping tightly to the leather coat. 'At what point did you think either of those things was not the case, brother?'

'At the point before you murdered an entire ambassadorial delegation!' He flung his arms out, exasperated and more than a little angry. His posture softened quickly, though, to one of appeal. 'What drove you to do this, sister, it is insanity, it is–'

'I am not your sister in this, Gerent!' she snapped, raising her voice for the first time in days. She cooled again in a moment, adding more gently, 'I am your queen. Reflect on that before you speak another word. I invite frank counsel from one of the greatest generals in the Kamidarian army, but I will not have disrespect,' she said, shaking her head, 'not after everything we have endured. Not after how they left my daughter, your niece, in that cargo hold. And used her as a bargaining chip to ensure our quiescence. Is that insanity, Gerent, or is it just?'

His face flushed, lips tight as a gorget as he bit back a retort. Royal guards stood at station in the room, even more silent and invisible than the queen's aide had been. Statuesque, they held their bastard swords tips to the floor, cold eyes staring through the slit between bronze helmet visor and veils of silver chainmail.

'The Imperium is not our enemy. I have fought beside the crusaders. They are good warriors. Noble.'

'And this admiral, this man Ardemus, you consider his actions noble?'

Gerent looked downcast for a moment. 'I know little of him and met him comparatively recently. I will admit, I did not take much of a liking to him, even as limited as our interactions were.'

'And yet, he speaks for the Imperium and treats us with disrespect. Spits on our grief.'

'Consider the cost of pride, sister.'

'It is more than that, and you know it,' Orlah replied, not asserting the distinction that she was queen this time.

Gerent let out a long, calming sigh. He sat down at a side table and poured himself a drink from a gilt decanter. 'Have you seen the reports? The tally of suffering for our people and their lands is long. It grows longer with the hour.'

'Of course I have,' she said, a little harshly before taking the edge off her words. 'I am not blind to it.'

He glanced up at his sister, offering a second glass to her, which she politely declined.

'Six years they had her, rotting in some dingy hold like forgotten cargo. It is undignified. Shameful.'

Gerent swallowed the drink in one impressive gulp, before pouring himself another.

'I know,' he said, voice like a shadowed rasp. 'But does that justify these lengths you have gone to?'

Emotion coloured her words again, red and hot. 'They are not far enough! But it is more than that. You've not seen the despoliation, brother, our lands driven under booted heel, ransacked.' She calmed then, the severity of the deed sinking in. 'I had to send a message.'

He sipped at the second drink. 'Was it as bad as that?'

'Rioting, vandalism, murder, and this is but a taste. Under their rule we would be a shell, a hollow fortress.'

'They are our allies, though. There has to a better way, one that does not end in outright war. The cost of it...' He rubbed his chin at the thought.

Orlah knew he was right. She had always been the decisive one, the natural leader, but Gerent was the more temperate. She would not have changed what she did. But, on reflection, she had been reckless.

'They came here to reap us, to take all we had made, all we had bled for in the years of darkness when none of us knew if there was still an Imperium to be a part of,' she said, tears well-ing, despite her anger or maybe because of it. 'And they did it *before* they gave her back to me.'

Gerent rose wearily to his feet, his own face heavy with grief. The pain of it all returned, over and over in an endless destruc-tive cycle. Orlah's voice grew faint as he took her in his arms, and he in hers, two siblings sharing their grief.

'You were supposed to protect her.'

'I know...' Gerent whispered. 'I'm sorry, sister.'

The grainy projection of Shipmaster Ithion emitted from the dais, his face grave.

'*They have well over a hundred warships as well as numerous lesser frigates and other carriers. A formidable armada. Our own fleet currently stands at forty-seven ships of the line, not including our high-orbit monitors and system-edge destroyers. Even with tac-tical advantage and the Iron Veil to stymie them...*' Ithion stalled, moistening his lips. '*Should they try to force a breach...*'

'Finish that sentence, shipmaster,' said Gerent flatly. He exchanged a glance with his sister, who sat on her throne in the royal alcove, the soft light from the lumens flickering across her face.

Orlah liked Ithion: he was a plain-speaking, straightforward man. Well groomed, he had a tidy beard, black as coal, with a face like old leather in his starched royal blue uniform with gold epaulettes. He had many years under his belt, but of late they had begun to show. It didn't diminish his war record. His sound admiralship had been responsible for the majority of the dead vessels drifting in the Iron Veil. He had also counselled as to the lacing of those gutted hulks with mines and other defences. Pride and confidence were in his blood, but standing before the pan-theon of nobles, relating this news, he looked uncomfortable.

Ithion raised his chin, back straightening. His chain of office, strung from collar to breast, shone as it caught the light. '*We can hold the picket line at the outskirts of the protectorate for half a day at most. And even then, we lack the numbers to prevent every Imperial ship breaking through. They will make landfall with more troops within hours.'*

'How badly can we hurt them, shipmaster?' asked the queen, her chin resting on a gloved hand. Less regal now, she wore a functional cuirass with a padded undercoat. Her Knight, *Lioness*, waited in the keep, though she knew Gerent would staunchly object to her taking to the field.

'To be frank, my queen?'

Orlah leaned back in her seat, leather breeches creaking, her golden helm resting on the arm. 'I would have it no other way, shipmaster.'

'Not badly enough. We can bloody them, but even low on ammunition and fuel they have enough to overwhelm us.'

Orlah chewed on that a moment, finding her brother's gaze as she considered the shipmaster's stark testimony.

'They came here to reinforce us, to fortify Kamidar for the crusade as well as acquire its wealth in fuel and materiel,' he said. 'A full-scale invasion doesn't suit that end. They want to cow us, not destroy us.'

'My thoughts exactly,' Orlah agreed. 'And no infantry, even one as formidable as the Astartes, will relish taking on our Knights in the open field.'

'Then what are we saying, your majesty?' asked Lady Antius, her image phasing for a moment as the signal weakened before resolving again. The majority of the nobles attended via hololithic projection. They had their own armies to marshal and little time to spend on travelling to the capital. *'That we fight them? The Imperium?'*

'The fleet of this admiral, not the Imperium,' Banfort corrected. He had his arms folded across a barrel of a chest encased in a black metal breastplate. Fresh sweat lathered his face and the light

smears of dirt from the cockpit of his war machine suggested he had already been in battle. *'For now, their forces are containable. Most linger in the hinterlands at the borders.'*

'We took captives at Runstaf,' offered Ganavain. Damp hair plastered to his head from wearing a helm suggested he too had seen combat.

'How many is that now?' asked Gerent.

Although the events that transpired in the feast hall had been bloody, the rest of the Imperials had been taken without much incident. Separated, disarmed, placed under immediate guard they had little choice but to capitulate. These were lesser officers, of platoon rank and no higher. They made demands, vowed their wrath but ultimately proved powerless. Orlah had slaughtered the delegation, fearing an assassination attempt and she had been vindicated in doing so. She had struck first and then matters had unfolded as they had. Innocent deaths were unfortunate but she could take no chances.

The captain of the Sovereigns, Gademene, spoke up. 'With your permission, my lord...'

Gerent gave it.

'With the troops and various aides that came with the Imperial delegation, we have upwards of five hundred men and women imprisoned in the barrack houses of the north quarter.'

'Is that wise,' ventured Banfort, *'to have so many enemy combatants sequestered at the palace?'*

Gademene bristled at this, evidently feeling his honour impugned. 'They are under heavy guard and watched every hour.'

'And what is the alternative?' asked Ganavain somewhat pointedly. Banfort did not reply.

'I heard two escaped,' said Lady Antius, changing the subject.

'Not under my watch.'

Orlah quirked an eyebrow as she met Gerent's gaze. It was foolish, she supposed, to believe that word of the two survivors of the feast hall massacre would remain secret.

'They are of no concern,' she said. 'The palace guards will apprehend them and they'll be taken prisoner like the others. It is only a matter of time.'

'Is there another way out of this?' suggested Antius. She wore her silver gorget and breastplate as yet unbloodied. *'One that does not involve outright war?'*

'You want to sue for peace,' said Banfort, sounding dubious. *'A slaughtered delegation – amongst them a warrior of the Emperor's own Custodians.'*

'An assassin,' Sheane corrected. 'Remember that. They sent two killers into our midst with the sole objective of slaying our queen.'

It was the first time the knight had spoken since the events of the feast hall. He was a rangy man with sandy hair and rough skin. He had a dark look about him, one at odds with the lighter-hearted man Orlah had once known. Gathalamor and the crusade had changed them all it seemed.

'Do you want peace, my liege?' asked Ganavain, ignoring the knight.

Orlah considered it again. She had been considering almost nothing else since she had spoken in private to Gerent. Temper cooled, she had no desire to see her people suffer, but the crusaders would have subjugated them. Instead of being treated as equals, they would have become slaves. She had not survived this long, sacrificed as much as she had to let that happen. But then Gerent's words returned yet again. *There has to be a better way.*

'I want only for Kamidar to prosper, and I want to lay my daughter to rest. She cannot go to the grove whilst we are at war. For now at least, perhaps a ceasefire can be brokered. It will give us time to consider our position, what to do about the Custodian, and buy our peoples some needed respite.'

The royal mausoleum lay on the outskirts of Harnfor. The ancestors of House Kamidar named it Sanctuary. It was here, under the lofty boughs of a nightvein grove, that King Uthra's bones resided and so it would be with Jessivayne. In holding with Kamidarian tradition, Orlah would see the body interred and pray over the remains. In ordinary circumstances, only a light honour guard would be needed to accompany her, but the Imperial occupation, even one largely driven to the borderlands, changed that. She wanted – no, *needed* to give her daughter the peace she had been denied for six long years. It could not wait.

'*Then I humbly implore us to deescalate immediately,*' said Lady Antius. '*We have reached a stalemate of sorts, so I suggest we use this time as an opportunity to reopen lines of communication.*'

Banfort looked doubtful. '*After what happened in the feast hall, do you really think our would-be oppressors will concede to parley?*' Banfort had always been amongst those nobles to promote Kamidarian independence. He had been vociferously against allowing any outside presence onto their native soil, Imperial or not.

'They do not know about the massacre,' said the queen.

'*An impossible task for us to keep it that way, your majesty. I say this with the utmost respect, of course.*'

Orlah nodded sagely, but it was Banfort who spoke up.

'*Their chief delegate, the Naval officer, Haster, still lives. The chirurgeons are tending to him as we speak. He could be used as a bargaining chip or proof of good intent.*'

'Are we to parade him, then? A lie to cool the ire of the army at our gates?' said Gerent, anger bleeding some colour into his words. It went against his code of honour and Orlah saw this same distaste reflected in some of the other nobles, but none of them were the queen's brother.

'If necessary,' she answered flatly. 'At least until the princess-regent is laid to rest.'

Gerent scowled. 'And then a return to war.'

'If necessary,' the queen repeated coldly.

'They will discover the truth eventually.'

'And I will remind them that blood has been shed on both sides.'

'I see a gulf of difference between the two, my queen. And so will they.'

'War is an ugly business, baron, any general or ruler knows this. This Lord Ardemus overplayed his hand. His agents acted recklessly and they were brought to heel. That is the narrative.'

'And if he still has aspirations to see you dead?'

'Then peace will be beyond the grasp of even the most gifted negotiator. I seek fairer terms for Kamidar. I believe we have an opportunity to do that. Ardemus will see the wisdom of what I propose or he will not. There is much riding on this for the Imperium as well as Kamidar.'

'I will state this now, so there can be no misunderstanding on the matter later,' said Gerent, addressing the entire council but with his attention squarely on Orlah. 'I am against this. Not the desire for peace. That I hold to, and will it to be so, but mendacity is unworthy of us. I will serve the crown as I have always done, but I will not be a party to these acts of subterfuge. We are knights, not politicians.'

Orlah regarded him sadly. 'Alas, dear brother, in this we must be both. Even you.'

Ardemus only half listened to his captains' debate. Their arguments rose and fell in fervour depending on the speaker, depending on whether they made the case for war or for peace.

An accord can be reached, uttered one.

We must show them whom they serve, bellowed another.

The Anaxian Line must be raised, declared a third.

And on it went.

They spoke of insult against the Imperium, of the crusade, of the wilful act of aggression perpetrated against them by capturing and holding the delegation. Some wanted war, others gave more moderate counsel, suggesting swift negotiation. All that Ardemus could think of was time, and how the grains slipped through the hourglass, its slender neck not unlike the narrow passage through the grave-yard of ships the Kamidarians had raised around their world, as effective as any minefield. In different circumstances, he might have applauded the ingenuity. He had tasked Adeptus Mechanicus scouts with assessing the threat posed by the dead vessels, assuming there was more to them than the mere wrecks they appeared.

The mines and other explosive devices had been discovered in the initial reconnoitre. Emplaced static defences had been revealed in the deeper layers of ships – weapon turrets, laser defence grids, missile pods. An impressive array. Half of Arde-mus wanted to charge the barricades regardless. The fleet could weather it, but the losses would be steep. He needed those ships. The crusade needed those ships. He also needed the Anaxian Line, or rather the Kamidarian part of it. If he wanted glory and not months of painful refit and repair, here or on some allied Imperial shipyard, then Praxis must remain intact.

He glanced again at the reports of missing vessels. It bordered on double figures. Mainly small frigates and auxiliaries, but the lack of a clear perpetrator was vexing, especially when ranked up alongside the current and more pressing concern of Kami-darian belligerence.

They had still received no word from the surface, all commu-nication apparently still jammed. He had a solution for that, but it still might not answer what had become of the delegation. He wanted rid of this problem, and soon. Perhaps it had been reck-less to place an assassin within the palace. It was a risk he had been willing to take. One that had not, to his annoyance, paid off. Remove the head of state and the rest would fall into line. Feudal rivalries would flare, unity would evaporate, any malcon-tents would be easily removed piecemeal. His political strategists had given him this counsel and before that he had come to the same conclusions. Ardemus still believed it. Even if Syreniel was dead, he hadn't exhausted every option in this regard.

Queen Orlah had merely beaten him to the punch. A misjudgement on his part. It would not happen again.

Lost in his own thoughts, he was only vaguely aware of someone trying to get his attention until the second time of asking.

'Lord admiral,' said the captain, his voice insistent. That bastard Tournis, always nipping at the pedestal. He wanted fleet command so badly it turned him into an even more insufferable prick.

'My apologies, captain. Please repeat yourself.'

'The matter of the Astartes, my lord. A lunar fastness in Kamidarian orbit has been discovered by our augurs. An outpost.'

That was interesting, though Ardemus queried the loyalty of the Astartes in this matter. One had to presume they had formed some kind of agreement with the Knight world. It was not unprecedented for Space Marines, who were often a law unto themselves and operated outside the bounds of strategic command.

'It has been suggested that we send an emissary to them in order to gauge their intent,' said Tournis, failing to hide his impatience. 'At the very least we could try to establish vox-contact.'

Ardemus' answer was stalled when a red-faced messenger, Second Lieutenant Renzo, interrupted the holo-conference. He had an ivory scroll case held in his outstretched hands.

'Sincerest apologies, lord, but it is urgent.'

The case bore the gold seal of the master of vox. Renzo proffered the scroll case like a godly offering.

'A missive from the Kamidarians.'

A few eyebrows raised at that. The grainy renderings of captains turned, momentarily disappearing to consult aides and strategists.

Ardemus scowled, wishing, and not for the first time, that Haster was still around. Renzo had piss for blood compared to that fine officer. He registered a pang of guilt and even regret that his old friend might have come to harm. He snatched the scroll case as an expectant silence fell across the room, barring the low hum of hololithic devices, as the gathered captains bated their breath. At length, he unclasped the case and broke open a wax seal to unfurl the parchment within.

He read the missive once, then again to ensure he had not been mistaken.

A curious quirk curled one side of his lips, a half-smile stillborn to confusion.

'She wants to parley.'

Five blocks of stone, each a square hewn by a mason's hand, stood in a pentagram in a small chamber lit by firelight.

As they had sat down, each man had slowly removed his helm. The helms rested at their feet, placed there solemnly in front of the stone blocks, visors facing forwards. Each had drawn his sword and laid it hilt first so the tips met in the middle like spokes in a wheel. A circle of blades.

The first, Anglahad, leaned forwards into the light. His face still clung to the dregs of youth, a little aquiline in aspect and with a short, grey beard.

'We swore an oath to Kamidar.'

Dagomir was second, edging into the light even as his brother faded back into shadow. Pain etched his face, a metal seal fused to where his arm had been cut off.

'We are crusaders, and the crusade has come,' he said.

A third, Apothecary Fulk, spoke next. He had a waxy cast to his skin and a metal plate riveted to the left hemisphere of his skull, the right patchy with dark, closely shorn hair. His nose was an arrowhead shape, his eyes perpetually narrowed.

'We serve the Imperium above all else.'

Last was Godfried, a rare moment when he allowed air to touch the face beneath his implacable helm. His expression held no guile, only utmost certainty.

'Two oaths were made. By fulfilling either, we break the other. The path before us is murky. Events unclear. To act upon hearsay or bare inference would be hasty. Unwise. A third oath was made to Bohemund. And above all else, before we consider pledging our swords, he must be avenged.' It was the most he had ever said in one sitting.

The fifth seat sat empty, for this had been Bohemund's and no Templar of the Black had risen to replace him. In Morrigan's eyes, none could.

They waited silently, patiently for their captain to speak his judgement.

They were torn between two vows: those they had spoken as Black Templars in service to the Imperium and the oaths they had sworn to Kamidar in the years of darkness. Godfried was right; they could not honour one of these oaths without breaking the other, and much remained in doubt. Without vid-feed and vox, they could not know for sure what had transpired between the fleets. For now, it seemed the ships had withdrawn. A disagreement that had either reached an accord or an impasse. Morrigan had no wish to stoke the embers of a flame either way.

Prior to this council of swords, Morrigan had sought out the reliquarius. On his knees, in a plain white chasuble bearing the Templar's cross, he had prayed for guidance. Revelation had been swift but disturbing.

A figure seated upon a throne, encircled by fire. It raised its sword and then its cup until the flames consumed it.

An ill omen, a warning.

He also saw Bohemund's death cruelly replayed, an old drama long since soured, and felt the dread pull of Blasphemy as it tried to gain purchase on his thoughts. His fists had clenched, the iron of his chains biting into flesh, drawing blood. Anger roared up within, girded by anguish, and he cried out to the darkness and the hollow helms of his dead brothers. None spoke, but that in itself was answer enough.

All of this returned in the moment at the council of swords,

his brothers patiently watching, and Morrigan rendered the only
judgement he could.

'These matters are unclear to us and I hesitate to act before we know more. I will speak to the queen and remind her of *her* oaths. Then we seek out vengeance.'

Chapter Twenty-Four

THE HAND

FOLLOW THE BLOOD

A SIREN'S CALL

They ran silent, engines cold, lumens dark, only the barest life support. The *Ruin* drifted fractionally in the stellar wake of distant solar flares, but she was a large ship and would not move far. Through a grimy oculus, Herek watched the far-off moon and imagined the lunar fortress stationed there. It was distant, not much more than a grey, misshapen orb, but the *Mourning Star* had made for it like it was a haven. Bleeding from her wounds, she left a trail a noseless hound could follow. The Red Corsairs had kept their distance, despite having damaged the vessel's long-range augur and any chance she had of detecting the *Ruin*. And for now at least, they had to wait.

Herek flexed his hand, the bionic, and felt the phantom pain of the missing appendage as if it had just been severed.

'It must be close...' he whispered to the darkness, his voice echoing off the walls of an old strategium now used as an interrogation room, though not in this moment. The scent of dried blood was thick and hung heavy without the air recyclers to disperse it. He had brought an offering. It squirmed in his flesh grip, but Herek barely noticed. One of the crew from the lower decks. One of thousands. Insignificant. They would not be missed. For was not that the cruel joke of the universe, that they were all just particles of dust? Inconsequential, the fulcrum about which only their own petty lives and desires revolved. Sustenance for the Dark Gods.

Herek wanted to change that. He wanted to matter. To be remembered.

But first he needed the sword.

Had he known how important the blade was back then, he might never have wielded it. Certainly, he would not have allowed a vengeful Black Templar to take it from him. The trade had seemed fair at the time, a head for a hand. Ever since the Rift, he had felt differently. Ever since *they* had come to him and made him the only offer that made any sense in a senseless universe.

You can matter.

He knelt, taking his wriggling captive down with him. The bloody iron of the deck was cold against his bare skin, for he was naked but for the short leggings of his armour's undersuit. For this to work, nothing could interfere with the casting, and as Herek was no magister or acolyte he had only the ritual and the words he had been given to call upon.

They would do the rest.

It chafed to be bound to another's will, but weren't they all servants of some uncaring god? He shrugged it off, slit the crewman's throat with a dagger. The weapon felt small in his hand, the concept of touch an abstract one since he was using the bionic and the haptic feedback was rudimentary. Kurgos had done his best, and Herek could hardly blame the chirurgeon for that.

As he parted the main artery in the neck, it bulged and blood sprayed forth, a thick pool of it that stuck to his knees, his shins. He felt it worm beneath the toes of his feet. He let the crewman slump to the floor, their last dregs of life eking through desperately scrabbling fingers that slowly lost their vigour and grew still. A mercy, for the crew suffered in the silent running of the ship to heat, to cold, to starvation and asphyxiation. This one had been relatively healthy. That was good, Herek needed strength for the ritual. A few final jerks and the body stopped moving, its blood spilled all over the chamber floor.

Dropping the knife, Herek set to work. His hands, metal and flesh, plunged into the blood, spreading it this way and that, making the sigils as he had been taught, murmuring the words that he had been given. He did it swiftly but with care. Any mistakes would be costly. When he was finished, he leaned back to inspect his work, breathless despite the low labour of the task. It was always this way. The ritual required vigour and so it took from what was in front of it.

The sigil grew hot, melting a thin layer of hoar frost that had built up over the deck, and the air filled with bloody steam. Then it began to glow, faint at first like a candle and then roaring like a campfire. Herek withstood the heat, though the body he had given up to it crackled as the flesh burned and blackened.

Smoke issued from the tips of the flames, snaking into a slowly coalesced form.

They were genderless, lithe and tall. Kneeling as he was, Herek had to crane his neck to regard them. He didn't speak, they knew his mind without the need for any of that. Focusing on them was hard for they jerked left then right and back again in continuous rapid motion, so fast they blurred. Words issued forth from the darkness of their form, gibberish, the language of tongues, no language, every language... *unwords*.

Only the caster of the ritual could parse them into meaning.

Herek didn't know how it worked, he had long since abandoned such foolish questions as the province of credulous, cowardly men, but his eyes widened at the first revelation.

'How...?' he rasped, his voice parched from the heat.

They answered, a stream of non sequiturs, and Herek winced as the pain of it hummed through his skull. Sweat beaded on his bare skin as the heat intensified. He would need to break off communion soon.

'And what else?' he asked, forcing the question through gritted teeth. *Gods! The pain of their presence.*

Another knifing answer, the heat like a furnace now and Herek the kindling. He bowed, as if a heavy weight had been slung around his neck.

'And what else?' he asked again, his instructions free flowing, every syllable a needle in his brain.

He bowed lower, reaching out, trembling fingers nearing the edge of the bloody ritual circle.

'It shall be done...' he croaked, scarcely able to breathe. The crewman's corpse was nothing but ash. 'My Hand,' he finished, and broke the circle with his fingertips.

Herek fell over, onto his back, skin burning, lungs aching. Every breath was like cinder and crushed glass. Coughed-up blood splattered his naked chest and then it was over. The air cooled, returning to the frigid climate of the void. He breathed. He lived.

Heaving himself to his feet, a groan dredged itself up from his body. He pushed a rusty square plate by the side of the door and it opened with a jerk of rusty cylinders. A small cohort of bent-backed serfs awaited him, not daring to meet his gaze. They trembled in their threadbare clothes, clutching the pieces of his armour. Three wretched serfs clutched Harrower, struggling with the burden and visibly dismayed.

Kurgos stood in the half-dark behind them, farther back in the corridor, but it wasn't the chirurgeon they were afraid of.

'He's in the lower decks again.'

'I thought we'd sealed them off.'

The hulking chirurgeon gave the equivalent of a shrug. 'He found a way in.'

Herek exhaled, and took up his axe. He didn't bother with his armour. There wasn't time for that.

'Where exactly is he?'

They followed the bodies and the blood. Rathek had been creative in his excesses, de-limbing, severing heads, painting the decks with violence. The lower decks were a stygian world, full of cramped tunnels and sewer stench. Chambers like abattoirs waited around every other bend and cold vapour hung in the air like a fog. It chilled Herek's skin.

Not all of the dead had been slain by Rathek's hand. They found some climbed into alcoves, huddling together for warmth, blue as azure, hard as ice. The Culler had left their sad memorial undisturbed. Others they found locked in violent embrace, two serfs with hands around each other's necks, scraps of barely edible rations spilled out on the floor between them. Another lay stabbed to death, stripped bare and murdered for their clothes. Rathek had killed the thief a few feet away. They were still wearing the purloined coat but absent a head. That, Rathek had taken.

The trail ended in the brig. No captives here: the entire ship was a prison and those aboard slave labour for Herek and his men. They heard screaming and Kurgos gestured in a direction.

'Gods...' cursed Herek. 'Has he still not had his fill?'

'It's getting worse, I think,' said Kurgos, letting Herek take the lead with Harrower clutched in both hands.

They reached a junction and Herek waited for the screaming. When it came again, he took a fork and Kurgos followed.

'Is he torturing them now?' he asked himself. The Culler's madness had always been about need, never sadism.

They found no further bodies and as Herek sped up, heading

for the source of the screaming as it grew louder and louder, he wondered if Rathek was hoarding them for some reason.

He took the head, after all...

Descending a set of steps, entering through a door with a bloody handprint on the metal, they found where the screaming was coming from. An oubliette, little more than a hole with blood-red footprints around the edge. Too large for an ordinary human.

Rathek was the one screaming.

As Herek rushed to the edge of the hole, he slammed Harrower into the deck, where it held fast. Dark at first, the oubliette was a portal to fathomless black, and then his eyes adjusted.

Sunk to his knees, Rathek was bent over with his head to the floor, shaking and screaming. The crewman's severed head sat next to him, the crown of the skull touching the floor so the neck cavity faced upwards like a bowl. Rathek had been dipping his fingers into the blood. The walls were covered with his writing, words in a language that Herek didn't understand but recognised.

'It's daemonic speech,' he said.

And whether it was the sound of his voice or for some other reason, Rathek's screaming stopped abruptly. He cocked his head like a canid reacting to its master's voice. Then he stood and began to write, feverishly, urgently.

Herek shared a glance with Kurgos. The chirurgeon was poised with a vial of serum but Herek waved it away. They watched him.

'He's listening,' Kurgos realised.

Herek frowned. 'He's deaf, Kurgos. What can he be listening to?'

'A siren's call... The sword, it's speaking to him.'

Herek looked again at the oubliette's walls, at the scratched markings, at the old language of prehistory.

'What do you think it means?' Kurgos sounded awestruck.

'It's a map,' said Herek, after a moment. 'It's telling him how to find it.'

Chapter Twenty-Five

PRISONERS

A TRADE

WARNING SIGNS

Usullis was going to get them all killed.

He had found an empty packing crate from somewhere in the hangar-sized barrack house and stood on it to rise above the throng.

'Release us,' he demanded to the air and the dark, directing his gaze towards one of the vision slits in the door. Several of the troopers had already tried to break that door, throwing their bodies against it, bruising their flesh and bones against foot-thick irynwood banded with metal. It hadn't yielded. Now, Usullis addressed it like the door and not the queen of Kamidar was their captor.

'As an Imperial citizen, I demand you release us. We are servants of the Emperor, here to enact the will of the arisen primarch. We are emissaries of the Throne itself, we are—'

'Beren...' said Ariadne, interrupting.

He looked down, dishevelled, dirty and pale. His indignation gave him courage but it was fleeting, a distraction. He looked confused, afraid. They all were.

'But we are held falsely. Unlawfully imprisoned, and when the lord primarch hears of this...' His voice trailed away, as he looked around at the weary faces, the men and women of the Astra Militarum, the adepts of the Departmento Munitorum. Tired, distraught, defeated. They sat in clusters, sticking to their units, disarmed, nursing cuts and bruises.

Ariadne reached out to touch Usullis' ankle.

'Come down,' she said. 'No one is listening. Come down,' she said again, 'or someone will listen and they'll take you away, and anyone you associate with. Come down. Please.'

He sagged, all defiance bleeding out of him as Ariadne helped him off the crate and back to the ground. She led him gently through the throng of bodies, back to where the adepts had gathered in one corner, a host of hollow-eyed faces, grey with fatigue and worry.

The Sovereigns had incarcerated them as soon as the transports had arrived at the palace. They had been ushered through the dark, down nondescript corridors, through back ways, always under heavy guard until coming to this barrack house. She estimated well over two hundred in this chamber alone, and only beds for half of that number. These were taken by the injured, and there were many. Mainly flesh wounds or shock, but some had it worse.

Questions had been asked, fervent, angry questions, about medicae treatment, about food and water. About the rest of the delegation. Ariadne had seen bodies under corpse shrouds on her way to the barrack house. They had been stacked in an alleyway, prepared for incineration she assumed. She held out little hope for the other delegates. It also left a sick feeling in her gut and diminished her hopes of a peaceful resolution to the crisis.

Despite their demands for fair treatment, nothing had been granted or promised. The Sovereigns who had detained and imprisoned Ariadne's group weren't rough but bordered on belligerent.

The Imperials were foreigners in a foreign land and the natives did not appreciate their presence. And every time she closed her eyes, back in the transport as it rumbled along the rugged roads and byways or here in the shadowy barrack house, she saw the few remaining Astartes lit up like a bonfire as the Knights destroyed them. As they destroyed Ogin.

A few of the troopers had field kits and had been allowed to keep them after being searched for weapons. These had already been put to use by the time Ariadne had arrived with the others, but they were already out of all but the most basic medical supplies. They needed counterseptic, morphia. Bandages and wadding would only accomplish so much. There had been activity at first, when the new arrivals had come. First excitement, the eager trepidation of news, then disappointment. A fight had broken out, several in fact, the Solians the main antagonists venting their fear and anger, reverting back to old tribal instincts supposedly drummed out of them by the drill-abbots and commissars.

There were no commissars here.

The few officers who had survived the battle at Runstaf, a captain called Rellion and a lieutenant by the name of Munser, managed to reassert order. Skulls were cracked, the antagonists held accountable. A sort of primitive hierarchy was established, led by the Mordian contingent, but it was fragile because the Solians had the numbers.

After the initial commotion had died down, Rellion conversed with the already incarcerated sergeants, but little could be discerned of their situation. Ariadne had listened, trying to blot out the nervous hubbub of the adepts around her. No one knew what was happening outside of the four walls of the barrack house. One of the sergeants said she believed there were more Imperial troops being held in the palace grounds and close by. Captain Rellion had nodded at this, as if to suggest that it made sense to keep the captives close together. Easier to watch that way. Quicker to execute too, though no one voiced that fact. The officers had gathered around an empty crate like some low-tech strategium to speak in low voices, casting furtive glances at the door and shuttered window slits, but no one heard and no one came.

Since then a sullen silence had claimed the room, the haunted faces made gaunter by the low-powered sodium lamps suspended by chains above. The lamps were the only source of light, barring the narrow slit in the door, and that only offered a sliver when it was opened from the other side. The shutters were limned at the edges, suggesting ambient light from beyond, but also sealed. Ariadne had been studying the shutters. Each slat approximately one foot long by three inches in width, three slats layered one atop the other like scales to each window. The sixth from the right-hand side of the door was bent slightly, from use or some previous incident, it didn't matter. It was far enough away from the door to be largely ignored by the passing guards and the damage just minor enough that a metalsmith had not seen fit to fix it.

'This isn't right,' Usullis babbled in a quiet, faraway voice, drawing Ariadne back to the moment. 'They cannot hold us here.' His breath was sour with fear and she smelled stale sweat on his body. Ariadne doubted she was any better. Without proper ventilation, the air was thick with the fug of despair.

She shared a meaningful look with Patrica that said, *Watch him...* The adept nodded and Ariadne laid a hand on her arm and then one on Usullis' shoulder.

'Try to get some sleep, Beren,' she said, and glanced at the damaged shutter before heading over to where the Solians had 'made camp'.

Given the size of the room relative to the number of occupants, Ariadne marvelled at how quickly it had become territorialised. It reminded her of penal legion prison yards, of which she had seen her share whenever taking on a fresh intake to bolster the regular troopers. Such men and women were given little from the Munitorum stores – a lasgun of low quality, a power pack capable of a half-charge, perhaps an old bayonet if they were lucky. But in her experience such individuals, those who had lived long enough to be called up to service in a penal legion, which was a death sentence however the commissars dressed it, were resourceful. Improvised weapons were common, smuggled in belt bands or boot soles, sometimes even ingested to be later regurgitated. Such men and women possessed a low cunning and credible inventiveness. It was that enterprising spirit born of a desire to survive that Ariadne needed.

She clutched a morphia phial in one hand, kept it close to her body. She had forgotten she had it, just something she had pocketed when helping out the medicae staff. A half-dose remained. By rights, she should have surrendered it to one of the officers, but Ariadne had another use in mind.

The Solians glared at her as she approached. They hunched in small groups, some standing, some sitting on stools or empty boot lockers, like flocks of rowdy crows ready to caw at the intruder. Ariadne walked on, head up, fear held in check. They parted for her, but as she passed she became aware of the ex-gangers closing up behind her, enveloping her. If any one of them chose to do something violent, it would be too late for the Mordians to intervene.

One particularly large Solian stepped into Ariadne's path. She wore a padded jerkin of flak armour, kill-marks etched in red over the left breast. More than ten, crosshatched over the rough material. She wore leather vambraces, her knuckles hard and calloused from use. A buzzcut shaped a thick skull, her eyes narrow, her lips pursed in amusement at the tiny adept standing in front of her. Heavy boots and baggy fatigues finished the look: a slum fighter used to killing with her bare hands. The perfect soldier for the Imperium, were it not for the obvious aversion to chain of command. Her arms and neck had scars from a discipline master's whip.

'What do you want,' she said, her voice deep and breathy, *'bean counter?'* She managed to say the term with the exact inflection to make it sound like the rudest invective. Ariadne took it on the chin. *When a predator has you cornered, show no fear.* She met the Solian's gaze and showed her the half-phial of morphia.

'To trade.'

The ex-ganger regarded the phial, her slightly widened eyes betraying her interest. She reached for it but Ariadne snatched it back. A brave move. Or a foolish one. The next few moments would determine which.

'Not with you,' said Ariadne with more confidence than she felt.

Snarling, the burly Solian advanced on her, and with nowhere to turn Ariadne thought about shouting out to one of the Mordian officers.

Show no fear.

She stood her ground instead, placed her feet, raised her fists. It must have looked ridiculous, the narrow-framed Departmento adept against this beast of a Solian.

'She means with me,' uttered a man's voice from deeper in the throng.

The beast stepped back, an annoyed look on her face, and the other Solians parted again to reveal a wiry-looking man perched at the edge of a table. He wore a sergeant's rank pins on a cut-down tan jacket that left his tattooed arms exposed. The jacket hung open, unzipped, to reveal a tightly muscled torso and an ugly red band of stitching across his stomach. He smiled, one boot on the table, the other hanging down to touch the floor. The very picture of insouciance. He ran a hand through his mousy, shoulder-length hair. A few days of dark stubble helped frame his narrow jaw. All in all, his features made him look avian, but Ariadne recognised him even without the flecked blood on his face and half a pack of wadding stuffed against his innards.

'She means me,' he said again, lightly jumping off the table to approach her. 'Don't you?'

Ariadne nodded.

'Crannon Vargil,' he said, introducing himself, though technically they had met before when Ariadne had her hands on the man's stomach, holding in his guts. 'Former clan leader, Bonetakers.'

Ariadne gave her name and credentials.

'So what have you got for me, quartermaster senioris?' he asked good-naturedly enough. 'And what do you want in return?'

She showed him the phial.

'I need a blade. Something strong,' Ariadne replied.

A ship alighted on a landing platform in the south ward of Gallan-hold. It had entered the atmosphere alone and, barring the pilot, had a single occupant. Nonetheless, a cohort of twenty Sovereigns stood at arms to meet the vessel as a landing crew hustled amidst its jet wash, scurrying with refuelling hoses and poised with fire suppressant.

As the ship's stanchions touched down against the polished apron of the landing stage, the crews came in, did what they needed to and retreated again. A few moments later, the ship's rear ramp unfolded and came to rest against the ground. The occupant stood in the doorway, framed by light from within the hold.

An officer with the Royal Sovereigns said something into a vambrace-mounted vox-receiver and the troops in gold and white parted to admit their queen onto the landing stage. Orlah had seen it all anyway but appreciated the caution. Up to this point, she still did not know which way the Black Templars would turn.

'Greetings, my lord,' she began, her voice carrying above the dying thrum of the down-cycling turbines. 'And welcome back to Kamidar and Gallanhold. It brings me great reassurance that you are here in person.'

Morrigan strode down the ramp, his votive chains rattling gently against his vambraces, one gauntleted hand against the pommel of a heavy sword sheathed at his waist. A red cloak flapped in his wake, ragged at the edges, for it, like he, had seen many battles. His many oath parchments and purity seals stirred too like old promises spoken anew to the wind. He went bare-headed, a helm strapped to his belt, and stared ahead with hard green eyes and a worn face that had seen horrors up close and seen them vanquished. His hair was black and cut short into a crest down the middle with stubble-grey scalp either side. A neatly trimmed moustache framed his upper lip, his chin the same dark wash as the shaven parts of his scalp.

As he reached the end of the ramp and took the last few steps that brought him within reach of the queen, he gave a shallow bow.

'Your majesty.'

Up close, Orlah felt the Sovereigns stiffen in readiness and trepidation at the Black Templar's presence.

'I can offer you refreshment, a sacristan to tend your weapons,' said Orlah.

'That won't be necessary. I will not be staying long. I come only to address the situation at hand and my warriors' part in it.'

Orlah suppressed a spike of annoyance but kept it well hidden. 'Invaders have come to Kamidarian soil. Am I to believe you will renege on your oaths to come to our aid?'

The gauntleted fist around the sword pommel tightened and for a moment Orlah thought she may have overstepped. She might be queen, but the Adeptus Astartes did not recognise such titles. They served the Emperor and His servants incarnate. That did not include Imperial dignitaries.

Morrigan came closer by a half step. The Sovereigns responded, edging closer too, a few with their hands on their weapons, but the Black Templar barely noticed them. Orlah had no doubt in her mind that he could kill all of the guards and her without breaking a sweat. Her entourage was for appearances only. Her heart thundered a little faster.

'They are not invaders. They are the Imperium, which I serve, which you serve.'

'Have you seen the ravages inflicted on my lands, Lord Morrigan? The citizens of Kamidar that have lost their homes and livelihoods? This Ardemus, who leads the armada that even now waits on our borders with wrathful intent, came here with a velvet glove hiding a mailed fist. How else should I respond? How would any ruler?'

'This dispute is not for the Black Templars to get involved in. Not yet. Whatever dispute arose, whatever blood was shed, that is the end of it. Pray it does not resume. I have urgent matters to address. Were that not so, I would seek out the truth of this and render judgement. But let me be clear. If this Ardemus acts against the Imperium's interests then he will be sanctioned.' He paused to stare a moment at the queen. 'As will you, your majesty.'

Again, the Sovereigns reacted. One man even half drew his sword. Orlah calmed them all down with a gesture. No sense in getting everyone killed now.

Morrigan gave nothing away of his inner thoughts, though his jaw tensed.

'Even as we speak, my chief aide and her negotiators are seeking a resolution, but I will have little choice but to defend myself if Kamidar is attacked without cause.'

Morrigan appeared to relax, though it was difficult to tell given how inscrutable most Astartes were. Orlah did know this meeting was all but over.

'I have faith... But if Kamidar is attacked without cause then the Black Templars will beseech the crusade to replace this man, Ardemus, with a calmer head.'

It was Orlah's turn to bow, which she did elegantly. 'I am ever in your debt, my lord.'

'The bloodshed stops, your majesty,' Morrigan reminded her, a waft of incense in his wake as he turned on his heel. It mingled with the reek of lapping powder and sacred oil, and the heady stench that all transhumans seemed to possess. 'If I am forced to return again, it will not be alone.'

He gained the ramp, heavy footfalls like giant drumbeats, and it closed behind him. In seconds, the engines started up, throaty and loud. Orlah retreated gracefully, her Sovereigns closing in around her as they left the landing stage. At the edge of the platform that overlooked the northward of the palace and the lands beyond, Orlah turned to watch the ship as it soared away into the night sky until it became a speck in the firmament.

She met Ekria a little later, as she made preparations for her departure to the royal grove.

'I take it, your majesty, that the Black Templars will not draw swords with us if it comes to it?'

'Am I that obvious, Ekria?' said Orlah, her gaze on the landbarge and the cargo hold where her daughter resided. *Soon,* she willed, *soon you will have peace.*

It was a long but bulky transport that went on six pairs of hefty tracks, three either side of the heavily armoured chassis.

'Far from it, your majesty. I merely assumed I would have heard by now had Lord Morrigan's visit gone as hoped.'

Orlah pulled up one of her leather gauntlets to tighten it around her hand. She still wore her battle gear, having thought only hours before that she would need to use it, but decided not to change. She would honour Jessivayne garbed as a warrior, just as she too had been a warrior. It seemed fitting.

'I had hoped they would hold to their oaths, but I suppose I am not entirely surprised. As biased as I am, I see how they are torn. Perhaps abstention was the best we could have hoped for at this juncture.'

Ekria nodded at the queen's sagely assessment. 'And without their swords?' she asked tentatively.

'I am forced to turn to other means for our protection, which is why I've summoned you.'

'Ah,' said Ekria. 'Destiny awaits for those who have the will to seize it.'

'Quite so,' remarked the queen. 'One of the old poets?'

'Very old, your majesty.'

Orlah nodded, her interest already moving on to other matters. 'Have Thonius prepare the archeotech.'

'It will not be easy to move from the catacombs, your majesty.'

'He will find a way,' she said, mounting the steps to the hold where she would ride with her daughter.

Chapter Twenty-Six

CEASEFIRE

FEAR OF DISCOVERY

LURKING IN THE SHADOWS

A ceasefire was agreed, a swiftly drawn treaty between the functionaries and factotums on both sides, the admiral's seal and the queen's royal edict making it official. And just like that the violence that had erupted so swiftly and so suddenly ended with the same abruptness.

An uneasy stillness fell across the fleet, which held at high anchor beyond the Iron Veil. The ships' bellies edged towards fumes, the crews' stomachs the same. But for the next three days all hostilities would be suspended. The reclamation forces would return to their landing sites, those that hadn't been driven there already, their soldiers stood down. The Knights would remain at the city borders. No captives would be freed, retained as insurance for the good faith of Praxis, but they would be fed and tended to.

Fragile peace would reign.

In his private quarters, nursing a glass of wine that he felt no desire to drink, Ardemus regarded the pict-capture of Haster again. It had been taken from a live vid-feed, freely offered by the queen as proof of good intent and the first lieutenant's continued existence. There was no audio and Haster had been seated under guard. Through this medium it was difficult to ascertain the man's condition, but he was conscious and appeared lucid. He had also greyed in his pallor, the washed-out complexion of someone carrying an injury, and not for the first time Ardemus wondered exactly what had transpired with the delegation Praxis had sent. Enquiries had been made about the rest of the party, the Custodian, Vychellan, in particular, but no specific answer had been given. They had the warriors under guard and that was all the Kamidarians would say.

Ardemus suspected they were dead, both of the Talons. Intriguing that the royals were not up in arms about Syreniel, for he was sure the Silent Sister would have attempted to fulfil her primary mission before succumbing to capture or death. He wondered what that meant and what else the queen had planned. He saw all of this as a ploy and the parley had done nothing to disabuse him of that notion. Every ship in the fleet stood at readiness.

Nothing had come through from the lunar fortress in Kamidar's orbit. A Black Templars garrison. Fleet intelligencers had discerned as much already but having confirmation was useful, if troubling. Ardemus didn't know how many they were or what kind of condition they were in, but he was glad they were standing on the sidelines for now. According to his intelligencers in the fleet, the Black Templars had sworn an oath of fealty to Kamidar and the queen, and he had no desire to reckon with such formidable warriors even with the Marines Malevolent in his corner. The fact they hadn't acted suggested they wanted no part in the dispute, which suited the admiral, but the stalemate chafed at his patience.

Once again, he considered whether they should just make a push through the Iron Veil and hang the damn consequences, but without just cause and whilst under a flag of truce, it would reflect poorly. No: for now, he would play the game. He still had Renyard in play, but no means through which to contact him. If all went to plan that would change soon.

He sipped at the wine, a vintage he had once enjoyed, but found it bitter.

Renyard had gone to ground, he and his entire strike force. They took shelter in the wilds, amidst cairns of stones, bleak scrubland and under the shallow boughs of skeletal trees. An army hiding in the open.

They had reached their target, a large iron tower inside a walled enclosure. It had a small garrison and a pair of Armigers at the main gate. A third, larger engine patrolled the compound in slow, ponderous sweeps. For now he waited, gauging his enemy's strength. He did so from distance, a mag-scope pressed to one bloodshot eye, the other clenched shut and pulling at his many scars.

Even far away, the larger war machine was impressive. He had no fear of it, but it was a fool who underestimated strength.

They had found her passing through one of the palace's common halls. She walked briskly, and projected a quiet air of authority. Her attire had a fine cut, trimmed in silver and accented with a gilded chain. A curved plate covered her left shoulder, wrought from silver and fashioned into the shape of a regal-looking bird with a ruby for one eye and a sapphire the other.

The serfs were vagabonds by comparison and bowed from her path. Even the haughty Sovereigns dipped their heads in deference. She had four of them in tow, with their tall horsehair-plumed helms and clutching glittering pikes and side-holstered shot-pistols. Queen's royal guard, the same ones from the feast hall.

Kesh hung back, silently urging Syreniel to follow her example. As a pathfinder, she knew much about stalking prey, but this was an entirely different animal and unfamiliar terrain. She would prefer a death world to this place and felt a gnawing in her stomach at every guard they passed, and wondered how much longer they could last before being discovered.

They had infiltrated deep into the palace now and any hope of reaching a landing stage, stealing a ship and escaping back to the fleet had faded to dust. It had been a foolish notion, and unrealistic. Their only reasonable course was to try to send a warning to Praxis, and word of the fate of the delegation. That meant finding a vox-station that could transmit beyond the planet's upper atmosphere. So far that search had proven fruitless. They needed a major comms hub or enhanced vox-array. Neither would be found in the palace exterior. That fact, and the guard patrols inexorably tightening their grip, had driven them inwards.

Syreniel had seen it as an opportunity, especially when they had seen the well-heeled royal equerry.

Lurking in the shadows of a servant's alcove, dressed in purloined robes, the pair waited for the guards to thin out ahead. Syreniel's fists tightened in impatience, her bare knuckles cracking. They had left some of their attire back in the stores where they had filched the robes, tucked away out of sight, anything they couldn't reasonably obscure with their stolen clothing. That meant Syreniel's vambraces and gorget. Only the bronze cuff remained. Kesh had ditched her uniform jacket. In the guise of servants, their chief advantage was anonymity. No one, not even the Sovereigns, looked a lowly serf in the eye. They had no faces, no identities. They were merely tools to do the nobles' bidding, silently and unobtrusively. Even so, Syreniel's eagle tattoo, the kohl around her eyes and the corpse-pale skin under the now absent gorget would not go unnoticed. She kept her head down, her hood pulled up.

Heading for their barracks or an alehouse, the guards went about their business and, after a few moments more, Kesh and Syreniel carried on. They followed the royal entourage, maintaining a surreptitious distance until the aide stopped and said something quietly to her shadows, who then departed without complaint or disagreement.

Kesh and Syreniel had already shuffled away to the edge of the corridor as the guards trooped past. Upon catching sight of the pair of humble serfs, one of the pikemen slowed and Kesh feared they would be undone until Syreniel eased off the strength of her limiter. At once, Kesh was hit by a deep repulsion and she pushed her tongue to the roof of her mouth to stop from retching. It repelled the royal guard, who suddenly thought better of his enquiry and marched on, catching up with the others. Syreniel re-engaged the cuff and Kesh exhaled her relief. Mercifully, the corridor was empty, barring the aide, and she was headed deeper into the palace precincts.

They hurried to catch her, keen to not lose sight of the aide now that they had found her. But she did slip from sight, moving sylph-like through the gloomy halls and corridors, and Kesh's heart leapt into her mouth when she thought they might have lost their quarry.

Turning a corner, more quickly than was appropriate for a servant in the palace confines, they found her again.

She stood in a patch of moonlight. It shone down upon her from a great arched window through which the stars and night sky were visible. And she was staring right at them.

'Beautiful, isn't it?' she said, and Kesh had to suppress the urge to run.

Something about her, the way she carried herself, her manner... it felt *off*. Or perhaps it was the sudden fear of discovery.

'It's called a lunarium,' she went on and eased closer. Her footsteps were soft and innocuous but Kesh's instincts were screaming. 'A place for stargazing.'

Why hadn't she called for the guards? Perhaps she thought they were serfs, lost in the wrong part of the palace, and had taken pity on them?

'How diminished we feel before the majesty of the celestial heavens,' she said, drawing ever closer.

Sweat drenched Kesh's back, her skin alive with prickling heat, although the chamber was cold enough to fog the breath. Kesh's jaw clenched, her limbs tensing. She felt Syreniel's presence and realised the Silent Sister was visibly shaking. Her limiter cuff was turned all the way off.

'How small,' the aide continued, closing, her mouth curling into a smile. 'How insignificant...'

'We need to leave,' uttered Kesh in a parched rasp.

Syreniel had become stuck, her feet rooted, her limbs taut enough to snap...

'Right now,' Kesh insisted in a harsh whisper and touched her arm.

And just like that they moved, backward steps at first, murmuring incoherent deference as together they turned and hurried away into the shadows and the gloom. No bells sounded, no guards came. All Kesh heard as they made their abrupt escape were those soft footfalls, impossibly light, until even that faded to nothing.

Chapter Twenty-Seven

ANOINTED

IRON BONES

FROM OUT OF THE MIST

Klaigen hissed, unable to mask his pain as the knife ran across his skin. Blood welled in his palm, thick and dark. He squeezed his hand into a fist and the blood dripped eagerly through the gaps between his fingers. It added to the steadily growing pool made by his brothers, a slowly congealing well shimmering in a clay bowl at the foot of the ritual stone.

The others stood around it, having made their pledge, crude bandages to staunch their wounds, their eyes hooded but as keen as the blade. Klaigen joined their ranks, a feral grin turning his mouth. Seven knights, seven warriors, made anew for the old god. For Hurne.

That left only Lareoc, who dabbed a bead of sweat on his lip with his tongue. He glanced to the stairwell, the stony spiral that led back up through the hollowed-out cave and into the larger caverns beyond.

But Parnius did not appear. And although Lareoc had not

expected him, his friend's absence stirred an anger in him that made him clench his fists. His jaw tensed.

Albia brought him back.

'Step forwards, Lareoc of Solus, and be anointed Lareoc of Hurne.'

The old priest gestured encouragingly to the former baron, his fingers gnarled but strong. The light from gently burning torches caught his eyes, one the green of untamed forests, the other the muddy brown of deep earth, a strangely alluring heterochromia. He had survived in the wilds, somehow, this wizened man, holed up in caves, living off the land. It had never really occurred to Lareoc before how remarkable that was. And yet, here he was, standing before him, hale and hearty enough, but wearing only a rough brown habit and hood. Winter alone should have ended him.

He didn't know where these doubts had sprung from, but now, at the cusp of the ritual, he wavered. Albia seemed to sense it.

'Hurne is of the earth and we are his children,' said the priest, his right hand inviting, his left carrying the knife handed to him by the previous supplicant. Dirt engrained his fingers and soil begrimed his skin, rubbed so deep it picked out the contours, the veins and imperfections. It was as if he had been born from the earth itself, an old root taken shape into the form of a man and made into flesh and bone.

Lareoc glanced again at the stair but it remained empty. The chamber beyond the light at its summit was cold, yet here in the deep earth it was warm, a heady, sweaty heat that pricked his skin.

I am unready, he wanted to say, but the memory of Baerhart shaming him again arose unbidden in his mind. He lacked the strength he needed. This is what Albia had promised. *The draught is but the beginning,* the priest had told him upon his return to the caves, *the opening of a valve to a natural spring of power. Drink of it. Use it.*

you by your brothers and sisters of the earth. All you do is take it.'

Lareoc looked at the ritual stone. A crude, misshapen rock, Albia had hewn it from the bowels of Kamidar and daubed the stag and spear upon it in a dark matter that could only have been his own blood. The clay bowl glinted with a much fresher offering.

He stepped forwards. He needed strength. He couldn't do this on his own. He took a knee, a knight pledging his sword.

'The letting of blood makes the oath...' said Albia, nodding sagely at Lareoc at the decision he had made. That gesture, that subtle thing, most of all gave him pause, but the moment of retreat had passed and the bowl was being raised by the seven. He would become the eighth, their leader, for Hurne as well as the rebellion.

'...and the dousing of the flesh seals it.'

Lareoc shut his eyes as he felt the blood anoint him, still warm, much warmer than he thought it could be, and all his doubts fled, subsumed by the ritual. When he opened his eyes again, Albia had daubed the stag and the spear upon his chest, his old fingers pushing pale lines through Lareoc's incarnadine skin. The sigils ran as the blood ran, joining with one another, forming a different mark but one that Lareoc had not the wit to see.

His brothers and sisters surrounded him, reaching down into the blood now welling at his knees, marking their own flesh in simulacrum of Lareoc's own.

He felt strong, empowered.

And the stairwell stayed empty.

He met Parnius later, at an outcrop of stone that jutted from the upper cavern mouth like a spear tip. Parnius had his back to him, arms folded as he contemplated the wind-tossed sky beyond, the small tussocks of gorse and wheatgrass riffling in time with his cloak.

'I am loyal to you,' uttered Parnius, his back still to Lareoc.

'I know that, Parnius.'

'But I do not trust the priest.'

'Faith requires belief, sometimes in the absence of trust.'

'He is a stranger to us, as are his motives.'

'Do you trust me, brother?'

Parnius turned, his face grave at first until it softened. 'I would follow you anywhere, my lord. But these *rites*, they disturb me. They should disturb you.'

'It is... strange, I'll admit.' Lareoc had since washed the blood from his body and changed his clothes, but the sheen of it still clung to him, and its fading metallic aroma. 'But it is strength, drawn from Kamidar's old roots. Earth and branch, Parnius. The ancient ways.'

'I had never heard of Hurne before Albia,' he said. 'I fear he came to us just when we needed him, when you needed him.'

'And what if he did? Is there harm in providence?'

'That depends, my lord, on where providence leads us.'

Parnius bowed, taking his leave. Lareoc let him go, his anger towards him long cooled, a pang of sadness in its place.

'In the end,' said the old priest, who had come in Parnius' wake, though how the squire had missed him Lareoc could not say, 'you will need to choose.'

'I know,' uttered Lareoc to the wind.

Another voice intruded, Klaigen. Urgent, breathless.

'A vox-missive, my lord,' he began.

As Lareoc turned to face the knight, he saw that Albia had gone. Nowhere to be seen. He was about to ask Klaigen if he had passed him on the way, but something in the man's expression made him do otherwise.

'What is it?'

'A ceasefire, my lord. Between Kamidar and the Imperium.'

Lareoc frowned, disappointed. He had hoped to make something of the inevitable chaos.

'That was fast.'

'There is more.'

'Oh...?'

And what Klaigen relayed next made Lareoc smile grimly.

At last.

Renyard had made a pyre of its iron bones, flames still flicking between the pieces of broken servos and pistons. Ten of his warriors had died in the assault, half of those belonging to the Sisters. He had expected more.

They had hobbled the Knight, first drawing off its lesser retainers and then ambushing the larger war machine. Its thick armour and ion shield were formidable, but melta weaponry, cleverly deployed, had seen the end to all that. *Sever the leg and the body will fall.* And fall it had, and a fallen giant, however formidable, will succumb to the onslaught of ants if it cannot move or defend itself.

Renyard had clambered onto the chassis of the Knight himself, using knife and axe like a mountaineer conquering an iron peak. As his cohorts had set about the stricken god-engine with charges and close-range weaponry fashioned to scythe through metal, dismembering and unmaking it, he had laid charges of his own. A pair of melta bombs magnetically fused to the torso. The blast had made a mess of things, left torn and congealed tongues of metal in its wake. Renyard had been forced to hack through what was left, a brutal and metronomic task that had eventually revealed the flesh-and-blood pilot within. He had fought, of course. Warriors with honour always do. A near-point-blank las-burn scarred Renyard's own faceplate from where the Knight pilot had shot him. They had even attempted to draw their blade from a scabbard, but Renyard had reached in by then, seizing the pilot's skull in one gauntleted hand and crushing it like an egg as the man had squirmed then screamed. Then there was silence but for the guttering flames overtaking his broken mount.

They had dragged the destroyed Armigers by chains, three Marines Malevolent to a length, three lengths per machine, and heaped them alongside the larger god-engine.

The mortal garrison had been less trouble. They had fought gallantly, but a man against a transhuman warrior was no contest. They died as all men die, in blood and terror. At least, this was Renyard's experience.

Its defenders slaughtered, only the tower remained.

'Lay charges around the base, enough to do a thorough job,' he said.

The Sisters set about this task, their scarred Superior nodding after receiving her orders.

Renyard watched them; he watched the Knights burn in the distance, the fire reflecting vividly against his dirty armour. Mustard yellow shone, but it was far from glorious. But war wasn't glorious. It was ugly. Renyard had always thought himself a good fit in that regard.

'See,' he said to the Marines Malevolent that had begun to gather around him, 'I told you gods can die.'

A loud crack of detonation rose above the dulcet crackling of flames, thundering across the barren plains. The tower collapsed a moment later, a slow-motion sag before crumbling utterly into oblivion amidst a pall of rising dust. It swept outwards, the dust cloud so thick that Renyard turned to his auto-senses for perception.

A signal registered on his retinal display, several miles east according to auspex. One of his men registered a silent interrogative. Renyard curtly dismissed it. He was walking, interrogating the signal. If there was someone else out here, someone who could send a warning, he would have to find them and silence them. The vox-jammer was down, but it would still take time for the Kamidarians to notice, and for someone to investigate the outage. If a report describing his presence and activities leaked out... Well, that could be problematic.

Clipped battlesign saw three of his men following sharply on Renyard's heels, the rest maintaining a perimeter. He ran, weapons mag-clamped to his armour, long strides eating up the yards with ease. After a few miles, he paused to check his bearings and refresh the signal return.

A single life sign. It had an Astartes ident.

He had been told the Kamidarians had made oaths with a cohort of Black Templars. If one of their ranks had witnessed the destruction of the tower... Renyard felt his potential problems mounting. He unclamped his bolt rifle and flicked up the iron sights.

Slowing his advance to a crawl, Renyard stalked towards the signal. A light rain was falling, flecking his armour with wet patches. Away from the smashed compound, mist gathered, turning into a thick fog the farther east he went. A weak sun shone watery and pale. Renyard kept moving.

An armoured figure resolved in the mist, unmistakably Astartes, its silhouette iconic.

Renyard raised his weapon to his cheekplate, aiming down the iron sights. Tacticus armour was durable and thick but weaker at the retinal lens of the helm. One shot, one kill. He didn't want a protracted fight. The warrior could have detected the explosion or even seen the smoke from the fires and be coming to investigate. He might not be expecting a hostile engagement from a fellow Space Marine. That split second of indecision was all that Renyard needed.

The figure emerged fully into the wan light.

Renyard relaxed. He wasn't a Black Templar. He wore white armour, though it was smeared with dirt and blood. Judging by the weakened bio-sign, some of that blood was his own. He staggered as he walked, obviously injured. A Storm Reaper, and therefore part of Praxis, probably with one of the reclamation forces.

'Hold there, weary traveller.'

The Storm Reaper looked up, as if seeing Renyard and his men for the first time. He clutched a long-curved blade in his hand, something indigenous to his culture. It looked serviceable enough.

'Have no fear, brother,' Renyard told him. 'You have found allies.' Up close, he made a rapid determination about the Space Marine's combat efficacy, a decision about whether to put him down to avoid carrying the dead weight or absorb an asset into his ranks. One did not offset the five lost, but it was a start in the right direction. One of Renyard's secondary objectives had been to pick up any stragglers should any be left. He fully lowered his weapon, a hand gesture to his warriors instructing them to do the same.

'What's your name, brother?' he asked, and voxed back to the kill-site to have a medi-kit prepared.

The Storm Reaper fought for the words. He had suffered but his Astartes physiology was healing him.

'Ogin,' he rasped. 'I am Ogin.'

Chapter Twenty-Eight

NO ESCAPE

BREACH

THROUGH A NARROW APERTURE

The palace wound around a spiral, one echelon leading to the next and rising from the lower wards to the upper royal quarters. Each precinct was a vast, many-chambered place, replete with halls and corridors, galleries and plazas. Parts of it, not limited to the bastion walls and watchtowers, were open to the sky. Others were sunk deep into the earth, utterly labyrinthine, and the province of the esteemed and powerful.

It had secrets and an abundance of shadows.

Kesh was glad of that. They had needed them. They headed inwards, east; at least it felt like east, and she trusted her pathfinder instincts. They kept to the fringes in the main, the austere and bare stone passages used by the servant classes. Kesh had overheard one referring to them as such and the name stuck. It ensured they steered clear of the heavier concentrations of Sovereigns, who appeared to be moving outwards, off to man battlements or other military stations in preparation for a coming conflict. If any were left still searching for the two errant Imperials who had survived the massacre, they were content to let them roam or at least not make especial effort to find them. Kesh didn't know if she found that comforting or quite the opposite.

She knew they *had* to get word to the fleet. Praxis must know what had been done in the queen's name. She thought of Dvorgin then, his corpse left unceremoniously in the corridor outside the feast hall, and wondered again what became of all the troops they brought with them. They could be dead too. She hoped not. She hoped for much more besides. Not least of which was the re-engagement of her companion.

Ever since the aborted attempt to find and assassinate the queen, Syreniel had become rudderless, following on behind Kesh, her thoughts opaque as slate. Kesh had reckoned the palace must have vox-stations. She had seen antennae from the landing pad when they had first arrived, ornate, beautiful and baroque but definitely antennae. Reach the fleet. Warn them. They could do that. Even two of them, lost and outnumbered, could do that. And then? Well, then the rest might not matter.

That line of thought had brought them here, through that spiral, working inwards, keeping their heads down and trying not to draw attention. A tactic that would need to change in the next few minutes.

The vox-station was manned and guarded. Three civilian operators in royal-blue uniforms presided over a bank of communication devices, monitoring audio traffic between the ships of the Kamidarian fleet. Two women, one man, each had a receiver cup pressed to their ear. One of the women had been fitted with a cranial implant, which effectively designated her seniority. She also took the central throne on the vox dais, the other two a foot lower at subordinate stations. A clear armaglass blister encased the comms operatives, its clean and clinical aesthetic at odds with the classical grandeur of the palace that surrounded it in carved marble and sculpted columns.

Four guards stood outside the blister, pikes and sidearms at the ready, long cloaks and tall horsehair-plumed helms. Sovereigns, their faces hidden by veils of silver chain. They looked like statues, as still as the grave.

Kesh watched them from a distance, another servant's alcove, another tense episode fearing discovery. She felt Syreniel's presence behind her, not her *otherness*, although her limiter was only partially engaged, but just the fact of another person's nearness. The Silent Sister had been on edge ever since their encounter with the equerry in the lunarium. Kesh found it hard to put the experience into words. An instinct, similar to the one she had felt in the feast hall right before the massacre, had urged her to retreat. They had not discussed it, but the unsettling memory of it remained between them like an unspoken argument.

Ordinarily, Syreniel's stillness verged on near invisibility, but she was agitated. Disturbed. Kesh didn't know which she found more unnerving, the stillness or this. The fact they had managed to evade capture for this long was in part due to Syreniel's pariah 'gift'. Kesh thought of it as a *shroud*. It had a way of dissuading attention, a repelling aura that averted eyes or deafened ears. They had become a shadow that no one wanted to investigate. Even reaching this point, there had been close calls. A turn of the head at just the right moment, a vox-summons to call away a troop of guards heading in their direction. The shroud had kept them covert.

Providence, Syreniel had signed.

Kesh tried not to think of it as a 'miracle'.

She turned to the Silent Sister, who had blended effortlessly into the shadows, and raised the four fingers on her right hand.

Syreniel nodded, and Kesh slipped back to allow her to come forwards.

This section of the palace felt remote and the corridors appeared empty but for the guards and the civilian operators, but all it would take was an errant patrol or a wandering servant to undo their subterfuge. A hooded robe would only work for so long.

Evidently, Syreniel thought so too as she began to edge forwards. Her hand went to the short sword now hidden beneath her borrowed robes.

Kesh grabbed her by the shoulder, and hissed, 'What are you doing?'

Scowling, Syreniel made the sign for 'kill and subdue'.

'And how quickly can you do that before one of them raises an alarm and we have an entire platoon bearing down on us?'

Syreniel gave the facial equivalent of a shrug that suggested she had confidence in her ability to silence the guards quickly. Kesh saw thirty feet of corridor, sparse enough that it resembled a shooting gallery to the experienced markswoman. Three soldiers could stand abreast and fire at an oncoming foe without fear of getting in each other's way, which left a fourth to vox for reinforcements. She also doubted that the operators were without protection, assuming the blister could be sealed and made practically inviolable at a moment's notice. If that happened, they were as good as discovered, even if Syreniel could take out the guards before they raised the alarm. If the Sovereigns didn't, the vox-operators would.

'We need to get closer,' Kesh whispered.

Syreniel curved her hands, placing the knuckles together. *How?*

An empty carafe and a salver had been left on a low table in the servant's alcove. Perhaps it had been forgotten or abandoned in haste. Kesh had seen no other servants in this part of the palace and wondered if they had been banished from the military stations until the crisis was over.

She picked up the salver with the empty carafe. As soon as the guards looked inside, they would know something was wrong. Assuming she even got that close.

'Stay behind me and keep your head low,' said Kesh.

They made it almost halfway before the first guard noticed them and stepped away from his post with an upraised hand.

'No servants allowed here,' he said, his voice tinny through the chain veil. 'Turn around and find an alternative way through.'

Kesh kept on coming, the salver held at chest height balanced on two hands underneath, just as she had seen other servants do.

'I said, turn around,' the guard insisted, moving to intercept her but not yet reaching for his weapon. His comrades had taken notice too and their stern regard fell upon Kesh and Syreniel.

She kept moving, feeling unarmed and utterly exposed. Her purloined rifle sat slung across her back, hidden away but useless.

Kesh gestured to the carafe, raising the salver slightly by way of offering. As soon as she spoke, they would know she was an imposter. Her Mordian accent would give her away. She made it five more feet before the lead guard drew his sidearm. The others had moved up too and readied their pikes.

The first guard was close enough for Kesh to see his eyes narrow.

'Shit,' she said.

'You're no serv—'

Kesh flung the carafe, spoiling the lead guard's aim. As the shot went off, thankfully wide, she threw the salver like a discus, hitting the man in the throat just below the chin. A markswoman's throw. As he buckled, dropping his pike and sidearm to clutch at his crushed throat, Syreniel had spurred into motion. She jinked left then right, her long legs crossing the distance to the other guards quickly. She incapacitated her first opponent with a palm strike to the solar plexus, hard enough to dent metal. Weaving around a hasty pike thrust, she grabbed the weapon's haft and used it as a lever to yank the guard around into his comrade before slamming one into the other and putting them on the ground. A swift kick to the head as a guard tried to scramble to his feet dealt with one. She cold-cocked the other with the pommel of her sword just as Kesh applied her rifle-butt to the nose of the first guard to put him out.

Four Sovereigns downed, none fatally, in under thirty seconds.

The vox-operators only needed twenty-eight.

As Kesh lunged for the door to the vox-station blister it sealed shut, the senior female operator having just pulled a lever. Her pale face turned to Kesh, the fear in her eyes changing into triumph when she realised the saboteurs couldn't breach the blister.

Kesh stared back, breathing hard, seething.

The senior operator said something to one of her cohorts in Kamidarian. A moment later, an alarm shrilled and warning lights bathed the woman's smug face in a crimson glow.

Dvorgin had a saying. He'd said, *'When facing peril, the threat of almost certain death, a man will do almost anything to gain a little more rope, to climb a little higher and escape the doom coming for him. Thing is, there comes a point when the rope runs out or the man realises he's not saving himself at all, that all he's done is gain enough to hang himself.'*

'Shit!' Kesh said again, somewhat unnecessarily. She glanced back at Syreniel, whose grave expression said everything she needed to.

No escape, no way to reach the fleet, and hunted by the Sovereigns, who now knew where they were. Shrouded or not, they were running out of rope.

'We need to leave.'

Syreniel bade her stand aside as she drew her sword. A whip-crack blow struck the hardened glass of the blister and bounced off. It left a mark but not so much as a crack. The vox-operators recoiled at first then, seemingly realising their invulnerability, began to smile, mockery in their eyes. She struck again, two-handed, but still the blister did not yield.

'This is pointless,' said Kesh, eyeing the shadows behind them warily. Then she had a thought. 'What about the weapon?' She gestured to where Syreniel had secreted it beneath her robes.

The Silent Sister shook her head. *A waste,* she signed curtly and had been about to strike a third time when she paused, turning to regard Kesh, who stared back in confusion. Syreniel had saved her outside the feast hall, a Talon of the Emperor rescuing a lowly pathfinder, and she looked at Kesh now as she had then, as if seeing something in her.

Shouting echoed from deeper in the palace, distant but growing closer.

Syreniel flipped the short sword around, lightly spinning it to catch the tip of the blade and then offered the hilt to Kesh.

'Hells, what do you want me to do? If you can't breach it...'

Try.

Kesh eyed the marks on the hardened glass, stout enough to repel a bolter shell, she reckoned.

Syreniel jabbed the pommel into her shoulder, urging her. *Try.*

Her expression was insistent. The voices were getting closer.

Kesh took the sword in one hand and, roaring, she swung.

The blister shattered, sheared right through, then broke apart, showering the vox-operators with glass. They recoiled again, terrified this time. Syreniel was on them in two breaths, incapacitating the senior and then the other two. She even disarmed the male, who had tried to reach for a pistol mag-locked to the side of the station.

Kesh regarded the shattered armaglass then looked at the sword in her hand. The vox-station stood open and at the ready.

She rushed inside, returning the blade to Syreniel then taking a moment to familiarise herself with the controls. They were standard template construct, like everything else made by the Imperium. Universal enough. She flipped the main levers to transmit wideband. It would be picked up by every station but it should also reach the fleet.

'This is Sergeant Magda Kesh of the Eighty-Fourth Mordian.' She gave her ident tag and Imperial authorisation code. And a silent prayer in the few seconds' pause. 'The Praxis delegation has been slain. Murdered in cold blood by the royal house of Kamidar...'

The Sovereigns entered the corridor, their voices raised in anger.

Kesh glanced over her shoulder at the fast-approaching guards. A sea of glittering pike heads advanced. She faltered until Syreniel drew her gaze.

Don't stop, she signed, then flicked a glance at the Sovereigns. *I will slow them down.*

It was a risk. The Kamidarians might have deployed scrying devices or have some other means of covertly observing the prisoner, but Ariadne had come this far. She had brokered with the Solians, who grew more belligerent by the hour, their fracas with the Mordians becoming ever more frequent. Insults, some less veiled than others, went back and forth. She heard muttering from her own ranks, most of it Usullis, who had recovered his bluster and aimed it at the scruffy gang-fighters turned conscripts. Discipline stood on a knife-edge and if a fight broke out, a *real* fight, she doubted the Kamidarians would intervene whether they were watching or not. And hemmed in as they were, it would be bloody.

They needed information, something else to focus on.

Ariadne had Crannon Vargil's knife and she meant to use it. Enfolding herself amongst the other Departmento adepts, she found her way to the sixth shutter, the one with the slightly damaged slat. Her colleagues acted readily as co-conspirators, gathering in front of the shutter as they conducted hushed conversations. Even so, Ariadne slid the knife slowly and carefully into the small gap in the damaged shutter and began to ease it apart. A narrow bar of light slid in, soft enough not to draw notice but not quite wide enough that she could see out. Using the jammed knife like a lever, Ariadne pressed down with her elbow. The metal creaked but no one heard it above the low hubbub of voices. Each incarcerated man and woman was locked in the prison of their own thoughts as well as the four granite walls of the blockhouse.

Pulling the knife back, Ariadne pressed her augmented eye to the shutter. The aperture she'd made was still narrow, but she could see out.

Light was low, and cast from flickering electro-sconces that fizzled in the rain. Her bionic eye compensated, piercing the gloom and revealing details that would have otherwise been obscured. Cold damp stone was everywhere. A lower level of the palace, she assumed, judging by the shimmer of the walls and the chill in the air. Sovereigns stood about in small groups. They blew on their hands to keep warm, talking to one another in murmuring voices. Low-ranked warriors, their cloaks were rough and their armour less polished. Not royal guard but gaolers. They appeared relaxed, either a symptom of their position within the Kamidarian army or because the royals didn't frequent this part of the palace. This was where the commoners dwelled. No servants either. No need for them in the absence of the nobility, Ariadne supposed.

Even from her narrow view, she discerned the blockhouse was outside in one of the outer palace precincts, open to the elements but surrounded by a high curtain wall. She just glimpsed the edge of it through the flurries of light rain. Several of the guards tugged up the collars on their cloaks and hugged their arms a little closer to their bodies. Across the wet flagstones of a courtyard was a second blockhouse. From what she knew about the size of the Imperial delegation, Ariadne reckoned on more prisoners within. The guards stationed outside practically confirmed it. A third structure, relatively central between the pair of blockhouses, must have been a guardhouse. Dim light issued from within, so she assumed it was garrisoned. It had a fortified tower surrounded by a shielded parapet. A turret gun sat ensconced at the summit of the tower, a heavy stubber. A guard in a rain-slicked cloak manned it. Another nearby on the same level lazily panned a search lamp. As its beam strayed over towards Ariadne she instinctively shrank away, but no one could see her and she had bent the shutter only slightly so as to avoid detection. The light passed on, she resumed her survey.

Despite the presence of the guardhouse, the troop numbers looked fairly thin and she guessed the bulk of the army had been reposted to the borders or the main gates of the upper palace in response to the volatility of the situation between the Ironhold and the Imperium. A major gate opened out from the courtyard; this led to the exterior palace grounds, for even hurried in the darkness to their place of confinement Ariadne had kept her bearings. She remembered the vehicle yard was nearby, north of this main gate. A second gate led inwards and Ariadne realised this place was a way station, a bulwark that stood at the mouth to the deeper palace. Further rings of defence would lie beyond it and that was why they had put the Imperial troops here: to keep them at arm's length and reduce the potential damage they could do should any escape. Not that this looked likely.

It took almost an hour, Ariadne pressed to the shutter, watching the guards coming and going, looking for a weakness, some useful intelligence they could act upon, before the inner gates opened.

A second tranche of guards filed out into the courtyard, their royal cloaks stirring in the breeze. The guard captain in the courtyard, his rank denoted by a bronze pauldron over his left shoulder, saluted to the leader of the new arrivals and listened as one of his betters gave him his orders. Ariadne couldn't lip-read, nor could she understand any of the Kamidarian dialects, but the meaning was clear enough: *Stay out of the way*.

The guard captain backed off, signalling to his men to make a path. Like the head of a driven lance, the Sovereigns led out a cohort of hooded tech-adepts, their dark crimson robes partly hiding their bionic enhancements from view. Many were hunched, red diodes where their eyes should be, glowing like campfire embers in the gloom. They were accompanied by a pack of grey-fleshed servitors pushing a bulky object lying on an anti-gravitic skiff. Ariadne rec-ognised the standard template construct from the Kamidarian barques and land-ships, but this version was designed for cargo, not passengers. The rain shimmered around it like an aura, repelled by a hard field of invisible light with only the halted droplets defining its shape. Harboured within was a device the size of a transport vehicle, as hefty and imposing as a tank. She didn't need to be a Munitorum adept to know this was a munitions shell. A massive one, the kind loaded onto starships for their primary weapon. A clutch of sacristans escorted the device, each one encased in a sealed suit of rough canvas material with a domed helmet. They carried rad-counters and used them to closely monitor their cargo. At the sight of the hazard-suited sacristans, several of the gaolers backed off, muttering to themselves.

Ariadne's breath caught in her throat when she realised what it was, then gasped when she saw it was not the only one.

Chapter Twenty-Nine

REFUGEES

LAY THE DEAD TO REST

TREACHERY AND BETRAYAL

Renyard knew a little about the Storm Reapers. He knew of their savage culture, of their strange sense of honour. Each man amongst them craved an honourable death. Renyard spared no thought for that. He would die, eventually. Sooner or later, something bigger and uglier than him would end him. Such things were seldom honourable. The concept held little meaning for him.

There is no honour in war, he thought, but despite his scorn for the newcomer he had been impressed by the Storm Reaper's endurance. Definitely injured – the limp he tried to hide and the perpetual grimace engraved upon his rugged face put paid to the lie that he was fully able-bodied – but he was still marching, still fighting. Renyard could respect that, as much as he respected anything apart from killing the enemies of the Imperium.

'Scopes,' he called to one of his men, and a moment later they were in his outstretched gauntleted hand.

First, he trained the monocular device on the palace. Not so far now, a few miles. It had a gaudy, ostentatious look to it. All spearing towers and grand marblesque walls. They had been more careful as they closed, the patrols of Kamidarian military more frequent, their defence lines thicker. They expected an attack but not one like this, he warranted. Here and there, the towering effigies of Knights prowled the horizon, but they were few and far between. Easy enough to slip by. They were looking for a war host, not guerrilla fighters.

A proximity detector *pinged* on Renyard's vambrace and he shifted aspect, panning east. His auspex had been set up with a simple long-range bio-scan, in case any more farmhands or land men wandered into their path.

His circle of vision alighted on a refugee train. He counted around a hundred citizens, some of them militia, and a cohort of fifty Kamidarian Sovereigns acting as bodyguards. Lightly armoured, lascarbines and pikes. Not much of a threat, but their path would intersect with his. To wait and let them pass would slow Renyard down and he couldn't be certain the guards didn't have auspex of their own. All it would take was a rogue reading and they would be discovered. Then those Knights wouldn't be so far away. Ambushing the jamming array was one thing, facing the war engines in open battle was quite another.

Passing back the scopes, he barked an order. Several of his men and the Sisters turned their gaze in the direction of the refugee train. The Marines Malevolent were the first to spread out. They broke in combat squads, two heading for the rear of the train; two the vanguard.

Renyard summoned the Sister Palatine to his side, the grizzled warrior with the scars.

'There'll be runners,' he told her. 'None make it out.'

She hesitated, the Palatine, her features frozen in unspoken objection, but Renyard quelled any potential rebellion.

'No survivors,' he reiterated, closing a step, a gauntleted hand resting meaningfully on the hilt of his undrawn sword.

The Marines Malevolent were already moving, bodies low, bolt rifles held close.

After a few seconds' pause, the Sister Palatine nodded, and snapped orders at her troops. They fanned out, east and west, closing the trap.

'There are civilians in that train.'

Another voice intruded, thickly accented, deep and noble. Renyard also caught the undercurrent of pain he was trying to suppress. He faced the Storm Reaper.

'Will you try to stop me?' he asked simply. 'Are you thinking you will put yourself between me and my orders?' He slid the blade from its sheath by two finger-widths. 'I haven't the time to debate, so just tell me now and we can get this over and done.'

Two of Renyard's men had stayed behind. Both had their bolt rifles readied.

'Ogin, isn't that what you said your name was?' asked Renyard when the stalemate continued.

Ogin nodded.

'War is ugly, Ogin. I'm sure you have blood on your hands.'

'They are innocent,' the Storm Reaper replied. He eyed the two Marines Malevolent edging into his peripheral vision but didn't appeared overly concerned by their presence. Nor did he reach for the exotic-looking blade he had strapped to his belt. Had he done that, Renyard would have drawn and killed him on the spot. He was wise then, or at least good at reading the terrain. He had heard that about the Storm Reapers too, though he assumed it was meant more literally in that case.

'No one is innocent in war,' Renyard told him. 'Not us, not them. Our only duty is to win.'

A little tension heightened the moment as even the Palatine paused to see how this would play out.

'Well, which is it?' Renyard pressed.

Ogin's face was like a storm cloud poised to break. He held it in, and backed down.

'I won't kill them,' he said with absolute certainty.

Renyard smiled beneath his war-helm and felt the old scars pinch. 'Yes, you will,' he said. 'It's what you were made for.'

Ogin stepped back and away as the Sisters resumed their advance. The Marines Malevolent bracketing the refugee train were almost in position.

A shout rang out from the train's forward sentries a few moments later. Then there was more shouting and screaming. There were children amongst the civilians, but Renyard had neither the capacity nor the inclination to take any prisoners. A lascarbine went off, a little energy shriek that saw the screaming worsen. Then came the deeper *boom* of bolt rifles and the trap closed and it was all over in a few minutes.

Silence followed and in it, through the drifts of fyceline smoke and the slumped and burst bodies, Renyard saw Ogin staring at him.

She walked in silence, hidden by the shadows of the nightvein trees. This grove, and others like it, had grown up around Kami-dar ever since Orlah had been a child and before that her mother and before that her mother's mother, and so it had always been. The largest, a violet arbour of breathtaking hue and subtle fragrance, housed the royal mausoleum. Sanctuary.

Orlah trod the winding path, a grav-barque trailing in her wake. The path led her to a broad clearing and a grassy mound upon which stood a white mausoleum, its marble columns climbed by gryfons, mantycores and dracons. The sword of Kamidar shone proudly, lit by the early morning sun through a gap in the purple-leafed canopy. She paused to breathe deep of the air, closing her eyes and touching the black garnet around her throat as a brief moment of serenity took hold. It was a needed balm. Her thoughts had been turbulent of late.

No priests, no ecclesiarchs here, the Kamidarian royal household buried its own dead. Orlah had assumed it would be Jessivayne laying her remains to rest in their native soil, but that blessing was denied to Orlah now. All that remained was to give her daughter peace.

A plot stood ready, the earth freshly dug, the gravediggers responsible having long since departed to leave the royals to their private grief.

'Brother...'

Gerent, who had walked behind the grav-barque as was tradition, stepped forwards.

Together they took Jessivayne from the grav-barque's padded slab. The body was heavy, the oils and unguents masking the odour of decomposition. They laid it down and Gerent deactivated the field engine that kept it suspended above the pit of earth. The field shut down slowly, gradually lowering Jessivayne until she touched the earth.

Orlah knelt as Gerent stood in respectful silence, her battle armour creaking, and drew her oighen from its lacquered sheath. The blade stung the skin of her ungloved left hand, leaving a thin trail of blood.

Blood had made her and so it would keep her. The droplets fell from Orlah's clenched fist, anointing the earth.

'I am a proud woman,' Orlah admitted after murmuring a prayer to the ancestors. 'But seeing her...' She faltered for a moment, the swell of emotion hard to contain, then continued, 'Seeing Jessivayne in this grave...' She gave a deep, steadying breath, fighting the trembling in her hands. She turned to face her brother. 'Can it be undone, Gerent? The war, all of this death and suffering?'

He sank to his knees, the soft soil yielding to his armoured weight, and clasped Orlah's bloodstained hands in his.

'It can. It will.' He smiled, despite the sorrow of the occasion. 'I am beyond pleased to hear you say this, sister. Mistakes were made on both sides, but I am confident we can reach an accord and become part of the Imperium again.'

'And what of Kamidar and the protectorate? Our heritage, our culture. All I see is a threat to that.'

'Threats will come, *have* come. Kamidar endures. It will always endure. But we are a part of a greater war now and we must take up our place in it.'

'They will want to execute me for what I have done.'

'Perhaps, but I doubt it. You are the sovereign and therefore best placed to ensure a bloodless transition from here on out. And you acted out of self-preservation to an aggressor.' His face saddened. 'Out of grief. These are all mitigating factors.'

Orlah gently broke his grasp so she could lay her bare hand upon the side of his face. She knew Gerent believed that, he had always believed in law and what was right. He held the galaxy to a higher standard than most. An unrealistic ideal but she loved him for it.

'Dear brother, I wish that–'

Orlah frowned, as a high-pitched shriek just at the edge of her hearing made her turn. Too late she realised what it was.

Before fire and destruction tore Sanctuary apart.

A thick veil of smoke hung like a funerary shroud. It tasted acrid even through her personal force field. Gerent's had collapsed, overwhelmed and overloaded. She saw him lying on his back, moving but not moving, his limbs slowly flailing in pain-drenched delirium.

Her thoughts swilled in her head, trying to piece together what had happened.

Treachery and betrayal...

She coughed, rolling off her back and onto her hands and knees so she could crawl to her brother. The trees had been felled in the blast and lay like broken soldiers, their branches twisted and jutting. Nightvein blooms drifted through the air with flakes of ash, violet and grey and white. It would have been peaceful but for the appalling violence that preceded it, and the ringing in her ears.

She crawled, breathing hard, her sword lost somewhere in the chaos. The mausoleum was destroyed, utterly. The columns split, its arched roof caved in. Even the graves had been unearthed. Yellowed bone protruded from soil and Orlah cried out at the sheer blasphemy of it. She wanted vengeance. Blood for blood. But first she had to survive. First, she had to reach her brother.

Her hearing had begun to return as she reached him, her vox alive with frantic enquiries about her wellbeing. She subvocalised a distress code but otherwise conserved her strength. Small fires had sprung up. The nightvein trees were burning like prophetic effigies. Some of the leaves burned too and trundled downward in lazy spirals like fireflies.

Gerent lived, though he looked bloody and grey. His armour had taken a hefty dent and a piece of shrapnel the size of a short sword was lodged in his left leg. He gasped for air, and Orlah assumed his ribs were broken too. At least he was conscious. And she heard her guards coming, the Royal Sovereigns she had left at the grove's edge. Less than a mile away. It felt like a hundred.

She had just got him into a seated position when the first of the Sovereigns broke through into the clearing, her face turning aghast the moment she saw her stricken queen and the baron.

'Your majesty...'

They spilled into the grove in a hurried flock, two Sovereigns dropping their pikes to help the baron. Captain Gademene went to the queen, his face awash with concern.

'Are you injured, your majesty?'

She shook her head, gestured to her brother. 'Get Lord Gerent away from here at once. Summon the chirurgeons. Is the land-barge still operational?'

Gademene nodded, then he paused at a message coming through the vox. His features paled, turning grim. 'We have to get you both out. Immediately, your majesty. The Kingsward and First Blade are on their way.'

'What is it? Who did this?'

The answer came with a tearing of foliage and the sonorous blast of a war-horn as *Heart of Glory* muscled into the clearing, trampling the few nightvein trees that were still standing. The shadow of the Knight fell across them like the cloak of death, steam venting from its joints and its recently discharged thermal cannon.

A shout rang out from a group of Sovereigns who were engaging the war engine, like ants attacking a mountain. The desultory sweep of *Heart of Glory*'s heavy stubber ripped them apart without ceremony. The survivors sprang for cover, hunkering down in craters or torn-up banks of earth as a second group, led by Captain Gademene, dragged Gerent away.

Orlah glared upwards defiantly, dwarfed by the iron god.

'A sundered name, for a sundered house,' she spat as the thermal cannon charged to fire.

Chapter Thirty

KINGSWARD

AN ACT OF REVENGE

SACRIFICES

At the last second, *Heart of Glory* angled its weapon up towards a different target. Close as she was, Orlah felt the backwash of heat even through her personal force field and was thrown down by the pressure wave. She scrambled, undignified, but this was gutter fighting now. Survival was all that mattered. And revenge.

The Knight fired again, a lesser charge, trying to fend off a persistent and deadlier enemy.

The few Sovereigns still alive inside the grove seized the queen, trying to get her clear, but Orlah shrugged them off. She backed away of her own volition, a few steps and nothing more. The vox in her gorget continued to relay frantically. Gademene pledging to return, amidst desperate urgings for the queen to flee. She stood her ground. She wanted to see this.

With a blaring of its war-horns, *Martial Exultant* strode into the ruins of the royal grove. Baerhart DeVikor, Lord of Harrowkeep and the Kingsward, had come.

'*No reprieves this time,*' he said, voice thundering from the Knight's vox-emitters. '*Justice lies at the edge of my sword.*'

Seeker crackled in the war engine's clenched fist, its gatling cannon turned aside in favour of destroying the traitor hand-to-hand.

Heart of Glory obliged, revving the massive chain-teeth of its reaper blade.

Then it charged.

Martial Exultant met it halfway, pounding in long strides across the grove, grinding fallen trunks and foliage underfoot. It swung and sword met chainblade in a flash of sparks of actinic impact.

They broke off immediately, one edging left, the other right, each seeking advantage.

It was not a duel in the traditional sense, not a match of feints and parries and thrusts. Knights are not subtle engines, such terms are foreign to them. They brawled up close, one iron god versus the other in a race to inflict the most vicious damage before their opponent. Ion shields and finesse meant nothing in such a contest. It was brutal and often short.

So it proved again.

The brawlers each gave two more blows before the decisive hit was struck.

Martial Exultant had raked several teeth from *Heart of Glory*'s reaper, its artificer blade having the better of it as the weapons slid apart. It swung again, wide then close, cutting into the other war machine's midsection.

Heart of Glory hacked down, a titanic blow that cut through the wrist, separating Seeker from its wielder and leaving it lodged in its own armoured torso. *Martial Exultant* staggered, oil and steam spewing where its limb had been severed. It brought up the gatling cannon and primed its missile rack as a weapon of last resort.

'*Where is your honour?*' roared Lareoc, his voice thick and resonant through his vox-emitters. He lunged and thrust with the reaper, pushing it with impossible strength through *Martial Exult-ant*'s armour until it pierced through its back. Then he dragged it upwards, a blunted blade missing most of its teeth, and tore through *Martial Exultant* like it was paper. *'Where is your honour now?'*

Orlah shook, despite herself, as she watched the Kingsward split in two, his engine torn from groin to shoulder, each half breaking apart from the other in a wave of fire and sparking electro-circuits. It collapsed and she could only imagine what mess the reaper had made of the Knight's pilot. Any chance, any hope of Baerhart's survival died when *Heart of Glory* crushed *Martial Exultant's* torso underfoot as it lay broken.

By then, the queen had lost all resistance and let the Sovereigns spirit her away. A brave few remained in a futile effort to slow the Knight down. Her last sight was of *Heart of Glory* slowly retreating into the mist, a fearsome white fog that had sprung up during the fight and was edged in red.

More horns sounded. She recognised the clarions of her First Blade, Sir Sheane, and Lord Banfort. Their Knights were abroad and coming.

Lareoc had known what he wanted, and it wasn't the queen. Not yet.

He felt drunk. Drunk and elated.

Baerhart, that insufferable bastard, was dead. And it had been a bad death. Inglorious, not even a corpse for a grave. A red smear.

Lareoc had left the grove as soon as the deed was done. He suspected the queen might have had defences in place and so it proved. He felt regret about Lord Gerent, for a man cannot help who he is related to by blood.

A heady scent filled his nostrils, like wet copper. He had enjoyed it during the battle, felt invigorated. Now it was cloying, overwhelming. Drunken buoyancy gave way to nausea and when he was certain he had slipped the queen's hunting dogs, he brought *Heart of Glory* to a halt and climbed out from his Throne Mechanicum.

The severance with his ancestors felt sharp, like a bitter sting in his skull, but the pain was fleeting. He needed air, freedom from the close confines of his iron god.

Klaigen met him as Lareoc had his hands on his hips, doubled over and sucking in heaving breaths.

'Remind me,' he said, between gulps of air, 'whom we have to thank for our good fortune.'

Klaigen laughed. 'Unknown, my lord. The message had an Imperial cipher.'

'Spies in the ranks, eh?' Lareoc smiled, shrugging off his nausea and the bite of aggression that made him want to beat his chest and bellow in triumph over his defeated foe. He still itched after his anointing, as if the blood he had bathed in could never be scrubbed clean. 'Gather the warriors, Klaigen. We march for Gallanhold and the queen. I've put the fear in her, killed her champion. It's time.'

Then he saw where he was.

A desolate tor, a ring of eight menhirs. And Albia stood within their cordon, the other Knights of Hurne beside him. The old priest stood over a ninth figure, one that had been bound in rope and beaten. Lareoc's eyes widened as he recognised Parnius. Then his surprise turned to anger.

'What is this?' He quelled a compulsion to draw his blade, hand resting on the pommel as he advanced on the old priest.

Parnius looked up through long, unkempt strands of hair. His face held onto fear and despite the gag in his mouth, Lareoc felt his friend's contempt.

'What is this?' he roared, casting around the other Knights of Hurne, but they looked back, as impassive as the stone menhirs.

'It is your path,' uttered the priest, calm in the face of Lareoc's wrath.

Lareoc drew his sword. 'Release him. At once.'

Albia went on, unperturbed at the length of steel being bran-dished at him. 'Strength, that is what you said. The strength to kill a tyrant.'

'I will kill her. She flees even now.'

'She *lives*,' Albia corrected, and in the eyes of his warriors Lareoc saw that same accusation reflected.

Uncertain now, Lareoc's blade faltered. Parnius regarded him still, eyes pleading.

'Why have you bound him?'

'To possess strength, one must take it. This is an act of will,' said Albia, without acknowledging the question. 'It requires sacrifice.'

Lareoc shook his head, not understanding. 'I have given. I have given all. Name, house, even honour. I have sacrificed.'

Albia pushed Parnius onto the ground, a hard shove that sent the man reeling. The fall jarred the gag loose and Parnius spat it out.

'He whispers poison, Lareoc,' he said, anger banishing fear and curdling it into something vengeful. 'This priest has come to us like a serpent, hissing lies. Turn back,' he said, 'turn back, I urge you.'

Lareoc frowned, a deeply unsettled mood falling over him. 'Turn back from what?' He glanced at the other knights, then at Albia, who smiled benignly, though his green and brown eyes were dead as winter.

From his rough habit the priest pulled forth a knife. It was a simple blade, old like a piece of flint, the edge shiny against the dull metal from where it had been repeatedly sharpened, and he clutched it by a crude handle of wound leather. Deftly, the old priest flipped the knife, catching it by the dark blade and offering it to Lareoc.

'Make the cut where you will,' he invited. 'Hurne cares not...'

Lareoc looked at Parnius then back to the priest. His heart pounded, filling his head with the drumming of blood. The copper reek came back, some psychosomatic effect but real enough to make him gag.

Behind him, he heard his war engine cooling, soft *plinks* of metal as the chassis met cold air, the gentle patter of rain against its carapace. Lareoc turned towards the sounds, his hope, his anchor, and saw *Heart of Glory* wreathed in mist. It knelt in a fashion, like a penitent warrior making his knightly vows, head bowed and the carapace hinged open where he had exited the Throne Mechanicum. He saw the seals where the sacristans had tended to its wounds, the reattached limb. It bore scars just as he did, a noble steed, a god of iron and steel, the honour of House Solus.

Then he faced Albia and the stricken Parnius, still cowed and beaten on the ground.

Lareoc took the knife, crouched down to his haunches and slit the bonds around Parnius' ankles and wrists.

'This is not honourable,' Lareoc said, his voice low and dangerous as he turned his eyes on the priest. It was as if a fog had parted, offering a glimpse of truth.

The other Knights of Hurne started forwards, some went to their weapons, but Albia held up his hand.

Parnius, trembling as Lareoc tried to help him to his feet, spat a curse and in one deft move drew the oighen from Lareoc's sheath and struck the old priest down.

'No!' Lareoc cried out, lunging for Parnius, trying to reach him.

Albia fell back, a strange smile on his lips, and without his will to restrain them the Knights of Hurne swept forwards, blades scraping against leather... and then stopped.

Parnius coughed, once, and then again, and on the second occasion spat up a thick wad of blood. It stained his tunic and he gazed down to where Lareoc had jabbed the knife in his side.

'No...' Lareoc's voice was scarcely a whisper, as he regarded first the wound and then the bloody knife. His hands felt like a stranger's. Then Parnius' legs buckled, he collapsed onto his side and breathed no more.

Lareoc sank beside him, cradling his old friend's head, wiping the sweaty strands of hair from his ashen face. 'No...' he whispered. 'Parnius...'

The Knights of Hurne surrounded him and he waited for them to strike him down, he *willed* them to. Klaigen laid a hand on his shoulder, so did Henniger and Martinus, until every knight was touching their lord.

'Sacrifice,' said Albia, as the old priest walked calmly into the circle of warriors, unharmed, untouched, whole.

Lareoc's eyes widened as he realised the depths of his damnation, the knife in his hand heavy with Parnius' blood.

Chapter Thirty-One

SPARRING

A WAR FOOTING

LORD LIEUTENANT

Ardemus saluted with his sabre, the blade held at the vertical.

'Again,' he commanded, adopting a defensive posture.

Sidar, the ship's master-at-arms, came at him with vigour, his own sabre dashing with silver streaks.

Moving deftly, Ardemus repelled every attack, his left hand always behind his back, his form expert and poised. He needed this, the sweat and exertion, the opportunity to blow off some steam. The fleet had been stuck at the outskirts of the Iron Veil for over two days. The hours had become wearing.

Steel crashed, ringing through the training hall, as Sidar upped the pace. Ardemus though was his equal, matching his foot-work, speed and ferocity. The admiral crafted a riposte and the master-at-arms barely blocked it. His opponent was on the back foot and Ardemus pressed, his blade as fast as a whip with a harsher sting.

'You move well, sir,' said Sidar between breaths, his face flushed with effort.

'And you are tiring, Sidar.'

A veteran, Sidar had fought in hundreds of boarding actions on the *Fell Lord* against pirates, xenos and worse besides. Some joked he had more scars than skin, the latter already the texture of beaten leather, but Ardemus had him on the ropes.

'I have perhaps lost a step, sir,' he confessed.

'Haven't we all, sergeant,' said Ardemus generously but didn't relent.

Sidar fell back under a rain of well-placed blows, each probing at his defence and hard as a hammer.

Ardemus had bulk and while his years in a commander's chair had seen a slight softening of his military-honed body, he still had plenty of muscle and knew how to apply it. All too rarely did he get to fight, and this hardly counted. Life or death, against the enemy, that was when a man learned who he was or what he had become. Deep down, he hoped he hadn't grown too soft sitting in his admiral's chair.

A brief spate of counter-attacks pushed Ardemus back, his drifting mind muddying his concentration, and for a moment he thought Sidar had him, but the master-at-arms overcommitted to his attack, seeking a swift resolution to the bout. Ardemus sidestepped a wild swing, trapped the other man's blade against his body and disarmed him in one deft movement. A lightning-flash whip of his blade brought the tip to Sidar's throat.

The master-at-arms smiled, breathless, shiny with sweat.

'Well played, sir.' He held up a hand when the blade remained. 'I yield.'

Ardemus nodded, and lowered his sword.

'Close,' he admitted.

His face darkened as Renzo entered the training hall. His second lieutenant looked distraught, clutching a data-slate in nervous hands.

'Out with it, then,' Ardemus growled. He nodded respectfully to Sidar, dismissing him. The man gave a slight bow and left.

'Sir...' Renzo began. 'We have received a vox from Gallanhold, the palace, sir.'

'I know what it is, lieutenant,' Ardemus snapped, and snatched the slate. He read the transcription of the vox-message in silence, his expression hardening all the while. After he was finished, he read the entire message again, then glanced at Renzo. 'Has this been authenticated?'

'Verified in triplicate, sir.'

Renzo looked like he was about to shit a frag grenade, whereas Ardemus had just heard one detonate in his mind. He thought again of Haster and that pict-capture, of what the man must have had to endure, of the horrors meted out under a flag of truce and cooperation.

The words on the screen were stark and coldly lit.

The Praxis delegation has been slain. Murdered in cold blood by the royal house of Kamidar...

And then Ardemus found his fire.

'All captains from across the fleet, conference in the strategium.' He was stowing his practice sabre and reaching for a towel to wipe away the sweat. No time to change, he'd grab a uniform jacket on the way.

'Of course, sir, at what hour?'

'*Now*, Renzo. Right now.'

He had sent in the Mechanicus breakers not long after the ceasefire. Covertly, they had begun the slow examination and deconstruction of the ships around the Iron Veil. Minesweepers had uncovered several fields of explosives, gravity bombs and rapid-burn incendiaries, chains of melta charges. They avoided the auto-sentry turrets and electro-mag arrays, laying down machine detection grids. But not every hollowed vessel contained traps and weapons; some were simply massive drifting hulks, as effective a barrier as any wall or spiked redoubt. These the breakers pulled apart, split them with chainblades or severed them with lascutters across their midsections. Slowly, they had thinned the Iron Veil, if only in part, and widened the aperture through which Praxis could make planetary approach.

It was a painstaking operation and vastly insufficient and behind schedule.

Ardemus scowled as he read the damage projections on a dataslate. If they forced a breach, Praxis would take casualties. Enough to reduce the military efficacy of the fleet. And then they would have to face the Kamidarians.

This, as it turned out, was not chief amongst his concerns as an incoming priority message appeared on the strategium's hololith array. Ardemus straightened his back and smoothed down his uniform when he saw the ident.

It carried Lord Guilliman's seal. Highest level authority.

After another second to compose himself, he answered the call.

A Space Marine in white power armour, and not the primarch, appeared before him.

'Lord Messinius,' he began, 'this is somewhat... unexpected.' A hololithic message meant he must be close. Ardemus felt his command under sudden threat.

An Astartes of the old order, a so-called Firstborn Space Marine, Vitrian Messinius was a grizzled-looking warrior, his features weather-worn with horrific scarring down one side of his face. He cradled his helm under one arm and had an ornate plasma pistol holstered to his hip. His right hand was sheathed in a power fist of staggering beauty. An aged countenance – if such a thing could be said of the nigh-immortal Astartes, and the term was a relative one – regarded the admiral, stern eyes like chips of stone.

The image flickered once then resolved in perfect clarity.

A privilege of rank, Ardemus thought to himself before the lord lieutenant and Guilliman's seneschal spoke.

'Is it?' he said.

Ardemus frowned, wrong-footed by the question. 'My lord?'

'Unexpected. You know why I am contacting you, Admiral Ardemus.'

'I heard you were waging war on the fringes of Segmentum Solar, lord lieutenant...'

'I was, and now I am here, at the system edge,' he answered levelly. *'The Anaxian Line is of paramount importance to the crusade. It has been deemed so by the primarch and thus it must be secured.'*

'A delicate matter has arisen, the... ah... *negotiation* of which has resulted in delay.'

'It is known. The situation cannot be allowed to continue.'

'The matter is in hand, lord lieutenant. And no concern of yours,' Ardemus added, somewhat boldly. He would not have this Space Marine telling him what was what. He may speak with the primarch's authority but he was not the primarch.

A cold edge entered Messinius' voice, one that seemed to stretch across the void and leave its chill in Ardemus' strategium. *'Do not think me one of your captains, to be ordered at your whim, admiral. I follow orders while they are relevant, but I serve one master and one alone. And I speak with his voice and I strike with his fist.'*

Ardemus was about to reply but Messinius cut him off, the Space Marine's presence suddenly cowing the ordinarily dominant admiral.

'I come bearing a message, an ultimatum, and I have journeyed far to deliver it and at no small cost. You must merely listen and then act appropriately.'

Suddenly parched of throat, Ardemus swallowed loudly. He waited for his directive.

'*The Anaxian Line must be secured,*' Messinius repeated. '*If you cannot accomplish this task then others will. If I speak expediently it is because the matter requires it.*'

'A sanction?' Ardemus dared venture, his voice smaller than he wanted it to be.

'*Exemplar protocol. An army musters even as we speak. I shall lead it.*'

Ardemus visibly paled, he felt a beading of sweat chill the back of his neck even though the room was warm.

'I shall not fail, lord–' he was about to reply, when the hololith blinked out and the room fell into humid shadow.

He had little time to compose himself, the meeting he had called was about to begin, but his brief conference with the lord lieutenant had left him in no doubt as to the urgency of their mission.

A few of the captains had begun to arrive, their hololiths flickering into grainy existence, one after the other, like ghosts manifesting in a dark hall. None spoke, and Ardemus barely gave them any heed. To any outsider it would appear as indifference, but in truth he was still thinking about the previous conversation and its ramifications. He glanced at his chron. Several minutes had passed since he'd sent Renzo off with orders. A second order had seen the troops aboard the *Fell Lord* muster for drop assault. He imagined companies of Storm Reapers, Marines Malevolent and Sisters of the Bloody Rose standing in serried ranks, their gunships idling on the embarkation decks. It was time to throw caution to the wind and hang the damn cost. His patience was spent and Kamidar's time was up. *His* time was up.

They had troops enough to take ten worlds, fifty even. Astra Militarum regiments clustered in ships' bellies in their droves. Ardemus felt his confidence renewed.

And Renyard had his orders. Disrupt, sabotage, misdirect. Be a lethal nuisance. And if he got the chance, kill *her*. She dies and the defiance dies with her. A pity they had failed to reach the native malcontents on the surface. Ardemus felt sure that, had they been able to turn the rebels to the Imperial cause, Kamidar would have already capitulated and the stalemate would have ended. No matter, the queen had given him the excuse he needed. Even Tournis, his greatest detractor, would not oppose an all-out attack now.

The last of the captains arrived, Tournis himself, coincidentally, and Ardemus raised his face to them all.

'Our plan is simple,' he stated, having already tight-beamed the vox-content to every ship in the fleet. 'Breach the Iron Veil, and engage the Kamidarian ships. They will outnumber us at first, but gradually we'll overwhelm them and use our numbers to force gaps in their pickets. Priority is the landers. I want to take this world, foot by bloody foot if needs be. It shall be left intact even if its warriors are not.'

He then turned to a broad-shouldered brute of a man dressed in Militarum uniform, festooned with medals and loyalty chains.

'General Tarrox will provide tactical.'

Tarrox bowed, his high collar straining to contain his bull-like neck.

'The Astartes and Sororitas shall be our spearhead, for the Militarum regiments to follow.' His voice was less refined than the Navy man, altogether gruffer. He nodded to the Holy Sister in red war plate, who attended the meeting via hololith from the embarkation deck, readying to depart with her troops. Neither Space Marine Chapter had bothered to send a representative.

'Our field commanders are Lieutenant-Colonel Sempner of the Eighty-Fourth Mordian, Captain Rognar of the 251st Catachan and Colonel Jordoon of the 9003rd Solian – north, east and west armies respectively. Every force is armed for Knight killing. Heavy armour from the Pyroxians and Vostroyans, under

Commander Vusoktich, in support. We will deploy fast and in volume. Our tactic is overwhelm and oversaturate. We cannot allow the Kamidarians to become entrenched. A swift and certain sword wins the day.'

Tarrox stepped back, deferring back to the admiral, who took up the baton with gusto.

'No one wanted this, but a peaceful transition is no longer viable, and the crusade waits.' He paused to moisten his lips, the memory of Messinius' stern gaze lingering. 'And mark me, if we do not render this world compliant, then Lord Guilliman will enact his own measures. A Legion-strength force is already being mustered and preparing to raze Kamidar to ash.'

None commented on the extremity of such measures or their apparent hypocrisy. It had been ten thousand years since the disbanding of the Legions, an edict driven by the thirteenth primarch himself and, according to legend, ratified by a conclave of his brothers. And here, in this benighted age, did Guilliman in contravention of his own ideals threaten to unleash that which he had proscribed all those millennia ago.

'This would represent nothing less than failure on our part, and that I will not countenance. Kamidar *will* be taken and the Anaxian Line will have its crucial redoubt. It has been sworn and so it shall be done.

'Brace for battle, ready your troops for war. I doubt the Kamidarians will go down easy, no worthy foe ever does, but we shall be victorious and repay their treachery with blood and a fierce resolve.'

He stood straighter, chin raised. The hour had come at last.

'To your duties. For the primarch, for the Avenging Son.'

Salutes and cries of affirmation answered this final proclamation before the hololiths snuffed out like candles in quick succession, leaving the strategium in soft shadow. The officers who were physically present marched out, bound for their own stations and ships.

And Ardemus was left to the dark again. His fists clenched. No one would take this victory from him, not even the bloody primarch himself.

The silence of the chapel held an unspoken accusation. Morrigan felt it, a more painful scourge than the barbed whip across his back. He had dismissed the serfs after the first few hours, taken the toughened leather handle of the whip and applied the lash himself. His blows were harder, unsoftened by fatigue, enough to break the patchwork of scar tissue over his body.

Frustration gnawed at him like a blunt knife applied to his skin.

They had sent out hunting parties, gunships and smaller craft, searching the void for any spoor, any small sign at all of the Red Corsairs. He had declared vengeance. All for nothing. The traitor had fled or else was lying low. All too easy to hide in the endless black, and Morrigan with scarcely enough hooks to bait his prey.

And so penance must be given whilst Bohemund remained unavenged.

The whip cracked loudly against his flesh, concluding a century of blows. Never enough. He could not flagellate his shame. It had become a part of him. Blood flecked the cold stone where he was kneeling, a crosshatch of red beads, slowly drying, from where he had flicked the lash. He set it down now, breathing slowly, drinking in the pain, letting it purify.

'O God-Emperor...' he began, closing his eyes as he beseeched the Master of Mankind for guidance, for a sign.

The flaming figure returned, shocking and stark in his mind's eye.

A sword, on fire, raised to heaven...
A cup lifted in supplication...

And then the vision changed, and the figure was no longer seated but standing and walking towards him, aflame. Obscured by heat and smoke, the figure was an ethereal thing, a wraith with its great wings like swaths of sackcloth extended, terrifying... *glorious.*

Morrigan wept at the sight, at the divine. For this must be an aspect of Him, a vessel into which a portion of His will, His essence had been poured.

But as the being closed, its wings faded back into smoke and the fire dimmed and a human face began to resolve, which then too faded into shadow.

He opened his eyes and found Anglahad watching patiently.

'All is in readiness, brother-captain.'

Morrigan nodded, and reached for his scabbarded sword.

Every attempt to reach Kamidar had failed. That in itself, Morrigan reflected as he stood upon the *Mourning Star*'s cold deck, was fairly damning. They had intercepted the deep-vox transmission from the palace, like everyone else in the vicinity, the serfs of Sturmhal rushing to bring news of it to their lord's ears.

At first, Morrigan had thought it must be an error, something lost in translation, but the ciphers and security codes were verified, the clarity of the message assured.

Nothing less than a slaughter, a delegation come in peace and killed where they stood. Amongst the dead, a Custodian, a representative of He on Terra. There could be but one answer to that sacrilege.

Morrigan had sworn a vow to Kamidar, he had done it kneeling before the queen herself, but he had also made her another promise, that if she forced him to return it would not be alone. He had wanted to stay out of the internal politics of Kamidar and Praxis, to turn his blade and his will to matters of personal honour and retribution. Now, he had no choice but to intervene. Resentment simmered in him and his patience was spent.

His prayers in the chapel had done nothing to cool his wrath. He would see it meted out instead in the warriors before him.

Over fifty Black Templars stood mustered in the embarkation bay. It was almost the entirety of Sturmhal's complement, barring the Initiates, and it left the fortress vulnerable. They had yet to find the Red Corsairs again, if they even remained in-system, though Morrigan was near certain they were not far away. He was counting on it. After the Black Templars had ended this internecine conflict, he would turn his attention back to Herek and vengeance for Bohemund.

Facing his warriors, Morrigan drew and raised his sword. Fifty something blades scraped free of scabbards in reply.

Half a century of Space Marines to subdue a world. He predicted a swift end to the conflict.

The land-barge thudded across the rugged landscape of Harnfor, pushing hard for Gallanhold. The pilot took the back ways, avoiding the main Spire Road for fear of further ambushes, but it was tough going on the tracked transport and Gerent grimaced with every jolt.

Orlah held his hand, a vice around her own, and watched the Sovereign medicae work. She had braced the baron's leg, having managed to remove the shrapnel as well as staunch the blood and bind the wound. Beyond administering counterseptics and a vial of morphia for the pain there was little else she could do. The chirurgeons back at the palace had been alerted and would be ready upon the baron's arrival. For now, he had been made as comfortable as he could on a long couch, his head resting on Gademene's balled-up cloak.

'How?' the queen demanded, her eyes on her brother and her face dark as a storm cloud as she addressed the captain of the Sovereigns.

'He took us by surprise, your majesty. I don't know how.'

She turned to him, her features contorted with anger. 'You are supposed to ensure something like this doesn't happen, Gademene.'

'I shall resign my commission as soon as the crisis is over, your majesty.'

Orlah dismissed that idea with an irritated snarl. 'Now isn't the time for histrionic gestures, captain. I need you and so does my brother. *Tell* me, how was this possible?'

'The sacristans managed to intercept and trace an outgoing signal containing your and the baron's whereabouts. It was bound for no Kamidarian settlement, outpost or military cohort. Therefore it can be assumed–'

'That it was sent to Lareoc.'

Gademene nodded.

'And the origin of this signal?'

'Nothing definitive, but it contained Imperial secrecy-ciphers.'

Orlah became as stone, her voice just as cold.

'They betrayed us. That bastard, Ardemus and his men. Attack us and they breach the ceasefire, but use a proxy...' Her face soured, her lips a tight, angry line. She knew Ardemus would fail to keep his word. Men like him always did. War was inevitable, she realised that now. This latest attack was all the justification she needed to fight back. 'How far are we from the threshold?' She referred to Gallanhold's outer marker and the far-most grounds of the palace.

'A few miles. At this pace' – Gademene paused to reckon on the number – 'less than half an hour.'

'As soon as we cross the outer marker, have Thonius raise our defensive shields.'

Gademene gave a fervent salute. 'It shall be done, your majesty.'

Through a vision slit in the side of the hull, Orlah saw the silhouette of Gallanhold on the horizon. It stood out magnificently, its white walls and soaring towers, the Gates of Ryn, so named for her great-grandfather, and the lesser portals to the various annexes and sub-precincts. And then her eye drifted upwards to the 'Long Swords', the macrocannons and other defensive guns that had kept Kamidar safe from attacks from the sky and the void above it. Her gaze lingered there, as her mind went to the archeo-tech her chief of sacristans would be preparing.

And the devastation it would unleash.

PART THREE

NO WAY BACK

Chapter Thirty-Two

BREACHING THE PALACE

RESTORING CALM

NO MORE

It had been a long trudge through hard terrain to reach proper sight of the palace. In the vicinity of its outer wards, the unkempt wilds, scattered holdings and farmsteads fell away to a city, dominated by the palace itself, a white pearl upon a crown of ivory towers.

They had crossed a threshold, a mile from the high walls: a literal one as it turned out.

Renyard felt the change in the air as he passed an unseen marker; the frisson of the actinic as molecules and atoms shifted, trembled and ignited. He was slow, slow to realise and slow to act, still turning, about to engage the vox and signal his men, when the Storm Reaper roared.

'Run!'

The Sisters had begun to move, faster than their Astartes counterparts, less arrogant, and more trusting of the lone warrior's instincts. The Marines Malevolent loitered, incredulous, seeking an enemy that did not exist but facing a threat deadlier and more insidious than an assassin's bullet. Renyard and four of his men were in the vanguard. As the air transformed in superheated strands of las, finally they ran.

It simply manifested, a las-field, a grid of burning, searing death. Renyard watched as it cut through one of the Marines Malevolent in the rearguard, slicing armour, undermesh, skin and bone, carving the warrior into neat segments, freshly cauterised. Others lost limbs or were cleaved in half axially across the midsection or bifurcated so the left side parted sagittally from right. Not all the Sisters made it – a pell-mell flight in full armour across uneven earth saw several fall or stumble. The las-field took them too. It burned the remains, slow cooking the severed pieces in the intense, ambient heat of the grid until the temperature reached such a point that metal became liquid and cloth, flesh and even bone became ash.

It was a brutal unmaking and more than halved Renyard's forces.

He sagged at the end of it, lungs burning from sudden and profound exertion, pushing even his enhanced Astartes physiology to near the limit. The survivors stood at the edge of the las-field, trying and failing to see their comrades through the hot, red light and the shivering haze that bled from it.

A few remained, enough for a half-squad of Marines Malevolent and a little more than that from the Sisters. The Storm Reaper stood amongst them, haggard on account of him carrying several injuries. His warning had saved this many. Renyard did not acknowledge it. He was trying to ascertain whether they had come under attack, but the las-field appeared to be a defensive measure. They had simply been caught in its region of activation. Bad luck and nothing more. The absurdity of war, which seldom cleaved to the crude poetry of men who spoke of honour and glory. Fabrications, both.

The calamity had brought them closer to the palace, which was nearing half a mile away now and looming large on the twilit once the vox was re-established. Regardless, they would need to change their tactics now, though his mission remained. Infiltrate the palace, raise havoc, find and kill the queen if he could. He had doubts about the last part, even when he had spotted the bulky, slab-sided transport surging for the gates an hour earlier. But he resolved to kill everything in his path in pursuit of his mission.

One of his warriors had crouched to a knee as he listened hard to the vox-returns beyond the las-field.

'Show me,' Renyard commanded and without hesitation the warrior turned the vox to *transmit*.

Dead air came through from the other side and the crackle of burning mechanisms.

Renyard nodded as if confirming a suspicion. He found Ogin staring back at him, eyes the colour of flint and just as sharp.

'No more sidelines for you, brother,' Renyard told him, recognising the look for what it was and not caring in the slightest.

The Storm Reaper did not reply. He turned his back and trudged on.

The land around the palace walls had been cleared in places to provide fields of fire for its defensive guns and the troops who garrisoned its ramparts, but it had not been done exhaustively. Copses of trees stood here and there, piles of stone ruins left to gather moss and weeds. Even the earth itself was uneven, rising in old burial mounds or sinking into craters half filled with brackish water. It provided cover, as did the onset of night.

Renyard waited in an old trench. It had been partially refilled, but the hint of yellowed bones protruded from soft earth as did rusty coils of razor wire. An old battlefield from an old war. It would serve. He had the scope pressed to his eye again, surveying the defences. A distance gauge ran along one side of the view. It marked the number of feet to the wall.

Sentries patrolled; they looked sparse and Renyard suspected the Kamidarian army had deployed farther out, ready to take the fight to the Imperium at their landing zones. They had slipped through the pickets of Knights and Armigers, his small force, now much smaller, moving covertly. They had split into two separate groups, each with their own important task. Renyard watched the skies for a moment but saw no telltale sign of invasion. Not yet. He had two of his men with him, as well as the Storm Reaper. He needed an eye keeping on him. Any sign of dissent and Renyard would do what he needed to. The rest were Sisters, their armour dulled by smeared black earth, as was Renyard's, as was his men's, and as was Ogin's. Stealth not force would breach the gate and once inside, they would wreak hell upon the Kamidarians.

A chrono ticked down on his retinal lens display, the countdown turning from green to red as it reached its terminus. As it zeroed, an explosion lit up the darkness, fire crawling thirty feet or more into the night. The hard booms of bolters followed, shot from distance and at several angles to simulate a greater number of fighters than there actually were.

The garrison reacted, as men who hide behind walls often do, with urgency and fear. Officers shouted, horns blew, soldiers armed with pikes and carbines scurried towards the commotion.

Renyard had a gatehouse in sight, a lesser entrance into the palace, confined to its outer districts, but a way in. The troops manning the guardhouse thinned, drawn like moths to the flame burning eastward of their wall.

As soon as they left, Renyard gave the signal.

They ran again, not in flight, but in eager anticipation of violence. Within fifty feet of the wall, two of the Marines Malevolent slowed enough to fire off a shot. They waited until a secondary explosion detonated in the same place as the first feint, the angry thunder drowning out their weapons. The sentry towers fell silent, their guards slain.

One of the soldiers on the gatehouse wall turned, alerted to danger but not knowing what it was or where to look. Renyard shot him through the throat, a messy death that brought further attention. He paid it no heed, leaving it to his warriors. He had gained the foot of the wall by then and, using his knife like a piton, began to climb.

Ogin was a few feet behind him, knife in hand too, features carved with grim determination.

The Sisters hit the gate, clamping krak grenades to its frame and fixings, and a melta charge to the door itself. The explosives went off loudly but the gate buckled, sagged and lurched open. They were charging through as Renyard and Ogin gained the battlements, a shocked and unprepared band of defenders greeting them as they landed on the other side.

They died swiftly, the Kamidarians, shot apart or cut down, the two veteran Astartes scything defenders like they were dead stalks in the field. No horn sounded, no bell rang. They had silenced the gatehouse and now came the descent into the courtyard.

Stronger opposition met them here or, rather, more numerous.

A platoon hurried itself from a guardhouse and began firing. By then, the Sisters and the two Marines Malevolent had engaged. One of the Sororitas fell, an unlucky shot that caught her just above the gorget, but the rest weathered the las-beams without injury and ripped the soldiers apart. A plume of fire from a Sororitas flamer did for most of them, their bodies like brown smudges in the conflagration, slowly curling in on themselves as they burned. Promethium tanged the air.

Now the Kamidarians realised the threat. Above, soldiers on the adjacent wall section had turned and started firing down on the interlopers. Renyard shot one and they spun on their heel to tumble off the battlement. He lost sight of them in the clusters of buildings in the courtyard interior and moved on.

Tossed grenades threw up confusion as well as bodies amongst the defenders' ranks as Renyard sought a route deeper into the palace through the clouds of smoke and increasing carnage. He found it, an archway leading to a secondary gate, and pointed a gauntleted finger towards his conquest.

They left another of the Sisters behind in the courtyard, her armoured body shredded by a mounted cannon the wall defenders had turned on their attackers. High-calibre rounds chased them all the way through the secondary gate but inflicted no further casualties.

After the hue and cry of the explosion at the eastward wall, reinforcements were coming. The rest of the Marines Malevolent and the last of the Sisters, their initial task accomplished, would make for the breach their comrades had made. Renyard could not wait for them. They would rally to him or they would be delayed by his pursuers. Bolster his troops or distract his enemy. Either outcome provided an advantage.

He moved quickly, the leading edge of a lethal sword. He had lost sight of the Storm Reaper and briefly wondered if he had fallen too or simply succumbed to his wounds. He had Marines Malevolent on either flank, edging just ahead as they moved into vanguard positions. The Sisters swept in behind, closing off the rear with gouts of flame.

The soldiers attacked more sparsely here in the narrower confines of the outer palace district. They came in threes and fours, bellowing pointless oaths before they died, picked off piecemeal by a superior foe. Serfs caught up in the fighting ran screaming. Renyard gunned them down all the same. A few of the soldiers showed more tactical sense, and gathered into a firing line behind an upturned iron cart. They managed to get off a volley before a Marine Malevolent's grenade blasted them and the cart into ragged pieces.

Through another arch, always moving inwards, closer to the palace core, and a large square opened up before Renyard and his men. A junction of some kind, it had two other gates, one leading to the upper wall defences, another leading inwards. Renyard made for that one, sensing their proximity to the palace interior.

More defenders here, a weary band of ragged guardsmen in scruffy cloaks and worn armour. They were milling about as Renyard and his warriors came amongst them, still smoking and carousing, evidently unused to trouble. Almost twenty fell to the first attack. The rest mustered quickly, troops pouring from a guardhouse in the middle of the square, men and women clutching hastily grabbed lascarbines and only half-dressed in armour. A heavy stubber mounted on the guardhouse watchtower spurred into action, muzzle flare roaring.

A precisely thrown frag grenade silenced the mounted gun a moment later, its crew blasted from the parapet and spilling earthward through smoke and falling debris.

The defenders bellowed, 'Kamidar!'

Renyard pitied them for their bravery as he charged to within close-quarter distance. Ferociously, he ripped into the soldiers, tearing limbs and pulping skulls. The humans had no answer as their pikes split and shattered against his armour. Six dead in less than a few seconds. The survivors had enough preservation instinct to fall back.

A spit of flame seared across a swathe of defenders, roasted them in their boots. More were coming, a phalanx of the so-called Sovereigns reacting to the attack. Two large barrack houses promised yet more reinforcements, though their doors were closed, their shutters sealed. Doubtless they were arming themselves.

Renyard turned to the Sister with the flamer.

'Burn it,' he growled, 'burn it all.'

Ariadne had fallen asleep against the wall but woke with a start at the sudden clamour. Her back ached like all the hells and she winced, briefly wishing her spine rather than her eye was the bionic.

A nervous-looking Patrica greeted her.

'What's happening?' Ariadne slurred, still shrugging off a fitful sleep. She hadn't been able to stop thinking about what she had seen through the broken slats. A weapon destined for use against the fleet she had no doubt, one they were powerless to do anything about. With waking came the present. Her nose prickling at a strange smell, Ariadne lurched to her feet.

'Is that smoke?'

A wild-eyed Usullis barged Patrica out of the way before she could answer.

'They're coming for us! It's an execution!' He was just crazed and loud enough that a few of the Solians took note. So did the Mordians in their half of the room, the barrack house still divided across the antipathetic regiments.

Still groggy, Ariadne tried to listen. 'Shut up, Beren. It sounds like... *fighting*?' She looked back to Patrica, who shook her head, eyes fearful.

But Usullis wasn't listening. He turned to the masses, gesturing madly with his rangy arms.

'They mean to murder us! Every one of us! Can't you hear it? It was only a matter of time. They're coming!'

A few of the Solians piped up, scared, angry. There was shouting. A Mordian sergeant tried to restore calm but took a punch for his troubles. One trooper shoved another. Then came a second punch. The dam broke then, that sliver of order that had held for the last hours, painfully under strain. A brawl engulfed the barrack house.

Pushed in the back, Patrica collided with Ariadne and the two of them were pressed against the wall as the brawl worsened. Usullis slipped through the fighting and found a perch atop a stack of equipment crates, emptied of their contents before the prisoners' incarceration. From this vantage he spewed his fear into the masses, fuelling their violence.

'We need to stop him,' said Ariadne, the fighting shifting enough that they were at least no longer pinned.

'How?' asked Patrica, looking hopelessly across the melee.

Ariadne pulled out the knife she had hidden in her shirt. Were she to brandish it, she had no doubt the knife would be taken and put to ill use. People would die. They still might. She dismissed the idea as a bad one. The smell of smoke intensified. It wasn't just coming from outside, from some distant fire. Tendrils of it were curling through the broken slat. Ariadne left Patrica and rushed to the window, jamming the knife hard and pulling the gap wider.

Outside, a battle raged. It was difficult to properly comprehend through the smoke and the hectic rush of violence, but she recognised Marines Malevolent moving through the black clouds and Holy Sisters of the Bloody Rose. Troops from Praxis.

An invasion?

The handful of warriors made that seem unlikely. They had engaged the guards. Through parting veils of smoke, she saw more coming, summoned from the palace interior. Then she saw Renyard, and a cold chill ran down her spine. He was gesturing to the barrack house, the barrack house that had been turned into a prison. A Holy Sister with a flamer turned her attention to it at his urging.

The cold chill turned into numbing fear as Ariadne swiftly calculated what would happen next. She smashed the butt of the knife into the slat, hammering at it frantically until it came loose. A wider shaft of grey light slid through the gap. Ariadne thrust her arm through it, desperate to get the Holy Sister's attention. She screamed at her not to fire, that they were inside and allies, but between the smoke and the clamour of the battle, the Holy Sister didn't hear or see.

She levelled the flamer instead.

Ariadne wrenched her arm back and grabbing Patrica, who had

been trying to get a glimpse through the broken slats, ducked down and thrust them both hard against the wall. A second later, fire burst overhead. It briefly spilled into the room, turning heads but not enough. The rest were still lost in the skirmish.

When her painful death didn't arrive, Ariadne returned to her window and braved a glance outside. Something had gone wrong. The Holy Sister was fumbling with her weapon, a nozzle malfunction or fuel to combustion engine failure.

Ariadne briefly closed her eyes. *Machine-spirits, be praised.*

Patrica joined her at the wall, so did several of the other adepts. Ariadne turned to them.

'Shout as loud as you can, but if she raises that flamer get down.'

She thought about scurrying to another window but the slats were sealed, impossible to prise apart with an improvised blade. Instead, she looked to the soldiers, who were laying into each other with gusto. Heads down and pressed against the wall, they all might survive the flamer. At least for a few precious seconds. Out in the open, the Mordians and the Solians would burn like braziers.

Usullis was still preaching terror and dismay from his 'pulpit', fomenting disorder and panic. Paying little heed to her safety, Ariadne headed towards him and into the melee. She tried to stay low, away from swinging fists and heaving bodies, but a punch caught her on the side of the face, a glancing blow, random but painful. She stumbled, almost fell. A boot struck her in the side. A shoulder barged her sideways. Bleeding from a cut to her head, Ariadne kept going, weathering the violence until she reached Usullis.

He was really raving by then, consumed by a terror that had slipped from its bonds and was running rampant. Ariadne grabbed his ankle and with one swift jerk, put the quartermaster senioris down. He stopped abruptly, open-mouthed in sudden shock before his head struck the crate and knocked him unconscious. Aching, grimacing in pain, Ariadne mounted the crate.

'Stop!' she pleaded. 'Stop fighting! They'll burn us.' She gestured frantically to the wall, where the adepts were screaming. 'Outside... They don't know... They think we're Kamidarian. Please listen.'

The fight had reached a crescendo, Solian gutter-brawling against practised Mordian pugilism. In truth, it was all chaotic and needlessly brutal. No one listened. They had been confined for days, tempers fraying. They only wanted to vent, to find an outlet for their anger. Common enmity would suffice.

'Please...' Ariadne begged, a nervous glance again to the wall as she imagined the imminence of their deaths, the conflagration surging through and consuming them all...

A gunshot, an utterly alien sound inside the barrack house, brought a halt to the fighting. Ears ringing from the blast, Ariadne saw Crannon Vargil, a barrel-pistol raised to the ceiling. He smiled, revealing two ranks of yellowed, buckled teeth. He thumbed back the hammer on the pistol.

'Always have a holdout piece,' he said to her, then addressed the mob. 'You'd best listen to this woman for she has our fate in her hands. Any who don't...' He gestured to the gun. 'I have five good shots left and they make quite a mess.'

The furore died at once, all eyes on Ariadne, but she could see they were already piecing it together. Soldiers from both sides began to help one another up, raw anger faded.

Ariadne found her voice again.

'Our allies are outside, and they don't know we're in here. They are fighting the Kamidarians. They think we're Kamidarian soldiers too and they're going to burn this place to the ground with us in it if we don't show them otherwise.'

After a short silence, the officers re-established order and sent troops to the wall, urgent but composed.

Several recoiled as Crannon Vargil fired off three shots, blowing out another window. Troopers sprang to the gap quickly, Solians and Mordians both, hollering to the warriors outside. Several banged on the door, three from each regiment hefting a bench between them and using it as a battering ram.

Fresh purpose filled the room, and unity. Ariadne nodded to Crannon Vargil and saw it reciprocated, a subtle thing, a knowing thing, one collaborator to another. Then she went to the window where Patrica was still shouting. She managed a glimpse outside, her bionic piercing through smoke. The Holy Sister was crouched behind a pile of rubble. She slammed the stock of her weapon hard like she was concluding some in-the-field maintenance. Ariadne couldn't discern much of the rest of the battle, but it felt like it was concluding. The Holy Sister rose from cover and swung around the flamer...

...before Ariadne saw a ghost in dirty white armour plunging through the smoke.

The guard had lain down his arms in surrender, but Renyard shot him anyway. He felt nothing but hatred for these people. They were his enemy and an enemy, whoever or whatever they were, deserved no quarter.

A clutch of civilians, the serfs who had become embroiled in the fighting, ran into his eyeline. Renyard turned his bolt rifle on them next...

Hate is the surest weapon.

...and was struck by something fast and heavy that hit like an assault ram.

Renyard sprawled, armour scraping against stone. Momentum pushed him ten feet or more but he turned as he rolled, coming up into a low crouch, gauntleted fingers dragging him to a stop.

The Storm Reaper faced him in a similar stance, a mask of fury on his face.

'No more!' he roared and sprang at the Marine Malevolent, his knife bared.

Renyard met him, slipping his own knife free, his bolt rifle having flown too far from grasp to reach.

Ariadne saw the clash through the narrow slit in the window. Ogin, alive and here. And fighting his own side. When she saw the civilian dead, huddled in corners but still blasted apart by mass-reactive rounds, she realised why. Ogin tackled the Marine Malevolent around the waist, stooping low as Renyard went high, and hoisted him up before slamming him back down. Renyard went down hard, but Ogin took a stab to his side.

He staggered back and Ariadne realised he was already wounded, but from before. He looked unsteady and for the second time, she feared for his life.

'Ogin!' she cried, fierce but afraid.

If Ogin heard her he didn't show it. His attention was on Renyard, who had backed off too, a raised hand instructing his men to stay out of it. The Holy Sisters watched on, having subdued the last of the Kamidarian guards, who knelt in rows with their hands behind their heads.

'I knew you'd be trouble,' said Renyard, switching his knife to a reserve grip and holding it at eye height.

'Jagun hak sang tal,' Ogin replied calmly, and spat on the ground at Renyard's feet. The Storm Reaper could barely stand.

The Marine Malevolent snorted in amusement. 'You should have stayed dead.' He launched at Ogin, knife raised for the kill, but stopped abruptly, a szabla suddenly protruding from his chest. Ogin had drawn and thrown it so fast Ariadne hadn't even seen it.

A bellow of anger came from the Marines Malevolent, ready to draw down on the warrior who had killed their captain, but the Holy Sisters turned their guns and shot them both.

'No more,' the Palatine echoed. Her scars made a ruin of her face but her meaning was clear.

Renyard had collapsed to his knees, blood gushing from the

wound, and ineffectually attempted to pull out the sword embedded in his chest. He managed to wrench off his helmet and the tapestry of his scars beneath made the Holy Sister's look like a mild disfigurement. An ugly smile curled his mouth, pulling at puckered flesh.

'See,' he began, and spat up blood, 'hate is the–'

Ogin yanked out the szabla and cut off Renyard's head. It lurched from the Marine Malevolent's shoulders and fell heavily like a ball of lead.

Horns were calling, Kamidarian horns. The enemy were coming.

Bleeding, Ogin walked heavily towards the barrack house until he was lost from sight. A few seconds later, the doors were breached and the prisoners set free. Ariadne joined the crowd of ragged but relieved Militarum troopers and Departmento adepts spilling out into the square. She shouldered her way through the mass, trying to reach the front. As she emerged into the square, Ogin was there to meet her.

'Hello, visha,' he said, and promptly collapsed.

Ariadne went to his side immediately, crying out, 'He needs a medicae!'

She saw the sky had changed, turning from night black to a murky orange. A chemical flavour tanged the air, she both smelled and tasted it.

A shield array, protecting the palace.

One of the Holy Sisters came forward, effectively stalling further analysis, carrying a field kit. She wasn't a Hospitaller or an Apothecary but she had stimms and sealant. Ogin groaned as Ariadne took the sealant and sprayed it into the clefts in his war plate. The substance stank foully but appeared to bind his wounds. She had no idea if it was effective but assumed his advanced armour systems and natural Astartes physiology would do the rest.

'You look like all the hells,' she growled, her face creased with concern. The air reeked of blood and smoke. Ariadne felt dirty with it and scowled. Such death, such senseless waste.

Across the square, the second barrack house was emptying of its prisoners. Several were looking to the sky too, evidently coming to the same conclusions. Ariadne saw First Lieutenant Haster amongst the ranks, alive but grey as winter. The man looked close to death but was at least conscious. Two Mordians had to practically carry him.

Apart from the Holy Sister with the field kit who remained with Ariadne and Ogin, the rest of the order had secured the square, but who knew how long that situation would last. The bodies of the Marines Malevolent still lay where they had died. That the Holy Sisters had shot and killed them spoke to the depths of callousness to which the brutal Astartes must have sunk. A melta wound had cored one, a gaping chasm through his chest. The other was riddled with the small craters of many bolter wounds. Ariadne doubted any here would mourn them. She wondered whether the truth of what had transpired here would ever see the light. She hoped it would.

Turning her attention back to her patient, she jammed a stimm syringe into Ogin's neck. Satisfied she could do nothing more, Ariadne wearily got to her feet.

'Don't die on me,' she ordered sternly.

Ogin gave a grimaced smile then his nostrils flared as the stimms kicked in and he rose shakily. He utterly dwarfed the Departmento adept and she was again reminded of his formidable strength and threat. That feeling of transhuman dread never went away. She turned to the Sister, her expression softening.

'Please stay with him.'

The Holy Sister nodded and Ariadne moved on.

She found Haster amongst the throng of Militarum, who were taking up purloined Kamidarian lascarbines as they prepared to fight.

'Sir,' she began, 'there is an urgent matter I must discuss with you...'

Haster turned to her, but before he could answer one of the wall guns spoke. A massive piece of ordnance fired into the sky. It shook the flagstones and trembled the tower into which it was ensconced. Through the uncanny radiance of the shield, Ariadne and everyone in the square followed the missile with their eyes as it soared skyward on a fiery contrail. It was huge, truly colossal, the roar of its expulsion deafening as it burned towards the upper atmosphere. And beyond. To Praxis.

'Holy Throne...' Ariadne murmured, powerless to do anything but watch.

Chapter Thirty-Three

VOID WAR

THE BURDEN OF QUEENS

TRUST IN THE EMPEROR

The meeting with Messinius had shaken him and Ardemus hated the feeling. He would crush it with a surety of purpose and a decisive hand. Unlike the training hall, where he duelled Sidar with sabre and dagger, here Ardemus wielded a fleet. Nothing less than the power to end worlds, the power of a god.

Only the Iron Veil stood between Ardemus and his prize.

The breachers had performed their task well here. At his order, large tranches of the graveyard of warships broke apart, detonated from within and split into smaller pieces to thin the debris field. The clear aperture through into Kamidarian space and the Iron-hold Protectorate widened.

The massive cathedral-like vessels of Praxis eased through it, a great shoal of them, slow like deep-sea leviathans. Two Astartes strike cruisers led the assault, like twin spear tips thrust into the fabric of the void, engines burning blue-hot. One was the dirty mustard yellow of the Marines Malevolent, edging to the fore with eager loathing; the other was the pearl white and sable black of the Storm Reapers, a wily hunter already gauging its foe. The Kamidarian fleet responded at once, their forward lances stippling the void in jabs of magnesium-bright light.

Shields flared against a slew of impacts minutes later, the strike cruisers driving hard and weathering the barrage before easing wide to allow for the larger vessels coming in their wake, grand cruisers and frigates, a queue of warships straining at the bit to loose their guns. An armada soon formed, a battle line of Navy warships burning hard for Kamidar's defensive fleet. Torpedoes speared from their weapon bays, filling the space between the two warring factions with a cloud of ordnance. Many were cut down by turret guns or hastily deployed interceptors, explosions blossoming against the night black like a Founding Day parade, but some ran the gauntlet. The first volleys overloaded shields, the second did the damage, and the first ship kills of engagement were registered. The Kamidarians held, firing back, and as the two sides closed the casualties worsened.

A cruiser broke apart, its superstructure cleaved in two from a nova cannon blast. Another simply fell dark, its critical systems damaged beyond repair, and drifted out of the battlesphere. One vessel, a frigate, collided with one of its fellows, the warzone now so crammed that all distance protocols had been abandoned. The two ships merged in a deadly embrace, armour plates shearing off to drift like dead leaves in the darkness. An explosion erupted in the bowels of the first ship a few moments later, rippling down its spine before overwhelming the second ship and taking both into the hells.

Ardemus watched the carnage through the ship's forward oculus from his command throne on the bridge. He had half an eye on the strategic display but preferred to look into the void, seeing the battle at maximum magnification, the great duel between godly warships.

Seldom had he witnessed such brutality in void warfare, but he could see the tide turning in their favour. Only a matter of time. Ship for ship, both sides were evenly matched. The Kamidarians were fine voidsmen, their captains decisive and well honed. They had many fine and powerful vessels in their fleet. But they did not have the numbers. Attrition would eventually swing the battle for the Imperium, whose vessels drove for the Kamidarian pickets like Horus himself was on their heels.

Another explosion lit the field of view, an Imperial ship, the *Implacable*, edging too close to the Veil and foundering on its debris. It caught a deep-void mine, the explosive detonating inside the *Implacable*'s shields, ripping through its armour and gutting half of the ship. The *Implacable* listed in the void, engines dead, until it slid into the debris field and became another husk consigned to the Veil.

Ardemus ordered recovery and extraction of the crew, sending relief transports to pick up the stricken frigate's saviour pods, which had started venting from the ship in panicked droves. The void was thick with them. Wings of fighter craft and interceptors darted around the escape boats, dog-fighting with the enemy, spry where the massive warships were ponderous. Even through the magnified oculus they were like insect swarms to Ardemus' eyes.

'Hold formation,' he willed of the main fleet, though each captain of Praxis was master or mistress of their vessel now, 'and push. Let's run these bastards from the field.'

The *Fell Lord* held back, the flagship the most valuable piece of the armada and therefore warranting protection. In truth, Ardemus wanted to keep it in reserve as the hammer blow that broke the Kamidarian fleet so he could be there amongst it all when he declared victory for the Imperium. No sense in losing the *Fell Lord* during the gutter skirmishes of the opening salvos or the initial scramble through the Iron Veil.

He was subconsciously planning his victory speech when an

urgent vox notification came through on the command throne's data-slate.

'Speak...'

It was Second Lieutenant Renzo, from his station.

'Lord admiral, contact aft, an Imperial ship.'

Ardemus frowned. With the fleet committed there were no Imperial ships aft. He leaned forwards in his seat. 'Name it.'

'The *Mercurion*, sir.'

The *Mercurion*, a ship of the line, missing ever since translation from the warp. Believed lost. His frown deepened.

'Status?' he said.

'Wounded, sir. They are requesting sanctuary. They report engine damage and imminent catastrophic failure of their reactor. Evacuation is underway.' Renzo paused to clear his throat. 'Our augurs have detected a flotilla of ships in pursuit.'

Ardemus chewed the information for a moment, deciding whether or not he liked the taste, and said, 'On my private hololith.'

A cone of grainy light extruded from the projector built into the arm of the throne. It depicted a badly limping *Mercurion*, ephemeral fires lighting up all down its flanks. Beyond it, like flotsam and jetsam, a dozen or more transports tried to escape its impending destruction.

A sudden flash of light briefly obscured the image, and a second later the *Mercurion* seemed to convulse and then explode dramatically, silently. Almost half the transports were engulfed, simply erased in a bright flare that left the *Mercurion* as a lifeless wreck in three major pieces and a slew of scattered debris.

A few moments more and the faraway shapes of the pursuing ships resolved. Even at distance, Ardemus could discern their provenance. Traitors. Haster had been right. Pirates in their midst after all.

The harrying scum have made their move then... Doubtless, they had waited until the bulk of the fleet was occupied with the assault.

Engaged to the fore and now to the aft... It wasn't ideal but he had fought his way out of tougher situations. Dispatch the renegades, overthrow Kamidar... they'd pin another medal on him for this. Ardemus smiled.

Dead air reigned over the vox.

Renzo's voice returned.

'Sir, the captain is still alive and in the lead vessel.'

'Emperor's mercy that he survived,' murmured Ardemus. 'Visual confirmation of Captain Phareg's presence on that skiff?'

'Negative, sir.'

'Audio?'

'All visual and audio comms are reported as down, sir. Analogue lex-datum only. They were using Navy battle-cant, sir, encrypted with Captain Phareg's personal ident-ciphers.'

At the rear of the formation, the *Fell Lord* was the closest viable vessel that could offer safe harbour to the *Mercurion* by almost two hundred miles. The pair of destroyers acting as the flagship's escort would take on no refugees.

'How far off are those traitor ships?'

'Within extreme weapons range in under half an hour sir.'

Ardemus chewed some more. He could not leave a man to die. And he wanted this victory, a chance to warm up his sabre before he put Kamidar to the sword. And if the rest of the protectorate had any sense they would stay out of it.

'Ready defensive turrets and open up eighth deck, bay six to receive them. Expediently, second lieutenant. We'll be in battle as soon as their heels hit our deck,' he said, trying to suppress a grin. He would pull the destroyers from the assault. More than sufficient against these dogs. He counted three traitor ships via the strategium as the lead vessel was identified by the *Fell Lord*'s datalogs. The *Ruin*.

Yours, not ours, scum.

'Have medicae greet the *Mercurion* refugees,' he said, 'they might have injured. And have the sergeant-at-arms raise a party of armsmen,' Ardemus added, almost an afterthought, 'just in case.'

The sky had turned the colour of amber glass.

It reminded her of bloodier days when she had fought for the kingdom's survival, as she fought for it now. Again.

'You are supposed to be resting,' said Orlah, not bothering to turn around when she heard her brother enter the lunarium.

Gerent limped awkwardly, the rap of a cane's ferrule on the marble floor as he made his way to his sister's side.

'I have rested. The palace chirurgeons are the very best in the kingdom.'

'They are not miracle workers, brother.' Orlah regarded him now, standing next to her. He looked pained, paler than before, with a twist of discomfiture to his features. 'You could have died.'

'So could you.'

Orlah returned to the view, of her lands, her people. Of the war at her doorstep. She didn't have the luxury of dying.

'I never did appreciate the view from this chamber,' Gerent conceded, following his sister's gaze. 'I always thought it whimsical that you spent so much time here, stargazing. But standing here now, I think I understand it better. You can see Kamidar, our forests and hills, our townships, the rolling lands of our youth. It's legacy, isn't it.'

'I only want to protect it, our culture, our history. I fear for its erasure, Gerent. I fear that's what the Imperium coming here brings. Our end.'

A moment of silence descended, calming, comfortable, each sibling enjoying the other's company, both thinking of elder days without bloodshed or fear or war. A pleasant memory but one that could not last.

Gerent sighed, dispelling the illusion with a shudder of breath.

'They know,' he said, 'what we did.'

'What *I* did,' Orlah corrected.

'It hardly matters.'

'It matters to me,' she said. 'It came from within the palace,' she added, her expression growing stern, '*inside* our walls, brother. It must have been someone from the delegation. A survivor. I was wrong to be complacent.'

'You were wrong about a great many things,' he countered but not unkindly. His voice was pitying and this stung Orlah more than his anger ever could.

'That's a matter of perspective. It cannot be undone and so I must look forwards.'

'Gademene will find them, whoever they are.'

'It's of no consequence now. We have enemies at our gates and soon to be in our skies.'

'The inner palace is sealed, and the Swordsworn surround the inner precincts and the Silven Gate. No one will set foot in here without first having to face them.'

'And you think that will stop *them*?'

She spoke of their erstwhile allies, the Black Templars, who had made several attempts at contact. The queen had refused every one. No sense in negotiation now. What could she even say to them? No, better to draw an honest sword and see who came out the victor. She had faced powerful foes before and triumphed, she would do so again.

'They have a path through the Veil,' she went on, 'and Morrigan as good as told me what would happen if I forced his hand.'

'Is that why you've had the sacristans toiling day and night?'

Orlah quirked an eyebrow. 'Little gets past you, does it, brother?'

'I'm not without informants of my own. I know what Thonius unearthed from the world roots,' he said. 'And I know you want to punish the Imperium for their betrayal. And kill Lareoc.'

'I wanted peace, to be left alone. I cannot have that, so I shall have to settle for this instead.' Her face grew stern, melancholy hardening into resolve. She felt Gerent's touch on her shoulder, the light tremble in his fingers. She touched her hand to his, wondering briefly how much morphia he was taking.

'Don't do this,' he said. 'If you do this, Orlah, there is truly no way back from it. The Black Templars might yet accept our surrender. We can at least still spare the people from the ravages of total war.'

Orlah's expression softened as she thought of everything she had lost and all the losses to come.

'It's already done.'

Syreniel bled from more than a dozen wounds. It was a miracle she lived at all, given how many pikes had been stabbed at her.

No, not a miracle, Kesh corrected, *not that.*

She supported the Silent Sister, whose arm looped over the pathfinder's shoulder as they staggered through the empty hallways of the palace. No one had challenged them, just a pair of serfs injured in the fighting and trying to find safe haven. There were so few Sovereigns anyway, and the pair stayed away from the guarded doorways. Any serfs they met barely met their gaze, as seemingly lost as they were. Kesh had no idea where she was going or what they would do now they had completed their mission. The fleet had been warned and knew about the massacre. Retaliation would surely follow. Perhaps the skirmishes in the outer palace districts were the start of it. Her mind went back to the fight in the corridor, the one Syreniel had given up so much of her blood to win, and was *still* giving up, a trail of it left in their wake.

Another miracle that they had not been found because of it.

God-Emperor but she hated that word, even to think of it...

'If we can reach a transport,' she breathed, struggling to support Syreniel's weight, for she still wore most of her armour beneath her torn servant's robes. Perforated as it was, it still made the

Silent Sister degrees heavier. 'Even a ground speeder. We don't necessarily need a flyer. There'll be troops on the ground by now. The open vox would be worth the risk, then we can–'

A hand on Kesh's arm made her slow and look down.

Syreniel was ashen and as she pulled her other hand away from where she had it clenched to her body, it came back dark red. She shook her head, and gestured for them to stop, for Kesh to set her down.

Mutely, she did, finding a place where they could rest. Syreniel sank down hard in a heap, her breathing badly laboured.

'Just a moment, that's all,' said Kesh, eyes darting furtively between the Silent Sister and the corridor ahead. She had the sense they were headed deeper but could not say for certain. The world had changed above, seen through several skylights, glowing with a dark amber radiance that reminded Kesh of an energy shield. The palace had raised its defences.

She had fought them of course. *All* of them, cut them down with her short sword. A dozen Sovereigns who had believed they would take her apart a piece at a time, that they could humble her. A Talon of the Emperor. The sheer idiocy of that still made Kesh laugh, in a quiet, vaguely hysterical way whenever she thought of it.

But then Syreniel had already been wounded and she was only half-armoured, carrying a borrowed sword. It had made the contest fairer but left the outcome unchanged. Apart from her grievous injuries.

'Perhaps there's a medicae or a chirurgeon,' Kesh was carrying on. 'I still have the lascarbine. I could make them treat you. Or at least steal a medi-kit... something.'

Syreniel held up her hand, the one dappled with her own blood. She shook her head again, slowly, and Kesh realised she would not be rising from this spot.

No, signed the Sister.

Kesh began to protest but Syreniel clenched her fist for silence.

I did not realise... I did not understand.

'Know what? You're not making any sense. We have to move now. We can't linger.' Kesh tried to help Syreniel up, but the Silent Sister shrugged her off, a snarl of anger contorting her features.

No. Trust in Him...

'How? I don't know what that means! Shoot a rifle to kill a target, find a trail or water in a hostile land, drag a comrade from harm's way. These things I can do. These things I am *trained* to do. They are like breathing, but this... I don't even understand what *this* is.'

Kesh was crying. She didn't know why or even when that had begun. She had lost so much, first Dvorgin and now this. Her terrifying and unsettling ally, the woman who had become her friend. Strange how she didn't really feel the repulsion of her pariah nature any more.

Syreniel reached out and placed a hand against Kesh's chest. The disc-shaped device was clenched inside it. Kesh took it numbly, still not understanding, wondering if she ever would, if it would even matter.

'How will I know what to do?' she said, pocketing the device.

Syreniel held her gaze but didn't answer.

Kesh stayed a moment longer, wiped her eyes with the sleeve of her robe and was gone.

Chapter Thirty-Four

A SAVAGE TAPESTRY

A HAMMER NOT A SWORD

I WOULD HAVE VENGEANCE

Spits of light stabbed across the darkness. A ballet of stately violence had engulfed the void around Kamidar, silent and destructive. The larger cruisers and capital ships duelled over great distances, exchanging salvos of devastating ordnance, where the smaller frigates and destroyers roved in packs. And amongst the starships, shoals of fighters and interceptors hunted.

Ardemus leaned back in his command throne and admired the show.

It was a savage tapestry, reassuringly familiar.

An alert registered on one of his many screens. The first of the landers were breaking through. As he had suspected, the sheer volume of Imperial ships had begun to tell against the smaller Kamidarian fleet.

He allowed himself a grim smile.

The Kamidarian pickets were withdrawing and re-entrenching against the onslaught. Praxis was losing ships too, more than he would have liked, but he had accepted that trying to breach the

Iron Veil by force was risky. It had also bunched the battle group together in a tight mass that made manoeuvring a challenge, at least in its initial phases.

He turned his attention to the void, eyes narrowing as he searched for his foe through the oculus. The *Fell Lord* had come about in response to the appearance of the traitor ships, turning slowly but surely until her prow faced the endless black behind the fleet.

Still coming... The three traitor ships had moved into a wide formation, the *Ruin* at the fore. Ardemus matched it, the destroyers on either flank, just below the flagship in the battlesphere.

A vox-message from embarkation deck four relayed that the *Mercurion*'s survivors were aboard. Ardemus dismissed it with a sweep of his hand and brought the *Fell Lord* to battle stations. Klaxons began to whine as red light flushed the bridge.

An opening salvo sparked from the lead enemy vessel, a desultory spit of torpedoes.

'Raise shields,' Ardemus uttered calmly, and his smile widened.

Somewhere nearby, a proximity alert began to chime before the augurs overloaded with static and white fire overtook the vanguard of Praxis.

The *Mourning Star* burned hard through the void. Repairs still glinted gunmetal grey in her otherwise black flanks, the welds not so long made and her scars still raw. She rode the black void like a dagger of night, save for the white cross of the Black Templars emblazoned on her hull. As the strike cruiser reached a marker several miles from the lunar atmosphere, she peeled away, heading to the galactic east, towards Kamidar.

'Do you think he is with them?' asked Kurgos, wheezing through the mouth grille of his helm. He almost sounded disappointed.

Graeyl Herek considered the question as he watched the ship through the forward oculus.

'A part of me hopes he is, another that he isn't.'

'He has become more cautious, I think.'

'Is that admiration?'

'Just an observation.' Kurgos wheezed a breath then continued. 'I am not the one who admires him.'

'Who would not?' replied Herek without hesitation, flexing his bionic almost subconsciously as the phantom pain of his missing hand briefly returned. Any man who could cut away a piece of him and live was worthy of his respect.

'How long do we wait?' asked Kurgos after a moment of patient silence as they watched the Black Templars ship recede.

'Not long. Just enough that they can't turn back, or if they do it won't matter.'

He glanced up through the narrow slit of the gunship's viewport as a shadow fell across his face. They had been here for several hours, the *Ruin* having left them far behind. The ironclad flanks of a bulk freighter edged into Herek's sight. They had taken her outside Styges and she had served the warband as a supply vessel.

'Why change ships?' asked Kurgos.

'If you want to breach a wall use a hammer, not a sword.'

Kurgos mused on that, the air gurgling and popping through his rebreather. 'That's quite the hammer...'

She was a colossus, far larger than the *Ruin*, a dull instrument to the other's rapier.

Herek grinned savagely as he looked upon her disfigurements. 'She's perfect...'

Praxis writhed like a struck nerve, thrashing amidst the detritus of its own debris field. Broken ships lay everywhere, indiscernible from the original graveyard of vessels ringing the world. They drifted, bleeding fuel, venting atmosphere and crew, fires flaring and dying like malfunctioning distress beacons. Pieces that had split off from the larger whole collided with other ships, tore rents through hulls. Shorn armour plates floated with silent grace as smaller fighters, powerless to escape, impacted against them, bursting like tiny incendiaries, candles in the endless black rapidly snuffed out.

Ardemus had felt the blast aboard the *Fell Lord*. She had trembled from its impact, the blind shields overwhelmed by an intense flash of magnesium-bright light. He was still blinking after the afterglow seared onto his retinas. Still recovering, reacting on instinct, Ardemus heard his own voice demanding damage reports.

An atomic. They had been hit by an atomic, right in the teeth of the fleet, which had closed ranks to push through the Veil and made itself an even better target.

The Astartes strike cruisers were gone. Not wrecked or destroyed, simply gone. Annihilated. Others joined their fate, and more ships besides, those caught in the outer ripples of the blast. He had no accurate count, not yet, but Ardemus knew it must be egregious.

The Kamidarians had been retreating. He had assumed it was because of Imperial aggression, the natives bowing to the superiority of his fleet. An error, and one he should have seen. A few ships had made it through, those at the extremity of the blast. They had launched landers, a heavy metal flock bound for the world's surface. Far from an overwhelming force. A bitter grind played out in his mind, of a war stretching on for months, years. Then he thought of the lord lieutenant, and the Legion that would raze the world to ash, and his career with it.

There was blood on his collar. Ardemus had only just noticed it and realised he must have hit his head. So much of the last few moments was still hazy.

The vox in his throne's armrest crackled and he answered it automatically, assuming more damage reports from the lower decks, but it was Sidar. It was difficult to make him out through the background noise but his ident-marker on the message relayed who it was clearly.

'*Admiral, we are under attack,*' he said calmly between las-bursts. '*Infiltrators aboard the evacuation ships.*' A quick and violent exchange of gunfire interrupted the audio. Ardemus heard raised voices. Not all of them were Imperial. Sidar returned after a moment. '*Captain Phareg is dead, sir. Executed. They were cultists. Hiding amongst the crew.*' Another shriek of las-beams. A scream. '*We've lost deck eight and are moving up-ship. We cannot hold them, sir.*'

Leaving the vox-feed open, Ardemus turned to his second lieutenant.

'Mister Renzo, seal all bulkheads from twelve to thirty-six. Rouse every armsman on the ship. We have been boarded.'

He raised a vid-feed of the lower decks, eight through twelve. Through the grainy resolution, he saw a ragged band of militia fighters spewing across the deck. They wore a motley collection of ex-Guard-issue flak armour and fatigues. Some had scraps of robes or went hooded. Several wore garish fright masks or else their faces were daubed with crude sigils. A swell of anger boiled up inside Ardemus at the sight of this vermin, then it cooled to fear when he saw the larger armoured figures moving through their ranks. Traitor Astartes. One turned to the vid-picter. It was almost as if it could see him. Ardemus suppressed a shiver, quelling his fear with indignation that a foreign invader had the audacity to try and take his ship.

'Lock them down between twelve and fifteen,' he ordered, after checking a ship schematic. 'Sentry positions at these junctions,' he added, marking them with a key tap. 'Engage all defences. I want them stymied, and I want them stopped.'

He got back on the vox.

'Sergeant, fall back to junction nineteen and consolidate with tenth and thirteenth squads. Slow them down as much as you can.'

'*Affirmative, admiral. I will do what I... Wait... they are flanking us. They're everywhere. We can't–*'

Ardemus turned to the master of the watch on deck, Sidar's second, and said, 'Bring up the heavy weapons from the armoury.'

Sidar's vox went dead.

'Do it quickly.'

He banged his fist against the armrest, just once. Despite the difference in rank between them, Sidar had been a friend.

He wished he still had Renyard or the Holy Sisters on the ship, but the entire complement had been committed to the planetary assault. They were on their own.

'Captain Tournis,' he began, after switching to ship-to-ship vox. 'Be advised, the *Fell Lord* is under attack. I repeat, we have been boarded, and have engaged enemy combatants to the Praxis rearguard. A warband of traitor ships.'

'*The* Valiant Spear *will divert course. I can have ten ships of the line to your position in short order.*'

'Negative, captain. Maintain course. Praxis has been struck a blow, we cannot further blunt our edge. Press the assault. The threat will be contained.'

'*But, lord admiral–*'

'See to the assault, shipmaster. Bring us glory.'

Tournis gave a reluctant sign off, and Ardemus turned his attention back to his own peril. The traitor ships had eased off, content to exchange salvos at distance now their trap had been sprung. Only then did he realise the stakes. They didn't want to destroy the flagship, they wanted to take it.

The first landers had breached the atmosphere. Orlah saw their distant silhouettes like dark clouds against the sky. The palace long guns spoke in answer, raking the air with fire-flash salvos of heavy ordnance. She watched as one of the foremost landers was hit and broke apart. Burning like a comet, it plunged downwards with smoke trailing from a dozen wounds, then disappeared behind the southern mountains and was no more. For every transport the flak cannons tore apart, another two crossed the gauntlet. The upper atmosphere was riddled with explosions, and tracer fire laced the air, but the sheer number of ships meant that some got through to make planetfall.

Ithion had held back the Imperial ships as long as he could. The Kamidarian fleet had weathered many conflicts and defeated many enemies but never against such overwhelming odds. Against such a dogged foe. The Imperium believed it was right, and the righteous were nothing if not stubborn, but Orlah knew something of righteousness too and would not be swayed. Nonetheless, the shipmaster had signalled his retreat as per his queen's command.

Preserve what remains, she had told him. *This is a Knight war now. A war of gods against mortals.*

She stroked the black garnet around her neck. Her heirloom, both jewel and clasp. Her gift to Jessivayne upon her ascension to the throne. A dream turned to ashes. Every time she needed reminding why she was doing this, she needed only to touch the stone and find her resolve.

Her eye strayed to one of her serfs, waiting nearby and ever attentive to the queen's needs. She wondered, and not for the first time, what had become of Ekria. Her aide had been absent ever since they had departed for the royal grove.

The matter would wait.

'Raise Thonius, and have him launch the second atomic,' she uttered, as calmly as if she were asking for a cup of wine.

'Sister...' Gerent hissed urgently through his teeth, but Orlah would not be baited.

'You said yourself, brother. There is no turning back from this.' She held his gaze. 'We win or we die. There is nothing in-between.'

'You would annihilate them?'

'I would do whatever is necessary.'

The serf returned a moment later, her manner apprehensive as she approached the queen. Orlah's quirked eyebrow asked the unspoken question. Thonius could not be reached, the serf told her. The long sword tower had been silenced.

That did not bode well.

Orlah had heard about the skirmishes in the outer precincts, but this was something more. She dismissed her concerns quickly, the barest flicker of unease crossing her face before she sent the serf on her way.

'Perhaps the Imperium would still accept our surrender,' suggested Gerent.

'This changes nothing.'

'Without the weapon...'

'We have other weapons. We'll need to commit to a longer war. Kamidar has been laid siege to before and she will be again. Our mettle has always proved the hardier.' Her agile mind was cogitating the possible scenarios, the calculus of war. There would be hardship, privation. They would endure it. The Imperium's resources were not inexhaustible.

'Please, sister. It will bring ruin down upon us. Upon our people.'

'*My* people,' Orlah corrected, feeling a brief flicker of anger. 'And you are too quick to capitulate. Have you already forgotten what they did at your niece's memorial?'

'That was Lareoc.'

'And who unleashed the motherless dog and set his teeth to our throats?'

'We do not know that for certain.'

'It doesn't matter. They took this road the moment they landed on our native soil and began to pillage everything they saw. The Imperium is a glutton, brother. It consumes and consumes, devouring everything and everyone, its appetite for conquest insatiable. We are nothing to it. A lesser cog to a fathomless, dysfunctional engine in its death throes. I would have us be strong. For Kamidar to survive on its own.' Her voice grew softer. 'And I would have vengeance.'

'Has there not been enough of that? When has enough blood been spilled to satisfy that debt?'

'When there are oceans of it! I will *not* relent and I will *not* surrender. Nothing has changed. An enemy has come, and I will see it vanquished like all the rest.'

'They will not stop. If this fails, they will return. And it will not be so discriminate. It will be a hammer and we shall be the ones annihilated.' Gerent coughed violently. He staggered, leaning heavily upon his cane and almost falling.

Orlah went to him, but he held her off with an upraised hand.

'I am all right, I just need a moment...' His face creased with agony as his body was wracked with tremors. At the queen's silent urging, two serfs were at his side. Gerent looked about to fend them off too but in the end relented.

As they gently shepherded him away to the chirurgeon, he gave a last withering glance to his sister. His face was grey as funeral ash.

'Ensure he is well tended,' she said to the serfs, who nodded in solemn assent. The uneven clack of the cane followed them all the way from the lunarium. As Gerent and his warders slid away into shadow, another figure was born of it, as if melting out of the dark.

Ekria bowed demurely.

'My queen...'

Chapter Thirty-Five

AJAX

BOY-SOLDIERS

OLD FRIENDS

The bulk freighter appeared on the augurs five thousand miles out. She had no weapons to speak of, barring the stubby anti-aircraft turrets bolted to her generous dorsal spine and she moved slowly on belaboured engines. A pack mule of a vessel, the *Ajax* was almost twice the size of a grand cruiser, a truly colossal ship that had been assembled in the void from the fusing of dense metals and prefabricated materials.

Any and all hails to the ship's captain were met with silence.

Hekatani watched it on the vid-screen as the ship grew steadily closer. As station mistress, the task of maintaining the sanctity of the void around the lunar fortress fell to her.

At four thousand miles, she sent a warning of direct action if the ship did not change course. On it ploughed.

At two thousand miles, the *Ajax* crossed an invisible marker, a prohibition zone that triggered numerous alerts throughout the strategium.

'Roll out the guns,' she ordered coldly. 'Bring that ship down.'

Across the fortress, embedded macrocannons cycled up to readiness and fired. Their plosive expulsions shook the moon rock around them, sending plumes of grey dust and billows of expelled fyceline rolling over the lunar surface.

Void shields blanketing the *Ajax* shimmered as the heavy payloads struck. The barrage was relentless, hammering at the bulk freighter's defences and stripping them back layer by layer. Hekatani watched it all via deep-void augur, the slow passage of the behemoth ship, the near-constant flare of its shields.

'What manner of bulk freighter has that many voids?' asked one of her crewmen.

'One that's being used as a battering ram.' Hekatani grabbed the handle of her console's vox-caster. 'Scramble fighters. Tell them to get behind those shields and target the engines. She's not stopping.'

Seconds later, four wings of fighters shot out from subterranean hangars, jetting into the void like cast spears. They darted in and out of formation, boosters flaring. The turrets aboard the *Ajax* juddered to life, swivelling and rotating as they thudded out a near-endless stream of anti-aircraft fire. Two of the fighters came apart as they were hit, shredded to atoms. Another took a glancing shot along the wing and spiralled helplessly into the bulk freighter's fuselage and turned into a fiery smear.

Inexorably, the *Ajax* crawled closer and now she disgorged her own fighters, birthed from her ventral cargo bays, a haphazard array of vessels, many of them heavy transports but all armed.

'Send wings five through nine,' Hekatani urged across the vox.

In the chill lunar atmosphere, a slew of fighters speared voidward. Missile silos came online next, emerging like square-edged crustaceans from the moon's grey earth. Turning on their axes, they sent forth their payloads into the darkness. The *Ajax*'s voids took the impact, flickered and collapsed.

Redoubling their fire rate, riding close to overheat, the macrocannons punched hard into the freighter's flanks. They chewed up armour, smashed away turrets. Slowly, she bled, venting fire and fuel, armour plates detaching and spilling like shed skin to the ground below.

Still, she ploughed on.

'Everything we've got!' bellowed Hekatani as the voidmaster mapped out a likely impact zone and signalled the evacuation.

As one, all of Sturmhal's defences turned on the *Ajax*. She burned prow to stern, driven by momentum more than power, pulled by gravity. She came apart just before the end, reactors blowing midships, the rear section jack-knifing as the forward section struck the earth, churning huge clouds of dust and digging a chasmal furrow. On she went, the guns powerless to do anything now, and kept going until she struck the fortress' flank. The rear section hit later, half a mile further up, breaking walls, collapsing towers, ripping Sturmhal open and leaving it gaping.

The fighter wings had switched targets now. They were duelling with the *Ajax*'s transports. Sheer void saturation made them easy to target but impossible to withstand. Dozens made landfall, their rusting hatches opening before their landing claws had extended, some even slewing to a halt on their bellies. Cultists in crude rebreathers and ragged battledress poured out. The lunar fortress had atmosphere, but it was thin and the gravity light. The cultists capered and leapt like beasts as they made for the breaches in the walls, the Black Templars bondsmen within rushing to meet them.

Skirmishes broke out, rapidly growing in intensity. The cultists were wild, fearless, amped up on some narcotic. They fell upon the bondsmen with knives or lengths of sharpened pipe. Hatchets and hammers. Blood hung in the low-gravity air, like red rain suspended mid-fall.

And Hekatani watched the slaughter through her vid-picters and prayed.

* * *

The *Ajax* had made a ruin of one side of the fortress. Even with all of its formidable defences, it had been broken open and made ripe for pillage.

Herek had no interest in any of that, though the cultist hordes provided a useful distraction to occupy the defenders. He ran in their wake, trying to keep pace with Rathek, who was charging ahead. No serum this time. They wanted him rabid. Every so often, he would stop, ear turned to the silent voice he was track-ing. The daemon spoor.

Kurgos did not follow. He remained with the cult demagogues, maintaining order. Besides, the chirurgeon wasn't built for speed. Not any more.

As they entered the breach, a band of Black Templars Neophytes moved into their path. The warriors looked young, not much more than boy-soldiers wearing the martial trappings of men. One shouted some litany or other, something about hate and vengeance. Herek had long since tuned out the hollow promises of his enemies. He gutted the first with his gladius, not bothering to unsheathe Harrower though she strained at the leash to be cut loose. The boy-soldier died with fear and surprise in his eyes. Not the glory he had been promised, Herek supposed.

Rathek killed two more, his twin swords whipping out with almost balletic grace to leave two heads parted from their necks. The corpses collapsed momentarily, dragged down by the weight of their polished armour.

Herek snapped the neck of a fourth, catching the boy-soldier's chainblade in his bionic fist and crushing it before wrapping an arm around his head and twisting until he heard the bone break. A fifth, the Culler impaled, a deft lunge catching the boy-soldier off guard and mid-slur.

The last three backed away, pale with fear, suddenly uncertain. Their tonsured scalps made them look like child-monks prior to taking their holy orders. The honour of the sword abandoned, they drew their bolt pistols but never fired a shot. Herek cut them down in a single blow, Harrower leaping from the scabbard into his hands and sweeping across the three like a scythe. Their bodies fell apart, cut into pieces, blood and offal spilling amongst their lovingly lacquered armour. How pristine they had been. How full of hope and confidence.

He whispered to her, apologising for sullying her blade with unworthy blood, but Harrower purred in his grasp, eager for more.

It had taken only a few seconds to dispatch these fledglings. As soon as it was done, Rathek sheathed his twin swords and bounded away into the ruins and the fortress proper, following the siren's call like a desperate sailor lost at sea. Every now and then he would pause to listen, heeding the pull of the warp as it led him on.

Slinging the axe onto his back, Herek ran after him.

Hekatani crawled. A piece of the bulk freighter had sheared off from the hull during its long, drawn-out destruction and crashed into the strategium. It had taken part of the rear wall and collapsed several adjoining chambers. From her low vantage, she saw the bodies trapped and unmoving under the rubble. Men and women she had served alongside for years. Colleagues. Friends. Some were shouting, crying out to be saved. Others whimpered in the darkness, dying but unaccepting of their fate.

Broken plasglass and chips of rubble crunched beneath her, opening up cuts in her uniform and skin. She kept on moving. Other voices were filtering through the dull fizzing of shattered lumens and slow-venting pressure from a busted bulkhead door. Unfamiliar, savage voices. They spoke in a strange dialect, coarse to Hekatani's ears.

A weapons chest was nearby and she made for it with vigour, pushing herself on her powerful arms, her upper-body strength considerable on account of the chair. Morrigan had offered to replace it with a grav-seat, but Hekatani preferred not to rely on technology. She wanted to stay strong. She was glad of that decision in that moment.

As she reached the chest, the savage voices grew much closer. They were in the room and the screaming ramped up then as they set upon the survivors. She heard something sharp cut into flesh. The wet splash of blood. A dying choke. Her gaze met with one of her crew, Lodren. A diligent logistician and an asset to the station. Fear had turned his face pale, his eyes widening as the savages culled their way through the injured. Silently, Hekatani urged him to stay where he was. The strategium was a large enough space, they could still slip away if they were careful, but Lodren gave a small shake of the head. Too much terror, overwhelmed by instinct. He scrambled to his feet and ran. A shot boomed out a few seconds later. It took Lodren in the back and tore him open.

Hekatani turned away, biting her lip to stop herself from crying out. She fumbled the clasp on the weapons chest but got it open the second time. A larger presence was moving through the chamber now, slow but indomitable. Its breath wheezed like a perforated bellows and its armour smelled of oil, blood and animal musk.

A hooted cry from her left told Hekatani she had been seen. The cultist sprang for her, tripping over a broken desk in her urgency, long lank hair spilling from a skull-faced mask, eyes wild with pain and hunger. She had a jagged knife, the cultist, still wet from the kill, and her armour looked pieced together from scraps. Scrambling to her feet, barely losing momentum, the cultist raised up the knife in a reverse grip.

Thrusting her hand into the weapons chest, Hekatani grabbed the laspistol, flicked off the safety and put three bolts in the cultist's chest. She fell like a puppet with cut strings, but the high-pitched whine from the pistol's discharge brought other attention. They hadn't seen Hekatani yet, though, there was too much wreckage, too much debris for all that. And other closer kills. A few of the crew even fought back, drawing the same conclusions as their station mistress and taking up arms. Las-fire jabbed back and forth but it was short-lived. Hekatani kept crawling, less cautious now, using all her strength, her left hand clamped around the laspistol. If she was going to die, she'd damn well make a fight of it.

A few feet from the exit, she heard the broken-bellows wheeze of the larger figure. Scrambling past a collapsed augur console and into the open, she saw it.

A Traitor Space Marine.

Clad in red and black armour, it looked like something from a nightmare, baroque and replete with chains and spikes. It walked with a pronounced limp, its helmeted head angled to one side because of the bulge on its back. Dried flaps of skin hung from where it still wore one shoulder guard. There were tools on its thick belt, syringes and cutters and other even less wholesome instruments.

And it saw her too.

It said something in its rasping, cancerous voice. The words made her head hurt, and though she couldn't understand them she knew they promised suffering. A long-handled mace hung by the renegade's side, the flanged head matted with clumps of bloody human hair. Clamped onto its back was a bolter with a saw-toothed blade attached to the muzzle.

As she rolled onto her back and scooted up onto her backside, Hekatani primed and raised the laspistol.

She had no chance against such a monster.

But it wasn't her who would have to vanquish it.

The broken door punched open, flying part way across the threshold to land with a plangent clang. A warrior armoured in black with a red cloak tossed over one side of his body stepped through the breach. He was wearing his helm, a white Templar cross bolted across the faceplate. The cultists, busy murdering at that point, stopped abruptly and began chattering eagerly. The traitor held up his hand and their voices died away almost immediately.

Hekatani edged back, shuffling using her elbows but always making sure to keep the renegade in sight.

Then the Black Templar spoke, his voice hard and metallic through his helm.

'I knew you were many things, Kurgos, but I did not think a coward was one of them.'

The renegade, Kurgos, seemed to be known to the Black Templar. Hekatani could not fathom what endless grudges and debts of blood the Astartes accrued over the centuries. Their understanding of honour and revenge was different to that of most mortals. And despite the fact that she wanted to be anywhere but in this place, she found she could not look away.

'Preying on the defenceless...' the Black Templar went on, and took three steps further into the room. He had not come alone. A band of hard-faced Neophytes were with him. Not his Sword Brethren, but still kin.

A hacking cough had the renegade convulsing and it took Hekatani a few seconds to realise Kurgos was laughing.

'I have no interest in children,' he said in a bile-filled rasp of Low Gothic, a language she understood. 'They're simply in my way.'

'Now, I'm in your way.'

'Dagomir...' uttered Kurgos, as warmly as if he were greeting an old friend, and again Hekatani wondered at the history between them. He sniggered, a hissing, crackling sound. 'Funny, two old cripples matching blades. How's the arm?'

Dagomir threw back his cloak, drawing his long sword with the same hand, the metal scraping noisily against the scabbard. The blade shone like silver fire in the flickering lumen light. His other arm ended in a steel-capped stump.

'More than enough to kill you, Kurgos,' he said, pointing the tip of his blade at the renegade.

The cultists, held at the leash until that moment like slavering dogs starved of meat, leapt forwards. Dagomir met them and for an eternity it seemed to be just him against the horde, scything effortlessly, carving bloody arcs. His lack of an arm appeared to be no impediment as he cut down the cultist dross like he was threshing wheat.

Then Kurgos entered the fray, long-handled mace swinging.

Hekatani dearly wanted to see the outcome of the fight but felt two pairs of strong arms lift her up and carry her from the strategium. Her crew were running, taking the chance to escape and spilling into the fortress' inner corridors. Saviour vaults had been fashioned into Sturmhal's design, places where the vulnerable station crew could flee if they ever came under attack.

Her last glimpse as she was pulled from the strategium was of Dagomir facing off against the hideously mutated renegade. Bulked by his many deformities, Kurgos dwarfed Dagomir but the Black Templar met him anyway, kissing the blade of his sword to his forehead in grim salute.

Chapter Thirty-Six

ION BARRIER

PLEDGING A SIDE

A MORTAL CUT

Breath held in her throat, Kesh waited for the Sovereigns to run past. She guessed from their urgent voices that there had been some kind of incursion in the palace, and it was drawing guards from their posts. For a moment she thought of staying where she was, hunkered down in the shadows until someone found her. After all, she had fulfilled Dvorgin's last wishes. What else could she possibly do? It would be easy to lie down and die here.

And then she remembered what Syreniel had last signed to her. *Trust in Him.*

Kesh tried not to think of her slowly bleeding to death in some bleak corridor of shadowed marble and felt a powerful urge to go back.

I am just a lowly scout, caught up in the affairs of demigods and monsters...

But she couldn't go back from this, from any of it, and clenched her eyes shut as she tried to think. The palace wound around a spiral and they had been edging further, deeper with every step. If she followed this path, she would eventually reach its heart and perhaps be able to strike a telling blow.

Trust in Him.

The guards had gone and Kesh hurried on, not knowing where she was headed. She slipped by two more patrols before crossing a narrow passageway into a wider, hexagonal junction. Here, the ceiling gave way to an expansive skylight of etched glassaic. Depicted in the glass was a knight of Kamidar but from ancient days, wielding a lance and slaying a dracon rampant by piercing its heart. A work of art, but it was what Kesh saw through the glass that caught her attention. A sky of dark amber, a shimmering ion barrier encompassing the palace.

The device suddenly felt heavy in the pocket of her fatigues, still covered by her stolen servant's robes. A killing weapon, an assassin's weapon. A brutal gift, now hers to give.

And when she moved on and rounded the next corner, Kesh understood its purpose.

The corridor terminated in an angular archway, through which she saw a large chamber crammed with machinery. She first heard energy capacitors, their deep insistent hum, and then saw sparks of light coruscating across thick brass coils. Ranks upon ranks of them, all powering the same engine.

An ion barrier generator, a more advanced version of the technology that powered a Knight's ion shield, and much deadlier. The operators had their backs to her, their attention on maintaining the machine through the many jacks and data-inputs drilled into their shaven scalps. Regardless, she closed on them slowly and carefully, remembering her role as a servant in the palace.

A guard had been posted at the archway and reacted as soon she came into his eyeline. He barked something at her in one of the Kamidarian dialects, which Kesh took to be some kind of injunction to stop. She still had the lascarbine under her robes but from the angle and the distance to the room, couldn't see how many more guards there might be.

When the guard's hand moved to his sidearm, Kesh made her choice. Parting her robes with a flourish, she brought up the lascarbine one-handed and shot the guard through the throat. It was an expert shot, truly exceptional and whilst on the move. Her marksmanship instructor would have been proud, but she was already running by then, her thoughts fleeing as instinct took over, her robes cast off behind her like a cloak in the wind, and coming up against a second guard.

He had his gun out, a long-nosed pistol pulled from a leg holster and jabbing shots at her. Kesh darted to the side, the hot beams from the pistol spitting wide but scorching marble. She kept on firing, not a wild burst but a controlled salvo that raked the column the guard was taking cover behind, forcing him out as the blasted stone slivers cut his face. He scowled, edging a half step away from the column.

Kesh already had the carbine snug into her shoulder, her off hand nestling the stock, as she put a las-bolt through his forehead.

By then, she had reached the archway. A sacristan in charge of the station lunged for a panel on the wall. Kesh shot it, wrecking the door mechanism and preventing a thick portcullis gate from slamming into her path. Without slowing for a moment, she advanced into the room.

The third guard had hung back and was lurking. She had seen her comrades shot to pieces by some hell-bent, dead-eyed assassin and had opted for an ambush. She came at Kesh swinging, a short sword in hand and readying to cut the interloper's head off. Kesh saw the attack late and barely got the carbine's bulky stock in the way. The blade hit factorum-forged metal and grated, giving off a shrill screech. For a few seconds, the two of them wrestled, Kesh fending off the guard's sword by keeping her carbine pressed against the blade, strength versus strength. An opportunistic kick took the third guard's leg from under her and she fell like a fully laden kitbag. The carbine had a deep gash in its workings, so Kesh turned the weapon about, almost parade-style, and smacked the heavy butt into the third guard's face as she was about to rise.

Breathing hard, heart pushing, Kesh turned her lascarbine on the operators. One had got to their feet and was reaching for a pistol.

Kesh held up the device, brandishing it high above her head so they could all see.

'No one moves!'

Whether it was her tone or the sudden shock of a stranger bellowing at them, the operators stopped what they were doing immediately.

In the few seconds she had, Kesh cast a glance over the machine. She saw several vid-screens describing power levels and other more esoteric data she didn't fully understand. A basic rendering of the palace in silhouette was depicted on one screen, a red outline tracing it that must denote the operational status of the ion barrier.

She turned her attention to the sacristan. 'How do I shut it off?'

He frowned, not understanding, so Kesh jammed the lascarbine's muzzle at the machine then at the man. A smile turned his lips, the bionic he had in place of his left eye glinting faintly.

'It can't be shut down.'

Kesh scowled. 'So you do understand me.'

'It can't be shut down,' the sacristan repeated. 'Not without an authorisation code.' He gestured to a runic keypad near to his station. The smile turned into a sneer and it took all of Kesh's resolve not to shoot the sacristan there and then. 'And I do not have it.'

Kesh gave a smile of her own, cold and without humour.

'Then I'll have to do something else.' She aimed the lascarbine into the air and fired a single shot. 'Out...' she shouted. 'All of you!'

Her meaning was clear enough without the need for the sacristan's translation. The operators filed out of the room in short order, glad to be away from the foreigner with the gun. Mere seconds after the last of them had departed, Kesh was hailed from outside.

'Imperial...' the voice began, male and authoritative. He managed to make the word sound like a slur. 'This is Guard Captain Gademene. I will give you one chance to surrender.'

Kesh's heart hammered, her first thought of Syreniel and whether they had captured her or worse. It was unlikely. If they had found her, she would have been interrogated first. That would take time. The guards had found Kesh not long after she and Syreniel had parted. She clung to the hope that the Silent Sister remained undiscovered.

Putting the thought from her mind, she edged to the archway and risked a glance around the corner.

Eight Sovereigns were slowly advancing down the corridor. They were being led by an officer wearing a silver breastplate, engraved with a snarling lion, and an ornate helm. A blue cloak flapped in his wake. An older man, tough but grizzled. This was clearly the one who had identified himself as Gademene. As soon as he saw her, he fired off a shot with his pistol and Kesh jerked back as the heat prickled the side of her face.

So much for surrender.

Sinking low, she fired a burst blind to force the Sovereigns to shatter and give them something to think about. The lascarbine gave a plaintive drone, the ammo gauge flashing empty.

Wishing bitterly she had not destroyed the door mechanism, Kesh turned her attention to the machine console. She only had seconds. Tossing the now useless carbine, she cranked every lever up to maximum and saw the power outputs all crest into red. Alert klaxons sounded, warning of the danger. Lightning arcs cracked frenziedly across the brass coils. The low hum became a scream as the power built, destabilised.

Shouts echoed from the corridor. They had heard the change

in the ion barrier generator and were coming to stop her. Kesh still held the device, glinting like a golden promise in her open palm. The red gem still blinked, primed.

No way out, and only this final duty to perform.

'I am a daughter of Mordian, born in darkness, I fear no shadow, not even death.'

Kesh pushed the gem with her thumb and threw the device at the machine as the first of the Sovereigns crossed through the arch.

First there was a great tumult like the world breaking, then light as bright as a hundred suns.

Then silence.

As the ion barrier fell, the launch bays of the *Mourning Star* opened. She lay at anchor at the edge of Kamidar's atmosphere, unmolested by the fleet, who had their hands full taking on Battle Group Praxis. What few outer atmosphere monitors had ventured her way quickly turned back or gave the strike cruiser a wide berth. Nothing in the fleet could match her and no sane captain would take her on ship to ship. Besides, the Black Templars had given their oath. And though they had not lent their swords to the queen's cause neither had they sworn for the crusader fleet. No shipmaster of Kamidar would risk that neutrality, but the sharp silhouette of the *Mourning Star* looked ominous suspended in the black.

She sat there like that, serenely powerful, gazing down upon the blue-green world beneath her. She had the perfect vantage, having bypassed the Iron Veil through a secret path shared with the Black Templars years ago. On the western hemisphere, the void war raged as swarms of minuscule landing craft quit the bellies of larger craft and made all speed for the surface like insects leaving the hive. Not all of the landers survived. Some fell to deck turrets. Others didn't clear their host vessel before it was destroyed and were caught up in the devastation. But many did. They breached the atmosphere then to brave the gauntlet of flak cannons and anti-aircraft missile silos.

All of this passed slowly, silently, as inconsequential as the seasons.

Until the *Mourning Star* vented her cargo, and in so doing pledged to a side in the war. Six drop pods launched in formation, their angular black flanks limned by the faraway sun. And in their wake came a pair of gunships, trailing the vanguard. The vessels streaked earthward, as sure as arrows, glowing with fire as they hit the atmosphere.

'You are right to demonstrate strength, your majesty.' Ekria moved closer to her queen, undaunted by the sudden chill in the lunarium.

Orlah's gaze was cut from ice. 'Where have you been?'

The open-ended nature of the question carried an unspoken accusation, but far from wilt before the queen's cold anger, Ekria answered smoothly.

'Gathering information and allies, my queen. There are enemies abroad in the palace. I wanted to know their movements.'

'I know about the infiltrators. Skirmishes, nothing more, and confined to the outer precincts. You were needed here.' Her chin jutted imperiously. 'And what allies?'

'As great as you are, majesty, every ruler needs allies.'

'Save the honeyed words for the more credulous nobles, Ekria, and speak plainly.' She scowled. 'What is wrong with you?'

Ekria bowed, dipping low, so her robes pooled about the marble floor like wax. If Orlah did not know better she could have sworn she was being mocked with this display of over-deference.

'I apologise, majesty. I have displeased you. But your enemies are closer than you think.'

She must have heard about the tower and the long sword cannon, though Orlah wasn't sure how she knew.

'You've had word about the tower?'

'Taken, my queen,' she said, rising again. 'A small incursion force managed to free the prisoners in the barracks.'

Orlah betrayed nothing of her feelings about this news and merely said, 'You are well informed, Ekria.'

The woman gave a humble tip of the head. 'I live to serve, majesty.' Then paused, as she often would, before uttering a less palatable truth. 'It would not be imprudent to make for safer haven. None would think poorly of you for that.'

Orlah's face clenched in barely suppressed anger. 'What are you saying?'

'Only, given the parlous state of things... that if the palace falls, no noble of Kamidar would judge you for being elsewhere.'

'I am to flee, give over my ancestral home to these interlopers, is that what you are saying?'

'Or if that proves unfeasible, if the way out is blocked, that sur-render could still be countenanced and none would think less of you. A monarch putting the needs of her people above her own liberty...'

'And life!' Orlah snapped, her rage bubbling over at last. 'My reward would be execution, the House of Kamidar left to pass in ignominy and shame.'

Ekria bowed contritely before the queen's ire. 'I have offended again, your majesty. I apologise. I merely meant that–'

Orlah sagged, her anger spent. 'Though perhaps you are not so far from the truth.'

'My queen?' Ekria quirked her head like an animal not under-standing its master.

'Not the response you were expecting?' Orlah asked wearily. She turned towards the great window that looked out upon Harn-for and the lands beyond.

The sky in the distance was thick with landing craft now and she saw the silhouettes of her vassal Knights advancing to the edges of what would be a dozen or more battlegrounds. Heavy tanks rumbled on the horizon, a slow trail moving into the heartlands to muster in armoured brigades. Closer still, the last of the refugee trains made for the cities and fortified settlements.

Ithion had done his best but the way was breached now and the Imperium flooded through it, multiplying by the hour like a rampant cancer. Kamidar would be overrun, burned from the inside out. God-Emperor, she swore she could hear screaming on the breeze. She was condemning her people to death, and only now, faced with it at the end of everything, did she see, as if she had overcome some malign influence and the scales had fallen away at last.

'Gerent warned me... he said it was folly. Have I really brought us to the brink of this? I think perhaps my brother had the right of it after all...'

'But, my queen...'

'There is no victory here. Only more misery. More grief...'

'And what about your daughter,' said Ekria. 'The vengeance she demands?'

A tremor passed through Orlah, the vestiges of her pain. 'I think perhaps enough blood has been spilled for the dead.' She wiped away a soft tear.

'And Kamidar? It will be defiled.'

'It is already on fire. How many more times must we burn? How many more times can we rise again from the ashes? Who will even be left after this to plant the seeds of our renewal if I continue on this path?'

She unclasped the black garnet almost subconsciously, letting it fall to the marble floor with a sharp *plink!* Opening the great window and deactivating its protective field with a verbal command, Orlah stood before the wreckage of her world and breathed. She tasted ash and smoke. Heard the crackle of fires and imagined the distant cries of her people.

I have brought them this terror through my own hubris. How am I any better than the oppressors at my gates?

A low rumble resonated through the palace, an explosion from the lower levels, and Orlah had to adjust her footing. There was a flicker of light and the air cleared of the actinic smell of the ion barrier as it fell. The volume of suffering and war increased. In the sky to the east, away from the main landing zones, she saw drop-craft in the brutalist teardrop shapes of the Astartes.

The queen sighed and gave a shudder of relief.

'It's time for this to end,' she said.

And gasped sharply as the blade pieced her side. Turning, she backed away from Ekria, who held a bloody knife.

'What is the meaning of...'

Her guards were dead. Throats slit. Dimly, Orlah wondered how long ago they had been slain. Both lay in still pools of their own blood. She turned her attention back to Ekria.

'How?'

Ekria smiled. Her eyes glinted, a flash of tapetum. A trick of the light perhaps, but one looked green and the other brown.

'It doesn't matter. You see what I want you to see.'

She *flickered*, like a half-glimpse out of the corner of the eye, so quick as to be almost imagined. An old priest in a rough-hewn habit, daubed in whorls and glyphs. An equerry of perfect poise, radiating trust and loyalty. A hooded and hunched figure, tall, its limbs enshrouded in robes of vermilion and gold, pale skin hinted at behind the shadows of its cowl, a thin chain hooked to its lipless mouth...

It blurred, a variety of smeared identities collapsing together in a confusing melange.

Then there was only Ekria again, after a lapse of only a half second.

Orlah clasped one hand to the wound in her side and drew her oighen.

'Brave unto the end,' uttered Ekria, or whatever it was that stood before the queen.

'Damn you...' She tried to take a step forwards and staggered. It suddenly hurt to breathe.

Ekria put away the knife, secreting it into her robes like a conjurer at a carnivale. 'That cut is mortal, I'm afraid.' She was backing away, the shadows coiling around her. 'But you're strong for a human. I'd say you'll suffer before the end.'

The darkness closed on Ekria like a glove around a hand, until only her voice remained.

'Embrace the fate you have always feared, an ignominious death to an assassin's blade. No honour left for you, my queen... and so ends the reign of the House of Kamidar.'

The words faded into nothing and Orlah was left with the echoes of her pained breaths. She had fallen utterly but Ekria, the *thing* that had become her, was right about one thing. She was strong. She would not die like this. Not like this. She knew of several ways out of the lunarium. She could reached the arming chamber if she wanted to, and from there, beyond the palace.

Gritting her teeth, mustering her failing strength, Orlah decided she would die with honour.

Chapter Thirty-Seven

THE HAND THAT WAS SEVERED

A SHARD BENEATH

FELLED LORD

After passing through the outer walls, the lack of defenders concerned Herek. He had followed Rathek, a breathless and manic charge into darkness, through gothic corridors and chambers, and the only impediment had been the occasional servitor or a guard in the wrong place at the wrong time.

They dispatched them all easily. The Culler killed what was in his way but ran past the rest, leaving Herek to take up his leavings. The trail of corpses was thin. Every door they bypassed with ease too. They were either open already or simple enough to breach. So when the path ended in the shadows of the silent reliquarius, Herek was unsurprised with what they found waiting for them.

Rathek stood poised at the threshold, chest heaving like a panting dog, eyes wild behind his helm's retinal lenses. He reeked of blood-sweat and oil from overstressed armour servos. It was darker here than the rest of the fortress, a place of solitude and reflection. Old bloodstains marked the stone floor in long slashes cast off by a flagellant's whip. Niches and alcoves harboured small shrines and accumulations of private belongings: a small shield taken from a warrior's armour, a laurel, a purity seal, amongst other ephemera.

Then there was the chapel's main shrine and the forty-three black war-helms staring emptily from their plinths. In the middle, one of the plinths was empty and Herek touched the flensed skull still attached to his belt, knowing what it was for. *Who* it was for. A great glassaic window framed the scene. It depicted Saint Sigismund, his black sword in hand, fighting a writhing basilisk. It shone golden but was ultimately hollow, just a memoriam for another dead fool. And its apex led the eye to a vaulted roof where strange, infantile creatures fluttered.

All of this Herek absorbed without feeling, but his heart quickened when he saw the sword.

She was held in a casket of armaglass, wrapped in chains and etched with faintly iridescent wards. They had even filled the casket with what he assumed was holy oil, such was their fear of her. Herek smiled. His severed, skeletal hand still clutched the haft.

Next to him, Rathek strained at the leash.

Two Black Templars stood between them and the casket.

Neither wore a helm. One was a giant, even for a Space Marine, his face impassive and scarred. He held a huge sword with its tip presently touching the floor. Godfried.

The other was Morrigan, a warrior who was yet to shake off that haunted look in his eyes that was apparent whenever he and Herek came face to face. There was resolve now though, as if he had come to some important decision about his fate. As if he, as if any of them, had any real choice when it came to fate.

Rathek shifted restively in his armour. The daemonblade was calling.

The Culler slowly drew each of his swords with a sound like metal scraping stone.

'I see no need to bandy tired words,' said Morrigan, as he finished wrapping a chain around his wrist. The broken links at the ends *plinked* against his vambrace. He pulled his own blade from its scabbard and let the hardened leather sheath fall to the ground when he was done with it.

Herek nodded, and unslung Harrower from his back. 'I agree.'

Godfried swung his great sword up into a knight's salute, touching the cross-guard to his forehead.

Rathek leapt to attack. He crossed the ground between him and his enemies in three loping strides and metal clashed with metal as his blades met with a heavy swing of Godfried's sword. Morrigan had been about to run on, to engage Herek, but Rathek threw his opponent back and aimed a thrust that the castellan had to parry.

The Culler then pressed, first a stab of his shorter main gauche to keep Godfried at bay and then a heavy swing that clanged against Morrigan's broadsword as the castellan had to improvise a hasty defence.

A shoulder-barge put Morrigan on his heels, and the wild swing that followed had him sprawling backwards. His war plate gave an ugly screech as it scraped stone. A retaliatory blow from Godfried went wide, Rathek dodging aside and then inside the Champion's guard to stab with the shorter blade. Godfried gave a clipped grunt of pain before shoving the Culler back with his shoulder, but by then Herek had slipped through.

He swung Harrower, hard and true, against the casket. A crack split the armaglass, wide like a jagged mouth but not enough to shatter it. Herek readied the axe for another strike when Morrigan regained his feet and lunged with his broadsword, forcing the renegade to turn the blade aside with the flat of his own. Metal chimed loudly in the vaulted place.

Morrigan leaned in, pressing his advantage, his broadsword raking against Harrower's axe haft. Another teeth-itching shriek as the weapons clashed. He was in close, the castellan, spitting fury, but his eyes were like cold and pitiless chasms. Herek lengthened his grip, inviting Morrigan closer still, and the castellan duly obliged. He headbutted Morrigan's nose, a sharp crack as the bone broke.

A roar of agony. Blood gushed down the Black Templar's mouth, matting in the moustache, spilling onto his gorget. Herek shoved, using the lengthened grip as leverage, and the castellan reeled, on his heels again, slipping. Herek turned at once, Harrower already in the right grip, and hacked into the casket like a headsman at the block.

A deeper crack this time, a slow seep of the sanctified oil within eking forth.

Still not enough.

He heard Morrigan bellow his name, and the heavy thud of his boots as he charged. Rathek got in his way, having slipped by the slower but deadlier Champion as he opened a cut in Godfried's flank, and swiped at Morrigan's defence. The broadsword came up, swift as silver, parried hard, and for the first time Rathek foundered. His sword arm swung away from his body, driven by Morrigan's momentum. A rapid thrust followed, piercing his breastplate, that went in halfway down the blade. He sputtered, coughing blood, and Morrigan kicked him hard to dislodge his weapon.

Herek struck again, a cleaving blow, a *killing* blow. He had slain ogryns with that swing.

The casket cracked like an egg, the armaglass shattering, spewing holy water like afterbirth, and the air crackled with pearlescent light and a thunderous, howling detonation. Pent up for years, the caged power harnessed within cut loose, the chains around the sword withering to charcoaled metal, the purity seals burning away to parchment-ash and liquid wax. It was like a bomb had gone off, the explosive energies rippling through the reliquarius and loudly toppling the vacant helms from their plinths.

Herek felt his body lifted into the air, grimacing as he fought against the overspill of power and lost. It blew him back, sent them all scrambling end over end like leaves before a roaring storm. Only Godfried held his ground, having rammed his sword into the floor and held onto the haft with both hands. He scowled as the unnatural tempest raged, a matter of a few seconds that stretched into centuries it seemed.

And then it was over and the daemon sword lay on the floor, whispering, only loud enough now so that everyone could hear it, and still clutched in a man's dead hand.

The Blasphemy was free. The sheer peril of that was not lost on Morrigan as he swept up his broadsword.

Herek was on his feet, swift to regain his wits and hell-bent on the fallen daemon sword, but Morrigan was faster. He hit the renegade like a freight hauler, heaving him off his feet and into the reliquarius wall. Plaster cracked. Herek rallied, shedding bits of stone and brick dust. Harrower had slipped from his grip and he drew a saw-toothed gladius, but Morrigan smashed that out of the way. A swift cut took Herek by surprise. It missed his neck but severed one of his horns, the filthy ivory nub like a diseased tooth as it hit the floor.

'Piece by piece,' Morrigan swore. 'You're mine!'

Herek blocked the next swing, stepping in close to trap Morrigan's arm. A hard crack of the elbow to his wrist saw the broadsword swing free on its chains from the castellan's gauntleted grip.

Unarmed, Morrigan swung a fist. A savage punch cracked cheekbone and broke the combatants apart as Herek reeled and staggered. The castellan crossed the distance between them, went low, tackling Herek around the waist. A crack split the wall as Herek hit it for a second time. Morrigan felt repeated blows to his flanks but only tightened his grip... and heaved. With a roar of effort, he lifted Herek bodily off his feet and slammed him hard against the floor.

Something wrenched free from the renegade's belt, rolling awkwardly into shadow.

The broadsword returned to Morrigan's grasp a moment later, hauled by its chain, his enemy still down and groggy. One quick thrust would end it. Vengeance for Bohemund at last...

Time slowed, as if cognisant of the moment. In that briefest of respites, Morrigan saw Godfried. The Champion was on his knees, disarmed and with the Culler poised to end him.

A decision made in a half second.

Bellowing 'Sigismund!' he charged Rathek the Culler.

Herek lurched to his feet, stumbling first before picking himself up again. Gods of Ruin, the Black Templars were fighting hard. Their zealotry and faith had made them even more dangerous. It had been many years since Herek had felt doubt. But he felt it now, the uncertainty of victory. The knowledge that he might yet fail in his task. He had a path, it had been ordained, but fate could be cruel and misleading. How many 'great men' had fallen to the promises of fate and destiny? A number beyond count, he was sure. These thoughts rattled through his mind, a flash flood of potentialities. He was hurt, but that pain gave him clarity. He grabbed Harrower, a half-fumbled effort that saw him scrambling for the haft. His head reeled. The part of his skull where Morrigan had removed the horn throbbed with an unquenchable fire.

Use it...

Something called to him, from the beyond. It knew his name. It made its promises. Herek knew what he must do.

All that mattered was the sword.

Rathek had turned to defend himself, meeting Morrigan with both blades. He forced the castellan to parry, a flurry of swift strikes keeping him off balance. It was long enough of a distraction for Godfried to take up his sword again. He swung, two-handed, the blow shattering Rathek's blade as he brought it up in defence. It kept on going, the great sword, burying itself in the renegade's side and flinging him halfway across the reliquarius.

Godfried sagged, bleeding from a dozen lesser wounds, his face a white mask of suppressed pain.

Morrigan glanced up from his injured friend. Herek had reclaimed his axe, was headed for the Blasphemy...

'He mustn't take up that sword!'

But Herek had no intention of *wielding* his former weapon. Instead, he raised Harrower one last time. He spared a look for Rathek, his comrade injured but some instinct making him crawl backwards on his elbow towards the sword.

Harrower trembled, eager. Hungry.

The daemonblade hissed as the holy water surrounding it turned to noxious steam, devoured by the presence within...

...until Herek brought the axe down in one titanic strike.

The Blasphemy broke apart. It simply ceased to *be*.

A coruscation of eldritch light, a momentary intrusion of the warp, filled the reliquarius. Whispers of the damned threaded the air and the faces of things best left to nightmare wavered on the edge of reality. It faded almost immediately, the host of partially instantiated horrors disappearing like a foul smoke and leaving only Herek holding a solitary shard.

The sword, the severed hand that once held it, everything was gone.

'Rathek...'

Herek grabbed the savage renegade by the back of the neck, holding him whilst on one knee, spent. That shard in his hand resembled a dagger, something old, primordial, even... mythic. Morrigan could feel ancient malice seeping from it.

Then he heard a cry from behind him.

NICK KYME

The veteran burst into the reliquarius, accompanied by a clutch of Initiates. The barest glance told of the battles he had fought and survived, his armour battered and rent in several places.

'Let's take him,' he declared, sword already drawn.

Morrigan's eyes locked with Herek's and in that moment he realised what the renegade was about to do.

'No...'

The shard cut the air, cut it like a knife shears fabric, and parted reality itself.

The doorway parted like an open wound. Darkness lurked within, and the faint susurrus of voices, indistinct as if Herek was hearing them from underwater.

For a moment he hesitated, confronted with the existential dread of infinite time and space. It hovered before him like a promise, a lure, just like the Hand said it would.

Then he grabbed Rathek by the shoulder and dragged him through the tear.

The renegades and their cultist scum were pinned down. Ardemus smiled to himself. Heretic Astartes or not, it would take more than this rabble to take his ship.

He watched on the vid-screen as the traitors tried to burn through the bulkhead doors. They had the dogs confined to three separate sections of the ship, their martial strength divided and effectively neutralised. His armsmen stood at the ready, hunkered down at key junctions and armed with every heavy weapon the ship's armoury could muster. If, and that was a big *if*, the traitors did effect a breach, they would be forced into a bottleneck of enfilading fire. Even Traitor Space Marines were not invincible.

Ardemus noted casually that the enemy ships had fallen away, pushed out his chest, feeling powerful again.

Purgation measures were being prepared: incendiaries and toxins deadly enough to burn through ceramite would be released into the compromised sections. Yes, it would ravage the ship in those areas, maybe even cause some minor structural damage, but it would eat through those infiltrators too and leave nothing but bones in its wake.

Then, once that was done, he would wrest back control of the battlesphere above Kamidar and bring that damn queen to her knees.

Already planning his victory celebration, Ardemus was about to bark at Renzo as to what was taking so long with cleansing his ship when a *tear* opened in reality itself. He could think of no other word to describe it, watching with a sense of incredulous detachment as two Heretic Astartes stumbled onto his bridge.

Shock then panic came in quick succession. Fifty or more mortals at their stations reached for weapons. Armsmen in tan uniforms and bronze armour ran to engage from positions at the periphery of the bridge. Only the servitors carried on, oblivious to the danger.

Sluggish from their... *transit*, Herek felt a las-beam touch his armour, a nervous and pre-emptive strike. He had a second to regard the scorch mark on his vambrace before Rathek pounced and the screaming started.

To call it a battle would be a lie. They fought, as most mortals do. At least at first. They called for their God-Emperor, invoking Him to smite their foes and then beseeching Him to save them from horror and death. It was an old and predictable refrain. Herek knew its tune well. He had let Harrower slumber. She was gorged on the thing harboured in the sword and would not stir for cattle. Instead, he laid about the mortals with his short sword and pistol. More discriminate than Rathek, who slaughtered one crewman after another, leaving limbs and chopped-up bodies behind him.

Herek shot a plucky officer through the chest. The shell detonated and spread the mortal around the room, showering his shrieking comrades with his still-warm viscera. The fear had them now, turning them into animals who scratched at the doors in an effort to escape, but some resourceful armsmen had long since sealed the room, not understanding who was trapped with whom. They battered and fought each other, and quailed.

Only one amongst them kept his resolve. An older man, he had a light blue uniform with gold finery. Rathek was about to gut him when Herek held him off with a warning hand. In truth, he was surprised that worked, but some of the Culler's lucidity appeared to have returned with the destruction of the daemonblade. It seemed the shard it had left behind, that which had brought them here, did not have the same effect on him.

A mercy for certain. Herek had feared he would need to put his brother down.

All of this went through his mind as he faced off against the old man. He glanced around at the carpet of dead, the broken and dismembered bodies in a red slurry about the bridge.

'Will you surrender?' he said in Gothic.

The old man, fear and anger warring on his ashen face, drew a ceremonial sabre from the scabbard at his waist and held it before him in a swordsman's salute.

Herek sighed in resignation, sheathing his sidearms but pulling Harrower from his back. She would feast after all, albeit only on a morsel.

'Very well then...'

Chapter Thirty-Eight

FLIGHT FROM THE PALACE

THE PROFLIGACY OF WAR

A LIGHT TRAIL OF BLOOD

They should be dead. Shot to pieces by Sovereign lascarbines, spitted on their pikes. Or annihilated by the lesser House Knights. Before the ion barrier fell, Ariadne had believed they would not escape the palace. That victory in the barrack house courtyard had been a false reprieve. But then it fell, by some miracle, and they could flee. It wouldn't be easy, though. Even now, as she helped to usher the troops, she heard the garrison being mustered. The Kamidarians wanted blood. Retribution.

She heard the clarion of war-horns. Armigers were coming. Against the palace guards, they had a chance. Against the war engines, they would all perish.

'Hurry! We move now...'

The prisoners had quit the barrack yard, first dividing into those who could still fight and those who could not. A few able-bodied stayed with the injured to defend them. One of the Holy Sisters, her wine-red armour like a beacon, led the group. She had removed her helm, damaged in the fighting. She looked young, younger than Ariadne had expected. Face smeared with dirt and blood, she had determination in her eyes and her shaven scalp was threaded with scars. Her name, Ariadne had learned, was Demetria. The rest, including Demetria's Palatine and Ogin, had made for the tower. Two hundred Militarum troopers, a handful of Sororitas and a lone Space Marine. They had done it because of her, because of what she had seen through the broken slat of a barrack house window. She couldn't decide if it was valour or stupidity. She supposed the two weren't so different from one another.

Passing under a high arch, Ariadne glanced over her shoulder at the looming column of the tower. Smoke spilled from the window slits. The weapon within, the weapon she had seen ferried through the barrack yard, had been silenced, it seemed, but the fighting still raged. Ariadne wanted to watch. Not the battle – she was sick of the war, of this pointless, internecine war – but rather she wanted to witness the outcome and know that Ogin lived. To have him return only to die in some heroic but potentially futile act seemed a cruel reward for his honour. When they had first met, she had thought him uncouth, a monster clad in loyalist clothes. She knew differently now, that not all Space Marines were like the Marines Malevolent; not all of them were inhuman.

And yet, as the wounded men and women filed into the vehicle yard, her thoughts remained bitter.

Such waste, such senseless bloody waste...

The profligacy of war.

She gave a glance to Usullis and the quartermaster senioris had the sense to be sheepish and look away. The mania that had seized him in the barrack house had faded. Only shame was left. She doubted he would try to censure her now. His own actions were more damning.

Crannon Vargil caught her eye. He had volunteered for protection duty. Some might call it cowardice but Ariadne found she could not blame the former gang-fighter for his sense of self-preservation. He still retained his swagger, despite the peril they were in.

'What now then, quartermaster?' he asked, a twinkle in his eye, but he could not entirely hide his unease. He wanted to be away from here and quickly. Technically, Haster had operational command, but he needed help to walk, his two retainers practically carrying the first lieutenant now, his grey flesh turned clammy to the touch. He needed a medic, not the responsibility of leadership.

A fleet of armoured vehicles stood empty in the yard, boxy and mounted on tracks for navigating Kamidar's rough terrain. They also had decent-sized holds for troop transport. Ariadne gestured to them.

'Can you get these vehicles started?'

Crannon nodded. 'Wouldn't be the first time I've coaxed the machine-spirits to see in my favour,' he said with a smile.

Putting thumb and forefinger into his mouth, he let out a shrill whistle and six Solians came running. Ariadne recognised one. It was the burly, buzz-cut monster who had looked like she wanted to wear the quartermaster's skin as a coat but who now gave her a surreptitious wink. Ariadne didn't know which was worse. Crannon barked a series of quick, curt commands. He used some gangland argot Ariadne didn't speak, but she could parse enough to understand that he had sent them to stir the vehicles into motion.

She was about to thank him when a roar sounded overhead, trembling the air, and Ariadne looked up. In the sky plummeted a distant flight of drop pods. They were like black spear tips, a white Templar cross painted on their sides. They rode the fire of chasing flak-guns, explosions blooming in their wake or inches wide of their arrowing trajectories. She saw one of the drop pods hit and it rattled in the air before spinning and pinwheeling. A flak-gun drew a bead on it and it burst apart. A second drop pod was winged and streaked away from the main group to crash land elsewhere, but the rest made it. As did the smaller specks of warriors and the gunship that followed them. With no ion barrier to repel the Space Marines or their craft, they streaked into the palace like bullets and down through a vaulted domed roof into the heart of Gallanhold before becoming lost from view.

As she had stopped to look, the train of injured had carried on, too weary to notice. The last of the stretchers appeared, watched over by a small rearguard of Mordian and Solian troopers. Ariadne's gaze wandered over to the young Mordian sergeant lying unconscious on the last stretcher in the line. They had found her wandering the halls, murmuring incoherently, after a small advance guard had led an aborted attempt to penetrate deeper into the palace. How she had reached them and where she had ultimately come from, no one, including the sergeant herself, could say. Ariadne remembered how she had reeked of smoke but did not appear to be burned in any way, her injuries unknown even as she collapsed at Lieutenant Munser's feet.

Munser's troopers had previously found another survivor too and this one Ariadne knew, albeit mainly from reputation. She was badly injured, more than a dozen puncture wounds piercing her silver armour. As the two came together, their stretchers moving alongside one another, Ariadne saw Syreniel reach out to clasp the Mordian's hand and wondered what must have happened between them.

A shout from up ahead: Crannon's ex-gangers had done their job and the transports gave out a throaty rumble. Ariadne saw Demetria hanging out of the cab of the head vehicle, organising the rest into a convoy. They would take the same route as the one used by her Sisters and the Marines Malevolent when they had penetrated the outer precincts. From there they would have to find a way back to Imperial lines.

As the last of the stretchers were carried into the holds, Ariadne clambered aboard. They were moving in short order and she only had time for one last glance at the tower, hoping that Ogin still lived.

It happened fast. Three insertion forces took the palace with speed and ferocity. The stunned Sovereigns reeled at the sudden, violent assault. Several cohorts simply laid down their arms and surrendered. Others had been penned in and effectively neutralised by the automated salvos of unmanned drop pods, carefully deployed to hold bottlenecks. The Armigers provided more resistance, either moving in packs or leading small groups of dedicated Kamidarian soldiers, but nothing could withstand the ferocious onslaught of the Black Templars.

In one of the palace banner halls, three squads of Sovereigns had erected a makeshift barricade and set up crew-served heavy weapons, an Armiger acting in support. They laid down thick swathes of fire as soon as the Black Templars breached the threshold, and three Astartes fell during the initial push. A heavy melta rifle took out the Armiger, coring the war machine through its middle and part vaporising its pilot. It stood stock-still, a perfectly cauterised hole running through it. A belt of frag grenades took out the barricade, blasting it wide open, and then the Black Templars were amongst the defenders with their blades.

At one of the incursion sites, a group of Sovereign sappers brought up demo charges and fortified tower shields to storm one of the implanted drop pods. They lost eight soldiers to the assault, managing to clamp on a single charge that tore the drop pod apart but halved their remaining number in the explosion.

A demi-company of Sovereigns laid an ambush in a narrow hallway, hiding in the servant alcoves and niches along the walls and arming their troops with armour-busting melta and plasma weaponry. As the Black Templars advanced through the corridor, the Sovereigns sprung their trap. They took out three

Astartes before the rest effected a break out and overwhelmed the defenders.

One of the last remaining Sovereign officers established a three-rank firing line in a high balcony overlooking one of the grand chambers. In the large space, a pair of Armigers held the lower floor and prepared to meet the Space Marines with maximum resistance. The officer could not have known the Black Templars had already cleared out both adjacent rooms to the grand chamber, nor that they faced Sword Brethren. When the Black Templars outflanked the defenders, first eliminating the two Armigers by hobbling the war machines with thunder hammers, they then doused the upper balcony with gouts of burning promethium. The officer made a spirited attempt to redress his ranks, hastily dividing his troops into two forces to meet the threat, but the battle was already over and lost.

Four Armigers guarded the main doors to the inner palace. They were a rarefied sort, the fabled Swordsworn, and amongst the queen's pre-eminent defenders. A cohort of Royal Citizen Sovereigns stood with them, armed with heavy lascarbines and plasma weapons. The soldiers were arrayed in four ranks, ten across. The first rank kneeled behind a wall of forcefield-augmented tower shields. Behind them, as a last line of defence, were the Swordsworn with thermal spears levelled at the entryway that led up to the doors. Reports were coming in via the lieutenant's vox, the Sovereign officer betraying nothing but grim resolve as one by one the Kamidarian defensive positions fell. He raised a voice augmitter to his mouth and his words boomed loudly in the closed space.

'This line and no further,' he declared. 'For the queen and for Kamidar.'

His troops echoed him and he hoped they were bolstered enough to hold their ground against Adeptus Astartes.

He didn't have to wait long to find out.

* * *

Anglahad led the Black Templars as they converged on the inner palace. His armour was scored and pitted with damage. The ceramite gleamed silver in places, but it was nothing. He had the Sword Brethren with him and they all bore similar scars.

Take the heart of the palace, end the war.

These had been Morrigan's orders and he meant to follow them.

Three more squads came in the wake of his spear tip, several carrying heavy weapons to deal with the Armigers they knew would be coming.

An outer gate barred further progress into the palace confines. It had been sealed and locked. The icon of a gryfon rampant clutching the sword of Kamidar in its claws shone in silver on its surface. Anglahad ordered melta bombs brought up to burn through it, and in short order the beautifully sculptured mural was reduced to melted slag, the metal running like wax. Through the still-glowing hole in the metal came a fusillade of las-fire. Anglahad and the other Black Templars standing by the breach immediately took cover behind the still-intact parts of the door. Las-bolts *pinged* noisily off metal. Several jabbed through the hole made by the melta bombs, raking the corridor beyond and shattering marble columns and flagstones. The ragged red beams looked like dagger blades.

Sharing a glance with the faceplate of Brother Lothered, who had brought up the melta charges, Anglahad gave a nod. The sergeant issued a curt battlesign and four of his squad moved up into position on either side of the gap as Anglahad fell back to join the Sword Brethren.

Las-fire still pouring through the holed doors, Lothered and two of his men primed and deployed shock grenades through the gap. Cries of pain and dismay echoed from the other side. Two seconds passed and Lothered and his warriors breached.

Anglahad followed, his preysight penetrating the smoke and electrical interference caused by the shock grenades. Several of the Sovereigns had been incapacitated, but those that retained their senses were making a fight of it. He saw one of the vanguard go down to a storm of las-bolts before the rest were amongst the enemy.

The Armigers had no such weaknesses as the ordinary Kamidarian troops, their thermal spears opening up the moment the first Black Templars made it through the breach. Four Astartes fell to the deadly heat beams, cooked in their armour, before the Knight-killing weapons could be brought to bear. One of the Swordsworn broke apart as it was stitched by the collimated fire of an Eradicator squad, the war machine dismembered and destroyed in the savage assault. A second was set upon by the Sword Brethren. Anglahad led the charge, braving the searing fury of the Armiger's thermal spear. Up close, the war machine engaged its chain-cleaver and Anglahad and two of his Brethren barely held it with their chainswords locked against the larger and more ferocious Reaper variant. Spitting sparks as the metal teeth met, his weapon's casing shuddering as it threatened to come apart, Anglahad saw Brother Hasiad smash the leg of the Armiger with a well-placed blow from his thunder hammer. At once the war machine buckled, its heavier chain-cleaver sliding loose and away in a shriek of protesting servos.

Pushing through, Anglahad and the rest of the Sword Brethren set about the stricken Armiger as it collapsed onto its back, desperately raking the ceiling with its thermal spear. They hacked at the war machine with zealous vigour, slowly and violently deconstructing it until all that remained was oil-slicked pieces. Standing atop the fallen chassis, Anglahad pierced the broken cockpit with a double-handed thrust of his chainblade to end it.

By then the last two Swordsworn had been destroyed too, but not before exacting a tally of dead and wounded amongst the Astartes. As the dust and smoke cleared, and the cries of the dying faded, Anglahad had two-thirds of his complement still active. He wrenched off his helm to grimly assess the damage, letting in the actinic smell of weapons discharge and the coppery hint of blood that threaded the air. The left helm-lens was crazed anyway, cracked during the fighting, so it was little use now. He fixed it to his belt. The chainsword hung broken in his grasp, the ritual execution of the Armiger proving too much for it. He clamped the weapon to his back and one of his Sword Brethren tossed him another. He caught the axe deftly, briefly assessing its heft and sharpness before nodding his thanks and approval.

He checked his vox for any word from Morrigan, but all comms from Sturmhal remained silent.

Anglahad still had a job to do. 'Lothered...' he began, trying not to let the fatigue show in his voice.

The sergeant consulted a data-slate set into his vambrace that displayed a detailed floor plan of the inner palace precincts. He gestured to a second door the Armigers and Sovereigns had been guarding, replying in a gravel-harsh voice.

'This is it.'

As they breached the doors, Anglahad expected resistance but the throne room was empty, as if whoever had been here had made a hasty exit. Cautiously, the Black Templars advanced. Their auto-senses lifted the brazier-lit gloom of the inner precincts, the brighter main lumens having been doused and left cold.

Several rooms branched off from this first chamber: a medical hall, where they found a terrified chirurgeon and his staff cowering at the back; a servants' quarters, now empty, with the scattered evidence of a hasty departure; a map room where war plans had been laid but ultimately abandoned.

The last fed off from the back of the throne room, a long and statue-lined gallery that ended in a large arched window overlooking the city and the province beyond it. Anglahad saw the war writ in smoke across the sky through that window and heard the ongoing battles where it lay open to the elements. Two dead guards lay on the floor, their throats slit.

A man stood before the window, his long shadow reaching back behind him like a dusky lance. He wore robes and walked with an ornate cane, and though he had the build and gait of a warrior his severe injuries were obvious. He was also unarmed. Anglahad gestured for his warriors to stand down and sheathed his own weapons as he approached the man alone.

'Have you come to kill me?' he asked, a pained rasp in a voice that had once been strong. The hand holding the cane gripped tighter, as if bracing for the inevitable. A few feet ahead of him lay an open trapdoor in the marble floor, a set of steps leading down into darkness. A trail of blood led to it from the window.

'No,' uttered Anglahad, and the man visibly relaxed.

'Then if you're here for my sister, she's already gone.'

Chapter Thirty-Nine

BLEEDING OUT

ON YOUR KNEES

TO THE DEATH

The arming chamber had not been far but felt like miles from the lunarium. Orlah staggered much of the way, a hand clamped to her side where Ekria, or whatever she or it had become, had stabbed her. Her mind reeled at the betrayal and the enemy that had been so close to her all this time. She began to second-guess every decision she had made and wondered how long she had been poisoned by Ekria's influence. Her father had told her of the entities beyond reality, for he had fought them back when he had been alive, but at the time Orlah had thought of these creatures as scary stories designed to cow a wilful child. When the darkness fell and contact with the Imperium ceased, her astropaths and Navigators had glimpsed *things* in the warp storms. Most who did were left raving and had to be put down; others simply perished, struck dead by what they had witnessed. Orlah believed her father now; she believed in manifest evil. What she couldn't fathom was how it had crept so close undetected.

That hardly mattered now. The slow knife had reached her

anyway and it would be her undoing. She cinched her armour tighter to try to staunch the wound, but by the time she reached the sacristans her trousers were damp with blood. She brought her hand up to the light of the subterranean lumens and it glistened wetly.

After overcoming the shock of suddenly seeing their queen amongst them, the sacristans and their attendants got to work. Orlah was already armoured so merely needed to mount and interface with the Throne Mechanicum. Ancient voices assailed her almost immediately once she was installed, some concerned, others angry on her behalf, many offering counsel. She silenced them all, her will the stronger, and urged her Knight to walk.

A Knight Valiant, *Lioness* was a peerless war engine clad in white and gold, its royal-blue banners emblazoned with the lioness of Kamidar. She should have run diagnostics on her armaments, a brutal pairing of thundercoil harpoon and conflagration cannon, but Orlah's mind drifted, flitting between reverie and dream. To old days of the glory of Kamidar; of Jessivayne in her arms as a babe; of Uthra in his prime before the sickening took him; of a kingdom in flames, brought back from the brink, and the triumph that followed. She saw feasts and the graves of noble warriors. She saw nightvein petals fluttering on an icy wind and felt the memory of its chill. She walked amid forests ablaze from Harnfor all the way to Wessen, a great serpentine trail of amber light, the smoke so thick she could barely see. And she crawled amongst endless fields of bones, the ossuary mounds climbing to the height of a mountain, their hollow-eyed skulls mocking.

And she wept for the passing of her world, the culture and history that would be forever lost.

By the time true consciousness found her again, the long and purposeful strides of *Lioness* had brought Orlah to the edge of a battlefield. Here she saw the burnt-out carcasses of Imperial tanks and the corpses of soldiers strewn across the ground like leaves.

It was quiet, like only a place of death can be, and only a single enemy remained. To the east, a red sun was rising like a bloody eye and it framed the other Knight ominously.

Orlah felt her life slowly bleeding out through the tear in her side, the interior of her Knight reeked with it, but she had enough about her still to recognise an old foe and spit through clenched teeth.

'A sundered name, for a sundered house...'

After killing Parnius, Lareoc had wandered in a daze. Adrift at first, a lost soul in the underworld of his own grief, he managed to anchor himself with anger for the old priest. Albia had gone though, as if spirited away on the breeze by Hurne himself, and his wrath for the mendicant had raced off unfettered. A wildness overtook him and even as the sky above Kamidar began to crowd with drop-ships, Lareoc raged on without purpose. The other Knights of Hurne stayed with him, albeit at a respectful distance. In the few moments of lucidity he had, Lareoc saw Klaigen nearby, close enough that the seneschal could keep an eye on him. He couldn't remember clambering back into *Heart of Glory* but proximity to the ancient machine restored some of his cognisance. The red haze lifted a fraction and he could think again. He wanted to vent his wrath and shed blood and oil, find a worthy foe to challenge. In that, perhaps, he could find again his honour. Thankfully, the invasion provided an abundance of targets.

Although he headed unerringly in the direction of the palace, Lareoc and his Knights hunted and slaughtered every enemy they came across. He remembered little of the kills, aside from the roaring exultation and weeping despair that came with every one. It took Lareoc a few moments to realise they were his shouts and his tears. He had only wanted his world restored to what it had been before the darkness, a fair and just world free of tyrants, yet he found himself making a different bargain.

The latest kill was an Imperial armoured battalion, and even now the details of it were fading. They had become separated from a larger army, an emergency landing perhaps, or simply wandered askew through poor navigation of a foreign land. It didn't matter. They were isolated and therefore prey.

Heart of Glory, though that name felt aberrant now, had bellowed a challenge from its war-horns and the attack had commenced. The Knights of Hurne emerged through white fog to encircle the Imperial tanks, who had consolidated into a defensive laager around their infantry. They had fought hard, the Imperials, as soldiers always do when they are trapped by a superior foe, but it changed nothing. Piece by piece, the Armigers had taken the battalion apart, their fury cold and unrelenting. Lareoc had killed their captains himself, *Heart of Glory* vanquishing the two super-heavy tanks leading the force. He tore them open, drinking of their pain and crushing them utterly.

His wrath spent, though he felt it growing almost instantly again like a restless cancer, he looked upon a hecatomb of men and machines. An icon blinked on the interior console, a guiding rune. He had almost forgotten about it and could barely remember engaging it. He had been tracking an engine signature and it had brought him here to this field of slaughter. The battalion were not his target at all, just collateral.

He blinked, as if shaking off a drunken stupor, and with red-rimmed clarity saw *Lioness* standing at the opposite edge of the battlefield.

Queen Orlah of Kamidar. Her Knight vox-clarions crackled as they were activated.

'A sundered name, for a sundered house!'

She gave a rueful smile. Fate had brought her here. To *him*. She had lost Kamidar, blind to the threat within her own court and driven by grief. She had erred, fatally, but she could see clearly now as a fresh-forged blade reflects the light. Perhaps it was the closeness of death, perhaps it was because she hoped to be reunited again with Jessivayne by the Emperor's side, but there was renewed purpose in Orlah. She had felt increasingly lost as the days wore on, but her hatred for Lareoc was a constant, as was her love for Kamidar. If she achieved nothing else with her death, she could at least remove the thorn that had irritated her ever since House Solus had become a traitor to the realm.

It was scant comfort but better than nothing at all. He had tried to kill her and almost killed her brother. A dishonourable act from a dishonourable man. He had been as twisted by his bitterness as she was. A reckoning then, at last. In her bones, she knew he wanted this as much as she did. He would never understand the sacrifice, what it had taken to hold the protectorate together. That was Lareoc's problem. His idealism got in the way of the pragmatic needs of survival. The arguments had been made long ago. He had chosen his road. It had made him an outlaw. Vengeance was well overdue.

'For the honour of Kamidar,' she whispered and felt the waves of approval from the Throne Mechanicum.

She engaged *Lioness'* actuators, stirring the Knight into a powerful stride.

Lareoc snarled, though the teeth that made it and the mouth that framed it didn't feel like they belonged to him. He felt strength just beyond the grasp of his outstretched fingers, a warm fount of power that could be his if he just reached for it. But these were not his thoughts nor the thoughts of his Throne Mechanicum, which had grown eerily silent. All these years, after she had betrayed his house, after Idrius and Golen. After every slain noble. Only he remained. And here she was... bleeding. Lareoc didn't know how he knew, but he knew. Orlah was dying but he would be the one to take her head. Kamidar was lost but he could do this, make the sacrifice matter. Sacrifice the queen, sacrifice her to... Hurne?

All he had to do was accept this gift. Take this strength.

Take it!

Give it to me...

A quiet voice resounded in his mind like an echo and when it wasn't immediately answered rose higher, louder.

GIVE IT TO ME!

And the strength to kill his enemy filled him like he was its chalice.

The thrill of combat teemed along every nerve as Orlah spurred her mount, and for a moment the greying haze of approaching death faded, replaced by the hot urge for retribution. *Lioness* crossed the ground to the other Knight quickly, battering aside the hollow shells of tanks and crushing boneless bodies underfoot. Nothing would keep her from this vengeance. Lareoc would pay.

As the distance between them ratcheted down in her heads-up display, Orlah fed power to the thundercoil harpoon. A gauge began to fill on part of her console, signalling the growing charge. A reminder from her dead grandsire through the Throne Mechanicum made her check the pressure levels on her other armament. The dial sat squarely in the green, the conflagration cannon primed and fully fuelled. She expected a pre-emptive attack and kept her ion shield at a moment's readiness, but Lareoc scarcely raised *Heart of Glory*'s thermal cannon and instead began to lope his engine towards her.

When *Heart of Glory* closed to within a half mile, klaxons began to wail inside the cockpit as the *Lioness*' armaments approached optimal range. For a split second, Orlah considered unleashing incendiary fire, but the other Knight's ion shield might raise and lessen the blow. And Lareoc was coming for her, his pace increasing with every stride.

She pulled *Lioness* out of its attack, halting abruptly to lock

She pulled *Lioness* out of its attack, halting abruptly to lock the motive actuators and launch the harpoon. A spit of crackling silver, it sped across the field between the two Knights in seconds, gas venting from ferocious pneumatic propulsion. The spear tip struck true, grapnels biting, driving through the Knight Errant's carapace and arresting its charge. *Heart of Glory* reeled, almost unbalanced, and immediately proceeded to hack at the chain conjoining it and *Lioness*.

Orlah felt the pull at once as Lareoc tried to free himself, but her engine was the larger and therefore unmovable. Her enemy snared, she engaged the electrothaumic generator and began to reel the Knight in. A feral smile curled her lips and she fed the power outwards, down the chain.

The harpoon hit like a mailed fist and Lareoc's head rattled against the side of the cockpit as his Knight staggered. He felt blood wet his cheek, trickling down from a wound in his temple. His Knight's reaper chainblade swung out automatically as he tried to cut the chain holding him, but the teeth slid off the heavy links. A jolt rippled through the engine, sparks firing off the console and electrical rivulets cascading over the interior. He received a shock, his nerves suddenly spasming and the smell of burnt hair filling the tight space.

Gritting his teeth, he forced *Heart of Glory* into a crouch, armoured claw-feet skidding against the earth as she dragged him closer. The stricken war engine twisted next, using its shoulder to create resistance. The chain pulled taut, shivering with tension. Up ahead, the other Knight's generator ramped up the power for its winch.

Heart of Glory stumbled but Lareoc swiftly corrected, kept his footing. Fall now and it was over, she'd be on him. He tried to turn again, the other way this time, folding into the chain. Another jolt ripped down the links but Lareoc held on, even though his bones felt like they were shaking apart. He yanked his shoulder and the harpoon tore loose, taking a chunk of chewed-up carapace with it. Breath halting, heart thundering far too fast, Lareoc found his anger and pushed *Heart of Glory* into a renewed charge.

The locked actuators kept her steady, but Orlah felt the sudden change in tension as the harpoon ripped free and came skittering back towards *Lioness*. Lareoc was coming with it, his Knight like a mongrel chasing a lure, chain-teeth fizzing along his blade so fast they blurred.

Orlah recalled the harpoon, almost felt it *shunk* into place and fired it again.

The barbed spear tip sheared into the other Knight's thermal cannon, punched right through the mounting joint that connected it to the shoulder and torso. It staggered as it was struck, like a prize fighter taking a surprise blow, but lost less momentum this time. The chain links went slack as *Heart of Glory* closed the distance, and she rammed the generator to maximum, hauling back the harpoon, tugging it hard with every iota of *Lioness'* power and ripping the weapon from its socket. The thermal cannon came away in a shower of oil and machine parts, slick enough that they reminded Orlah of viscera.

It barrelled on, stumbling, wounded shoulder lowered, reaper blade low to the ground. A klaxon chimed in her Throne Mechanicum, the conflagration cannon at full murderous readiness. Her breath came in hiking leaps now, her skin as cold as winter frost. A gaunt and greying face looked back at her in the reflection of her visual display.

She could die later, but not before him.

Lioness fired the cannon, unleashing an inferno.

Heat and flame blinded Lareoc almost immediately. It slammed into *Heart of Glory*, merciless and unrelenting. His internal systems went crazy, the fire ravaging already damaged circuits, fusing servos and melting wires. The cockpit became an oven, the leather of his gloves splitting and melting as he fought to hold onto the controls. Every display screen flickered, cracked. Several blanked, turned black. Smoke insinuated itself through compromised joints. He kept going, though he felt every tortured step, his Knight's movements slowed to a near crawl. Something cracked; Lareoc heard the sharp *plink* of distressed metal and the telltale shearing of a previously hermetically sealed unit. The fire got in and he burned.

Lips blackening, flesh searing, hair ablaze, Lareoc gave off a choked howl.

She had him now, buckled to one knee and roaring like a pyre.

'Bastard...' she seethed, pouring on the hurt, spending every drop of fuel until he was ash. Orlah smelled blood on the air, her own. The cockpit reeked with it, she felt it slosh gently against her boots. When she looked down, her entire side was sodden and dark. It rimed her armour plate in a ruby wash. Black pressed at her vision, edging inwards, threatening to overwhelm her. Orlah held it back, determined to see this through.

She opened up the vox-emitters and heard a ragged, half-rasped voice that she knew must be her own.

'Was it worth it?' she roared. 'To defy your queen, to betray your lands. Beggar-knight. You die as you were meant to die, on your knees before *me!*'

I would never serve a tyrant, and it's you that betrayed your lands. Rather a beggar-knight than a vainglorious despot. You were a blight on Kamidar.

He would have spoken but he couldn't speak. Smoke filled his lungs, choking him, and his mouth had long since melted shut. His teeth were locked in a grimace. If the other Knights of Hurne were close, he didn't know it. This was about honour.

They would not intervene. Lareoc would forbid them anyway. His end neared as his flesh burned, but something wouldn't let go. It welled up within him, starting out as a sense of injustice and becoming something entirely more volatile as it bubbled up to the surface and broke loose.

Strength filled his arm, his body; it batted back the flames for a few seconds. His hand, clawed with agony, made a fist. Orlah had stepped in close to finish him, thinking of him as defeated prey.

'I will never die on my knees!' Lareoc roared, his fused lips tearing apart, his voice resonant through the vox-emitters and coming from somewhere deep within.

The reaper blade swept upwards, edged in flame like some sword of myth. It cut through *Lioness*, gutting her from groin to shoulder, passing the neck joint and severing metal and cables. Beheaded, *Lioness* staggered. Her torso hung partly open, exposing the pilot within, who looked on, blanched with terror and fury. Orlah's eyes widened, a breath came and held, then another, harder than the first, and then no more. She died with her vitriol written forever upon her face.

Lioness fell still and Lareoc sagged in the Throne Mechanicum, still burning as darkness took him.

Lareoc woke. He was strapped to a medi-slab, his horrific burns swathed in counterseptic gauze. Even with the morphia drip in his arm, the pain was like being burned alive all over again. He screamed at first, to the darkness around him, at the gods who had cursed him, at the allies who had abandoned him.

As the echoes of his accusations faded, a lumpen figure advanced on him through the gloomy light of the infirmary. The room looked Imperial by the design, what little he could discern of it anyway, but the creature before him was anything but.

It wore battered, baroque armour, rimmed in studs and spikes. A brass rebreather was clamped to its face. The war plate looked like it had seen recent battle, and was bent and split in places. It was red and black, a heraldry Lareoc did not recognise. But he knew the wearer was a Space Marine, and he suspected the broad stripe to which it belonged.

'Am I alive…?' Lareoc croaked and the effort of speaking made his eyes water.

The Astartes nodded, slow and purposeful. 'You are saved,' it said with all the harmony of a wheezing bellows. 'Our drop-ship found you and your warriors. You are with us now.'

'*With* you?'

'I am Kurgos, this ship's chirurgeon.'

'I am alive because of you?'

'Not only because of me,' said Kurgos, taking a few laboured steps backwards.

In the warrior's place, Lareoc saw a face he knew and immediately strained against his bonds, teeth clamped in a snarl.

'That's good,' said Albia, 'nurture it, *feed* it. Let it sustain you. You're on the Path now, Lareoc. All of you. Klaigen, Henniger and the rest. Hurne's Path. Although you will come to know him by a different name.'

Lareoc spat the reply, jaw clenched. 'I. Will. Kill. You.'

Albia chuckled and for a fleeting second his image changed, becoming that of a robed female servant and then a hunched and hooded figure clothed in dark red and gold, before settling again into the guise of the mendicant priest.

'All in good time, disciple, all in good time.'

Herek attached the admiral's flensed skull to his belt. The bone was still bloody, he'd had to work quickly and crudely. A few tufts of hair remained too. He would attend to it later.

He felt the presence of the knife shard in his scabbard. Harrower felt it too, agitated and irritable. He still didn't know how he'd done it. First he'd been *there*, staring down the Black Templars' blades, then *here* amongst the cattle. He didn't question it too deeply. The mysteries of the universe were mysterious for a reason. Let the scholars debate the metaphysics.

The ship was theirs, that was all that mattered in the moment. A few stalwarts had held out, sections of resistance that dug in when they realised what was happening, but they'd been rooted out. Once they had opened up the doors trapping his troops, once he had sent the Culler into the ship, it didn't take long. His own crew served the bridge now. The cultists and Imperial traitors he had brought on board. Kurgos lived, which surprised him. The chirurgeon had returned via one of the gunships fleeing the wreckage of the Black Templars stronghold. He had served his purpose well, drawn Dagomir and the others away just long enough for Herek to get what he came for.

But now it was time to leave. The naval battle was breaking up, the natives put to flight, and they had already fended off more than one hail from the two destroyers in the flagship's retinue. But what a ship she was. Herek had not seen finer.

A signal from one of the crew told him the cargo was aboard, and not only the defectors. *They* were here too. The Hand.

Herek prayed the Dark Gods were watching, then gave a nod, and without further warning the *Fell Lord* plunged into the warp.

Chapter Forty

SURRENDER

OUR OATHS FULFILLED

DAUGHTER OF MORDIAN

Kamidar gave its surrender in the sixth hour after dawn. Word had reached the generals. Queen Orlah was dead and the de facto ruler, Baron Gerent Y'Kamidar, had ordered all fighting to cease. It didn't happen all at once and the war petered out in a series of ever smaller and more remote skirmishes until every front received the message. Galius and Vanir, which had been spared the brutal rigours of the war, had meekly acceded to the Imperium's will without complaint. Some claimed they had exchanged one ruler for another, but the truth was they were simply grateful to remain unscathed.

Tournis, field-promoted by a conclave of his peers to admiral, issued a stand down order to Praxis and her fighting forces. Despite several attempts to contact the flagship, there had been no word nor sign from Ardemus or the *Fell Lord* since his sudden disappearance. Mechanicus adepts could only surmise a warp engine failure or freak ignition. Whatever the case, it had cast the *Fell Lord* and her entire complement into the empyrean to

Throne only knew what fate. The risks, plunging a vessel into the warp in such close proximity to the world, were monumental and little hope remained that the *Fell Lord* had survived its parting. The two destroyers that served as her outriders and retinue had been devastated in the unscheduled translocation. Parts of the ships remained but they had been sealed and left to drift when fleet ecclesiarchs had deemed the wreckage irrevocably tainted.

A more even-handed man than Ardemus, if less ambitious and inspirational, Tournis allowed a period of grace for the Kamidarians to recover their dead, observe any necessary rites and otherwise prepare their townships and cities for the arrival of the Imperium. The admiral-elect gave a speech across global and orbital vox that the protectorate would be made ready for the Anaxian Line. He called upon all citizens of the Imperium, non-Kamidarian and Kamidarian alike, to come together for the crusade and the desperate plight facing all mankind in this, its darkest hour.

The transition was not without rough edges, much hostility remained, but without the incendiary elements of the Marines Malevolent, who had been entirely annihilated in the ground war, and the former admiral's distemper, no further blood was shed. Tournis reassured Kamidar's citizens that where possible their traditions would remain and that respectful concessions would be made to help preserve their culture.

Of course, Ariadne knew this amounted to little more than talk. She had been part of the crusade for years and knew what it needed and what it had to do to get it. Even had matters at Ironhold not deteriorated as they had, it would not have changed the fact that Kamidar's sovereignty was about to be erased. It would become a redoubt world of the Imperium, a vital piece of the defensive infrastructure that would support and supply the front lines of the war.

She had reached Outpost Theta by the time the ceasefire came.

They had lost only eight of the injured, the hard journey across the wilds of Harnfor too much for the poor souls who sadly succumbed to their wounds. It was not a bad tally, all told, though the sting of it still hurt.

As she rung out her jacket, having found an empty basin to wash away the blood and the stench of the hard days, she reflected on how tired she felt. The hollowness of her anger. Such waste, such avoidable waste. So many dead. She had just finished listening to Tournis' speech for the fifth time. It had been playing on a loop every hour, across every band and frequency. He was a decent man, the captain – *admiral*, she corrected herself – but a dour one. What he had in fairness, he lacked in charisma. She doubted the appointment would last long.

She checked her chron, the hustle of the camp unfolding around her as men and materiel made ready for what came next. The acquisition forces would muster again, the natives would be trampled again – albeit with more like a velvet slipper than a mailed boot, but crushed all the same.

As she looked up from her labours, arms drenched in the suds from low-grade Munitorum soap flakes, Ariadne saw a smiling face trooping towards her.

'Are you cleaning, visha?'

He looked well, she decided, but couldn't entirely hide the pain. He tried to hide something else, too, and she thought it might be grief. She had heard about the fate of the Storm Reapers' strike cruiser and knew there weren't many left in the battle group. That pain, though, it had been engraved into him somehow and she doubted, despite his inhuman constitution, that he would ever shake it.

'Not exactly. I do feel filthy, though, and am sorely tempted to climb in this bloody bucket.'

'A hard war,' Ogin agreed, wistful for a moment.

'An unnecessary one.' She couldn't help the bitterness but made a mental note that she should try to check her tone. Unfriendlier ears might hear it as heresy and she had no time for that kind of groxshit.

'Aren't all wars unnecessary, visha?'

Ariadne kinked an eyebrow. 'That's a strange thing to say, coming from you.'

'Perhaps I only wish for peace, heh.'

She snorted. 'Now I know you're joking.' Her face grew serious again. 'But this one was unnecessary. It need not have happened. What did you call it?' She frowned, remembering. 'Grushälob.'

Ogin smiled but his eyes were sombre.

When he made no other reply Ariadne carried on, scrubbing her jacket with even greater vigour.

'It never should have come to this. We need to learn from these hard lessons. Our allies can't become our enemies. Too much is at stake.' She stopped, blowing out a breath, cheeks red with effort. 'I am going to petition Tournis to be reassigned. Away from here, somewhere in the crusade with fewer bleak memories.'

Ogin raised an eyebrow. 'You will leave Praxis, heh?'

She wasn't sure, the true emotions of Space Marines were sometimes hard to discern, but she thought he might have been slightly hurt.

'Reassignment isn't guaranteed,' she replied, and stared at the grimy water, not knowing why she felt suddenly abashed. She looked up. 'It could take time. I don't even know if it's possible, and I'll do my duty regardless.'

Ogin nodded and Ariadne found herself surprised at the warm feeling at his apparent approval. He outstretched an immense and gauntleted hand to her.

'Then I shall bid you fortune and favour, visha,' he said. 'I will miss you as I war across the stars, though perhaps our paths will cross again.'

She took his hand – well, a finger really – and grasped it

awkwardly. She smiled back, a little uncertain. It was like shaking hands with a carnodon, the fear his presence evoked never quite going away.

'Perhaps they will.'

The empty reliquarius echoed to the chime of his armour against the stone floor as Morrigan took a knee. He went unhelmed, his weapons sheathed as he proffered the skull to the waiting plinth. The others had already been restored from where they had fallen during the fight, the chamber resanctified after Blasphemy had been released. All evidence of its presence and that of the renegades had been scoured away. The smell of soot and char still bit on the air, warring with the scent of holy unguents.

Morrigan reverently laid the skull down, murmuring a prayer. After all this time, Bohemund had been returned. He closed his eyes and wept for what would be the last time for his brother. Then he rose, unchained no more, his bindings tightly wrapped around his wrists and forearms, the broken links reforged.

The others rose too, their presence behind him suddenly noticeable again as Morrigan ended the reverie.

'What now?' asked Dagomir, the sound of his cloak heavy as it fell around him.

'Our oaths to Kamidar are fulfilled,' offered Anglahad. 'I heard the baron give his blessing himself.'

Godfried grunted, either in agreement, or at the tacit implication that the will of some royal held the Black Templars to their duty rather than the oath itself, but the outcome was much the same. They were free of their obligation to the Ironhold.

'A sword, on fire, raised to heaven,' said Morrigan, recounting his vision. 'A cup lifted in supplication. Then I saw the figure stand, and it walked towards me aflame, ethereal, a wraith with sackcloth wings.'

'What do you think it means?' asked Anglahad, ever inquisitive.

'It means we have near sixty warriors here and their blades are ready for war,' growled Dagomir, ever eager.

Morrigan faced them, his closest brothers, his Council of Swords.

'Herek still lives and whatever he took from that blade, whatever he *did* to escape us, I would know of it and destroy it. Destroy him. But the crusade has come, it beckons us to war. We shall answer.'

They left the Reclusiam behind, sealing it shut and barring it from without. Sturmhal had served its purpose. It would remain, a fortress empty of its warriors. Those who stayed behind would act as its custodians. The *Mourning Star* would be the Black Templars' chapel now, their fortress.

A figure seated upon a throne, encircled by fire. It raised its sword and then its cup until the flames consumed it.

The memory of the vision returned, crisp as parchment in a fire. An ill omen, a warning.

Morrigan had faith the purpose of it would be revealed to him. Great deeds were at work, great deeds.

First light, then fire.

It touched but did not burn. No harm befell her.

In the shadows of the catacombs as the bone hoard came crashing and the dead things hungered, there was the light. Then a feeling of weightlessness, and the beating of soft wings. Wings that turned black, made heavy with soot. The memories converged, collided, confused, but the message they imparted was the same.

A miracle.

Kesh woke in her bunk, shivering despite the heat, dappled with cold sweat. They had let her rest, though the medicae had cleared her for active duty, having found no injuries to speak of. She still didn't know how that was possible but she knew she was remembering things, not just Kamidar but what had happened on Gathalamor too. Fragments at least, pieces she was afraid to reassemble.

She reached for the chron looped around her neck, finding reassurance in its presence. In the interim between fleeing the palace laid out on a stretcher and being temporarily billeted here in the camp, she had found an enginseer to put the keepsake on a long chain so she could wear it. She wondered if Dvorgin would mind, then decided he probably wouldn't. A pang of grief welled up as she touched the metal and she tamped it down again. They were shipping out, no time for any of that. Back with her regiment, the Mordians pressed and polished for duty. Except, she felt different. Not herself, even if everything around her was as it had ever been.

It was dark in the billet, though a few stray rays of early morning sun crept in through gaps in the slatted windows. An old farmhouse, decent enough lodgings for the last couple of days on Kamidar whilst the Departmento organised the muster out.

Her rifle had been found in some lockroom in the palace and returned to her. She took it from the soft leather case, ran her hand along the freshly lacquered stock. She'd need to strip, clean and reassemble it later to her own exacting standards. Her fingers trembled though, as they made their journey down the weapon; she wondered if she should talk to the frater about it but decided against it. What would she even say? What could she say?

The sudden hint of movement from the corner of her eye and a queasiness in her stomach made Kesh turn.

'Oh, hello,' she said, 'I'm surprised to see you up. I actually thought you were dead.'

Syreniel looked tall and imposing in the shadows. Her armour had been patched in many places, suggesting the sheer number of wounds she had taken, and a greatsword lay strapped to the Vigilator's back. Like Kesh, the Silent Sister's armaments had been returned to her. She gave a mute nod.

I am leaving, she signed.

Kesh started packing up the rifle. 'Off to a different front?'

Terra or Luna. It depends...

That made Kesh pause. She had seen pict-captures but never actually been to Terra. Few in the ranks had.

'Something serious then.'

Something stirring.

Kesh felt her heart jar a beat and had to steady herself on the edge of the bunk. She almost dared not ask the question. 'Does that have something to do with me?'

Not just you. I must seek out the commander of the Silent Order. She will have answers. A pause then, the barest betrayal of unease crossing her face. *I hope.*

'I am shipping out soon,' said Kesh when the silence stretched and before it grew too awkward. 'Back with the Eighty-Fourth.'

Another nod.

Be mindful, signed Syreniel, though failed to elaborate on what she meant. Instead she held out a coin-shaped talisman. It looked like it had come from her armour and was made from silver with a winged lightning bolt engraved onto the surface.

A sigil of my order. A mark of sisterhood. If you ever need it.

Kesh stared open-mouthed. A gift from a Talon of the Emperor. It felt warm to the touch.

'But what will I do with–' she began, but when she looked up saw that Syreniel had already gone.

The muster horns were sounding. Kesh pocketed the talisman and picked up her rifle bag, hands shaking. She didn't know what came next and the not-knowing scared her, but she was a daughter of Mordian, born in darkness. She feared no shadow, not even death.

Her hands steadied and she opened the door and made for the landing strip.

Epilogue

AND NOTHING MORE

STAND DOWN THE LEGION

THREE SHARDS

The bodies had been removed and the blood scrubbed from the floor, but the stains remained.

A tech-priest shuffled through the now quiet confines of the lunarium, resanctifying the various mechanisms, ensuring that whatever taint had visited these halls was gone, at least in the machine sense. Ecclesiarchs had come too. They had blessed every hall. Sanctioned psykers had been brought in, observed diligently by their handlers, and it was they who had detected the residue of something *unclean*. Received wisdom was that they might never know what had caused it since only its fading echo remained.

A disappearance had been reported, a high-level royal func-tionary, an equerry of some standing, but she was never found, alive or dead. This concerned the tech-priest little, for his task was to ensure the machine-spirits were in alignment, a final stage before the palace could be restored. A vault had been uncov-ered, something deep in the lowest levels, and the tech-priest sorely wished to see it, but he was of middling rank and thus such secrets were denied to him. He did know that the vault had been sealed and the entirety of its contents confiscated and proscribed by his order.

Still, he could not help but wonder what it had contained. So preoccupied was the tech-priest with his thoughts, a reason perhaps for why his status was only middling, that he almost missed the small gemstone and its chain. It had been discarded and had ended up tucked away in a corner, forgotten by all. He stooped as he saw it, reaching out with mechadendrite digits which began a subtle haptic analysis as soon as they made contact. A black garnet. It took three point seven seconds for the mineral analysis, which, for a nanosecond, registered something unknown before normalising. The tech-priest paused for another nanosecond, eventually ascribing the anomaly to a machine error and within standard parameters, concluding that the item was a simple decorative gemstone and nothing more. Pocketing it in his robes, he moved on with the rest of his duties and after a while the lunarium fell to silence again.

They stood at readiness at the system edge, vessels arrayed, his forces mustered.

Vitrian Messinius had been on the bridge of a battle-barge when word reached him of Kamidar's surrender and with it the rest of the Ironhold Protectorate. He listened patiently as a Chapter-serf relayed every detail, including the succession of the new ruler of the world and the bizarre disappearance of Admiral Ardemus and his flagship. This last fact warranted further scrutiny: it was an unsolved detail, the kind that tended to bother the lord lieutenant because he knew such things had a habit of becoming problematic. Nothing could be taken for granted, not in this perilous era in which the Imperium found itself. He would relate these matters and the status of the Anaxian Line to his primarch at the earliest possible convenience.

He looked to one of his officers, Nevius, a Primaris Marine

and one with a decent measure of experience. The officer's face remained impassive as he stood by the lord lieutenant's side, patiently awaiting his next order. Messinius gave it, and imagined the war host he had gathered slowly breaking up and returning to their respective armies. It was no small feat to disband such a force but it would be done regardless.

'Stand down the Legion.'

Herek had not expected to come here. His ship, the *Fell Lord*, and his entire fleet had emerged from the warp guided by them, the Hand. As a voidfarer of several centuries, he had seen much of the galaxy. He knew where most of the major strongholds were and who had last laid claim to them, but he didn't know this place. This was strange territory and he wondered if, even given the appropriate cartograph, he would have been able to find it again without them to guide him.

They had told him their name was Augury, but Herek found he preferred not to think of the name, and especially not speak it aloud, for it was as if they could hear it, hear you, and all your secrets would suddenly be laid bare.

Nonetheless, he had earned this meeting, this moment, and he was determined to be a part of it.

A shadowy hall led from the docking spikes where the ships had laid anchor. From here to a stark black landing hall and a platform that descended deep into the heart of the place. Herek went alone, leaving Kurgos in charge in his absence. The chirurgeon had already begun to see to the Knight lord's recovery. The Kamidarian and his warriors would be useful in the days to come. Every Hand had their own followers, a necessary precaution in such a cut-throat order. Herek had ambitions to be a part of it and understood that an opening might have already presented itself. As he trod the strange halls of this place, he hoped his offering to the Warmaster would hold some sway in that regard.

It had an uncanny air, a sense of being slightly out of kilter. And it had an unusual resonance. Herek felt it in the deck plate under his feet, in the walls as he reached out a hand to try and capture what was making him so uneasy. A background hum persisted, a sort of *frequency* but not in any code or language he could parse. He thought he heard machines, or *a* machine, a distant grind and churn of ancient metals like the mechanism of a rusty clock.

Here and there, what appeared to be black obsidian layered the walls. His reflection peered back from within the glassy panes but it was inexact, some of the details were wrong: his remaining horn longer, his eyes blacker, a rune seared into his forehead. It hurt to look at these false faces, and not for the first time he wondered if he had been too hasty in coming here alone.

After what seemed like hours, though he had the sense that time moved differently here, he came to a vaulted chamber where several figures draped in shadow awaited him. He had not realised he was late, but felt tardy nonetheless.

It was the court of the Hand, he knew it in his marrow.

Augury met him at the chamber's entrance; hooded and red-robed but pale like something from the deepest ocean that has never felt sun. Their brown and green eyes glistened from within the shadows of their cowl. Their movements were ever a mystery to the Red Corsair. They had their own schemes, of which he knew only a few details. That Kamidar had survived and civil war had been averted did not appear to sour their mood. Both sides had bled themselves during the conflict, and were left weaker as a result. And the Knights of Hurne had defected entirely, a fine prize to strengthen Augury's forces. His mission, he knew, had been of paramount importance. The sword, the shard. It was everything. Augury had drawn the eye of its defenders and, despite Morrigan's intervention, Herek had prevailed. He did not wish to consider what would have happened had he been unsuccessful.

But Augury was not alone, for this was not a court of one.

A second lounged upon a rotten wooden throne, his dirt-encrusted and gauntleted fingers tapping out a steady rhythm against the arm. Death Guard for certain. Seven raps, a pause, then seven raps. On and on it went. The drone of flies provided a buzzing chorus. Herek forced himself not to listen. A third claimed the shadows as his own, tall and emaciated, his overly wide mouth curved in a sickle grin. The reek of sorcery clung to him as doggedly as the flies to the slovenly Death Guard king. The fourth wore a long caul of black cloth, sigils of the Machine Cult stitched into the fabric. A triumvirate of retinal lenses slowly cycled in appraisal, their light dulled by grime. Unseen appendages writhed beneath this one's robes, and Herek caught a glimpse of both metal and pale ophidian flesh.

It stole his breath to be amongst such a gathering, but he let none of his awe show.

The four formed a circle, each at a different cardinal point. A fifth, an old warrior Herek recognised from something akin to myth, and not of their coven, stood apart from the others. He was a shrunken form clad in ancient and formidable armour. The Dark Apostle of the Word Bearers nodded to Herek as he breached the edge of the circle, filling him with a mild disquiet at what Kor Phaeron knew of him, for they had never met before this moment.

Herek hated them all, but forgot his loathing as he felt a subliminal call, like a siren's song, to the middle of the circle. Augury beckoned with a long, taloned finger.

'Destiny awaits for those who have the will to seize it,' they told him.

The round dais raised the ground by half a foot at least, and sigils had been carved into its surface that shone with the same lustre as the obsidian walls. Herek faltered for a second, and made sure not to look too closely into the black glass. Instead, he allowed his eye to be drawn to the three shards lying in the centre of the dais. Each was a jagged piece of a greater whole, and had been arranged next to each other as if placed there reverently.

Even several feet away, he could feel the power of the shards, and hear the whispering of their secrets. In his mind's eye, he saw priests of an ancient cult and a king laid low by treachery. He hissed in sudden pain, clasping a hand to his side, and then again to his neck as if a blade had been drawn across it.

Gasping now, unable to hide his discomfort, Herek looked at his hand but found no blood. His side was unwounded, his throat unslit. They were echoes, he realised, old deeds made by an old blade. The one he carried trembled in the scabbard, suddenly agitated after long hours of quiescence. Herek felt the undeniable compulsion to join his shard, the one he had retrieved from the daemon sword, to the others. It *pulled* magnetically to its kindred pieces, and who was he to deny such power?

Without realising, he had crossed the dais and was standing before the other shards. He fell to his knees in supplication, over-awed and overwhelmed as a name hissed through the cracks and crevices of the old ritual chamber.

Erebus.

He made his offering.

And then felt a presence suddenly come amongst them. Herek raised his eyes, glad he was still kneeling. Even via hololith, their authority was undeniable and an old emotion Herek had once thought buried, one he thought he had evolved beyond, resurfaced.

Clad in black, a huge pelt of fur draped across hulking shoulders...

He faced the Warmaster. They all felt it, in spite of trying to hide it. Fear or its equivalent. Abaddon's gaze lingered on Herek, who had to fight the urge to look down; an anchor dragging at his neck.

The Red Corsair's sense of relief when that gaze shifted was palpable. It alighted on the four shards, the chiselled face betraying no emotion. Then he uttered three words.

'Gather the rest.'

And was gone.

Appendix: Notes on the Crusade

After many notable successes in Imperium Sanctus, by the time the Indomitus Crusade passed its fifth year, earlier impetus had bled away, and a large number of battle groups found themselves mired in expanding warzones across the galaxy. This slowing of reconquest was by no means universal, and large areas of the Imperium to the galactic south of the Rift found themselves, if not totally safe, at least safeguarded by the presence of Guilliman's armadas. Some fleets continued to blaze across the stars. Alas, successes such as the lightning advances of Battle Group Thetera of Crusade Fleet Octus across the Veiled Region and its subsequent, dramatic relief of Bakka, or the daring actions of Commodore Hyspasian in the heart of the Segmentum Tempestus, were the exception rather than the rule.

MULTIPLYING WARZONES

Elsewhere in these addenda, we have detailed the rising menace of the necrons of the Nephilim Sector, increasing ork activity in the north of the Segmentum Tempestus, the Plague Wars of

Ultramar, the bloody stalemate at the Nachmund Gauntlet and the uprisings orchestrated by the Word Bearers, one of the most notable of these being in the Segmentum Solar. These were, however, by no means all the dangers facing the Imperium.

CHAOS DIVIDED

The forces of Chaos remained the Imperium's greatest threat, yet as the crusade went on, the feared assault on Terra did not come. The galaxy instead began to see increased factional activity within the wider Chaos forces, often centred upon the personal goals of various Legion remnants and their insane daemon primarchs. The Death Guard, arguably the most cohesive of the old Space Marine Traitor Legions, were active in multiple warzones, with the ancient and evil warlord Typhus being spotted across the galaxy. Although their greatest numbers were to be found in Ultramar, they brought plague and woe to many other sectors. The Word Bearers showed remarkable purpose, with a large contingent operating worryingly near Terra, while the returned Magnus the Red gathered his scattered acolytes as he strove to build an empire within the galaxy centred upon the twin worlds of Prospero and the Planet of the Sorcerers. Questions continued to be asked by the greater sapients of Imperial government as to why Abaddon had not made his move. Citing these self-interested actions by the Traitor Legions, one answer offered was that Chaos carried the seeds of its own destruction, and that process of dissolution had begun again. Wiser heads rejected this optimistic proposition, sure of nefarious plans on Abaddon's part that had yet to come to fruition.

XENOS OPPORTUNISM

Every species in the galaxy found their territories rocked by the opening of the Great Rift. Many lesser beings were destroyed, and even heavyweights such as the t'au on the Eastern Fringe were forced to launch the Fifth Sphere Expansion to discover the fate of the failed Fourth Sphere Expansion, following its disappearance with the advent of the Cicatrix Maledictum.

Despite these challenges, a rising number of hostile xenos actions were also beginning to bite. In the Charadon Sector, we saw eruptions of multilateral war as xenos, Imperial and Chaos factions made unremitting slaughter of each other. Meanwhile, tyranid hive fleets pushed their tendrils deeper into the galaxy, and their genestealer cults took advantage of the Noctis Aeterna to infest and overthrow isolated worlds. Across the length and breadth of the galaxy, great necron dynasties also stirred, alerted by their ancient machines to the rising tide of Chaos.

In Imperium Nihilus, other stranger alien beings were stirred up by the great cataclysm. Though communications across the Cicatrix Maledictum remained tenuous, rumours of Enslaver plagues and hrud migrations reached the ears of Guilliman's Logisticarum. There were even unsubstantiated reports of a break-out attempt by the hyper-violent barghesi, long confined to their home systems by Space Marine blockade.

THE PERILS OF THE WARP

Warp travel remained difficult in most parts of the Imperium. As already discussed, the upheaval caused by the Great Rift affected the currents of the warp as much as it did the fabric of the physical universe. Long-established, reliable empyrical routes withered overnight, while new, fast streams opened up areas of the cosmos that were previously hard to access. Compared to warp travel before the Rift opened, any journey through the empyrean was fraught with peril. Journey times were wildly unpredictable. Ships went missing with a frequency that before the Rift would have caused enormous consternation, and yet came to be regarded as normal. Time as well as space was affected. Guilliman himself was among the most affected by this. Travelling more than any man to direct his titanic venture of reconquest, his appearances seemed to make little chronological sense, and by even the most generously elastic dating system, on more than one occasion he appeared to be in several places at once.

These temporal anomalies brought logistical problems aplenty. Gatherings of strength were incredibly hard to orchestrate, with component parts of task forces arriving weeks, months or even years apart from one another. Bizarre occurrences such as ships arriving before they left became commonplace; others vanished into the past. It is surmised that the fate of such chronologically displaced vessels was horrific indeed, dragged across the materium into the maw of the opening Rift. With all manner of sanity-troubling events being reported across the Imperium, the Ordo Chronos was busy indeed throughout those years.

A LACK OF SUPPLY

Despite the growing network of fortress hubs, redoubt and bastion worlds laying a logistical web across the fractured sectors of Imperium Sanctus, the factors discussed above made supply of Imperial fleets incredibly difficult. Not even the Avenging Son himself, the acknowledged master of organisation, could surmount the obstacles of Chaos and xenos depredation and temporal-spatial disruption. In desperate need of men, equipment, food and water, the crusade fleets were forced to extract materiel from the unfortunate worlds they fought to protect. In this tome, the rebellion of Queen Orlah and her Iron Kingdom is laid bare, but she was not the only ruler of an Imperial world to first greet their saviours, then turn upon them as the needs of their guests became apparent.

By decree of the Imperial Regent, any senior crusade commander could commandeer resources from a world as an *Exacta Amplius*. Supposedly, these extra demands were to be offset against future tithings, albeit at a nominal rate that favoured the Imperium far more than its subject worlds. In reality, the demands of those crusade fleets forced to harvest Imperial territories could outstrip enormously the ability of the world to sustain itself, sometimes to the point of destruction. It is true that there were instances of rebellion against central Imperial command driven by largely political concerns; planetary governors left to their own devices for centuries often take exception to imposition, as has been the case throughout history, but other acts of defiance were born of sheer existential desperation.

Take, for example, the mining world of Frentius in the Ob System, whose entire population of men, women and children were conscripted by Battle Group Omnius of Fleet Decimus to fill the places of crew killed by a plague of parasitic mindworms. Group Captain Essene generously waived exacta obligations for twenty standard Terran years for this service; a mere token formality, for the mining galleries were left entirely stripped of people and machinery. Or consider the refugee fleets fleeing worlds coreward of the growing Maelstrom: gathered into a vast armada in search of a new home, they were left without food, fuel or protection when two battle groups of Fleet Sextus, recently decimated in combat by the hordes of Huron Blackheart, had to choose between their own destruction or that of the largely civilian flotilla. Upon hearing tales of such additional 'tithes', a substantial number of worlds became fractious, with many attempting to secede from the Imperium altogether.

These incidents happened time and again, and yet that has always been the lot of mankind, to suffer as individuals so that the species and the God-Emperor might live on. Those subjects of Terra who forget this are no better than the pawns of Chaos that the Emperor's glorious armies do battle against day and night, and deserve no more mercy than they.

ABOUT THE AUTHOR

Nick Kyme is the author of the Horus Heresy novels
Old Earth, Deathfire, Vulkan Lives and *Sons of the
Forge,* the novellas *Promethean Sun* and *Scorched
Earth,* and the audio dramas *Red-Marked, Censure*
and *Nightfane.* His novella *Feat of Iron* was a *New
York Times* bestseller in the Horus Heresy collection
The Primarchs. For Warhammer 40,000, Nick wrote
the novel *Volpone Glory* and is well known for his
popular Salamanders novels and the Cato Sicarius
novels *Damnos* and *Knights of Macragge.* His work
for Age of Sigmar includes the short story 'Borne
by the Storm', included in the novel *War Storm,*
and the audio drama *The Imprecations of Daemons.*
He has also written the Warhammer Horror novel
Sepulturum. He lives and works in Nottingham.

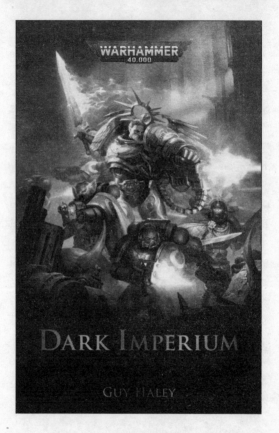

YOUR
NEXT READ

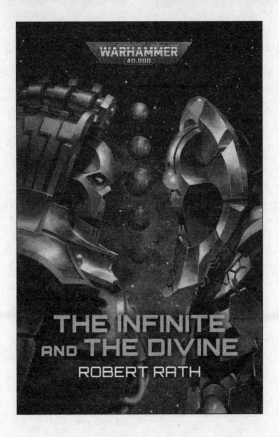

THE INFINITE AND THE DIVINE
by Robert Rath

Trazyn the Infinite and Orikan the Diviner are opposites. Each is obsessed with their own speciality, and their rivalry spans millennia. Yet together, they may hold the secret to saving the necron race…

YOUR
NEXT READ

THE SOLAR WAR
by John French

After years of devastating war, Horus and his forces have arrived at Terra. But before they can set foot on the Throneworld, they must first break the defences of the Sol System. Powerful fleets and cunning defences bar their path – but can anything hope to halt the advance of the Traitor armada?